MILORD'S PLEASURE

She turned as she felt his touch. "MacLachlan!" she cried out.

"Aye, indeed, lady!" he said. "Tell me, did you know my name before or after you tried to slash my throat?"

"You could have called out, you could have said my name, your name. I was scared to death—how could I expect to see you? How can you be here? The rebels were attacking us . . ."

"We rode in behind them, milady. They took flight."

"I'm at a loss, milord. After all this time, you come here now, today . . ."

"Milady, I have come to take charge," he informed her.

"Of what?"

"Of you," he said flatly. "And Aville, of course."

"Ah, but *perhaps* you are not welcome here.'

"Ah, but *perhaps,* my lady, you will feel differently after tonight. After our wedding."

She stared at him, the blood draining from her face. "A wedding? Tonight? Because the king demands it? At the king's pleasure? She stood, hands on hips, furious. "A wedding tonight? In a pig's eye!"

Suddenly she found herself plucked from the ground as if she were weightless and set atop his stallion before she could protest.

"Indeed, milady. In a pig's eye or no, the king's pleasure or my own. There will be a wedding tonight!" He leapt up behind her—his arms came around her . . . and a wall of shimmering red fire seemed to sweep within her . . .

DANGEROUS GAMES   (0-7860-0270-0, $4.99)
by Amanda Scott

When Nicholas Barrington, eldest son of the Earl of Ul-
combe, first met Melissa Seacort, the desperation he
sensed beneath her well-bred beauty haunted him. He
didn't realize how desperate Melissa really was . . . until
he found her again at a Newmarket gambling club—being auctioned off by her father to the highest bidder. So,
Nick bought himself a wife. With a villain hot on their
heels, and a fortune and their lives at stake, they would
gamble everything on the most dangerous game of all:
love.

A TOUCH OF PARADISE   (0-7860-0271-9, $4.99)
by Alexa Smart

As a confidence man and scam runner in 1880s America,
Malcolm Northrup has amassed a fortune. Now, posing
as the eminent Sir John Abbot—scholar, and possible
discoverer of the lost continent of Atlantis—he's taking
his act on the road with a lecture tour, seeking funds for
a scientific experiment he has no intention of making.
But scholar Halia Davenport is determined to accompany
Malcolm on his "expedition" . . . even if she must kidnap
him!

THE KING'S PLEASURE

Shannon Drake

Zebra Books
Kensington Publishing Corp.

http://www.zebrabooks.com

Prologue
Lovers and Other Enemies . . .

The Year of Our Lord 1357

The door to the tavern opened and Adrien MacLachlan stood there for a moment, his towering form barring the entry as he surveyed the place.

He was a knight, one of the most famed of all King Edward III's fighting men, yet tonight, he wore no armor.

He'd been warned of the tryst tonight, and had come clad like many of the cutthroats who frequented the ill-famed establishment. He wore a simple brown tunic over his soft linen undershirt, hose and boots, and voluminous dark cloak with a hood which hid both his features and the weapons he had chosen to carry—his magnificent Toledo sword and the rapier-honed knife in the sheath at his calf, its usage learned from his Scottish relatives. They had learned the bitter lesson that fighting could come quick, fast, close, and at any time.

He surveyed the tavern and satisfied himself that she had not come as yet; then he entered and made straightway to a crude wooden table near the wall where he could sit with his back to that wall, see the doorway, and keep a keen eye on all those who entered there. Seated, he ordered a tankard of ale from the richly-bosomed wench who strode the place, diving and darting through a clientele of most seriously questionable character, for the place was rumored to cater to murderers, knaves, and thieves, and it was known that any evil business could be pursued here. At the table to his left, a black-toothed seaman watched him warily, commenting to an equally scurvy-looking companion in whispers, and Adrien was well aware that they were contemplating what wealth might be upon his person. Ah, well. He could have had help coming here. Any number of good, brave fighting men might have joined him. But this was a personal matter, one he meant to keep from the king. Her life might depend upon it.

He prayed that his informants had been right, that she was coming here. For if not . . .

Fear and fury seized his system, stormed throughout his blood. How could she be so foolish, take such chances? Did she think herself so strong, so powerful, or merely so damned noble that she could command the base instincts of dishonest men to her own purposes? Dear God, but he wanted to set his hands on her tonight . . .

In so many ways.

Duty demanded that he be here. The little vixen deserved a lashing at a stake, and she was, dear God, his responsibility. But it was equally true, too, that he had the sense and wisdom to see what she could not: she was a fairer prize to seize than one with whom to bargain. And in his heart, he feared for her and knew that he would die for her, die inside if harm were to befall her.

Ah, there! His heartbeat quickened.

The door opened. A figure stepped into the tavern, which was filled with smoke from the boar that spit fat over the fire in the great hearth. The room was in a haze.

Like him, this figure was clad in a dark, sweeping cloak.

Actually, he mused ruefully, it was a room full of figures clad in cloaks.

But he would have known her anywhere, just from her movements. He had known her most of her life. Seen her grow into that graceful sway and ease of motion.

She pushed back the hood, just slightly, that she might see around the room. He quickly lowered his head, then raised his eyes again, Indeed, it was she. Anger seemed to boil his blood once again, yet he contained and controlled it and tried hard to study her objectively. He could not. Were she the poorest of peasant lasses, she would have drawn the hunger and envy of the richest and most noble men. Lashes like ink swept over emerald-green eyes. Her face was delicately boned, exquisite. She was tall and slender, yet beneath that cloak, curved beautifully, perfectly. Seductively.

And she had come here to meet a man. A Frenchman. An enemy. Ah . . . there!

From another corner of the room, a man rose and came forward, eager to meet her. He, too, was clad in a dark cloak, but the hood had fallen back and his features were clearly visible. Comte Langlois, a man in the service of the French king. Adrien had seen him a few times from a distance on the battlefield.

The comte reached the girl in the doorway. Both their heads bowed. He indicated the stairway leading to the private rooms above the common floor.

Adrien blinked hard, gritting his teeth, fighting the wave of red fury that all but engulfed him. *She should have learned. She should have learned her lesson with him before!*

He clenched and unclenched his fists beneath the table, taking deep breaths. He had to keep a clear head.

The two went up the steps. Seconds later, Adrien followed.

Danielle d'Aville had never been so frightened in her life, but she had learned quite early that a show of courage was almost as good as the real thing. She had also learned that a regal manner could be a tremendous strength in itself, and it was a ploy she never hesitated to use.

Yet there was more to her uneasiness tonight than fear. She was also sick at heart, torn cruelly within. Once she had made a vow, a deathbed vow, and because of that, she owed a warning to King Jean. It was all she intended to give, and it was the last time she would ever seek to help Jean, but even in that, she knew she betrayed King Edward. And worse . . .

Oh, God, she did so much worse . . .

And the man now at her back made her uneasy tonight. Comte Langlois, a striking, charismatic man, the rage of the French court. He had always been courteous and proper before, but tonight . . . tonight, he looked like a predator. She bit into her lower lip, dismayed and aware that she had summoned him here with a few half-truths to receive his help in getting her to Jean.

He led her down a darkened hallway, deep into the far back of the building. There he pressed open a door to a room already alight with a candle's glow. A carafe of wine awaited on a table with a wedge of cheese and loaf of bread. A fire burned; the cover had been drawn down from the bed, which seemed to dominate the crude room. It had been arranged as if for a lover's tryst.

She spun around and stood, straight and regal, and waited. Comte Langlois entered behind her and leaned against the door. He was a handsome man with flashing dark eyes, a lean face with a trim beard, and flowing dark hair; she thought again that he looked like a vulture—or a wolf!

"There was no need for so elaborate a set-up," she informed him coolly. "I arranged this meeting that you might bring a message to the King of France. You will be amply rewarded."

"Ah, lady. How can you be so like ice when I have risked life and limb to come here—to your rescue?"

"How so, sir?" she said carefully.

Langlois was still against the door. She heard him slide the bolt behind him. Her heart began to race. Dear God, what had she done? He walked to her, and she fought for control, certain still that she could best him with her wits, no matter what his intention.

He caught her hands, bowing as he held them, like the most gallant of knights in the most chivalric of times. "Alas, my lady, it has been said that Kind Edward's plans for you have not met with any desires of your own, that there is all but open warfare between you—and the Scottish savage of King Edward's choosing."

Cold seemed to sweep along her spine. She longed to wrench her hands free.

Outside, flattened against the doorway in the shadowy corridor, Adrien MacLachlan arched a brow high, once again feeling his temper begin to simmer and brew.

"I wrote to you because—" Danielle began to Langlois.

But the comte quickly cut her off. "Ah, lady, if there is no consummation of your vows, then you are free, and the good French king can bring matters before the pope."

Adrien's fingers wound into fists at his side. No consummation of vows, eh? He'd like to consummate his fingers right around her throat! He tested the door. Bolted. But it was constructed of flimsy wood, and one butt of his shoulder would take it down. He started to move against it but paused, waiting for Danielle's next words.

Danielle was damning herself and her foolishness for thinking that this man might actually have had the welfare of his king in mind. Comte Langlois was interested in himself—in having her, and Aville. Still, she needed to play this carefully. "Perhaps there are other matters we can discuss at a later date. But this matter must be settled first. Perhaps it would be best if you escorted me to King Jean and I gave him my information in person," she said. She felt a chill again. His dark eyes narrowed and took on a cunning and determined glitter. "Comte, I don't intend to offend you. You are surely a worthy nobleman, but there are matters at stake of greater importance than myself and Aville."

In the hallway, Adrien clenched his teeth so hard he feared they might crack.

"But think of it, lady," Langlois interrupted, his voice gutteral. "King Jean would be pleased. We go to the French king with our love an accomplished thing, and a marriage can thus be surely arranged—and you are free from that savage, heathen lout! Lady, you led me to believe that there would be great reward for me if I were to help you. I will have that reward.

Now, dear sweet beauty! Since there is nothing at all between you and the savage—''

"Comte, I have a message for King Jean! Think of his anger—''

"Think of his pleasure that you may be claimed by a Frenchman rather than that arrogant Scottish bastard!''

She stared at him, growing outraged, furious with herself. She had tried to put just enough in her note to entice him to meet her, but Langlois was assuming she had given him an invitation to wed and bed her!

Oh, she had to think, for were he to touch her, she would most surely long to die; something inside of her would perish—her heart and, perhaps, her soul as well.

Her temper suddenly got the best of her and she wrenched her hands free and stared at him with all her hauteur she had learned from a childhood at court among the King and Queen of England and their royal brood. "No!"

She pushed impatiently past him and for a moment, her manner prevailed. Langlois fell back. But when she would have kept moving toward the door, he suddenly caught her shoulders and wrenched her back before him. He was angry, dark eyes glowing. "I had meant to be gentle. Seduce you, my lady, and seal our pact with your willing agreement. But though I have served loyally, lady, I am one of the lesser nobles of the French king's court and am in dire need of the lands and finances that come with your French holdings. Ah, milady, not to mention how I have hungered for your beauty! I swear, we *will* go to the king as lovers, needing only his blessing to legalize our union!''

"Not in a pig's eye!'' she swore, and kicked him soundly where it would do the greatest harm.

He bellowed in pain, doubling over. Danielle shot away from him, but his fingers snagged into the fullness of her cloak and she went down with a hard thud in a tangle of coarse brown wool, the breath knocked out of her. Stunned, she struggled to breathe. Then Langlois was on top of her.

"Dear lady, I had meant to have this done upon a bed, but if the floor be your choice . . .''

She struggled to free her wrists and managed to slam the side of his face with her open palm. She thought she heard the sound of an explosion, but she could not be sure, for he returned her blow and her head was ringing. She wiggled and thrashed, desperate and determined, and not untalented in the art of self-defense. An elbow to his throat, nails down his cheek . . . but could she prevail? Langlois was a knight trained to combat, one who wore massive steel upon a warhorse, and though perhaps she might have the wits to defeat him, in the end she might not have the strength.

"Sweet Jesu, milady, by God, will you just be still! I'd not hurt you, if you'd just let me touch you—" Langlois began. Then he was suddenly quite silent. He wasn't staring at her, but at something . . . someone else. A towering, cloaked figure who stood just behind her.

The she knew what the sound of the explosion had been— the door shattering. And the man who had broken it down loomed over them.

He was very tall and broad-shouldered; his presence dominated the room. His hood hung back from his face and his features, chiseled like stone, rugged and striking, were in no way hidden. His hair was thick, fire-blond, while his brows and lashes were a deeper honeyed shade, adding to the effect of his gaze. Eyes of true gold stared down at them both with a deadly glitter.

The sword in his right hand was pointed at the Frenchmen's throat.

Adrien! Danielle thought, and though she was desperately grateful for the Frenchman's downfall, terror and dismay filled her heart. Adrien. Oh, God. He had caught her. She had only meant to warn Jean, and nothing more.

Adrien—oh, God.

He might well hang her himself. She had thought he was away, fighting; she had never imagined that he might discover her in this endeavor! He had been gone again, fighting his never-ending battle, and it had been so long! How many times had she lain awake, longing to see him . . .

But not like this—oh, God, not like this! In his eyes she saw deadly fury.

Yet he spoke so calmly.

"Touch her, my good man, but once again," Adrien warned, "and I shall sever that protrusion of your lower body that makes you act like such a fool . . . before I lop off your head!" His voice was almost pleasant, yet deeply chilling, and Danielle felt a wall of ice come sweeping down upon her. Langlois rose slowly and carefully, for Adrien's sword remained at his throat where a pulse beat furiously against the flesh.

"Now you, Danielle," Adrien commanded, his eyes on Langlois and not on her.

She rose, cheeks flushed with humiliation.

"How—how long were you standing there?" she asked.

"Long enough," he said, and did not glance her way.

"And you let him maul me so—"

"You seemed to be doing fine on your own," he snapped curtly. "In fact, I was not at all sure you desired a rescue, since you were so intent on this assignation."

"Aye!" cried Langlois. "Indeed, I am the man to come to the lady's rescue, and indeed, my lady, you needn't fear now. Who is this lout? Be aware this house is filled with men loyal to the French king, men who will mow down this English knave!"

"Call them," Adrien suggested, his voice little more than a whisper, his eyes glittering like twin fires from hell. Despite herself, Danielle trembled, then spun around with fear, for she could hear the pounding of footsteps along the hallway. A fat man in an apron, obviously the proprietor of the establishment, ran into the room, followed by two big men armed with knives.

"Do you need assistance, milord?" the fat man demanded of Langlois.

"Indeed!" Langlois cried wryly, for it was quite obvious he stood in discomfort, a sword tip still at his throat.

"I seek no trouble with you, and with the dead already upon my conscience, I'd not add more corpses here!" Adrien informed the gathering, not a muscle twitching. "I don't intend to kill the comte, just leave with the lady—"

"She came to me to escape the English!" Langlois cried. "You will not leave with her—I mean to wed her—"

"Well, that, sir, cannot come about, for she has a husband," Adrien said dryly.

"No true marriage—"

"True in every way." Adrien said. His eyes lit upon Danielle and she struggled to breathe as she felt the touch of gold fire. He looked from her back to the men and smiled icily. "I would be delighted to prove it, if the lady is not willing to admit it. A midwife can be called."

"But—" Langlois began.

"Alas! I am aware that the lady used her wiles upon you, milord comte, and she does so exceedingly well! Unless one knows her, of course. Which I do. You were duped, sir, and that is why you draw breath this very instant." He stared at Danielle, a hard, rueful smile curled into the corner of his lip.' "She is charming, is she not? But as I've said, I know her well, and you, sir, should now be warned to beware of such devious and seductive charm and beauty! I'll let you live to-day . . ." His eyes left Danielle's face and he stared sharply at Langlois, "But if we meet again, sir, you die!"'

Langlois gasped, realizing just who had accosted him. "MacLachlan!" he cried out.

"Indeed." Adrien inclined his head. "Ah, yes! I am that savage, heathen Scotsman. Comte, *c'est moi.*"

For a moment, Langlois looked decidedly ill. Adrien's reputation for expertise in tournaments and in battle was well known throughout the Christian world. A flick of the wrist, and . . .

But Langlois seemed to think Adrien outnumbered.

"Take him!" Langlois cried out, and the two cutthroats started forward to do his bidding, the one to the right of the proprietor raising a honed blade and slashing down with tremendous strength.

Yet the man was a simple barroom brawler; Adrien had spent his life learning to do battle. Steel met steel, and Adrien drew back first, as swift as mercury, and the man fell to the floor. A cry flew from Danielle's lips.

"Seize him, fool!" Langlois shouted to the second man, who

started forward, stared at Adrien's blade, and swiftly retreated. Langlois let out a strangled sound which was silenced when Adrien's swordpoint pressed against his throat again. "Adieu, milord comte! I should kill you, but I will spill no more blood than necessary over this treachery. She did summon you."

Danielle stifled a cry when Adrien's fingers wound around her upper arm, for his hold was like steel, with no mercy. She found herself blindly propelled out the door. His fingers then entwined with hers as he raced her down the hallway, pausing as he neared the stairs, for more men had come up to meet him.

"Get me a weapon!" she cried.

"Not while I draw breath, milady! It would fester in my back!"

"I never brought arms against you!"

"I beg to differ!"

"You've too many men to fight!" she cried. "You'll kill us both, unless you've men of your own waiting below."

"I came alone."

"Alone!" she cried in dismay. It seemed that all of the tavern had risen, and every man was reaching for a weapon.

"I try not to invite witnesses when I am hoping to prevent a rock-headed little wench from endangering herself in the act of betraying the King of England—not to mention me!" he retorted.

A crimson flood rose swiftly to her cheeks even as he cried out to her again. "Get behind me. Close. And if you even think to betray me here again, I swear before God, I'll live long enough to make you regret it!"

She had no choice but to obey him, for he still held her fingers. She'd had no intention of giving him the least resistance, but it seemed that he was more furious than she might have imagined, even knowing him. Fear seemed to fill her heart anew as she realized that even now, as their lives were threatened, he would not be surprised at any betrayal from her.

There were numerous men to meet his sword, men practiced at illegal professions, but none of them so perfectly trained to battle and hand-to-hand combat. His first blow took the man at the top of the stairs, who fell backward, hurtling the others down like felled trees. Adrien stepped over them swiftly, dragging her along. His strength was tremendous. When a huge fellow charged them at the foot of the stairs, he swung her hard to the side before him, stepping aside just in time for the man to crash headfirst into the stairs.

"Duck!" Adrien charged her, and he did so as well as a cutthroat's sword arced above their heads. Adrien rose, his sword swinging, and their attacker fell. He spun around, slicing the man who had come behind them, even before she had time to scream out a warning. He stepped over the dead men, wrenching her along with him. Another, in front of him, fell at a thrust from his sword. The others fell away, watching them.

He swiftly led her from the tavern, out into the night.

He might have come without armor or companions, but he had brought Matthew, the swiftest of his four war stallions. He saw the gelding she had taken from Prince Edward's stables, untethered it, and slapped its haunches, sending the animal on its way. Then he pushed her ahead of him, throwing her atop Matthew before leaping up behind her. She didn't look back, yet she could hear the roar of anger as men grouped together again and found their courage to follow. Adrien kneed the animal. The horse began to race. She felt its majestic power beneath her and the hard-muscled chest of the man behind her, hot and vital. She closed her eyes, leaning against Matthew's neck in the wild ride as branches and leaves slapped at her face and tore at her cloak.

Matthew left the others far behind, and in time, Danielle became aware that they were out of danger, that Adrien raced on out of fury. He slowed when they came to the river, reining the stallion in at the bank. Both bridges were far downstream to the east.

He nudged the horse forward.

"It's freezing!" she cried out in protest.

"You might have killed us both—and you are afraid of a little water?"

"I am afraid of nothing."

"You lie, for you had best be afraid of me tonight!"

"If I would fear you at all, it would be because it appears you intend to drown us!"

"Nay, be glad of the water. Perhaps my temper will be cooled."

They entered into the water. The cold was brutal.

"Oh, you can just go straight to hell!" she snapped, praying that he attributed her shaking to the coldness of the water and not to the wild stirring within her.

They reached the opposite bank and once again, he began to ride hard. The breeze whipped against her soaked clothing and she shivered anew. They rode on and on. Then she saw the stone walls of her own fortress of Aville.

The gates opened as they neared them and rode quickly in, then closed behind them at an invisible command. Adrien rode the stallion straight to the door that led to the manor keep. In the darkness, a groom stirred when called to take Matthew's reins and care for him.

Danielle could scarcely walk when she was set upon the ground, but he was in a mood to grant no mercy as she tried to elude him, hurrying for the hall. He caught her arm, not allowing her a moment's respite. She prayed to see a familiar face. Rem, Daylin, Monteine . . . anyone.

But the hall was empty.

"Upstairs, my lady!" he commanded, and she had little choice as he dragged her along to the master's chambers.

She found herself all but thrown into the room, spinning to stand at the foot of the carved, four-poster bed, while he paced before the massive fire that burned in the huge fireplace.

She looked longingly to the door. She was shaking, for she knew what she had done. Treason against the King of England. And worse: she had betrayed him.

"No servants will attend you here tonight, milady. When I discovered your foolish treachery, I saw to it that I could bring you back unseen. These are no longer games you play with me! You and your indignant protestations of innocence! This was treason, Danielle. The servants have been sent out for the night. Don't look to others for help."

"I look nowhere for help!" she lied.

"Nay, lady?"

She refused to respond, but despite herself, she shivered wretchedly; her clothing felt like a glove of ice.

Suddenly he ceased his pacing and stared at her, seeing her discomfort. "Get those things off!" he roared. But she lifted her chin stubbornly, fighting a threatening rush of tears. "They are causing you to shiver," he snapped.

"I shall shiver if I choose."

"Indeed, you shall shiver, but because *I* choose—I want you to shiver in abject fear!" he growled. And as he started toward her, she took a step backward, crying out quickly. She was an idiot; she could hang for her offense.

"As you—command!" she gasped.

He halted, glittering eyes still offering her no hint that his anger might abate, his temper relent. But as her cloak fell to the ground, he turned to the bed, drawing from it the soft covering of Flemish wool. He waited. She gritted her teeth and cast off her shoes and hose, tunic and chemise. His searing gaze swept contemptuously over her, and he cast the blanket her way. She quickly wrapped it around herself. He drew his own soaked cloak from his shoulders, letting it fall, and stood in simple but expensive garments that hugged his muscled frame—hose, shirt, and tunic. He was every bit as tall as their renowned Plantagenet king, as well-versed in war, grown hard and solid, muscled like steel, in its pursuit. Indeed, she had learned the strength of those muscles, and felt a quivering deep within her even now, which she fought valiantly to ignore.

She inched her chin up, standing very still, determined not to cry out. She could explain, but he would never believe her.

"Sweet Jesu!" he swore soundly. "Edward does not deserve this hatred on your part!"

She forced herself to remain calm. "I wished no harm to Edward. I don't hate him. I merely sought to warn King Jean—"

"King Jean is well aware there will be battle, and what aids the French king injures the English one! To help Jean, lady, you do great hurt to Edward!"

That gave her quite a tug upon her heart, for she felt for Edward as she did for Adrien. So very often, she had loathed him. Had been infuriated by him, determined to defy him, to defeat him.

And yet . . .

She loved him as well.

"My God!" he said suddenly, his voice thick and trembling with renewed anger. "Do you know that heads have rolled, that necks have been broken, for far less than you attempted this night? Good Lord, I should strike you down, you little fool!"

Guilt assailed her again. She could not let him see it.

"You are Edward's lackey," she ventured. "You have gained everything through him."

"Including you?"

"Including my lands and titles!" she whispered.

"Would that I had been deprived! And, aye, lady! I am his lackey, I am his man, and I warn you now, don't ever forget it again, or that you are my wife!"

"Well, sir, you came for me. I was duly stopped in my efforts. And I know that you will judge me and sentence me as you see fit—you condemned me when I was innocent. At least this time I am guilty of hoping to see King Jean live! But as you are in such a wretched mood, I am well aware that there's nothing else I can say to you this evening. I cannot apologize for what I meant to do. I have never lied to you about my loyalties or—emotions." But she *had* lied. She'd never let him know that trying to remain loyal to old vows had slowly become harder and harder, that she had long loved him as fiercely as she fought him.

She certainly couldn't tell him such a thing now. And indeed, she needed to tread very carefully. She had crossed him before, and paid the price, but she had never seen him quite this angry.

Don't think of it! she warned herself.

Head high, she started walking across the room. He had turned his back on her in anger once before. If only she could escape his fury now.

He watched her for several moments, not making a move, one brow arched high with amazement.

But she didn't make the door.

"Oh, no, milady! You're not leaving tonight!" he assured her, his long strides allowing him to beat her soundly to the door. He blocked it with the formidable wall of his body.

She stepped back, struggling anew for some dignity, pride, and control.

And courage.

"I should flay you to within an inch of your life!" he snapped out so suddenly that she jerked back, biting into her lip.

"I had to—"

"Ah, yes, the hell with the English blood in you—you had that French vow to keep! Well, that somewhat explains why you would so wretchedly use the very king within whose household you were raised."

"Then give me over to the king!" she cried out, alarmed at how desperately she pleaded. "Let's end this—"

He shook his head slowly. "End it? We've barely begun."

"Surely," she mocked, "you are needed elsewhere. You are the king's champion. Have you no enemies to challenge tonight? No dragons to slay?"

He smiled. "No dragons this evening for me, my pet. Just one for you. Me." His glittering gold eyes narrowed dangerously. "Tell me, milady, just what did you write to that dolt, Langlois? You had taken no vows? No marriage was consummated?"

Color stained her cheeks. "I merely said that I needed his assistance."

"You were willing to lie with him to reach the French king?" he demanded.

She shook her head, blood draining from her face. "You were there! You know that I was not—"

"Ah, yes, my love, thank God that I am aware you were not willing to give anything away—for free."

"How dare you—"

"How dare you ask?" he demanded, cutting her off, his voice deep and husky with fury.

She was still for a moment. The room seemed tight and small.

Once, she had been determined to deny him. Maybe she had

been afraid even then of the tempest he would create within her heart. Maybe she had always known that if he touched her but once . . .

Adrien continued. "You seduced him with promises of your hand in marriage. Sweet Jesu, milady, but you speak of vows! I remember the vows you made to *me*, quite clearly, if you do not. Every vow."

He was walking toward her. It was all that she could manage to keep from screaming aloud, from running madly and wildly, only to slam herself against the wall.

"I remember the vows!" she whispered.

He stood just inches from her, and she felt his tremendous strength and heat as if he touched her. His eyes raked her with their golden fire and now she did move back again, just inches, yet he followed her. She stood to the far wall and he set a palm against it, leaning closer to her still, and smiling once again.

"Ah, milady, do you know what astounds and dismays me most?" he demanded.

She wet her lips warily. "What?"

"That you could say that our marriage had not been consummated. Indeed, I remember even that first night so very well!"

"Aye!" she cried, newly alarmed, for he had thought her guilty of treachery that night as well. She decided she must go on the offensive. "You threatened to prove to that rabble tonight that our marriage was real. You call yourself a knight! You speak of chilvary—"

"I seldom speak of chivalry. And I merely informed the fools that a midwife could be summoned to prove that you were no sweet, innocent lass!"

She gasped. "You would have had me—"

"I would have given nothing to those wretched fools, milady, even to prove to your too-amorous but well-besotted Frenchman that you are *legally* and in every way very much a wife—*my* wife. But there is something I do most earnestly intend to give you!"

She swallowed hard, fought for courage, narrowed her eyes. "And what is that, milord tyrant?"

"A jog to your memory, milady wife. I had not realized I had so failed in my husbandly duties that you could forget such a thing as the consummation of your marriage."

"Oh, you fail at nothing!" she cried out. "And my memory is just fine. I haven't forgotten a thing—"

She broke off, gasping as she found her blanket wrenched from her and thrown to the floor. She recognized the glitter in his eyes as more than anger and she caught her breath in dismay, thinking of the times when she had longed for him, ached for him, and yet . . .

He would not forget what she had done tonight, and he would not forgive her, and she couldn't even fathom where they would go from here. She hadn't been his choice for a wife; her memory, especially now, seemed far more keen than he could ever fathom. As seconds flew between them, she felt the years cascading past, the pain, the anguish, the Black Death, the loss of so very much to them both.

"No . . ." she whispered.

"Damn you," he told her.

She tried to wrench away. He would not allow it.

"You will remember who you are."

"And to whom I belong?" she cried in protest.

"Aye, lady, indeed!

His lips touched hers. They burned, they were fire, like his eyes . . . they ignited the seeds of desire deep inside her, aroused her mercilessly. His palm cradled her cheek, his lips and tongue caressed her mouth. She closed her eyes, aware of nothing but her senses for several seconds . . .

Dear God, no, he would never forgive her this time!

His lips broke from hers.

She struggled from a fog, trying to remind herself that she knew him well, that he held her in contempt and distrust for this night's work, and that she would be made to pay.

"Please . . ."

She heard the word, and was surprised to realize that she had issued the plea herself.

For a moment, he was equally startled. "Ah, lady? Beg mercy, would you?"

The taunt in his voice brought her eyes flying open full upon his.

"Not in a—"

"In a pig's eye?" he suggested, using her term.

"You are the worst of knaves and I'll never beg anything of you!" she promised, pushing wildly against his chest to free herself.

But his hands were suddenly upon her wrists. His eyes were burning into hers once again, and they were dead still together while the flames snapped and crackled in the hearth.

"Indeed, milady, tonight, by God, you will please me! For I want everything that I have remembered, the hungers of so many nights appeased. Aye, please me. Ease away the rage. I demand it!"

She found herself up and in his arms, and falling into the softness of the bed that had awaited them, his body wickedly hot as he pressed her nakedness down into the coolness of the linen sheets. Again his lips caught hers. With pressure now, with fierce demand. She tried to twist from his assault, felt the liquid flame as his tongue pressed past the barriers of her lips and teeth, entering into her, filling her sweetly. His hands raked over her naked thighs and hips, rose to cover and caress her breasts. His weight held her still; his hands commanded a magic of equal power, his lips seduced with ruthless hunger. He rose above her, casting aside tunic and shirt with an urgency that tore the latter, yet he didn't seem to notice. She swallowed again, feeling the tremors fill her that had from the start when she gazed upon his body. He was bronzed and scarred upon the shoulder and chest, incredibly beautiful nonetheless, for his taut muscles were temptation in themselves, the copper sheen of the fire that danced upon them as haunting as the flicker of flame that drew a moth to a fire's deadly heat.

She would not touch, she would not fall, she would not burn in the flames . . .

But she would, for he drew her hand to his chest, where it

lay upon the thunder of his heart, the softness of the crisp red-gold hair. And she met his eyes still when he drew her hand ever downward, enclosing her slender, trembling fingers around the great shaft, life and fire itself. His body shuddered massively, yet his eyes pinned her still and when she would have gasped and drawn her touch away, his fingers curled around her own and a half-smile curved his lip.

"Lest you forget!" he whispered, and she discovered herself meeting his eyes, trembling within, and longing for him in the most traitorous way. Yet his gaze held her until he eased himself downward, parted her thighs, met her eyes once again. She cried out, trying to twist away again, knowing his intent. There was no escape. He ravaged her intimately with tongue and touch until it seemed that she plummeted into an abyss, writhing, gasping, and crying out again . . .

Burning in the flames.

He rose above her, entered her. His fingers entwined with hers at either side of her head as the fullness of him thrust into her, deeper, deeper still, deeper again. She closed her eyes, yet felt his fierce gaze upon her, and opened them again.

"Lest you forget *me* . . ." he whispered.

She could never forget. Never, never.

Not this tempest, not this fire. Not the man, tension and steel above and within her now, not this reckless beat and thrust, climbing, thundering, demanding . . .

Sweet, mindless pressure spiralled within her. Honeyed pleasure doused her body and soul even as she felt his last shuddering thrust impale her, the stream of his seed fill her. She closed her eyes tightly, dismayed by the hot tears that threatened to spill as he moved away from her.

Already, he was rising.

Tonight he had come for her.

But her fate had to be decided. Come the daylight, he had to ride to battle, and she was a traitor.

It was war. As it had always been, from the first time they had met. Aye, she had known him forever. Perhaps she had loved him just as long. Been his enemy as long.

Alas, no!

Longer.

For war had begun before they met, before she was even born.

And thus their roles had been cast.

Part I

To the victor . . .

Chapter 1

The Castle of Aville
Fall, 1336

"I know how to breach the walls," Adrien MacLachlan said.

No one heard him. Edward was in a rage. Sweeping his great mantle behind him, the towering Plantagenet king shouted again in fury. "By God, this is madness! I, Edward, the warrior king, cannot breach walls held by a woman!"

Around his campfire, the king's most illustrious knights held silent against his wrath, deeply frustrated themselves. They were muddied, weary, bloodied, and cold. It had seemed a simple enough measure to take Aville, a small fortress situated on land within Edward's own duchy. A fortress held by Lenore, daughter of the late Comte Jon d'Aville, a second cousin to the Valois king.

It was rumored that the French king hid within the walls, and thus, King Edward's preoccupation with taking the fortress, despite the countess's talent with boiling oil, flaming arrows, and other methods of defense.

"Can't someone give me advice?" the king demanded.

"Sire!" Adrien cried. "I know how to breach the walls."

Edward, hearing the boy at last, spun around. His ward, the Scotish lad, stood at the entry to the tent.

The boy was just ten, but he was already tall and showed great promise of strength in the breadth of his shoulders. His golden eyes were steady and shrewd, and along with his growing prowess with arms, he had a keen desire for knowledge, spending many of his free hours with his head buried in books. He also showed great courage, Edward thought, to come upon this gathering at his tender age—and offer advice.

"Ah, the Scots lad is going to advise us!" Brian of Perth groaned angrily. He was in a foul mood, having received a burn on his shoulder that day. "Get on out of here, lad!"

"Wait!" the king commanded, his cold blue gaze putting Brian in his place. "The Scots have been known to teach us many a lesson! Come in, boy. I'll listen to any piece of tactical advice at this time!"

Adrien MacLachlan stepped into the center of the circle, closer to the fire. He kept his head high, his shoulders straight, aware that he must give an impression of wisdom and strength far greater than his years allowed. His father had taught him well.

"A poor man, even one with noble blood, must be a strong one, boy. If you would survive these troubled times, my lad, I would create a great warrior of you. Most importantly, impoverished men—aye, even defeated men, such as ourselves!—must excel, and thus, in the end, become the victorious. Never accept defeat, my son. Not when you fear a stronger opponent. Not when you have taken the first blow. Never surrender, for the only surrender there can be is death itself. Fight hard, boy, fight with your wits as well as your brawn. Never be afraid to learn. Then fight for honor, fight to carve a place for yourself in this fine harsh world of chivalry and death. Fight hard, and so, my boy, you will conquer even kings!"

Not long ago, Carlin, chieftain of the clan MacLachlan, had said those words to him. Grandson of a Scottish earl, kin to the family of the late, great Robert the Bruce, he was then suffering the defeat of the forces of Robert's son, David II, as

Edward of England set another pretender, another Baliol, upon the throne of Scotland. Because of that unrest, it seemed to Adrien that he had been born fighting. Constant battle with the English had stripped them of crops and livestock. Baliol was on the throne, but the MacLachlans fought for David II.

But one day, as battle ebbed, he had seen his father in the midst of a group of well-armed knights. One mounted man stared down at his father; he recognized that man as his greatest enemy—Edward III. Adrien had been certain that the English king had come to kill his father. And so, nothing, not even life itself, had mattered.

He ran across the fields, his small dirk in his hands. With a cry of rage, he had flown at Edward and nearly toppled him from his horse. He'd had his dirk at the man's throat, ready to strike, when his father pulled him from their enemy.

"Nay, lad, nay!" warned Carlin.

"Hang the boy!" a man cried. "Your Grace, he all but slit your throat."

But the king dismounted and came forward, tipping up his visor. Adrien saw a pair of bright blue eyes, a handsome face framed by golden hair.

"Hang him? This son of so valiant a warrior himself, a man come to make his terms with me? I think not! The lad has just shown more courage—and skill, I might add—than a score of you, my finest!"

There was a bellow of laughter from some of the men.

"Laird MacLachlan!" the king continued. "We are well met—your honor is thus preserved. If it is your will, this fine son of yours will reside at my court and be raised with my oldest son as his constant companion. I will keep him safe, and you will no longer harry my northern borders."

"Aye, Edward, King of England!" Adrien's father agreed.

"Nay, Father, I'll not leave you—" Adrien began, but his father closed his lips with his hand, and later, in the ruins of the family fortress, Adrien was told the truth of it.

"My boy, we've fought him good and long and hard, but he's an enemy I respect. He doesn't realize that the Scots will never accept a Baliol upon the throne, but one day, I warrant,

David Bruce will be back. But we starve here. I need you at the king's court. I need to know what happens among the Englishmen, I need them to take on the expense of training and arming you. I pray that you will go now and give the King of England all the loyalty and obedience you have shown me. I love you, son. I couldna' be prouder of you.''

Soon after they had ridden south, the king of England had summoned Adrien to stand before him again. He had stood, grave, his hands behind his back. "Your father was one of the finest fighting men I knew, boy. You must always be proud of him, for all men respect his memory, Englishmen and Scots.''

"His—memory?''

"He sent you with me and made peace because he knew he was dying. And among your unruly tribesmen there were many who might have been willing to kill you for your family holdings—such as they have fallen to be! Lad, your mother was Lady Margaret of Meadenlay. Her brother has just perished in battle—his son succumbed to fever last week. You have inherited English lands in the south, and are now, my boy, the Count of Meadenlay and Laird of Reggar. By your father's will, I stand as your guardian, and you will remain in my service.''

And so, he became to be with Edward now, and dared to speak to the knights here. He had taken part in some of the assaults against the walls. The king's men grudgingly acknowledged his abilities—some gained in Scotland, and some learned from the same master swordsmen who trained the king's own sons. But their assaults were all for nothing. Like the others, he had seen the beautiful Lenore d'Aville upon the ramparts, ordering down the rain of flaming destruction which had fallen on the English. They had called her a witch, a temptress, seducing men to their deaths. For it was true. Great knights stared up at her, captivated by the sight of her ebony hair blowing in the wind, and death had fallen upon them. Even Edward raged, claiming his men were bewitched.

"Speak up, Scotsman!'' the king commanded.

"We must dig a tunnel,'' Adrien said.

"A tunnel!'' Sir George scoffed.

"Would you continue sacrificing men to the boiling oil and

oatmeal the countess casts down each day? When we could so easily dig beneath her defenses, get a man in to open the gates, and fight then in fair hand to hand combat?''

''Bah! We keep up the battering ram, break the portcullis!'' roared William of Chelsey, an experienced knight.

Adrien spoke swiftly. ''Think again! Hear me! At what great loss, sire? And what if there is a double portcullis, with murderer's slits above? More men will die, trapped in agony as the countess rains oil or arrows upon them.''

Robert of Oxford, an older knight who had long served the king, spoke up in the boy's defense. ''He has studied the architecture of these castles, sire,'' he said quietly.

Edward eyed the boy. ''I'll see more of this plan. You will draw it out for me. Robert, get parchment. Show me, boy, show me what you have in mind.''

With Robert supporting him, Adrien did so, explaining how such strategies had worked years before for Roman and Greek conquerors on different types of structures.

''Sire, I do suggest,'' said William of Chelsey, ''that our young Scots lad—with all his book knowledge—he be the one to enter the castle, and thus bring about its downfall.''

''He's but a decade on this earth!'' Edward snapped.

''But willing to go, sire!'' Adrien said excitedly. He trembled, afraid, and yet eager. Fear was not a bad thing; letting it defeat courage was. He longed to be the warrior his father had told him he must be. He was anxious to prove himself to the king—and to himself.

In the end, it was determined that he would go.

Preparations began; Adrien's strategy was put into play. Men slinked to the walls in the cover of rain and night. Miners tunneled deeply. If they were discovered, they would surely perish, for the defenders of the castle would flood their tunnel and drown them all.

But the tunnel was not discovered, and Adrien managed to get within the walls, unseen. Under the cover of darkness, he chopped the ropes that held the gates, and the English troops came charging through.

Caught within the castle walls himself, he fought that day

against a dozen Frenchmen determined to place his head on a spike above their walls; he fought desperately, for his life, and he fought afraid.

But he did not let the fear defeat him, and that night, though the English knights and nobles and infantrymen teased him, they toasted him as well.

Within the castle walls at long last, Edward III, King of England, watched the flames dance. Christ's blood! He was weary. He had never expected to fight so exhaustingly here— only to discover that the French king was *not* in residence here after all!

He swallowed down the contents of a chalice of fine claret as he stood before the hearth, easing his tensions somewhat. But then, Robert of Oxford entered behind him.

"I have brought the countess," Robert said.

The countess! the king thought furiously. Despite his many good points, Edward III was a Plantagenet king, and all knew that the Plantagenets were a passionate and rare breed of men, prone to rages. In a rage, he was formidable. He was a towering man, a warrior king who held his power in his own two mighty hands.

He had learned early that it was necessary to do so. His grandfather had been the great King Edward I—the Hammer of the Scots. His father, the unfortunate Edward II, had lost Scotland to Robert the Bruce. Edward II had been a weak ruler who had formed intimate liaisons with evil and crafty supporters—and fallen prey to an invasion of his country by his own queen and her lover. Edward II had been captured, forced to abdicate to his son, then cruelly murdered.

Crowned King of England when he was fifteen, Edward had not been unaware of his position, or his past, or of the sins of either of his parents. His father had been weak, his mother had been called the she-wolf of France. His mother's lover, Roger Mortimer, the Earl of March, had held complete sway with her, and Edward had not been king long before being warned that Mortimer wished to seize the throne himself. But the people, nobles and the commons alike, were up in arms against Mortimer.

And so, when Edward was eighteen, Mortimer met his death, hanged on the common gallows at Tyburn. Edward knew from that time on that he must be a strong king. His first son, Edward of Woodstock, was born that same year. He swore to himself that he would build a powerful monarchy, restore respect for the royal family, and rule with both power and compassion. He was blessed with a good queen, Philippa of Hainault, and though she was no great beauty, she was warm, intelligent—fertile, the good Lord bless her!—and quickly beloved of his people.

Yet not even Edward's best intentions, nor his affection for his wife, could change the fact of his Plantagenet blood, and tonight, he paced with an energy and tension to match that of the leopards of his blazon and arms.

It had been nearly three hundred years since the Conquest of England, nearly two hundred since Henry II and Eleanor had brought the titles of their own French lands into the English monarchy. Granted, John of England had lost a great deal of the English royal holdings and prestige in the first years of the thirteenth century, but certain lands had remained strongholds. Kings of England had been calling themselves kings of France for many years, yet Edward had a better reason than most to do so, for his mother, Isabella, she-wolf of France that she might have been, had also been the daughter of Philip the Fair. Three of her brothers had taken the French crown; all three had died childless. Claims through the female line had been debarred by the parliament in Paris, and the crown had gone to Philip of Valois, a cousin of the three deceased Capetians, then to Edward himself. Edward argued that although females themselves might be barred, he was a male, and a more direct descendant of Philip the Fair.

Edward knew he hadn't really the strength of men and arms to seize the French throne, but Philip was now after the duchy of Acquitaine, perhaps the most important English possession left upon French soil. Philip also threatened Edward that there would be no solution to the problem of Acquitaine until Edward granted the Scots their rights, and he'd be damned if he'd let the French dictate to him about the Scots!

So Edward had come here to do battle with his French cousin—and done battle with a woman instead.

"Bring her in," he commanded now to Robert.

As she was led into the room, Edward awaited a cry for mercy, a word, but her head remained high. Her hair was blacker than the night, streaming free down her back. Her gown was a soft purple, hem, neck, and sleeves trimmed in fur. Her eyes were green, a blazing emerald, meeting his with no apology, and certainly no plea for mercy. She was slim and lithe, the gown molding to her. The soft, clean scent of rose petals seemed to surround her; her face and gown were perfection. He didn't know if it was the sweet scent sweeping over him, or perhaps the one sign of her agitation, the wild rise and fall of her breasts beneath the fur-trimmed bodice, that suddenly created a new emotion within his anger—desire. Fierce, powerful, undeniable.

Her face was perfectly sculpted. If he touched it, he thought, her cheeks would feel like silk. Her long, ink-black hair would tease and arouse the senses.

She stared at him with calm, defiant contempt. Even now she hadn't the sense to beg mercy. Perhaps she felt that her noble blood would protect her. Dear God, but she was wrong.

He took a step toward her, furious that he could want her so when she had so blatantly defied him. By God, he had the power to execute her if he chose!

"Witch!" he charged her, and his hand cracked hard across her face, so hard that it startled her from her imperious stance, sending her down upon a knee. He stared down at her, a moment's remorse seizing him. But then her face raised to his once again, and her eyes seemed to gleam with the brilliance of a thousand gems.

She rose to her feet, cheek reddened, and cried out, "You are no king here! The great Edward, the great warrior! Making battle with children, burning crops, slaughtering animals. You may take what you will, but no one will surrender to you, no one here will beg mercy from you!"

And with those words, she threw herself at him, nails clawing for his face. Stunned that anyone, man or woman, would dare take such action, he threw his arms up just in time to defend himself. Still, her impetus brought them both crashing down upon the wooden floor before the hearth. Fighting desperately now, she sought to free herself from his weight. The fire blazed all around them. It caught upon the blade of the tiny knife she drew from her pocket to use in her defense, and in doing, so sealed her fate . . .

He caught her wrist, seized the weapon, sent it flying. He took hold of her beautiful mauve gown, and the sound of the fabric tearing seemed incredibly loud in the otherwise silent room. The blazing green fury in her eyes seduced him anew, along with the feel of her now naked breasts.

She let out a cry as a demon light in his own eyes clearly told her that she had lost her battle. Her fists rained upon his shoulders, denial tore from her lips.

She fought him until she could fight no more. And he didn't give a damn. He was the conqueror, and he took her with a fury, mindless of her innocence . . . yet in the end, his anger abated, and he became gentle, captivated by her perfection, her sweet scent and silken flesh.

When it was over, when she lay curled away from him, determined that he would not hear her sobs or see her tears, he was shamed. That he should feel so, of course, angered him all over again. "Beg mercy now," he said harshly, "and I will see that you keep your life, even if innocence is lost."

She was silent for a moment, then with a sob she whispered, "No one here will surrender, or beg mercy!"

He thought then that he barely knew her, and yet he was amazed by her, fascinated and infatuated.

He thought of Philippa, of the fine family she had given him, of the love she nurtured within it. Philippa, expecting another child. Sons, to give him a strong house, and a strong rule, with his kingdom secured with a multitude of heirs. She was with him often in his camps, alongside as he fought his battles . . .

But she wasn't here tonight. And admittedly, he had been a man to take what he wanted before.

"Perhaps," he murmured suddenly to the girl, "you will beg mercy, in time."

He picked her up—she hadn't the strength left to fight him—and brought her to the master's chamber. He kept her there throughout the night, made love to her more gently, and let the wildfires within his blood run free.

But she never did surrender. Or beg mercy.

When morning came, he left her to go campaigning once again, the castle held secure by Robert of Oxford.

Philip VI of France gave word that he would meet Edward in battle. The King of England waited, ready, eager to fight.

But word came then that Philip had made a hasty retreat back to Paris. Edward's advisors all warned him that he had been left with nothing but barren earth, and that he should take his troops back to Hainault, and there spend the winter.

He determined that he would do so, yet some of what he had taken and conquered, he was loath to let go. As he made his preparations to travel in the great hall of the castle at Aville, and in the midst of other matters, he sent Robert to bring Lenore before him once again.

He had spent each night with her since he had come to the castle, held her, savored her youth and beauty and pride. Indeed, she was something of a witch, for even now, he realized that he cared too deeply for her.

He determined not to meet her gaze, and looked back down at the document he was about to seal and sign. "Lenore d'Aville, it is my intention that you will be brought to England. From there, negotiations with your kinsman, the King of France, may begin for your release."

"This is my castle, and you cannot hold it! And you mustn't bring me to England!" she cried out. She moved toward him angrily, but he caught her hard, determined to remind her of his power. He smiled slowly. "Beg mercy?" he suggested.

"And would it be forthcoming?" she demanded.

He shook his head. "Lady you will come to England, and there be housed within the great tower of London."

The king had one night remaining in the castle at Aville before he had to travel on. He conducted business late into the night, then came to the master's chambers. It was late, but still, she remained before the fire, bathed and naked except for a soft fur about her, her long hair streaming down her back, one bare shoulder catching the bronze of the firelight.

She said nothing when he swept her up, nothing when his desire for her soared and peaked. She lay beside him, and he thought that she slept. But she spoke to him then.

"Let me go!" she pleaded.

But he shook his head. "I cannot."

When morning came, she slept, and he looked down upon her, and knew that he was bewitched. She had touched him as no one ever had. But indeed, he was king.

And he had to ride out that morning.

That winter, Edward III became closely allied with the Flemings, who would pay him homage if he would take on the title and arms of France. He had the fleur-de-lis of France quartered with his own leopards for his banner, which aggravated King Philip. Philip told messengers that he was not displeased that Edward, who was his cousin, might take on the French arms—he was merely displeased that Edward would quarter the leopards first, as if the island of England might be as great as the nation of France.

Edward returned to England. Queen Philippa bore him another child, a boy, and he was named John. Yet as Edward celebrated this fine news, he received a message that it was urgent Robert of Oxford see him. Edward felt a tug at his heart, for he had sent Robert on to London with Lenore.

Good Robert, loyal Robert! He was nearly as tall as Edward himself, a strong and valiant knight, more than sixty years old now and still as straight as an arrow, a gentle man despite his prowess at warfare—the best of men.

Robert congratulated the king on the birth of his son, then said, "Though I am certain I am the only one aware of the lady's condition, there are many very aware of your special interest in the Countess d'Aville. With the queen so recently delivered of such a fine boy, I'm certain that the news of a royal bastard would not be welcome to her. Also, there is the lady herself, and I must tell you that I have come to care very greatly for her.''

Edward stared at Robert for several long moments. Even thinking of the girl could stir his blood, and despite the circumstances, he was ridiculously pleased that she was, indeed, going to bear him a child. He told himself that it would make her pay for her initial defiance of him—she would be reminded of the English king every day of her life once she bore his child.

He leaned back in his chair. ''I will see that the Countess d'Aville is married to a proper lord immediately.''

''To someone kind as well as discreet, I implore you!'' Robert urged him.

The king smiled. ''The kindest and most discreet man. I am now preparing to go to battle once again with my dear cousin, Philip. A naval battle, and I will need you, too, old friend. But first, we will settle this matter here and now, by proxy. Lenore will be married within the week.''

''But to whom—''

''You, my old friend. You will wed the lady. The Count of Gariston has recently died, and left no heirs—therefore, I grant you the land and the titles, and a new bride to bring to them. The castle at Gariston is exceptionally fine, one of the most ancient in the country, yet the old count was a crafty—rich!— fellow, and it is a fine, warm place to abide.''

Robert nodded. ''Sire, I am exceedingly grateful for the holdings. I am too old for such a young bride.''

''Older men have married younger women,'' Edward said.

But indeed, Edward was glad of Robert's age. He did not care to imagine the raven-haired beauty with any man other than himself, and thus it seemed an older man the best choice for Lenore. He could not keep the two from being together, but still, Lenore would remember him while lying in her husband's arms.

Three days later, the Countess d'Aville was married by proxy without her knowledge or consent.

In the tower, she heard only that she had been married to an English baron. She kept her peace, waiting, until Robert of Oxford returned to her, awkward and silent.

"Dear God, what has he done to me now?" she demanded, pleading for an answer.

He cleared his throat. "He has wed you to me."

Robert was deeply dismayed to see the tears that rose in her eyes. He came to her upon one knee, taking her hand in both of his, offering his most profuse apologies. "Dear lady, I am heartfully sorry that you are pained to be saddled with such an old warrior. I love you beyond words, and am happy to act as husband or father, however you would have me."

Lenore set her free hand atop his silvering hair. "Robert, I cry for the land that I will never see again, the people I loved, the ancient castle walls that were my home for so long. With all my heart, I assure you this: of all the men that Edward might have chosen in his kingdom, there is none I might have been more pleased to wed."

He rose from his knees. "I will get you from this place before the child is born. I swear, Lenore, I will love and protect the babe, and from this moment, the child will be mine. I will see you safe, then I must make haste to attend the king again, for he is ready to go to battle once more."

"He will spend his life ready to go to battle," Lenore said quietly.

"You mustn't hate him too much. I will strive all of my life to make up to you what he has done."

"I don't hate him!" she whispered softly.

It was all that she said, yet, looking into her beautiful eyes, Robert realized that she was very much like the king herself. She would fight unto the very end for her own rights. But though she might have defied King Edward, she cared for him in her own way, just as the king had fallen as deeply in love with her as he had dared.

"I will do all that I can—"

"Dear Robert! Nay, I will do all that *I* can to bring happiness to you! There is only one wish that I have, and you cannot grant it."

"And it is?" Robert demanded.

"I wish to go home!" she said softly. "To Aville. I do not hate the king, but . . ." She touched her swollen abdomen. "I would like the three of us to have a chance as a family."

"Ah, lady! I serve the king!" Robert whispered miserably. "And yet, perhaps, if his campaigns prove successful, he will allow me to take you home."

"Perhaps," she agreed, and smiled tenderly.

Edward prepared to battle the French fleet. When the enemy ships began to move, he determined that it was time to attack.

The English pitched into the fray with cogs, broad-beamed merchantmen, while the French were better equipped with proper war galleys.

Though it was fought at sea, the battle was fought with every weapon imaginable—arrows, swords at close range, even stones thrown from ship to ship to rain down death.

Robert of Oxford fought bravely through the long hours of the first day.

That night, while the English king's troops celebrated their first day's victory, a messenger arrived and quickly sought out Robert of Oxford. The count was the father of a baby girl, healthy and fine in every way. His countess, Lenore, begged that Robert take the greatest care of himself, and come home to care for her and their child.

Happiness enveloped Robert. He'd been alone all these years. In his old age, he had a family.

But the next afternoon, when an outstanding victory was all but achieved by the English, a French ship seeking escape sent a rain of arrows hurtling down upon the English vessels.

One found its mark deep within Robert's chest. His men gave chase to the ship, still following his orders. After she was caught, run aground, boarded, and taken, Robert allowed the surgeon to study the arrow in his chest, but he didn't need the sorrowful man to tell him what he already knew.

The wound was mortal.

"Send for the king," he entreated his men. He was in no pain, but he felt a numbness that promised death.

"A priest, man, summon a priest!" called his second in command. "And for the love of God, someone find the king!"

Men rushed in around Robert, tears in their eyes, for he had always been a gallant and courageous man.

A priest arrived; the last rites were given.

Near death, Robert at last saw the golden head of his king above him. "Sweet God, but I cannot go on without you, old friend!" Edward said.

Robert whispered. Edward leaned closer.

"Grant me this, on my deathbed!" Robert pleaded. "Grant Lenore freedom to take—to take the babe home to Aville. Before God, Edward, I beg this of you!"

His voice had grown louder. He found the strength to grip the king's arm. "Protect the babe. Stand as godfather to her—send her home with her mother."

He leaned back, exhausted.

"Robert, save your strength—"

"Edward, give me your promise."

"Aye, man, you've my promise!" the king cried harshly. "Now fight the shadows of death, Robert, as you have fought my enemies. Dear God, my good old friend! Fight now—!"

But Robert's eyes closed. He lay at peace. The valiant warrior had lost this battle. Robert of Oxford was dead.

"Sire, do we send the body with word to Lord Robert's lady in London?"

Startled, the king looked up. It was Adrien, grave and sorrowful, who had asked the question. Adrien, who had often fought by Robert's side, admiring the man's patience, wisdom, and loyalty. Adrien, reminding him of his duty.

"Aye," the king said sadly.

"Sire, shall we arrange to give the Lady Lenore escort back to Aville?" Adrien asked.

The king looked at the boy. At eleven, he was tall and gangly. His eyes were bright with a golden wisdom that went well beyond his years. He expected the king to keep his promise, and Edward was well aware that he must do so, if only to keep this remarkable young lad's loyalty.

"Aye," the king said. Ah, Robert! he thought of his old friend. Noble even unto death, he had forced Edward to grant the lady freedom. "Nay" Edward said then, "I will see Robert's child first. We will send for the countess. I will stand godfather to the babe as I vowed. Then . . . then Lenore may return to Aville," he said wearily at last. "With advisors from my own court, she will surely hold it well for me."

Lenore arrived in the Low Countries when her babe was but a few months old. She stood with the king in an ancient cathedral by the shore, she in mourning, the babe in her arms, the king stiff and cold as he watched her. Jeannette d'Este, the French widow of an English knight, was godmother, and would journey back to Aville with Lenore.

The ceremony was elaborate, as befitted that for a child who would have a king for a guardian. During it, the king held his infant daughter in his arms. She was endowed with a headful of raven-dark hair. Her tiny cheeks were round and rose-tinted, but her features were already fine and delicate and beautiful. She had a little rosebud of a mouth, a small, straight nose, fine, high bones, skin soft as silk.

Her eyes were emerald.

She lay perfectly still in his arms, staring up at him as if she challenged him, and if she were only a bit older, she would have fought his hold, and demanded she be set down.

Lenore would not look at the king during the ceremony. When she talked to others, he saw that she deeply mourned Robert. She was pale, slim, and beautiful still.

That night she was to stay in a Dover manor, held by Lord Huntington. The king had meant to keep his distance, but as he brooded through the evening, he realized that he could not.

That night, a servant summoned Lenore to come alone to another guest wing within the manor. She was ushered into a bedchamber with a large hearth and a table before it. Seated at that table, features drawn and brooding, was the king.

Fear pricked at her heart. She kept her distance from him. "Milord King of England!" she said softly. "I know you gave my husband a promise that I should return home. Surely, sire, you could not fail to fulfill such a vow."

Edward sighed deeply and stood, running his fingers through his hair. "Aye, lady, I will honor my vow."

"Then—?"

"I have summoned you because I had to see you. Had to hear your voice."

"Indeed," Lenore said, for he walked toward her then, and she felt a buckling in her knees. "Perhaps it is well, for I have not had the chance to congratulate you on the birth of your new son."

"Truly, you are a witch to taunt me now in so gentle a tone."

"Edward, will you or will you not allow me to go?"

"On my terms," he said.

"And they are?"

He walked away from her, hands clasped behind him. "Should anything ever happen to you, the child is given over to my care."

Lenore was silent for a moment. "Why?" she asked.

"She is mine by right."

"She is yours, but by no right."

"Perhaps you will not believe this, but in my way, I have loved her mother."

"Will I leave here if this promise is not given?" Lenore asked softly, tears filling her eyes.

"You will leave in the morning, if the winds grant a crossing."

She sighed after a moment. "I will abide by your will then, milord king."

"Will you, Lenore?" he asked her softly. He had come close again. So close that she remembered too well everything that had been between them.

"When morning comes, I will set you free, I swear it! But by God, lady, perhaps we will never meet again!" he cried, his voice grown tense and passionate, his words, indeed, a vow.

Lenore closed her eyes briefly, struggling for breath. She met his demanding gaze once again. "So be it then!" she whispered fiercely in return.

And once again, felt his touch, his hands upon her arms, his lips so near her own. She heard his voice, oddly hoarse as he entreated her, "Ah, lady, that you would not hate me so!"

"Sweet Jesu!" she cried. "That I could not hate you more!" And with her words, she found herself lifted, imprisoned in his arms.

But in the morning, a fair wind rose.

And as the king had promised, she was free. With her infant in her arms, she stood upon a cliff and looked out at the English countryside.

I shall never return, she thought, and felt a shiver. The cold swept through her, seeming to haunt her. Nor, she thought, would she ever see the king again, and yet . . .

Her hands trembled. For she was suddenly quite certain that the babe she carried would, one day, come back.

Just as the king had kept his word, so would her own promise to Edward of England be upheld.

"Milady, may I help you?"

She looked back to see Adrien, the Scots lad with the striking golden eyes who had mourned Robert so deeply. He stood near her, tall and strong and grave against the cold wind.

"Your ship is ready to sail, milady," he told her quietly.

"Aye, Adrien. My thanks, if you'll take the babe?" she inquired softly, for the way down was steep, and she knew the lad was far more sure-footed than she was.

She handed him her daughter. He held the child awkwardly. The babe instantly began howling. Lenore found herself smiling as he struggled to hold the lass more securely.

"Can you manage?" she inquired.

"Aye!" he said indignantly.

At the landing, he returned the babe to her. "She's quite a temper," he said.

"I'm afraid so."

"She's not much like her father," he said apologetically.

Lenore lowered her lashes. Her infant daughter proved to be more like her true father daily, she was afraid.

"Time will tell, as she's just a babe!" she told him.

"You loved him very much," Adrien said, and she saw how he mourned Robert. "The babe's father."

She smiled. "Indeed, very much." No lie was spoken. She had loved Robert, deeply. And she hated the fact that she loved the king, but she loved him as well. That was one of the reasons she was so desperate to leave.

"Aye, Adrien!" she said. Then she kissed his cheek swiftly. She knew the boy's strategy had been part of the downfall of Aville, but she knew as well that Edward would never have relented, and she did not blame Adrien, knowing full well that a seige might have brought about more deaths.

He flushed slightly. "God speed you, lady."

"And you, Laird MacLachlan! Until we meet again."

Again, she felt a strange tremor. They would not meet again. And yet she had a strange feeling about the handsome young MacLachlan. As if their lives had become intertwined the day Aville had fallen.

The wind blew cold.

As she had said, time would tell.

Chapter 2

Danielle adored her mother. She held her own court at Aville, and with a smile, a tilt of her chin, and coolly spoken, totally authoritive words, she kept everyone within it under control.

Even as a child, Danielle knew that her mother's house hosted both Englishmen and Frenchmen, and that her mother was deeply distressed any time she heard that even minor fighting had broken out between the two countries. Thankfully, as the years passed, Aville was not involved.

Among the many men who visited Aville, there were those, both English and French, who sought her mother's hand in marriage. One of them, Roger, the Count of LacLupin, was exceptionally charming, and Danielle was very fond of him. He brought her presents every time he came. She was certain that her mother cared about him, too. She came to her mother's chamber one night when Roger visited, crawled into bed with her, and asked, "Mother, why don't you marry Roger?"

Lenore smiled. "He has not asked my hand as yet."

"And if he does, you'll marry him?"

Lenore was silent a long time. "I don't know."

"Why not?"

"I don't think that I wish to marry again. For many reasons. It would be very hard to make you understand."

Doctor Coutin, a physician who had trained at the fine university in Bologna, kept a manor in Aville and was now her tutor. He had told her that she had an incredible mind for a child—a female one at that. She could *understand.*

"You must obey the King of France, is that it?" she asked, pressing her mother for an answer.

"My love, the King of England is the one I am compelled to obey first. He seized this castle, and proved that he is duke here, and I have been returned here as countess through his permission alone. By right, he owes his fealty for these lands to Philip, my cousin, but since he claims himself to be King of France as well—and since he has the military power here!—Edward of England holds sway over the future of us all. He is also your godfather. Your father served him. And he can give orders, when he chooses."

"The King of England can make you do something you do not want to do? But mother, just tell him no!" Danielle's world revolved around her mother's household, where Lenore's firm but gentle words were law.

Lenore laughed, and the sound of her laughter was strange. She tousled Danielle's hair. "My sweet, trust me, kings have the power to try very hard to make people do whatever they choose."

"But you mustn't allow the king to make you do anything that you do not want to do."

"Ah—never surrender!" Lenore said, and still she sounded strange. "Ask no mercy."

"Never surrender!" Danielle agreed. "Ask no mercy."

"Ah, Danni, my little love! Alas, it seems we can lose battles though we do not surrender them, and then again, sometimes mercy comes when it has not been asked. Men will do what they are determined they will, and often, our wits are all that we have against them, and against their strength, wits are not always enough."

"Pardon?"

"I am rambling!" Lenore laughed.

"Did my father make you do things you did not wish to do?"

Lenore hesitated, then took her chin between her hands. "Robert of Oxford was one of the finest, gentlest, most chivalrous knights ever to draw breath. He would have fought any danger for you—real or not, man or dragon!"

"You loved my father very much, didn't you, milady?"

Lenore hesitated several seconds. Her voice was husky, something like a strangled whisper when she answered. "Yes, I fell in love with—your father. Enough questions. Now, go to bed, my sweet!"

She set Danielle upon the floor and kissed her forehead. "Go! It is late. Call Monteine, and she will see you in."

Monteine was the youngest daughter of a knight killed while fighting the English. She had told Danielle that Edward's armies had ravaged every town in France they had come near. She detested the English, and Danielle could certainly agree that they had done very cruel things to the French.

And now, it seemed, the English king—who thought Aville owed him allegiance!—was preventing her mother from marrying Roger. The king was a monster, and Danielle knew very early on that she hated him. She hated the story about her parents, of course. King Edward had been furious with Danielle's mother for keeping the castle against him, and he had kidnapped her back to England, but it hadn't mattered because Robert of Oxford, who had been Lenore's escort and guard, had fallen madly in love with her, and she with him. He had been one good Englishman, so Danielle grudgingly decided that there must be one or two others as well. Tragically, her father had been slain just after her birth. Danielle was certain that her mother mourned him still, and they said Masses constantly for his soul. Danielle was proudly convinced that he had been the bravest and finest of all knights—even if he had been English. He had left her vast holdings in England, and she was a countess there, too, in her own right, just as her mother was Countess of Aville. He had been a very great man. It made her feel good to realize that everyone within her household seemed to agree with her, those who were French, and those who were English.

When she was about to lose her temper, which seemed far too often, even to her, she tried to think of Robert of Oxford, who had always been calm and fair. In his honor—for she had heard he loved learning—she worked hard with her tutors and masters. Her days were filled with lessons. She sang, she rode, she learned to stroke the lute. She learned to read, for she loved to do so, and Lenore believed that men prospered far more than women because their minds were expected to be far more expanded. "You'll never regret knowing how to read!" Lenore assured her daughter once, and so Danielle studied all the harder to please her mother. She was to learn Latin, Spanish, French, Flemish, and English, and no one thought a thing of teaching a child all languages at once. Doctor Coutin taught her the theories of Hippocrates and other great men, the beginnings of medicine from the Greeks and Romans. Her mother was so practiced with herbs and healing, she knew that she must be as knowledgeable as well, able to give advice to the surgeons and barbers who were not nearly as well-educated as doctors.

She learned to ride expertly. She insisted, by her tenth birthday, that she was too big for a pony, and must have a fine horse. She was given one—a very special mare. She received the horse from her mother's distant cousin, Philip, the King of France.

He arrived at Aville with great ceremony, a striking man despite the fact that he seemed old. He arrived with all manner of retainers, and all of Aville—including the Englishmen there—had scurried around wildly in preparation for his arrival.

Monteine helped Danielle dress in special finery in a silk underdress and a fur-trimmed tunic in ivory. Even her hose were silk that day, and her hair was dressed in flowers. When she came to the great hall where she had been summoned, she paused, entered, and grinned in response to the elegant smile given her by the Valois king.

"Ah, my lady cousin!" he declared. "This child may exceed even your great beauty."

"Indeed, merci, my lord!" Lenore said softly.

Philip came to Danielle, capping her head with his palm. He bent down to her. "If ever you need me, little cousin, remember that you must call upon me!"

Danielle nodded, tongue-tied for once, pleased with this great man's attention. "I've brought you something," he said. "A mare. She is outside, big enough for a girl who is quickly growing to be a woman. You must go see her."

Impetuously, Lenore hugged the king and kissed his cheek. He was deeply pleased with her show of affection. "Go see your mare now. Her name is Star, and you will get on quite well, I am certain."

Danielle ran out of the entry to the keep. As the French king had promised, the mare was there. She was big and beautiful, bay-colored with a star upon her forehead. With the help of a groom, Danielle patted the mare's nose. When Monteine came to the stables to tell her it was late, she insisted that she had to thank King Philip.

She started to enter the great hall, but realized then that her mother and Philip were deep in discussion. Philip was talking and her mother was nervously pacing the room.

"He breaks all his treaties, he is coming against me again, and he is determined that he will claim to all that he is King of France!" Philip said, vastly agitated. "Even now, we gather men and prepare for war again. He will never take Paris, I swear it, and I will beat him back to the farthest borders of his own domains! If you would but agree to marriage with Roger yourself—or give me leave to have the child wed to a noble Frenchman! Someone who will give me a strong alliance against that wretched Plantagenet cousin of mine!"

"Philip! I tried to fight him once—I bought you time upon that occasion!" she reminded him.

"I am the King of France!" Philip roared. "Your kinsman. I can command a marriage for you—or the girl!"

"You can command what you will, but if you don't lower your voice, war will break out here and now. Edward's loyal men, Gascons and Englishmen, fill this place! You would lose if you were to try to fight here now. You must take care, for you are fighting him to keep your title to all of France, and losing a battle here would not help your quest!''

''I'm not sure it matters!'' Philip said angrily. ''I've an army at my back, preparing to take on his!''

Lenore sighed deeply. ''Philip, please, you put me in a precarious position. Let me think on this!''

''I must leave, but I'll return before he can press an attack upon me,'' Philip said. ''Lenore, your daughter should have been betrothed by now. Why have you hesitated—''

''I have not found the proper man—one who might be satisfactory to me, to God—and to two warring kings!''

''One of us will shortly take the matter out of your hands,'' he warned softly.

''Philip! I beg of you—''

''Lenore, tonight I will leave you,'' Philip said. Danielle still hid against the door as he kissed Lenore's cheeks. ''I am in your debt, for once. You did buy me time against the wily bastard! But don't forget—I am the King of France.'' He turned to leave the room. From the hall, his retainers saw him prepare to leave, and all jumped up, ready to follow him.

He all but ran into Danielle, just outside the door. He touched her cheek gently.

''Thank you for my horse!'' she told him.

''Care for her gently!'' he said. He paused then, studying her. ''My God, but you are a young beauty!'' he told her, and strode on by. Then, with a great amount of tumult, he took his leave.

She didn't want her mother to catch her up so late, so she went to bed and awaited Lenore, for her mother always came to see that she was safely in. But that night, Lenore did not come to her. There had been a fever outside the castle—a smith had died of it, along with one infant boy and an old peasant woman—and that night, the fever made its way into the house. Danielle dozed, then awoke when she heard running footsteps and cries in the night.

She crawled out of bed. Monteine was not in her adjoining bedroom. Danielle wandered into the hall, and saw that servants were rushing to and from her mother's chambers. She ran among them, pausing in the doorway. She had stood there just hours before while her mother spoke with the French king in the vast space before the fire by the light of the windows. Now Lenore was far across the room in her massive bed, her black hair splayed out across the pillows, her features frighteningly ashen against the white linen sheets.

Danielle cried out, and rushed to her.

"The child!" someone shouted.

But Danielle had thrown off whatever hands tried to stop her and come to the bed, crawling atop it.

"Danielle, come away!" commanded a voice, and she realized that it was Father Giles, her mother's friend and confessor. Doctor Coutin was there as well, gravely standing just away from her mother's side.

"Mother!" Danielle cried.

Lenore's beautiful eyes opened and fell upon her. She tried to reach for Danielle's hand, but could not. Danielle caught her hand, crying out again. "Mother!"

"Dearest love!" Lenore managed to whisper painfully. Her eyes began to close again.

"Lenore, save your strength!" Jeanette entreated.

Danielle's eyes fell upon those of Doctor Coutin.

"There's nothing more to be done," he said gently.

She looked to Father Giles.

He met her gaze, and found pity for her. "Lenore is dying!" he said sorrowfully, staring at the others. "Let her daughter speak with her. It is all they will have."

Dying? Her mother? No, no, it could not happen! "Mother!" Danielle cried then, lying beside her, holding her, as if, with her own slender body, she could hold her mother to life itself.

Lenore was whispering again. "Yes, Mother, yes!" Danielle said, crawling closer to her mother's lips. "Ask me anything, ask me anything . . ."

"The king," was all she heard at first. "You must honor the king. Care for him, you do not know . . . he will care for you. Danielle, do you hear me?"

"Yes, Mother! Yes, but—"

"Honor him. Keep him safe."

"Mother, I swear I will do whatever you say. But you mustn't keep talking, you must rest. You can't die . . ."

Her voice trailed away. Lenore was not answering her. And something about her mother had changed. Her body had been afire. It was as if that fire had suddenly been extinguished.

"You must come away now, Danielle," Father Giles said. "Monteine, take your young mistress. She must leave this place of contagion!"

Monteine came forward to take Danielle, sobbing still.

"No, I cannot leave her!" Danielle cried.

"Child, she has left us already!" Father Giles said, not unkindly.

Tears sprang to her eyes. She tried to cling to her mother's body. She was dragged away by Monteine and Jeanette while Father Giles gave orders to other servants as to the care of the body.

Danielle thought that she would never bear the pain. She sobbed herself into exhaustion, and from there, into sleep.

By the morning, she could no longer mourn, for the fever had seized her.

The plague had come to them, and throughout Aville, people fell sick—the poor, the rich, the peasants, and the nobles. A full half of those inside the castle fell ill.

And half of those who fell ill, died.

Danielle drifted in and out of light for days, sometimes knowing that she had lost her mother, sometimes knowing that she was close to death herself, and caring little. By the sixth day, however, the fever pustules that had formed on her burst. Her body began to cool. She was going to live.

She gained full consciousness one morning to learn that despite the fever that had raged all around them, the beautiful, beloved Lenore d'Aville had been buried with all care and ceremony.

Father Giles had waited until after the services to succumb to the fever himself, and perish.

Losing her mother was agony. For days, Danielle, still very weak, lay in bed and wished that she might have died and gone to heaven with both her parents.

Jeanette told her that it was a sin to want to die, that she was a countess, that she had to learn to accept God's will with fortitude. She had always been so very wise and mature; she must be even more so now.

Danielle didn't want to be wise or mature, and she didn't know why she should accept anything about God—God had taken her mother. But she was too desolate to argue with Jeanette.

The weeks passed, and she gained her strength again. The dead were all buried; the fever had done its damage, and passed them by.

She became dimly aware that people within her household were talking about battles once more—it seemed that the English were ready to make war again. Danielle still hadn't roused herself enough to care.

But she awoke one morning to discover that Monteine was in her room, her face damp with tears, muttering as she packed trunks full with Danielle's belongings.

Danielle sat up and demanded to know what she was doing.

"Countess, we are going to the king!" Monteine said.

"The king?" Danielle replied, perplexed. She bit her lip, remembering that she had promised her mother she would honor the king.

"It seems that there are all kinds of legal documents," Monteine said with a sigh. "Your mother made arrangements for your care in case of—in case of her death!"

"Why must we leave? Philip could care for me here—"

"It is not Philip who will care for you at all! Your mother has placed you into the care of your godfather, the King of England. Danni, your father was an English lord—you know that well enough. You have heard the stories over and over again, you have told them over and over again. And Robert of Oxford was a baron well admired by the king. But, oh God, that my life should come to this! The Lady Jeanette and I are to remain your retainers. We are duly summoned before the King of England—even as he plans another attack upon the French!"

At last, Danielle felt aroused from her pain and lethargy.

She slipped from her bed and ran in her nightdress to Monteine, throwing her arms around her. "We'll disobey such an outrageous summons! We will not stay with him. We—"

"Oh, Danielle!" Monteine said, and sank down before her, hugging her close. "You cannot disobey! There's going to be a terrible battle, and if you were to try to run somewhere, it would all be the worse! Edward has great strength in Gascony. People would be up in arms, there would be more battles, more deaths. Forgive me! He is your guardian—he has the right of your life, of your future in his hands, and you must not anger him! I have been wrong to instill my feelings in you!"

Monteine was not wrong—Edward was a wretched monster with illusions to the throne of France. Everyone, even little children, knew that.

"You must honor him!" Monteine told her earnestly.

"I will never honor him!"

"Shh!" Monteine pressed her fingers to Danielle's lips. "He has men here in the castle—you could cause us both grave harm!"

"But the King of France just came here!"

"To visit his lady cousin only, an act the English and the Gascons loyal to their duke could not rebuke, for though Edward is the superior here, by ancient rite, he holds these lands of the French king. And though he even claims that he is the French king, Philip rules in Paris, and it is doubtful that even such a warrior king as Edward of England will ever truly lay claim to all of France. He will never have the surrender of the French king and all of France."

"He will never have *my* surrender!" Danielle assured her. "And I am convinced that we could escape—"

"To do what?" Monteine asked with dismay. "Starve in the streets? You don't understand! Edward has prepared a great force against Philip once more. The English king has landed on French shores and begun to ravage the land again."

"If he fights Philip, we should go to Philip," Danielle said with simple wisdom.

"Trust me, my lady," Monteine said softly, "Philip cannot

help you now. He has no strength here, and he will be occupied with his coming battle with the English king.''

Danielle stood stubbornly silent. She watched as Monteine packed her things, feeling frozen in place. She felt like crying, except that she had cried so much over her mother, she just didn't have any tears left.

I will never honor the Englishman! she vowed again to herself in silence.

And she thought again how she had sworn to her mother as Lenore lay dying that she would honor another king.

Someday, sometime, she would do so. She might be forced to go to the English king now, but she had given her mother a vow. A sacred vow. She would hold all the loyalty in her heart for the house of Valois—even if she was now being all but abducted by a foreign monster with illusions of grandeur.

Edward had not seen his natural daughter since the day he granted Lenore her freedom from English shores. Nor had he seen Lenore, Countess d'Aville, since that time.

Still, her death had grieved him more than he dared allow himself to show. It was natural that he should order numerous Masses said for her soul—she had been the widow of Robert of Oxford, his dearest friend and retainer. Yet there was no one he could tell that a small piece of him had perished as well, for the lady's beauty and spirit had set a lock upon his heart. Even as life had gone on, as Philippa had continued to prove herself the best of queens, he had remembered the woman who encaptured him and defied him until the very end.

His thoughts, however, by necessity were deeply occupied by the masses of troops he had brought to these shores, and with his plans for strategy and battle.

He had almost forgotten that he had sent for Danielle when there came the sound of footsteps across the floor in the hall of the manor he had seized, and then the clearing of his steward's throat to draw Edward's attention from his intense study of the map before him.

He looked up, words freezing upon his lips, all else forgotten as he stared at the child who had come before him, just ten feet in front of her ladies.

He trembled suddenly. He had once thought that the child would force Lenore d'Aville to remember the King of England for all her days, rue her defiance of him, and remember well the nights they had shared. His pride had demanded that she do so.

Alas, Edward was the one who would now rue his own temper.

He would be the one who would never forget.

Emerald-green eyes blazed out at him furiously from a delicate face of perfectly formed beauty as she surveyed the king, her godfather. Her hair, sweeping down her back, was lustrous and black, deeper than a raven's wing. Her smile, when she offered it to Lady Jeanette, who had come beside her to urge her to go forward and bow down to the king, was like the burst of a sun's ray, sweet and seductive.

"Come to me, child!" the king commanded.

Her chin inched high as her green eyes surveyed him with defiance and wariness.

"Come, child," Edward repeated, growing impatient. He had forgotten his war for a moment, but he never forgot that he was king. "Come closer!"

"I am here already, milord!" she replied serenely.

"Come closer."

Danielle d'Aville took one small step toward him.

Indeed, the king thought, she was her mother's daughter.

He rose, and spun on the two ladies accompanying her, Jeanette and Monteine.

"You have been entrusted with this young heiress, and you have been sorely lacking at your task, Lady Jeanette. By God, this is insufferable! I shall have you replaced—"

"No!" the girl cried suddenly, rushing before him then and falling down quickly upon a knee. "Sire, I humbly greet you!" she cried out, just as she had been taught.

Those emerald eyes touched him, but there was nothing humble whatsoever about her. She stood. "You mustn't blame my ladies," she said. "I have been properly schooled—they have taken great pains. But no one, King of England, can command another's heart and what lies within the soul."

Edward stared at her incredulously. So the little vixen had a will about her. But she also had some compassion in her—along with her reckless pride and courage.

But no child of his—acknowledged or no—was going to defy him for long.

"You!" he warned, pointing a finger at her, "are my ward, young lady. And you will learn in the future to do as I command as your guardian and your king. I know that you understand my words full well."

"Indeed, I understand a great deal," she replied. She stared at him with her blaming eyes, and he thought, by God, she is like Lenore, coming down from heaven for her revenge.

"I will make you honor me, girl," Edward told her. She didn't reply then, but Monteine stepped forward, urging her to do so. "You must ask the king's mercy—for us all!"

But Danielle smiled, staring at the king. "If he is such a great king, he will be merciful. I do not beg mercy, my lady."

The king felt a soaring streak of anger.

"You will now reside in my court, my little lady," he informed her. "And if you give me too much difficulty, you will be beaten."

She was staring at him, her fury ill-concealed, when Philippa suddenly swept into the hall, his wife who had willingly followed him into so many battles. She gazed at him, a brow arching at his obvious temper. Then she smiled at the girl. "Ah, it is Robert's daughter at last, is it?"

With her motherly kindness, she did what Edward hadn't dared, and embraced Danielle. "Oh, but you're beautiful! Your mother must have been quite lovely, for you're not a thing like your dear, departed father! You mustn't fret—you will be with us until you are safely full grown and wed."

Philippa left the room with her, and Edward thought that Lenore had soundly bested him in the end. This child of theirs was destined to plague him until death.

"Out!" Edward commanded Danielle's ladies, and both departed the chamber with haste.

He stood and paced for several minutes, feeling the knotting tension of his anger like a cape around his shoulders. He didn't like losing battles—especially to his own children.

"You! Little witch!" he whispered to the air. "Lady daughter, you will learn to surrender to me."

He felt a shiver snake down his spine again, and though he would not admit it, he knew he might be wrong. In time, the little emerald-eyed vixen of his own creation would surely try to force him, the king, to beg mercy. No. He'd not have it. In time, there would surely be another man to deal with her. In fact . . .

He realized that he now had another pawn in the political game of marriage. Hmmm . . .

He would need a knight of impeccable courage—and indomitable strength. A will of steel as well as muscles of rock. A man to whom he could entrust vast lands in both England and France.

He began to think as the king. Danielle was incredibly wealthy, what with her Gariston holdings and the fine castle of Aville. Both commanded powerful military positions, tremendous riches in manpower and agriculture. An army could be fed from the fields of Gariston alone; thousands of fighting men could be drawn from those who dwelt upon the lands of the little countess.

Though she was just ten, infants were often betrothed upon the very day of their birth. In a few short years, she would be marriageable. Her husband might well need all of a knight's prowess and strength. Edward had to take great care, for she could not be wed as his own child, but as a royal ward. She would need someone powerful in himself, and deserving of reward . . .

Someone with a will of steel.

Someone who did not know the meaning of the word *surrender*.

Chapter 3

August 25, 1346
Crécy

"The prince is down! Dear God, Edward, Prince of Wales,
is down!"

Adrien had been fighting just feet from his friend and lord,
Edward, eldest son of Edward III. He swung himself about and
ran the distance that separated him from Edward upon the
bloody field of battle.

The battle here had been long in the coming.

The English had landed eighteen miles southeast of Cherbourg at St. Vaast la Hogue after a fine, smooth crossing of
the Channel. But there, it had taken them six days to regroup
and begin their march toward Paris through the Cherbourg
peninsula. When they came to the mainland, the king's army
split into groups of three. Edward, Prince of Wales—who had
been knighted by his father upon their landing—was given
command of the vanguard while his father led the central line
and the rear guard was commanded by the experienced warrior,
the Earl of Northampton.

The three groups marched through the countryside, laying

waste, seizing prizes, booty, and noble prisoners to be held for ransom. Caen was taken. There the king plotted and planned, and on July 31, they spread out again in a broad column. Philip of France had taken the *Oriflamme,* the majestic battle flag of the country of France, from its place of honor at the Abbey of Saint-Denis, and he had ridden about himself, demanding his feudal service from knights and men-at-arms, letting out a cry that the French must defend their country from the pillaging English. Philip's first defense was at well-defended Rouen, and the bridges over the Seine had been destroyed.

The French and the English troops kept pace with one another, the stretch of the river all that separated them. Philip slipped into Paris. The English rode north, for Edward was determined to meet up with his Flemish allies.

The march had been grueling; they had moved sixteen miles a day with all the wagons and accoutrements for battle, keeping up the pace despite the harrying attacks of French patriots. They neared their Flemish allies, but paused there, separated by the River Somme. The ever-growing army of the French began to press their ranks.

The English king searched high and low for a crossing, and at last discovered a tidal causeway across the mouth of the river where the waters were shallow. Across the river, they confronted the enemy and defeated the forces sent to attack them on their crossing. The French retreated with heavy losses.

Philip's army moved off. The English spent tense hours awaiting another attack, but it didn't come. Philip rallied his forces back toward Abbeville, and stayed there the night of August 25.

At dawn, the English army surveyed the countryside. Adrien, at Prince Edward's side, listened to the initial plan. The forest of Crécy would secure the rear of their line. The three devisions of the English army would draw up along the hill that led to it. The village of Wadicourt would provide protection for the left flank of the army. The cavalry, the knights and the men-at-arms, would fight on foot.

They were drastically outnumbered by the French and the French allies, but they were exceptionally well led and disciplined. There were perhaps twelve thousand English fighting men that day, and some estimated that there might have been as many as sixty thousand men beneath Philip and his French commanders.

The English had brought with them some tactics learned through English defeats. Deep holes had been dug before the front line, trenches ready to entrap the unwary. The English had learned their usage when they were soundly defeated at Bannockburn by the Scottish king, Robert the Bruce. A tremendous dependence was being put upon the English archers—the plan being that the attacking troops could be riddled with the arrows, and would mire in the trenches in confusion before moving on to hand-to-hand combat, where the English numbers were so poor in comparison to the French.

The strategy, the discipline, had served them well. Philip's contingent of highly respected Genoese crossbowmen were first into the fray, just as the sky let loose and it began to rain. They were experienced fighting men, but they broke ranks when the English longbowmen began to return their hail of deadly arrows. Other French troops rushed in even as the Genoese tried to retreat, or reload their heavy weapons.

French horses crunched upon the skulls of their own allies in the confusion and bedlam.

Some forces did get through, fighting their way up the rise. There Adrien fought hard and savagely, battling the enemy with all the skill and power learned and earned through years of constant war and training. His armor was heavy; he had learned to carry the burden to protect his flesh and blood. His suit, however, had been crafted in one of the finest German armories—the king had seen to it that he had been fitted for it, and refitted. Mail and leather for movement at the joints, attached plates of steel designed to ward blows away from the vital points. Steel points on his gauntlets gave him added weapons if his sword should be lost. His helm, or bascinet, protected his skull while his visor guarded his face—and somewhat obscured his vision. Today, his strength and training stood him well, even against men far older, thicker in the shoulders and chest.

The fighting was fierce, and he prayed his strength would not fail. Again and again he met new opponents, lifting his sword, slashing hard, seeking enemy weak points, just as the enemy sought his. He raised his sword high against a Frenchman with a visor formed like a boar's head.

The man fell.

It was then that he heard the cry that Prince Edward was down. He moved with lightning speed to the side of his prince.

Enemy knights, seeing that the English prince was in danger, rushed forward, seeking to use the advantage against the young prince. Edward's standard bearers were helping him to his feet in the casement of his heavy armor. Adrien quickly moved into the breach to stave off the French knights swarming in like flies.

He knew his own strength and power. He was perhaps half an inch taller than the Plantagenet prince, and though constant training had given him a heavily muscled torso and massive shoulders, he had been taught that he must learn to move with swift grace despite his size and the bulk and weight of his armor. He raised his sword again and again, watching all the while as more men came to join in the attack. He felt to a knee, bracing against a blow that came from a mounted knight, then rose as swiftly as lightning, swinging with such speed that he caught his opponent in the vulnerable crevice at his side. The man fell, his horse screamed and floundered in the mud and blood that had become the floor of the hilltop.

In the frenzy of combat that followed, Adrien found himself cut off from his fellows. He had meant to shift the fighting from where the prince had sought to regain his balance; he had succeeded all too well. Man after man came after him. His strength waned and he knew that he must use his wits, watching every opponent, weighing each man's measure. He could afford to make no wasted strikes, for his strength could not last forever. He took one charging horseman with the dirk at his calf, ducked low to avoid the charge of another, and watched as the horse sent its rider crashing against a tree. Two more men he battled by hand, seeing the one from the corner of his eye, swinging his sword arm to fell the one before completing the movement which allowed him to catch the other straight in the groin.

Both men fell.

But there were more to replace those he had taken. When he looked before him then, he saw that a good dozen heavily armored Frenchmen stood before him, ready to rush in to attack. As he faced them, they began to call out.

"Surrender, man!"

"Throw down your sword!"

"Do so with honor now, and we'll take you whole!"

"Keep fighting, and we'll slice you gullet to groin!"

"Surrender, by God or by Satan!"

By God or Satan, it could not be so.

He remembered his father's words. *Never surrender!*

Death would be his surrender.

He smiled beneath the steel of his visor. Shook his head slowly. And faced the enemy. Madly, perhaps, yet he was certain that whether he did or didn't fight, they meant to slice him—gullet to groin. He had taken down too many of their number to seek mercy.

"Milords, I do not surrender!" he returned, and with a wild Scot's battle cry, he raced forward, startling them by attacking rather than seeking to make a defensive stand.

Death might well have brought about his surrender against so many, except that, even as another rush of men swept forward to meet his onslaught, he suddenly found himself with aid. Twenty good English knights rode into the fray, the king at their lead. The dozen Frenchmen fled, some of the English in pursuit.

The battle, for the day, was over. The French had launched at least fifteen attacks, and been repulsed with tremendous losses each time.

King Edward had come upon Adrien's position with a retinue of knights just in time.

The king dismounted from the white horse he had ridden to lead his men that morning, striding quickly to Adrien. As he doffed his visor and bascinet, his gold hair glittered in the sun. He paused, surveying the carnage around Adrien.

"Scotsman, you've done well. Extraordinarily well."

Adrien was startled when the king suddenly drew his sword. "Kneel!" commanded the king.

"Sire—" Adrien began.

But Prince Edward was with the king by then, and he called out with his deep, rich voice to his friend. "Adrien, good fellow, my father means to knight you here and now!"

Still startled, Adrien fell to his knees. He was dimly aware of the king's words, of the sword falling upon his shoulders. He was duly knighted.

He stood, more stunned by this sudden turn of events than he had been by any action in the battle.

His father's words had proven true. He had been knighted on the battlefield. An odd pain, long suppressed, seized him. He wished that Carlin, Laird MacLachlan, might have lived to see this day.

Father, let me not fail you, he prayed suddenly. He had never forgotten Carlin MacLachlan, nor all that he had learned from his proud, wise father.

Cheers went up; he found himself hoisted high by a number of men, and then the king warned that the battle had ended for the day, yet the French were not quit of it. More war would be waged on the morrow.

The French did attack again, come morning, but by the afternoon, Philip had found himself soundly in defeat at Crécy. More than four thousand French knights and nobles lay dead upon the battlefield.

Knights and nobles . . .

No one bothered to count the bodies of the lesser men, the peasants and freemen with their pikes and staffs.

There were tremendous celebrations. On the following day, a Requiem Mass was said, and then Edward prepared to move on, determined to take Calais.

But before the army moved again, Adrien found himself summoned to stand before the king.

Over the years, he had been summoned often enough.

There had been the time when David II had returned to rule in Scotland. The king, who had supported Baliol, told Adrien the news dispassionately. "You've proven yourself a tremendous asset, my young laird. You're as tall as any Plantagenet, you've honed yourself sharper than steel. You've fought in God knows how many tournaments and taken God knows how many prizes."

"Sire, as you know well, I need to win those tournaments. My armor and household are expensive."

"Indeed, and your own holdings don't provide quite enough. I understand. Tournaments are good for young men. You must keep winning them. My point here is that I've really no right to keep you from serving David. I'd prefer you stay in my service. You will soon see the rewards of your efforts."

Adrien, who had become best friends with Edward, pretended to give the matter great thought. "I will stay with you if I am granted two promises."

"You would demand promises from a king?" Edward roared.

"Aye, your grace."

"And they would be?"

"First, sire, that you never ask me to fight against the Scots."

"Aye, lad, I'd not ask that of you."

"And secondly, that you promise not to decimate *my* holdings when you're fighting in the border regions!"

Amused, the king had given him his promise. Now, as he was about to face Edward again, he wondered at the king's intent this time. He had been knighted on the field. Given expensive horses.

What was the king about now?

Edward had been at some business with the Earl of Oxford, but he dismissed the earl, who nodded in acknowledgment to Adrien as he passed him by. They had both been fighting with the Prince of Wales. Adrien was startled to realize that his English peers seemed to believe that he had saved the life of the prince on his own.

"Ah, Adrien!" the king greeted him. "I was most impressed, most impressed. That wily old father of yours promised me I had the makings of a fine warrior at hand. It was a good alliance I made with him that day. He'd be a proud man today, as I am. I wanted to tell you again what a fine service you performed in the fighting—and that I'm heartily glad you did not choose to go and serve David II, but remained with me.''

Adrien cleared his throat. ''Thank you, sire. But the prince outdid himself as well. And the men were deeply pleased with you as well, sire, for it was known that you set each of us out there, including your own son, to fight, and that you numbered us all as worthy to hold your lines.''

The king waved a hand in the air. ''I am deeply proud of my son. Proud, indeed. But at the moment, we're discussing you.''

''You have commended me, sire.''

''Ah, yes! But that was a splendid moment I came upon! Men fallen all around you and a host about to storm you again, demanding that you beg quarter! And what was that you said in return to them all?''

Adrien, puzzled by the king's good humor and something akin to glee over the matter, frowned. ''What I said, sire?''

''Aye, lad, tell me again what you cried out to the enemy! It was glorious!''

Adrien didn't remember what he might have cried out in the midst of battle. He shrugged, and then he remembered. He had cried out words his father had taught him. ''I refuse to surrender—I was foolish perhaps, but I'd not have begged mercy of those wretches, not when we'd fought so long and hard.''

The king sat back, smiling from ear to ear, blue eyes alight as if he'd just been told the most humorous joke.

''Let me hear it again, I command it!'' the king said excitedly.

''Sire, I—''

''Tell me again, Adrien! These words, today, are sweet music to my ears. Again. I insist.''

''I refused to surrender or beg mercy—''

''Ha! Never to beg mercy!'' the king exclaimed.

''My lord, I must admit, I was quite immersed in the battle and—''

"Never mind, never mind!" the king said, and he waved a dismissing hand, turning back to his camp table and the parchments strewn across it. But he looked up at Adrien again, still smiling with the greatest pleasure and amusement. "You may go now."

Still puzzled, Adrien turned to leave. But the king summoned him back once again.

"Adrien!"

"Aye, sire?"

"Be aware, my good man, be most aware! Your future from this day forward is assured, and all the rewards that you might imagine will be yours—simply for the taking."

The king started to smile again, a strange smile as if he were harboring a secret joke close to his heart—and taking much more pleasure from it than Adrien's prowess in battle. Edward waved his hand in the air again. Adrien was to go.

Yet as he departed from the king, Adrien felt a slight chill of unease snake down his back.

Just what did Edward have in mind?

He didn't have long to ponder the question, for when he left the king, he was met by the prince, who cast a palm hard against his back as they walked together.

"So what great prize is my father giving you for your service today?" the prince asked, in good humor himself. "Even the old knights who still like to call you the Scot were talking about you today, my friend, extolling your virtues to the heavens. So tell me, what did Father give you? Were I king, I might well have created an earldom for you! You surely saved my life."

Adrien arched a brow to his friend. "I stepped into a gap where I was needed, and I was knighted on the field. That in itself—"

"Oh, come!"

Adrien shrugged. "Your father was a little strange. He didn't give me anything. He seemed—I don't know, as I said—strange. He was excited, and amused. And at the end of our conversation, he did assure me that my future was well secured."

"Ah, well, then, to the future! He must have something

exceptionally fine in store for you. But for the present—we're young, we're great warriors—victors! And to the victors, my friend, belong the spoils!''

''Meaning?'' Adrien inquired.

''Meaning we've a case of some of the finest French wine—and a bevy of defeated French beauties awaiting us who are quite willing to entertain victorious Englishmen.''

''Defeated French beauties?''

''Ah, my friend, young, French, feminine—merchants, if you will. An exceptional class of—''

''Ah. Whores!'' Adrien said wryly.

''The best, the brightest, the prettiest to be found. And the Lady Joanna will never know,'' Edward teased.

Adrien paused and looked at Edward, surprised that the prince was aware of his growing relationship with Joanna, daughter of the Earl of Warwick. What Edward didn't seem to realize was that it was not a deep, desperate passion that lay between them, but a fine friendship. If he gave thought to his emotions, he did love Joanna, but because they thought so much alike, they could laugh easily together and hide away to read—something that was not considered a great activity within the Plantagenet realm of action and vigor. Joanna sympathized with his past; he rued with her the iron hand her father kept upon her. They talked sometimes of marriage, because their friendship might well make it a very good one, and since Joanna was one of three daughters, her father might find Adrien, one of the king's favorites, a suitable son-in-law. But as yet, they had not asked leave to marry, and the future of their dreams remained vague, even to them.

''I am not yet affianced,'' Adrien said. ''And Joanna is a lady, while I assume your fine French women are not. Lead on, my prince, to whatever diversion we, as warriors, require!''

Edward laughed. ''My father's reward comes later—what I would give you for my life comes now!''

The prince and his friends strayed from their battle camp to a house deep in the woods. There they were entertained with music, dancing, roast boar, fine wine. One of the women had a sweet, gentle voice and played the lute well; her face was an angel's, her voice like silk, her words as bawdy as a warrior's might be, and her eyes as devilish as Satan's own. When her last song was finished, Adrien walked into the woods with her. That night, he was young and victorious; the fires of youth soared quick and high.

But when he had bid the pretty whore good night, he discovered that he did not want to remain with his companions, carousing away the night. He was still brooding over the day—not so much over the battle that might well have claimed his life, but rather over his conversation with the king.

He found Matt, one of his trained war stallions. He had four, named from books in the bible, Matthew, Mark, Luke, and John—and he rode into the night, steering away from the main camp, and riding by the water.

Once again, the question plagued him.

What did the king have in his mind?

Chapter 4

Being a ward of the King of England did not mean that Danielle would soon set foot on English soil.

Month after month went by with Edward intent upon taking the impregnable town of Calais.

Danielle spent most of her time with the queen, who, despite another pregnancy and her cumbersome size, seemed not to notice the difficulties of day-to-day life while residing with her husband and his army. Functions went on in the king's hall outside the walled town while men battered at Calais daily. Edward had begun his seige in September, right after the battle of Crécy, and he had done so with the determination to remain for the duration of a long struggle. The king had built up a town of wooden buildings outside Calais to house his army for the winter and even as the inhabitants inside the walled city were slowly starved, life went on outside it in a close to normal way. The little English town was built around a central market-place, and enterprising Flemish merchants came twice a week to hawk their wares. Smiths and coopers set up shops; barbers and surgeons opened their doors. Since the seige was such a long affair, the knights amused themselves by raiding the countryside, yet while they were not raiding and ravaging, they

determined upon a more chivalric code of action, challenging
one another to contests and even challenging the French knights
within the walls. By chivalric code, the Frenchmen could leave
their walls for the tournaments, then return to them.

Danielle attended the tournaments as a lady to the queen.
They were quite bearable in a world that otherwise bewildered
and grieved her, for she watched daily as the French people were
battered. The tournaments were different, for often enough, the
French knights won, and no one found it amiss that she clapped
and cheered the valiant young men in their contests.

It was during one of these tournaments that she was first to
see Adrien MacLachlan. He was to become a thorn in her side
from that day forth.

The afternoon had begun with a great sound of trumpeting.
There was no snow upon the ground, but the day was crisp
and cool. Only a strong sun overhead kept it from being too
cold to venture out. Danielle, seated just to the right of Philippa
and the royal brood, was deeply intrigued to see the coming
contest. Jean d'Elletente, reputed to be one of the finest knights
ever to fight in the Christian world, a Frenchman by birth and
loyalty, was ready to joust with a young English knight. Danielle
didn't know his name.

She was shortly to learn it . . . and never forget it.

Sir Jean d'Elletente was introduced with tremendous fanfare;
his victories and exploits were expounded. He appeared on a
massive silver horse with fringed feet, tail, and mane, a tunic
atop his coat of plate and mail, his bascinet secured over his
head. His visor, one that gave the impression of a snarling boar,
was down over his eyes. He carried his lance high, bearing it
even higher as he rode dramatically before the king, bringing
his horse to a halt that threw up great clumps of mud and earth.
He was cheered, more fully from behind the walls of Calais
than before them, but the code of chivalry was strict, and even
the English gave homage to a knight of his reputation.

"A token for a French knight!" cried Sir Terrell Henley,
master of the tournament.

No one rose immediately—they were, after all, an English
audience in the stands. Someone would have stood soon, how-

ever—the queen herself, if need be—for there were definite courtesies to be observed, among the women as well as the men.

Danielle found herself leaping to her feet, tearing the silk fall from her headdress, and coming forward to stand just center of the box where the onlookers sat.

Cheers went up for her—for the courteous and polite behavior of King Edward's ward. Danielle was little aware of them as she tied her silken banner to the lance lowered her way. The French knight raised it high, winking at her, and she smiled. Once again cheers went up, and then Danielle turned to take her seat.

D'Ellentente's joust combatant was then introduced, and Danielle gave little heed to the name.

"Sir Adrien MacLachlan, Laird of Reggar, Count of Meadenlay!"

Trumpets sounded again, and Edward's knight rode forward from the lists.

A cobalt tunic covered the plates and mail of his armor, and his horse's saddle was adorned alike in the deep blue with edgings in gold and silver. His shield was decorated with his coat of arms, a design with three roaring lions set atop a field of three running leopards. His helmet, bascinet, and visor were simply fashioned, with no elaborate pretension to any animal. Steel covered the man's face, shaped in human form. Only his eyes were visible, and though Danielle couldn't discern their color, she thought that they glittered beneath the sun just as brightly as the steel of his armor. Atop his horse, he seemed very tall indeed, as if he might be even taller than the King of England himself.

Danielle decided that the man had simply chosen to ride a very big horse, and so gain stature himself.

"A token for an English knight!" called the master of the tournament.

The queen rose swiftly to her feet. At her side, the king smiled as his lady tied her own silk scarf about the lance of the Englishman, who inclined his steel-clad head to her in thanks.

"God go with you, Adrien!" she called to him.

"God is my right, my lady!" he called in return.

Pompous fool! Danielle determined.

The combatants were called back to take their places. Trumpets sounded again. With earth flying from the mighty hooves of the horses, the men rode to their opposite sides before the royal box, and the master of the tournament commanded them to prepare to joust.

Then it began. The very earth itself seemed to thunder as the huge war horses ran with all their strength, seeming to run straight for one another.

Each man carried his lance, the point covered, ready to strike his opponent. Closer and closer, dirt flying, earth trembling . . .

The men came together. Clashed. The sound of it was shattering.

But neither man went down.

They returned to their sides where each man's squire rushed forward to supply him afresh as he threw his broken lance to the ground.

Once again, the horses charged.

Running harder, harder . . .

The clash again, shattering, near deafening. A horse screamed. And a man was down.

Danielle leapt to her feet with the other onlookers.

The great Frenchman was down!

Down, but not defeated. The Frenchman's squire ran to him with his sword while MacLachlan remained astride his mount. Then MacLachlan raced to his side and dismounted, took his sword from his squire, and strode swiftly back into the fray to meet his opponent on foot.

The crowd seemed to cry out simultaneously as the mighty swords first clashed. Then, to Danielle's pleasure, it seemed that the Englishman gave way, falling back under the power of the Frenchman. The Englishman might be tall, Danielle thought, but she had seen a number of these tournaments now, and she was quite confident that the Frenchman's maturity would serve him well, for he was the heavier of the two.

But then the Frenchman pressed forward with an aggressive

attack, and his opponent so smoothly side-stepped him that the
impetus of his movement sent him pitching forward, his blade
catching deep into the earth. Unbalanced, he fell forward to
the ground. He was a seasoned fighter, and quickly rolled in
an effort to leap to his feet again, but too late.

The Englishman already stood above him, the capped point
of his sword just above the Frenchman's throat.

Everyone leapt up again.

The cheers and shouts were deafening, even more so when the
young Englishman pulled his sword back, bowed in deference to
his opponent, and reached out a gauntleted hand to help his
enemy to his feet. Every bit as chivalric, the downed Frenchman
accepted the assistance and the two rose, bowing deeply
together. D'Elletente then returned to his horse and squire, while
MacLachlan strode forward, sheathing his sword, unlatching his
visor from his bascinet, then lifting the whole of his helmet
from his face.

Danielle saw instantly why it seemed his eyes glittered so—
they were gold, or as close to that color as eyes might truly
be. Not brown, not green, but some color in between, as bright
as a sun's ray. He had a full, rich head of deep red-gold hair
to complement his eyes and the fine strong features, hard and
unlined. He came instantly to the queen, bowing to her first,
and then to his king. Edward remained standing. "Remarkable,
Milord MacLachlan. Remarkable! Name what prize you would
have of your king!"

MacLachlan hesitated just a moment, then said, "Sire! I
have been informed that David of Scotland raised an army, as
commanded by Philip of France, and came against your barons
in the north of England."

"That's true," Edward said, eyes narrowing. "He was met
by my barons at Neville's Cross near Durham, and is even now
my prisoner. If you would ask his freedom—" the king began,
anger in his voice.

But MacLachlan spoke quickly, "Nay, my lord, I would not
ask what you could not give. I merely ask that you offer him
mercy as you keep him in prison and remember he is your
sister's husband, and beloved of the Scots."

"All that is granted. You ask nothing for yourself?"

MacLachlan grinned. A handsome grin, with a devil's own touch to it.

"The time will come, milord king."

"Ah, but will you always be victorious?"

"Sire, it is my plan."

Laughter arose.

"I suppose, my young lord, that your time will come!" the king said.

"My thanks, your grace," MacLachlan said, lowering his head to the king once again before quitting the field—amidst another thunderous rise of cheers.

Danielle, deeply disappointed that the charming and talented Frenchman had not won, did not watch the victor quit the field. At first, she was only dimly aware of the conversation around her as men and ladies chatted about the daring young MacLachlan. "He defended the prince like a wildcat at Crécy!" Someone said.

"So young!" came another soft, feminine sigh.

"Rest assured, he has been brilliant from a very, *very* young age," the queen supplied. "Edward told me that as a lad, MacLachlan was the military mind behind his siege of Aville, and that the castle fell because of the lad. Aville was taken, and returned to the fold of those loyal to the king!"

The castle at Aville . . .

Her castle!

She knew the story well enough. King Philip had needed to escape Edward. Danielle's mother had defended Aville, allowing the English king to think that Philip remained within the walls, while the French king escaped. But despite her mother's valiant efforts, the castle had fallen, and Lenore had become a prisoner.

And so, Danielle thought, I am here now—the king's ward. His prisoner, she thought, just as her mother had been.

And now she knew why. MacLachlan! Her fingers curled into her palms as she sat. Her hands formed fists. Great knight indeed! And his intent was always to be victorious. What nerve! Every man paid the price of his actions.

As of that night, Danielle began to have sweet dreams in which she managed to take on the knight herself—and slice and dice him to ribbons. She wished desperately that she could challenge him on the field, but he was a knight, and she was not quite eleven years old.

One night, not long after the tournament, she saw pepper on the table. She stared at it, reminding herself that she hadn't the strength, power, or position to challenge MacLachlan on the field. Battles had to be fought with what weapons were at hand.

She was seated far down from the king and his knights— the fighting men taking the seats of precedence—and she thought long and hard about what she intended to do. Pepper was a prized and valuable spice, but a bit too much of it could cause discomfort. She looked down at MacLachlan, whose handsome face was fixed in a smile as he laughed at something said by the queen. For all the damage he had done, he found far too much humor in life. Perhaps a bit of pepper could make him quit laughing.

She slipped from her seat and around the high table, and pretended to speak with the queen herself. While doing so, she casually filled his wine chalice with a generous supply of the pepper.

She bowed humbly to her godfather, the king, aware that Edward's eyes narrowed suspiciously, and that the nobleman by the king asked questions regarding her, commenting on the luster of her hair.

She sat down with the king's young son, John, just barely her senior, at her side. She liked John. She knew he considered himself superior as the king's son, but he was also proud of his older brother, the prince, quick to smile, wonderfully digni-fied, and always ready to help her. His eyes, light blue and yet penetrating, were upon her.

"Are you angry, Danielle?"

"Angry?"

He leaned closer. "I was watching you last week at the tournament when my lady mother was talking about the siege of Aville. Your face went white, like parchment. I thought you'd dig holes in your own flesh. Aville was taken before you were born—you mustn't let what happened then upset you.''

''I'm not angry,'' Danielle said, stabbing a piece of meat from the dish set between them. But just then, there was a strangled, choking sound, followed by tremendous coughing. Danielle didn't look up.

''Why, it's Adrien MacLachlan!'' John said.

She looked up then. MacLachlan's face was blood red. He reached for a fellow's wine and drank it down, stilling the spate of coughing that had seized him.

''My God, Adrien, what ails you?'' cried the king.

It took the man just a moment to speak. ''Nothing, sire. Nothing, I think. Just a cup of—bad wine. Seasoned wine,'' he added after a moment. ''Nothing more.''

Danielle looked quickly back to her food, eating rapidly. She felt John's eyes upon her, but he said nothing more. In time, she dared to look up at the high table again. MacLachlan had regained his normal color. His eyes moved around the room.

And remained puzzled, she was quite certain.

Those gold eyes fell on her then, and for a moment, she froze. Just the touch of his gaze made her tremble and feel warm inside. Afraid.

He wanted people to be afraid! she thought. The brave warrior, the man who tore down French castles and bested French knights.

She wanted to tear her eyes from his; she didn't seem able to do so. But his gaze moved on and she realized, to her vast relief, he would have no suspicion that one of the king's wards might have any reason to wish him harm.

The siege of Calais went on eternally, or so it seemed to Adrien. As to strategy, the king had determined to starve the people into submission.

Calais, standing at the point where the Channel was the narrowest, was a difficult place to take, for it was defended by a double wall with towers and ditches.

In the end, Calais fell. The people had been starved into submission; the last rat had been eaten. Edward sent men in to negotiate with the governor of the town. The messengers came back to King Edward, and as the French had charged them, they begged King Edward to spare Calais. Adrien was there when Edward's chief negotiator, Walter Manny, told the king that the people of Calais would hand over the tower and town, everything, if only they were allowed to leave.

"There's not the slightest prayer!" the king bellowed. Of all places, none had seemed to infuriate him quite like Calais. He had lost many men to pirates from the town—of that, Adrien was well aware. And Calais had held out for a very long time. Adrien feared the king's wrath against the people, becuase it was so unreasoning.

"Sire!" Adrien said, "I beg your pardon, but think on this! You are a noble king. You should not have to look back on this great battle as if it were murder!"

"Murder?" Edward said, eyes narrowing.

Walter Manny quickly stepped into the conversation again. "My lord Edward, what if you were to send us to defend some stronghold! How much more happily we would go, knowing that you showed mercy to others, and so, if all else should fail, mercy might befall us as well!"

The argument went on. In the end, Edward somewhat broke down, lifting a hand to the lot of them. "This is it! Six of the most important men in the town are to come to me. Heads and feet bare, ropes around their necks, and the keys to the castle and the town in their hands! The rest of the town will have my clemency. These six men will be mine to do with what I will!"

The message was brought back to Calais. Adrien walked before the walls of the town, heartsick as he heard the wailing inside.

But soon after, the men came, six of the most important and influential citizens.

King Edward came from his quarters to the field directly outside his hall. He was surrounded by his barons, his family, and then by everyone in the near vicinity who saw what was happening.

Adrien edged his way through the crowd, already praying that some way might be found for the king to be merciful to even these, the chosen citizens of Calais. The poor men were all but corpses already, shirtless, ribs showing through thin skin.

All six men fell to their knees before the king. One spoke for them, and did so eloquently, telling Edward that they had come so that the people of Calais, who had already suffered grievously, might be spared. They put their lives into Edward's hands and prayed for his mercy.

There was not a sound to be heard. Then the jagged note of a lady crying sounded on the breeze. The six brave men of Calais had moved many a heart, so it seemed.

But not the king's.

"I have had mercy!" Edward roared. "By God, I tell you I will not be swayed in this!"

Adrien started forward, as did Walter Manny, Ralph Basset, and many others.

"My king—" Adrien began, but Edward was quick to cut him off.

"Laird MacLachlan," Edward said, a taunting note of the Scot's accent to his voice, "I would grant you much, but in this, I warn you leave me be! And you as well, Walter. These six are mine. You will send for the executioner! Their heads will be struck off immediately!"

At that moment the crowd suddenly gave way. The queen, heavily swollen with another child, came before her husband. She fell down to her knees before him in a gesture of humility that again brought a hush to the crowd.

She looked to Edward, tears straining her face. She was more beautiful than Adrien had ever seen her.

"My lord, my husband!" she cried out. "I have followed you into many a campaign at peril to myself, and to your children. I have travelled rough waters, rugged lands. I have never asked anything of you. I do now. I beg you, through the blood of Jesus Christ, that you give these men unto me, and unto mercy."

"Sweet Jesu, lady, but I wish that you were home now, anywhere but here! I would not deny you—"

The king broke off for a moment. Adrien saw that he was looking over the queen's head, past the bowed heads of the condemned men of Calais. Frowning, he tried to determine just where the king looked.

He was staring at the children. John, a handsome lad, and another. Robert of Oxford's daughter.

Adrien felt a strange sensation as he watched her. She was so much like her mother. Tall for her age, and very beautiful with her raven-black hair and bright green eyes. He always felt a touch of poignancy remembering Lenore; they had defeated her, but every man among them—even the very young ones such as himself—had fallen a little bit in love with her.

Still, it seemed strange that the king might be looking at her daughter now.

But he turned back to the queen then, grasping her hands. "My lady, I grant you that I owe you much, and that you have asked for nothing. No one else could have swayed me here. I cannot refuse you, no matter what the right of my fury!"

He turned. A wave of cheers arose and people called out the queen's name, blessing her.

The queen rose, shaking, amazed that she had managed to change the king's mind.

The two executioners, hooded for their craft, turned away.

"Rise, rise!" Philippa entreated the men of Calais. They were shaking too hard to do so.

"Help me . . ." Philippa said. Her eyes touched upon Adrien's. "Adrien, please . . ."

He hadn't realized that he had been standing as if frozen in place, still looking toward the place where Robert of Oxford's daughter had stood.

He gave himself a quick shake and rushed forward, helping the queen with the shaking men who were all blessing her then, trying to kiss her hands, weeping.

Others stepped forward then. The ropes were taken from the men's necks and Philippa assured them gently that they must come to her chambers, where they would be clothed and fed.

The men were walked away, the crowd dispersed. Adrien found himself still standing in the field before the king's quarters. He stared back toward Calais, aware that they would enter it now, then looked back toward the king's residence.

She was suddenly there again. Her emerald eyes were on him like twin green daggers, ready to slice into his heart.

"Milady?" he inquired, and bowed—somewhat in jest.

She didn't reply. She spun about as if she were the most regal lass in all the world.

He found himself laughing softly as he turned to walk away. It had been a good day. Mercy had at last been wrought from the king; Calais had fallen. He was young, and the very world lay at his feet.

That night, he forgot the girl with the emerald green eyes. He didn't know then that the time would soon come when he would not be able to forget her.

Ever again.

Chapter 5

Once they had returned to England, Danielle discovered that she had her own apartments in the king's household. Lady Jeanette and Monteine continued to serve her. Doctor Coutin arrived as well, summoned by the king to come as her tutor. Danielle was happy to have her people from Aville, but despite her determination to remain a subject of the French king, she found herself making friends at Edward's court as time passed. A number of the ladies who served the queen were kind to her, intrigued by her history, and ready to take her beneath a matronly wing. She enjoyed the king's son, John, her friend, who was aware that she remained homesick for Aville. He would allow her to learn with him in the fields when his sword and horse masters would teach him, and he would applaud her when she learned well.

The Scottish king remained a prisoner of the English monarch. An uneasy truce continued between the French and the English.

Days became weeks, weeks became months. Years passed. Danielle was nearly fourteen when death—in a different form than that caused by war—came to threaten the hardiest of English warriors. The Black Death. It had scourged the East, riddled Europe. Now, it had taken hold in England, and there wasn't a man alive who did not fear it.

For the gentry, royalty and nobility, the only defense against the disease was to run from it and into the country. That was perhaps why the king decided at last that it was time for Danielle to be brought to see her English inheritance, her father's lands and fortress at Gariston.

Although Aville remained her home and she believed she would return one day, she was not opposed to seeing Gariston and was, in fact, happy to see her father's holding. Robert's memory remained sacred to her. She was also aware that the queen herself had been married at an age younger than she was now, and she was anxious to escape the court where she was well aware that Edward—who had thus far firmly turned down every offer for her—could easily choose to use her soon as a marriage pawn. Out of sight, she might well be more out of mind.

To her surprise and annoyance, Laird MacLachlan was to be her escort for her first visit to her holdings. She discovered the annoying situation when she came down a hallway at Winchester and saw MacLachlan with Lady Joanna, one of the queen's women who was exceptionally kind, lovely, and pleasant. The two laughed and teased very intimately in the hall, and Danielle paused behind a column—startled that someone as sweet and wonderful as Joanna might be seduced by a man like MacLachlan.

"This will not take long—Gariston is but a day's ride from here. Ah, Joanna! Can you imagine! I am the rage of the battlefield, the best in tournament and against foe, and for my prowess I now discover that I am to be nursemaid to an arrogant young countess!"

"Adrien, she's no longer a child. She's a sweet, intelligent young lady. A beautiful girl," Joanna countered.

"Aye, she's her mother's daughter, with a witch's eyes! I believe she thinks she is queen here, as royal as a prince or princess."

"Adrien! She lives in a court foreign to her. She lost both parents."

"My lady, that happens quite often."

"I'm sorry, I had forgotten your past, for it seems we have known one another forever. As to the Countess d'Aville—"

"My young charge, the witch?"

"I find her charming."

"Because you are the kindest creature in Christendom!"

"You must be kind to her," Joanna said.

"I will get her to Gariston as commanded and return as soon as possible. Then we must bring our petition to the king."

Danielle watched as Joanna, with her bright blue eyes and sable hair, ran a delicate finger down the warrior's cheek. It was a pretty motion, and somehow stirred Danielle's heart— or perhaps would have done so, had the warrior not been MacLachlan. "My dear Scot's laird!" Joanna said softly. "Aye, indeed, I would love to wed you. But . . ."

"Aye, but?" he demanded, glowering fiercely.

"Do you know, my noble laird," Joanna asked softly, "that you do not truly love me?"

He seemed taken aback by her words, startled. He caught her hands, frowning. "Joanna, I have loved you a long time—"

"There's a difference being loving and being in love."

"Joanna, men and women are often wed as total strangers! Think of all that we have!"

"I do. And I am grateful. I just wish that—" she broke off, shrugging.

"We will wed—we are both happily agreed!" Adrien announced.

Joanna laughed softly. "Ah, Adrien! Indeed, we will wed, for you are my great and indomitable warrior, and I defy my father—or, heaven forefend, the king!—to stop us!"

He was going to kiss her. Danielle was deeply upset, hearing that MacLachlan was to escort her anywhere—much less to her noble father Robert's home. And she certainly didn't want to watch anything tender between MacLachlan and Joanna. She turned quickly on her heels, determined to escape them both for the moment.

She heard a sigh, and then a moaning sound that gave her pause. Afraid that Joanna might be suffering, she looked back.

Joanna wasn't suffering. She was clinging to MacLachlan, who seemed towering, all height and steel, as he held her.

Oh, he was a wretch! Danielle thought. By sheer luck he had taken a fine French knight at tournament, and now it seemed that he also had Joanna at will.

Danielle bit into her lower lip, unnerved by the strange warmth that filled her. She realized again that she might soon find herself a marriage pawn. She was considered an incredible prize because of her vast holding and watching these two, she felt newly afraid. Joanna wanted to be with her warrior. What would marriage be if a woman despised her partner?

Just how long would the king refuse all petitions for her hand, and why did he wait?

Dismayed that she had stood watching the two, Danielle, her face on fire, all but ran down the corridor until she stopped, holding the wall, gasping for breath.

Then she froze as she heard the booted footsteps of a man close behind her.

She shot quickly into an alcove and waited. A moment later, Adrien MacLachlan walked on past her. She held her breath while she watched him open one of the chamber doors and disappear into the room beyond it.

Private apartments lined this corridor. Only those most honored by King Edward were given these rooms. Many a knight slept atop another in the crowded sleeping chambers at court. At times, some even slept in the hall.

How could Joanna love MacLachlan? He didn't deserve her. He had gained everything in life by his treachery against Lenore and Aville. And now, he was to escort her to Aville. How could the king be so cruel? Could he possibly think that she didn't realize how bitterly MacLachlan had wounded her family?

She backed away as the door to his room opened. His squire came out, his laird's boots in his hands. Danielle hurried along the hallway to escape, yet discovered that they walked in the same direction, toward the massive kitchens.

She pretended to have come for an herb as a headache remedy for the queen. As she waited, she saw MacLachlan's squire sit on a bench to polish the boots. His task quickly accomplished, the lad moved away, while she still waited.

Curious to see where he had gone, she spun around, knocking an earthenwear jug off one of the great wooden work tables.

It plopped straight into a boot. Gasping as she quickly bent to retrieve it, she discovered that the jug contained honey—or *had* contained honey. Most of the sticky substance was now in the boot. She stared in dismay, then bit into her lower lip as she smiled. She hadn't even done it on purpose, but MacLachlan was getting what he deserved. God, she decided, was on her side.

Adrien lay in bed awhile after he awoke the next morning. It was early, and he didn't like the task of escort that lay before him.

He stared at the ceiling in his chamber, wondering when he would be able to speak with the king regarding Joanna.

A private audience with the king might be difficult now, since he was being sent on a fool's mission with the girl. And the king had determined to hurry to the countryside himself; they would all be leaving that day.

Adrien had yet to see the plague, but he'd heard enough about the awful black fever to know that it cared little whether a man was noble or peasant, strong or lean. The best thing about it was that death often occurred with lightning speed. When it did not, pustules formed all over the body. Some people survived when they burst . . .

But many died, in great pain.

He did not fear death; he had faced it too many times. But he was afraid of his own weaknesses, and prayed that the disease would not strike him down.

The fear of the plague did not make him any more pleased to be leaving Joanna, even though she had assured him she would take the greatest care. "My noble lord, with the queen's permission, I can either travel to my father's marsher estates, far west of where the sickness encroaches now, close to the

Welsh border, or else . . . I can journey to see my friend, the
Countess of Gariston and Aville.''

The thought of Joanna arriving at Aville was a pleasant
enough one, and maybe her father would give her permission
to come. Adrien chafed anew that he had waited too long before
seeking a marriage with Joanna, but there had been so much
that was comfortable and easy between them that he had not
imagined things could go wrong. Her father liked him, he liked
her father. Since he had come home, their relationship had
deepened; she had slipped into his chambers at night, and
though the thought of behaving nobly and sending her away
had crossed his mind, the hungers and fires of youth had burned
away any idea of restraint. Making love to her was pleasant,
like everything else about her, comfortable, easy. If he awoke
upon occasion at night to discover that he felt that something
was just a little bit lacking, it only served to make him remind
himself very fiercely that he loved her and intended to marry
her. She would make an excellent, loving mother for the sons
and daughters he intended to have, a multitude of children,
strong and indomitable, in his father's memory.

Not wanting to act as Danielle's escort would not change
things. Edward had firmly assured Adrien that he was in dire
need of his service. It was an important journey, since the
countess had never set foot upon her English holdings before
and it was necessary that the lady realize that her father had
been an Englishman, a knight honored by the king. Edward
apparently wanted the girl taught that her holdings in England
were rich, and to be managed responsibly.

Adrien was certain that Edward was irritated with the girl's
. . . *Frenchness.* But since she had grown up in Aville, and
surely knew a number of her Valois relations, Adrien wasn't
quite certain what else she could be. Still, the king's attitude
toward her seemed strange altogether. He would sometimes
stare at her broodingly from his chair in the great hall at dinner.
He would speak of her beauty with pride, then state furiously
that she must be kept well beneath his thumb because she had
a dangerous and reckless streak that he recognized well. Adrien

could only assume he was referring to the lass's mother, the spell-binding Lenore.

She was a danger—indeed. Adrien wasn't at all sure of what he had done to draw her enmity, but he had the suspicion that she was the one to have peppered his wine outside Calais. He had caught her eyes upon him at times, and they glittered with a wild, green fire. She was always an angel in Philippa's presence, and she seemed to care for the queen, dropping her eyes like the sweetest innocent when Philippa was near.

But Adrien had seen her as well in the courtyard with the king's son, John, learning swordplay from his master and never retreating from any situation. He wondered suddenly if she was aware that he had been involved in the taking of Aville—but that happened before she was born. She couldn't really be aware of it. No—she had just decided that she didn't like him. Pity. She was going to have to tolerate him, and do so courteously.

Adrien rose. He slept naked, and when he washed, he was glad to douse his chest and arms as well as his face, for the coldness of the water helped to awaken him.

He dried himself and paused where he stood. Ah, well, he was stuck, and that was that. If he remembered just how kind a mentor Robert of Oxford had been to him, and just how much he had admired Lenore, he could make the journey in honor of the two.

He donned his hose, shirt, and tunic, still telling himself that the coming journey would end soon enough—all things did.

Adrien had just talked himself into something of a better disposition when he sat at the foot of his bed to don his boots. He shoved a foot in his left boot hard and immediately started at the sticky slush he felt through his stocking. "What in God's name . . ."

He pulled out his foot. It was covered in golden slime. Honey!

His voice rose as he swore vociferously, threw the boot down, and stared at it in amazement.

"Who . . . ?"

Who, indeed. His eyes narrowed. The little French wench

herself. She with the wide, glittering emerald eyes, raven hair, and deceptive beauty.

He slammed his boot down and hobbled with his honeyed foot to his door, threw it open, and stumbled out into the hallway. As it happened, one of the girl's companions, Monteine, was hurrying down the corridor just as he appeared. He caught her arm, spinning her around to face him.

"Milord!" she cried in surprise.

"Where is the little witch?" he demanded.

"Milord, I'm not at all certain to whom—"

"Milady Danielle d'Aville. Where is she?"

"Preparing for her journey, naturally, I swear it—"

"Where?" he all but roared.

She jumped with alarm, gesturing down the corridor. "Down there, second door. But milord—"

He heard no one. Heedless of his sticky toes and stockinged feet, he hurried down the corridor. Her door was slightly ajar—he slammed it inward.

She stood alone in her room, folding a garment. She was startled by the shuddering of her door as it slammed, but she didn't jump back—she barely paused in her actions. She stared up at him, an ebony brow arching with regal disdain.

She looked far older than her thirteen years. For the first time he realized that she had grown very feminine curves, and that her face was perfectly molded. Her delicate features gave her an air of dignified maturity as well, as did the green fire in her eyes, the hike of her chin.

"Milord?" she inquired, her tone regal and patronizing.

He smiled. He stepped into the room and closed the door behind him. "Milady. You are the king's ward. Poor little French orphan, adapting to all things English! Well, I knew your father. And he would not want his daughter to mature into an insufferable brat! If you would play pranks on me, Countess, you had best take care, for you will pay the price for mischief with me!"

She didn't move a muscle or betray the least fear. In fact, she had the audacity to appear aggrieved herself. She kept her tone low and cool as she replied, "You don't dare touch me, milord. I am the king's ward."

"You don't deny—"

"Milord, if you will please vacate my chambers?" she inquired softly.

"Vacate!" he exclaimed. "Vacate. Ah, milady—"

He didn't know quite what he had intended—maybe just to strangle her then and there. But he had come halfway across the room to her when he heard his name called with a slight sound of alarm to it.

Called by the king.

"Adrien!"

He gave pause, steeling himself, and turned to face Edward.

"Have you a difficulty?" Edward asked. The girl's companion, Monteine, stood uneasily behind the king. Adrien could well imagine that she had gone tearing down the hall, all but screaming that one of his knights was about to do some dire evil to her young mistress.

"I fear so, sire," he said evenly, his jaw remaining tight. "I awoke this morning to find that my boots were filled with something other than my feet. Strangely, I believe the sweet young countess here to be responsible!"

Edward's eyes quickly fell upon Danielle. Adrien thought that the king didn't doubt it in the least, but he frowned, demanding, "Milady?"

"Milord king?"

"Are you responsible, as my Laird Adrien believes?"

"If he is such a warrior, why would he tremble over something in his boots? And, indeed, sire, why would I wish to bother with his filthy footwear?" she returned, her voice soft with amusement.

"Your Grace," Adrien said flatly, "it seems milady is well in need of some discipline! She is favored by you and the queen, I am well aware. But sire, you have charged me with her welfare, and I'll not tolerate such behavior!"

"She's my responsibility *now,*" the king said with a sigh, "And therefore, out of your hands. But come with me, Adrien, I'd have a word with you."

The king started out of the room. Monteine rushed toward Danielle, glancing uneasily and guiltily at Adrien.

Adrien should have followed the king. But he paused, then took a menacing step toward the girl. She didn't recoil, but this time, he thought with a minor sense of triumph, she did seem to start and go just a shade pale.

"Milady, trust me. Try something again, and the king will not be about to protect you!"

"Alas!" she cried. "And what will you do now? Bring about the fall of Aville again? But it has already fallen—the king already holds it! Use trickery to take knights superior to your own strength and ability? Just what will you do?" To Adrien's amazement, she suddenly took a step toward him, hands clenched before her tightly. "What a perfect life you've created, Laird Adrien, on the misfortunes of others. Perhaps things shouldn't always be so perfect. You don't deserve all you've gained through the ruin of Aville! You assuredly don't deserve Joanna—"

"What?" he snapped.

"The king has summoned you!" she reminded him suddenly.

"What did you say?" he demanded anew.

Monteine, pretty brown eyes wide, hurried behind Danielle, holding her shoulders. "She said nothing, Laird Adrien—"

"I said that you don't deserve Joanna. She is gentle, kind, and sweet. And you are just like that wretched lion on your shield, roaring, scratching, clawing—grasping!"

Once again, he found himself taking a step closer, lifting a finger beneath her nose.

"And you, milady, are quite likely to get a sound switching soon—with or without the king's consent!"

Since he was itching to take her right over his knee, he determined to make an exit on that line, spinning after the words, and forcing himself to quit her chambers quickly. When he came into the hall, he was surprised to find Edward alone in the corridor—awaiting him there.

"She lived too long among the French," Edward said with a sigh. "I should have demanded that Lenore send her to me upon occasion, but then, there were so many battles to be waged and while Lenore lived . . .'' His voice trailed and he looked away, but then stared at Adrien hard again. "Perhaps you could go more gently with her.''

"More gently?" Adrien said incredulously. "That would all but invite her to come into my room while I slept and slit my throat!''

"Come now, it isn't that bad.''

"She needs discipline, sire.''

"You were far younger than she when you brought about the fall of Aville. There were times then when my own men— as well as the defenders of the place!—thought *you* were in need of some discipline.''

"I had discipline ground into me by your chosen masters, milord.''

"Be that as it may, the girl remains my concern. I cannot let you discipline her, as it stands. However . . .'' The king said, and cleared his throat, "that is a situation I wish to change.''

"I beg your pardon, sire?" Adrien said warily.

"Ah, my boy!" Edward clapped a hand upon his shoulder. "You and the lass are much alike, did you realize that? As much as I long to take a hand to her as well at times, I am deeply impressed by her fire and spirit. And loyalty! You must remember, Adrien, as yet, she's spent much more time across the Channel then she has spent here. Remember what an adjustment it was to leave your family in Scotland? To serve a different king?''

Adrien stood very still for a moment. "I remain loyal to David of Scotland. Even though I serve you and he is your prisoner.''

"I have dealt fairly with him.''

"I know. And so I remain your servant, Edward,'' Adrien said quietly.

"Indeed. My servant. And that is something I wish to discuss with you.''

"Aye?" Adrien said, growing evermore concerned and careful.

"I wish to bestow on you land worthy of the finest man! And a wife of the fairest form and beauty!''

Adrien's heart skipped a beat. "I had meant to speak with you for some time on the matter of marriage, milord. I—"

"I have pondered this for some time now," Edward said, firmly interrupting him. "I wish to betroth you to the Lady Danielle d'Aville. She becomes your responsibility to discipline as you will. If you're not ready for marriage you may wait, as long as you are legally betrothed. Not only is the fortress at Gariston an excellent one, the land is some of the richest in the country, the sheep are plentiful, the grain grows with greater vigor than any weed!"

Marriage! To the green-eyed little witch who was out for his throat? "Edward!" he gasped, "I meant to beg for the hand of the Lady Joanna—"

"Ah, Joanna! Sweet, fair, and lovely. But not for you, my boy! She's too gentle—you need a touch of fire—"

"So you'd give me a . . . young shrew?"

"Surely, lad, you cannot be blind. Danielle is young, but she already grows to a greater beauty than even her mother possessed. Aye, she's a spitfire, lad, but she'll keep you intrigued, when your blood would cool from the hunger for a less vibrant lady. She's young, but mind you, older than many a bride. Danielle is now thirteen, nearly fourteen. Philippa was but twelve when we wed. You needn't marry for a few years, if that is your wish, but the betrothal will give you the power of regent over the lady and her land. And there's more, naturally. The Earl of Glenwood, overlord to milady's English holdings, is recently deceased of the plague, his wee babe and wife along with him. The title and holdings remain vacant, and those would be my gift to you upon such a betrothal."

Adrien felt the blood drain from his body. *Most men would crawl through broken glass and kiss the king's feet for eternity to hear such words. Many men had begged the king for the hand of his French ward. Outside himself, looking upon the ragged boy his father had tried so hard to teach and train, this was an offer of power and wealth he had never imagined. The title of earl! What incredible riches and heritage he could pass onto the grandchildren of Carlin MacLachlan . . .*

But he had sworn that he would wed another.

"I shall never again be offered such a great boon, your grace," he said quietly, "but I must decline. You see, I love Joanna."

"Bah, son! She is a dear friend! An advisor, a mentor, lad, but not for you. Adrien, I believe you are forgetting something."

"Sire?"

"I am the king. I refuse you permission to wed Joanna."

"Sire," Adrien protested. "I have served you well—"

"And that is why we will say no more at the moment. Think on my offer—take the lady to the castle at Gariston. When we meet again, we will speak of it then. Make haste to leave this place now! There are more and more deaths being reported! The plague spreads wantonly here!"

With those words, the king hurried by him.

"I'll be damned if I'll do it!" Adrien promised the air in the king's wake. "I do love Joanna!" He did, in his way, care for her with all his heart. She was his best friend. She was gentle, kind, beautiful, in truth, everything desirable in a wife.

While he was being offered a young spitfire who longed to gouge out his eyes. Lenore's wild daughter. In his eyes, she remained too young for marriage, but she was already beautiful. Indeed, she was a young temptress just beginning to realize the power of her face and form, one who could dazzle, flirt, and manipulate when she chose, and make noble lads follow her about the castle with their tongues dragging upon the dirt. She was arrogant and superior. The greatest temptation in the king's offer might well be the power to put the lady in her place.

How deeply dismayed she would be to find herself handed over to his keeping! Ah . . . tempting!

But she would spend her days despising him.

While Joanna loved him.

He had vowed to wed Joanna.

But he swallowed hard. To be an earl . . .

Chapter 6

The day was beautiful when at last they set out. For Adrien, however, it promised to be a tedious ride. He was accustomed to long marches, often over enemy territory, with foot soldiers and wagons trailing along as well. This was different. He rode with his squire, Daylin, a freckle-faced lad of fifteen eager to prove himself, and to serve as well. Ten of his men-at-arms accompanied them, along with another ten soldiers who had ridden in to do service from their young mistress's own county of Gariston. Lady Jeanette and Monteine were with them, along with a seamstress and maids, a Doctor Coutin, who had been imported from Aville to continue to tutor the lady and administer to her and her household, and a French cook who had once served Danielle's mother and was reputed to create sheer magic out of food. There were all manner of carts and wagons containing the lady's belongings and those of her women. Although the ride should have taken no more than a day, it would take two since they were so heavily encumbered.

It didn't seem to help that the young countess seemed as impatient as he to move along quickly. She rode a fine horse, a bay mare with a white splash on the forehead, nearly sixteen hands high but far more slender and elegant than the destriers

Adrien was accustomed to. He was riding Matthew again, with Mark in tow along with the baggage—Luke and John remained at the palace at Westminster.

The old Roman roads, at least, were good. No heavy rains had fallen lately, and the paths were broad and clear. Adrien began leading the party, but became so preoccupied with his own thoughts that Danielle d'Aville soon rode ahead of him. Scowling, he urged Matt forward.

"My lady, an escort is intended to keep you from danger," he told her.

"There's no danger to be found in the countryside," she assured him, not slowing in the least and barely turning her head to reply.

He gave Matt a nudge with his heels and came abreast of Danielle's mare. "Cutthroats and thieves and creatures of evil design," he told her sternly, "can be found anywhere, my lady."

"I haven't seen any," she said coolly, "other than those who have been ordered to accompany me."

"Milady, you cannot imagine what other evil creatures may exist, since you are traveling with an escort of armed men!"

"Then I would imagine that my escort of armed men could protect me riding five feet behind as easily as they might riding five feet forward."

Ah, just once! Just once he'd love to have her over his knee! Just once . . .

He struggled fiercely for patience and control. "Get back behind me, my lady. And if you are even considering causing the least bit of trouble, remember, the king is no longer with us for you to hide behind, and I am in command."

"Don't be absurd," she told him smoothly. "I would never hide behind the English king."

"It was well that he came to your rescue when he did, my lady, or else you would have felt the force of my wrath."

He was nearly abreast of her then and she turned her head back just slightly. Emerald eyes narrowed sharply, disdainfully. "You'd not have touched me, milord."

"And why not?"

"I am a countess."

"I am a count."

"I am a ward of the king."

"Ah! So, you are still trying to hide behind him!"

"I never hide behind anyone, milord."

"If you don't believe in hiding, then tell me the truth. Did you put the honey in my boots?"

She paused, giving the matter thought. "Aye, in a way. It was actually an accident."

"Honey accidentally came to be in my boots?"

"Aye."

"And pepper came accidentally to be in my wine?"

That startled her a bit, but she quickly recovered, "The pepper was quite a while ago. And it was not an accident. Nor do I keep it a secret that I consider you an enemy. You should have the good sense to stay away from me!"

"Why? I shall simply put pepper in your *milk* and honey in your bed, and a sound hand upon your noble little *derrière* if you cause me any more difficulty."

"Oh, you will have more difficulty!" she assured him.

"Why?" he demanded.

"Because it's your fault I'm here now!" she exclaimed furiously.

"I beg your pardon—"

"Aville is a wonderful fortress, a great fortress! My mother could have held out until Philip could come to her rescue if it hadn't been for you."

She knew her history well. "You weren't there at the time, milady."

"No, but I know that you caused the fall of Aville and found the king's favor in the destruction of my home."

"Your home was never destroyed and you must surely be aware of that. The king ordered no retaliation against your mother or the town at all."

"He made her his prisoner and forced her back to England!"

"And she married your father there, and was allowed to return home and govern Aville again after Robert's death!"

She was not appeased. She stared straight ahead as they rode, emerald eyes flashing. "None of it would have happened at all if you hadn't made the fortress fall—"

"Sweet Jesu, cease!" he cried in sudden aggravation. "You saw the siege of Calais. It is far more merciful when a stronghold is taken quickly. Had a siege continued for any length of time, many more would have starved and died at Aville. And, my dear young wretched one," he added, his temper wearing thin, "perhaps it's time to think about this—your home is really here! You were born in London. Your father was a loved and favored servant of the English king—"

"And my mother was a cousin to the French king."

"Distant cousin."

She waved a hand in the air. It was no matter. "I am of the house of Valois. And Aville would have remained so. You alone brought about the fall of the fortress."

"I alone? The king and many brave men would be quite offended by such a statement. I was a boy—"

"You chose to make your way through the defeat of my mother and my people. You forced her to become the king's prisoner, and he tortured her, and when he was done there he dragged her back here—"

"Dear God, give me patience! Lenore was never tortured, and I don't believe she ever told you such a thing! And perhaps you should remember, just for good measure, that it was your father who asked as he died that the King of England be your godfather!"

"Sir, you will not change my feelings on this matter. My mother died reminding me that I must honor my king. I do not care to ride with you."

"If you fall back and allow me to lead, you will not exactly be riding with me. And bear in mind, I am the one sent to do a wretched duty here!"

She muttered something impatiently about what he should do with himself. Rather shocking language for a young countess, and Adrien imagined she had learned it spending time with the young princes and their men-at-arms.

She started to move away from him but he caught her horse's bridle, stopping her, grinning suddenly. "Think on this! Had it not been for me, milady, you might not even exist! For you are a mixture of French and English whether you wish to admit it or not, and would not *be* at all had Aville not fallen.''

''Then I'd still not be subjected to you!'' she hissed.

''Don't be subjected then, Countess. Fall back now!''

''I am trying to do so!''

He released his grasp upon her mare's reins. She did not just fall back. She swung her mare around in a sharp turn, riding back to fall in place toward the center of the line with Doctor Coutin.

Adrien looked up to the sky, amazed to see that it remained clear, that it was still a beautiful day. It felt as if his entire body was in knots. His fingers were like iron around his reins. Ah, if Joanna were but with him!

Dusk began to fall. Gentle colors to combat his mood filled the sky. They came to Hendon, where they would stay the night. Sir Richard Aisling, the king's appointed sheriff there, strode worriedly out to the courtyard to greet them.

A slim, grave old man, Sir Richard greeted him with courteous enthusiasm, then asked worriedly, ''None stricken among you?'' He crossed himself. ''Praise God, but we have escaped the Black Death so far, and though I'd not deny the king or wish any ill upon the poor little countess—'' He broke off. Adrien realized that the old gent was staring at Danielle, who had now ridden up beside him. ''Why, she's quite the lady, isn't she?'' he murmured, then collected himself and bowed deeply to Adrien.

Irritated, Adrien leapt down from his horse. He helped Danielle dismount—despite the fact that she didn't want his help.

Then he turned to Sir Richard. ''No—none of us has the least touch of fever, and indeed, I am anxious to keep the countess safe and well myself.''

Sir Richard sighed and managed a smile. ''Then come in, come in, bring the lady and her women into the manor. Your men may find their meals and lodging in the stables and cottages yonder. ''Darby!'' he shouted out, calling to a young groom. ''See to these good fellows, and the horses, too, lad, for the night's rest. Milord MacLachlan, Countess Danielle, if you will follow me, please.''

They followed Sir Richard into the manor, where a meal awaited them on the table in the hall.

It was a pleasant, clean place, with sweet-smelling rushes, a crisply burning fire, and the appetizing smell of well-roasted meat. Adrien was pleased to see that Danielle's manner to him before Sir Richard was courteous, if cool. They shared a small, intimate meal and Adrien found himself watching Danielle as they dined, startled to realize that to many a man, she would indeed be a prize. She ate delicately. Her hands were small, with long, elegant fingers and pretty, rounded nails. Her eyes sparkled with her words, her laughter was melodic. She had chosen to enchant Sir Richard. By the time they finished the meal, in fact, Sir Richard was all but convinced that King Philip of France was a poor, maligned fellow, and that they should cease all actions against the French.

Adrien found himself on his feet. ''I think it's time the young countess headed to bed, Sir Richard. I want to get an early start in the morning. I wouldn't want her sleeping in the saddle, nor would I want to carry her all the way.''

Danielle, of course, was instantly on her feet. ''You needn't fear, Milord MacLachlan. You'll not be carrying me anywhere. Sir Richard, I thank you for your hospitality, and I bid you good night!'' She made a wonderfully grand exit.

When she had gone, Adrien excused himself. ''I need to get some sleep as well, Sir Richard. I am anxious to reach Gariston, for I am even more anxious to return from it and see to the welfare of a friend in these very troubled times.''

''Troubled, indeed!'' Sir Richard lamented, crossing himself. ''It is dreadful—each day the death toll soars higher and higher . . . England may well be decimated if this plague continues to strike so ruthlessly!''

Adrien should have slept well. He'd enjoyed a fine dinner and gone to bed weary, but he tossed and turned all night and awoke feeling as if he hadn't slept at all.

He rose, washed and dressed, then summoned Daylin and told his squire to make sure that Danielle was roused and ready to ride along with her ladies.

"The countess is up and in the courtyard, milord. And I've saddled Mark for you today," Daylin told him, helping him with his mantle. "The men await your word to mount up and begin the journey."

"Good. We shall bid Sir Richard thank you and good day, and be gone," Adrien said, exiting his chamber to a narrow corridor, and from there down the steps to the empty great hall and then out to the courtyard beyond.

As Daylin had told him, his entourage was assembled. Danielle sat upon her mare, apparently serene. He thanked Sir Richard and inclined his head to Danielle. "Are you ready, milady?"

"Most assuredly, milord."

She seemed anxious, even in a good, if mischievous, mood. Adrien lifted a hand in final salute to Sir Richard, and their entourage started out, snake-like and slow, leaving the manor behind them.

Adrien rode at the fore, half closing his eyes, letting Mark move along at a steady pace.

Perhaps an hour or so after they had begun, he became aware that Danielle was abreast of him, moving ahead of him. They came upon a rich expanse of field, and she uttered a little cry of delight and nudged her heels strongly to her mare's sides.

The horse leapt forward and began to run, smooth and sleek, elegant and fast as the wind.

Adrien swore softly and took off after her. No matter what he said, she didn't seem to realize that there might be dangers awaiting her.

He had all but caught her when he suddenly realized that something was amiss. The girth upon his saddle was loose, so much so that even as he raced, the seat was giving. In seconds, he would be thrown off along with it—and trampled beneath the heavy hooves of his great war horse. Swearing, he threw himself against Mark's neck, arms wrapping around it. Just in time. The saddle gave.

And was trampled beneath him as they raced on.

He slid to the horse's back once again, reining in as Daylin anxiously rode abreast of him.

"Milord—"

"I'm fine! Have the others wait here until I return. I am going for the countess!"

He raced on ahead, so angry that there seemed to be an explosion of red swimming within his head. He caught her just as she neared a new forest to encompass the old Roman road. She turned back, startled and alarmed by his appearance.

As well she should be.

"What—" she gasped to him as he rode down hard on her. She backed her horse carefully away, but not quickly enough. He leapt from his own and grabbed her mare's reins, holding the animal still.

"What!" he roared. "Pepper is one thing, milady. It causes a cough. Honey in a man's boots is an irritating inconvenience. But this time, my wretched little witch, you came damned near to killing me!"

"I don't know what you're talking about!"

"But you do."

"I'm telling you—"

"My saddle!" he hissed furiously, and then he had her. Reaching up, he caught her around the waist and dragged her down.

"I didn't touch your saddle," she said scornfully, gritting her teeth as she stood stiff against his hold.

"Daylin knows how to secure one, milady. And since you readily admit your mischief—"

"Mischief I admit when I am guilty!" she retorted.

"Unless you realize that you are finally about to pay the price for it."

"Get your hands off of me!"

"Not this time! Milady."

She protested, wildly struggling against him. "Let go of me this very second or I shall see that the king—"

"If the king were to hang me from the highest tree for my intent, milady, it would not sway me from it now!"

He was incensed. His heart still pounded from his near plummet from his horse's back, and he was determined. There was a tree stump five feet away and he strode to it, dragging her with him as he sat, then pulling her irrevocably down over his knee, despite her desperate struggles to free herself and pummel him in return. Within seconds he had landed a good number of sound whacks upon her very French *derrière*. He was barely aware of her cries and shrieks of vengeance and fury. He didn't even stop to think until he felt her perfect teeth biting into his thigh and then he gave her his hardest whack of all, one that caused her to cry out—and cease trying to bite. He became aware then, of her person. Of the lush, tempting curves, her sweet scent. Startled, he set her back on her feet and rose, walking toward her with menace as she backed away from him, then stood dead still and defiant. He pointed a finger at her, keeping his voice harsh with anger. "Not another prank. Not a single little thing, not a one, to be done against me, do you understand?"

She was shaking, fighting tears, and surely, fighting the temptation to fly at him and scratch his eyes out. Her eyes sizzled their pure green fire. Her dark hair was a wild tangle that gave her a surprisingly sensual appearance. He discovered that he had to remind himself that although marriage was a game and brides could be very young, he had always preferred more mature women; Joanna was now nearly twenty-one.

"You bastard!" she cried. "I did nothing!"

"Your *nothing* nearly killed me!"

She remained outraged. He'd never seen her eyes glitter with such a fire and promise of vengeance. "You are wrong! I am not guilty! If you are such a fool, it's a pity that you were merely *nearly* killed and not completely so! Oh, sir! You will rue this day. I am not idly threatening you—I will tell the king what insult you dared upon me—"

"You may tell Edward anything you like, milady. Tell him I sprouted horns and a demon's tail. The king has given me free rein with you, milady. In fact, he has suggested that I should be entirely responsible for your behavior."

She was startled. Her eyes grew even wider, her face paler.

"You're lying. I know that you are lying. I am the king's ward. You cannot possibly have the right or deserve—"

"Ah, yes! You were rambling on once before about what I did and didn't deserve, weren't you? Hmm. I didn't deserve Joanna. Because she was so kind and sweet! Well, it seems, Countess, that the king agrees with you."

"Good! Joanna will then have some good and gentle knight."

"If the king has his way. And I will have a little shrew, a tempest, a wild little creature—"

"As you deserve!"

"So you say! And alas, you, lady, as well will have what you deserve. A roaring lion, grasping, clawing!"

"What are you talking about?" she cried out. "I don't understand what—"

"Ah, but I am trying to enlighten you! Pay attention! The king has suggested that I should have *you*, milady."

"No!" she gasped out in a strangled voice.

"Indeed, yes!" Adrien said, smiling wryly and speaking quite pleasantly. "The king thinks an immediate ceremony would be best. However, I am against marriage with one your age, and the king is well aware of that. Yet he sees a betrothal now, one which puts me legally in charge of your estates— and your precious little person as well! I would be your master, milady, your sole guardian."

"You!" she croaked.

"Indeed, me! Grasping, clawing, roaring, wretched horrid lion of a knave that I may be!"

He enjoyed a moment of complete satisfaction, fully aware that his taunting words had tormented her far more than the spanking. He couldn't resist the temptation to go on and he turned idly from her, continuing slowly in a thoughtful voice.

"A tempting proposition," he told her. "Very tempting. A knight can always use a greater income and I have been promised that Gariston is a rich county, indeed. But—" he said at last, "thus far, I have turned down the king's most generous offers regarding your placement. I will marry the Lady Joanna."

He frowned, hearing a thump behind him. He turned quickly,

curious about the sound and intrigued to discover her reaction to his last words.

But there was to be no reaction. His tough-as-steel young countess lay in a little pool of silk and ebony hair in the soft grass. The mere suggestion of a marriage between them had managed what no threat or action had managed to do.

Silence her.

She had passed out cold.

Chapter 6

Staring down at her, he had to admit that she was growing into an exquisite—and dangerous—beauty. Then a wave of guilt washed over him because she was young and, despite herself, afraid. With a soft sigh he told himself that he had to be more patient.

Maybe not. She had deserved it. Ah! Perhaps it was difficult to admit as well that the very idea of marriage with *him* had been so horrible that it had caused her to lose consciousness. He shrugged, smiling slightly, and reached down to scoop her up into his arms. He ran his fingers lightly down the length of her cheek.

"Danielle."

After a moment, she stirred. Her eyes seemed very wide, innocent, vulnerable. Dazed. Then she looked up, and her eyes met his and widened. "I'll never marry you."

He smiled. She was quite well, and still fighting. "Good," he assured her in return. "I'll never marry you."

"But you said—"

"I told you what the king suggested. I never said that I had agreed."

"Then—"

"I love Joanna," he said determinedly. "And I am going to marry her."

"Oh," she said, still staring at him. Then she swallowed hard. "I'm all right. You could set me down . . . please."

He did so, a hand still supporting her until he saw that she was really standing on her own.

Then she drew away. Her chin tilted, her head lifted, and she spoke very softly to him. "I did not touch your saddle," she said with tremendous dignity, then spun around and at a rapid speed, walked toward the field where the others waited.

Following behind her, Adrien saw Daylin dismount from his horse in the blink of an eye and bend down to offer Danielle assistance.

Danielle didn't need assistance. She'd had the big bay mare with her as long as Adrien could remember, and she'd never had the least trouble leaping atop it. But she smiled prettily at Daylin and accepted his help. When she was seated atop the horse she looked down at the young squire and thanked him in a soft voice.

Daylin blushed so vividly that his freckles disappeared.

An extra saddle was taken from one of the supply wagons and when his mount was readied, Adrien tightened the girth on his saddle himself before he leapt atop his horse and lifted a hand to their party to begin the ride again. "Come!" he called, and started out at a brisk trot while the others fell into place.

How odd. She had been so willing to admit so many things! And then today . . .

Today, when he'd dragged her down and handled her like a child, she had denied any part in what had been done. Well, he had been longing to take such action for a long time. He wasn't going to feel guilty.

She kept her distance from him then. After a while, Daylin rode up close behind him and since Adrien much preferred to be alone, he sent his squire ahead to see that the road before them remained clear.

But Daylin soon came back riding hard. "Milord!" he cried, face pale, red hair wild. "Milord, we must fall back, off the trail! Friars are coming this way, heavily laden with a wagon of plague dead for mass burial!''

Adrien rose in his saddle, looking back at his entourage. Life was full of little ironies. Landed knights and noblemen seldom drew aside for any reason, but the plague could make them scurry like desperate rodents.

"Draw the wagons far off the road and move deep into the woods!'' he commanded. He rode Matthew now and turned him around and rode hard along the snake-like trail of his party, making sure that all heard him and obeyed. Just as they cleared the old Roman road, he saw the first of the brown-clad, tonsured friars making his way slowly around the curve, waving a pot of smoke and incense to warn others that they approached— and to somewhat allay the terrible stench of death.

"Sweet Jesu!'' he whispered softly, crossing himself as he saw the entourage approach. Bodies lay piled atop bodies and more bodies, some half-clad, some fully dressed, as if they had been struck down even while they worked, and died so. Arms and limbs of gentry entwined with arms and legs of peasants, workers, farmers. He stared, feeling enormous pity. Then he suddenly remembered that he was in charge of an impressionable young lady, and he turned around to seek her in the woods.

He didn't have to look long. She was quite close behind him, dismounted from her mare, staring even as he stared. Her eyes seemed even more startlingly green than usual, for her face was pale, like snow, surrounded by the ebony wealth of her hair.

He leapt down quickly from Matt, catching her shoulders, drawing her against him.

Surprisingly, she didn't fight his hold. But neither did she turn to him to hide her eyes from the sight of the death wagon. He felt her trembling.

"Don't look!'' he commanded her. At that moment, she seemed very vulnerable.

For the moment, it seemed, Danielle had forgotten that he was her dread enemy. For that same moment, he felt the pain and compassion within her and wanted to protect her.

"Don't look!'' he repeated.

She shook her head. "I've seen the plague before," she said, but he could feel her trembling. But this once, she did not fight his supporting arms, and her voice quivered when she spoke. "I watched my mother die," she reminded him.

She slipped from his hold then, sank to her knees, crossed herself, and prayed as the friars passed by with their heavy burden of death.

When they were gone, there was silence. The sun beat down and cool air swept by, rustling the leaves. At last, the sounds of birds chirping came again.

Then it seemed that everyone was talking.

"We shouldn't breathe—" cried one of the armed guards from Gariston.

"We have to breathe, man. What are you, daft?" returned another.

"We must move quickly, quickly, milord!" Daylin said to Adrien.

"Aye, milord," agreed Doctor Coutin. "The Black Death cannot be stopped by a knight's armor or a noble's silk—it will attack where it pleases. Keeping clear of it is the only defense I know. Though it sounds cruel, we must hurry on, and be careful when we come to Gariston, that once we've entered, we keep others out!"

"Let's move onward!" Adrien said. "And make Gariston quickly then."

Men began mounting their horses. Adrien turned toward Danielle, but she was already mounted and ready to ride.

They rode hard in silence, and the hours passed quickly.

Coming out of a forested section of the Roman road, they reached a vast field that stretched across a wide valley. Then they saw Gariston before them, up on a hill, looking almost like the fabled Camelot beneath the dying sunlight of the day. Rich farmlands with a plentiful dotting of cottages, stables, and barns surrounded a moated fortress with high stone walls that seemed to gleam and glitter against the deep greens and golds of the fields. The Norman engineers who had built the original fortress had incorporated the natural flow of the river into the structure. The water did not lie stagnant around the fortress,

but moved in a swift flow around it, heightened now by a brisk
breeze. As the king had sent a messenger ahead days ago, they
were expected. The great drawbridge lay down across the water.

Adrien found himself assessing the place with an appraising
eye. The king had assured him it was a rich inheritance, and
indeed it was. He could see flocks of sheep upon the distant
rolling lands—acres and acres of rich, productive land. The
fortress appeared to be in excellent repair, and he was anxious
to see inside it. Gariston surely supplied the king with a multitude of fighting men-at-arms, and with a rich income as well.
The feudal system of life was simple. Villeins worked the land
they held from their lord or lady. A portion of all goods went
to the lord of the manor, a portion to the king. In turn, the lord
protected his villeins, the king led his country, and he and his
knights upheld the realm. The king expected service from his
landed knights and nobility. Equipment was expensive, horses
were expensive, a good set of armor could impoverish a man.
Thus, a holding such as Gariston was a rich prize for any man
to claim.

The countess was indeed a rich young lady.

He realized she had ridden by his side, that she stared up at
the great fortress and vast lands equally intrigued.

" 'Tis quite an inheritance your *English* father left you,
milady," he told her.

She turned to him, chin high. "Indeed, I imagine you find
it tempting. I'm ever so glad you are so enamored of Lady
Joanna!" She nudged her mare and went racing before him
once again.

He swore to himself and came riding after her. Her mare
was a swift creature. She tore across the fields, cutting through
flocks of sheep, and reached the bridge before he caught up
with her. Even then, she but slowed to a trot to cross the bridge
while he followed behind. In the vast courtyard of the castle,
he leapt down from his horse and came to her, sweeping her
down from her horse whether she wanted the assistance or not
as the rest of their party filed into the enclosure.

There were three towers in a circular enclosure. Massive
doors to the eastern tower were opened to the day, and it was

from these that a tall, slim man with a creased face and a headful of silver-white hair came hurrying out. "Milord, milady, welcome!" he called to them. He was Sir Thackery Milton, longtime steward of Gariston. Adrien knew him. He was loyal, shrewd, and intelligent, the perfect man to manage such a wealthy estate.

He saw that Danielle smiled at the old steward, pleased as she greeted him, instinctively liking him. Yet he was touched with a shade of unease watching her then, for he couldn't help but think that hers was a dangerous smile. One day, that smile might move men . . . where they shouldn't be moved.

"Welcome, welcome!" Sir Thackery said. "A long ride, eh, milady?" he asked.

"Not so long!" she said cheerfully. "What is long is the time it has taken the king to send me here!"

"Then come in, explore, and see this wonderful place," he told her. "Milord MacLachlan," he said to Adrien, "if your squire will see to the men, young Jacob there will see to the countess's women. And I will show you and the countess the fortress castle of Gariston."

Adrien nodded, giving the order to Daylin to see that his men were quartered, then following behind Sir Thackery and Danielle. The great hall, taking up the whole of the east tower's ground floor, was a fine place worthy of any man. Heavy tapestries lined the walls, along with a display of weapons, swords, pikes, halberds, maces, and knives. Two full suits of fighting armor stood by the entry, and two full suits of tournament armor stood far across from it by the massive stone mantel and hearth. A heavy, finely carved table stretched out from the hearth, while a rich fur rug lay directly before it, surrounded by heavy chairs in a golden oak to match the table. A tray of wine was set on the table. Sir Thackery poured a goblet to offer to Adrien, who was smiling, pleased with the place.

"A fine hall," Adrien commented.

"Indeed. Come up to the master's chamber," Sir Thackery said. "Ah! Forgive me!" he told Danielle. "It is now the lady's chamber, is it not?"

She smiled her acknowledgment and followed closely behind

Sir Thackery as he started up the broad, sweeping stairway to the level above. There was but one door there, and a rise of stairs that continued on upward again. Sir Thackery opened the door with a flourish, and they stepped in.

The hearth was identical to that in the great hall below, huge and crafted in stone. The fire that burned within gave an unsual comfort and warmth to the room, for fortresses such as this could often be drafty and cold. A huge canopied bed stood across from the hearth, while before it was another rich fur rug, surrounded by cushioned and tapestried chairs. Across the room was a table with another set of chairs around it, set before the archers' windows so that light might stream in. A door led to a privy and a marble-topped washstand, which held a pitcher and water.

"A fine place, indeed, Milord MacLachlan!" Sir Thackery said.

"Very rich," he agreed.

"Come above, milord, for there is a guest chamber above this master suite where it is said that William the Conqueror housed his own family upon occasion. I'm sure you will find it quite comfortable."

Sir Thackery started out and Adrien followed him, but paused to study the finely carved mantel.

"Excuse me, milord, but this is *my* room," Danielle said. "Sir Thackery awaits to take you to yours."

A brow arched, he turned back to her. She might have forgotten his treatment of her when the plague victims passed by, but she remembered it now. Her eyes were pure green fire— she was obviously anxious to be rid of him. And she was delighted in the richness around her, relishing the fact that it was all *hers*—and not his.

He fought the temptation to reach out and drag her over a knee again. Instead, he bowed deeply to her. "Countess, with great pleasure, I leave you to your solitude."

With that, he again started to follow Sir Thackery, who had gone on up the second flight of stairs. He was surprised when she called out to him again.

"I didn't touch your saddle, MacLachlan."

He turned around, arching a brow.

"I didn't do it," she repeated. An irritated and yet injured note touched her voice then. Her eyes were brilliant, she appeared very regal and feminine. She looked beautiful, and, like Lenore, seductive. "I tell you," she said firmly, "I was not guilty, and you owe me an apology."

He didn't reply for a moment, swayed by the vehemence of her words.

But he knew better than to allow her to sway him. He crossed his arms over his chest, surveying her. "I've yet to receive an apology for what you did to my wine or my boots."

"I never touched you."

"Sir Thackery awaits me," he said, and left her.

The guest chamber was nearly as comfortable as the master's quarters. That night, Adrien slept deeply and long. In the morning, he learned more about the layout of the castle. Danielle's ladies and tutors were housed in the south tower while the north tower was the domain of the knights and men-at-arms.

He spent hours in the great hall with Sir Thackery, going through Danielle's Gariston accounts and finding that the place was, in truth, all but a Camelot. Sir Thackery trained the men-at-arms himself, no blight had ever touched the fields, and the countryside was peopled by numerous craftsmen as well as farmers. There were two blacksmiths, three coopers, three stonemasons, at least ten good carpenters. There were seamstresses, metalsmiths, millers, and more. The sheep were some of the finest in all England, and the revenues from the sale of wool to the Flemish were generous.

Adrien commended Sir Thackery for his excellent management of the estates, assuring him that the king was well pleased with his efforts.

"I'm glad that my good lord Robert's daughter has come here at last. He was a very great man, and it is good to see his bloodline follow here!"

Adrien agreed that Robert had been a great man.

Sir Thackery suggested a hunt for the following day, since

the forests were rich with game and there were now many more mouths to be fed at the castle. He had been entrusted with the care of the Glenwood Forest, since the old earl had died without an heir, and the king had yet to choose a man upon whom to bestow the title, estates, and income. "Deer are plentiful, wild boar as well. Ah, and the birds to be taken! Pheasants and fowl fill the air. We've a fine selection of hawks and falcons for the chase, and it's a good day's pleasure, Laird MacLachlan."

Adrien wondered for a moment why so many people chose to use the Scots accent when addressing him, since he had been away from his father's country so many years. He didn't mind. No amount of time could erase a man's roots, and though he was Edward's knight, he never forgot that his first language had been Gaelic and that he was Carlin MacLachlan's son.

"I should enjoy a day's hunting," he agreed, then excused himself from his host and exited the hall to walk around the fortress, assessing everything he saw.

Out in the large expanse of courtyard, men and women plied their trades. A barefoot girl walked with a flock of geese, a cooper sat upon a stool beneath a thatch-roofed hut, nimbly transforming oak shavings into a barrel. As he walked down along the row of craftsmen, Adrian saw a goldsmith fashioning a circlet and he paused, watching the delicate work as the artisan welded tiny beads into the design.

"A beautiful piece, milord," the bearded craftsman called to him. "Worthy of a lady a man such as yourself might call his own."

"Indeed it is," Adrien agreed. "When will you be finished?"

"When would you like to have it?"

Adrien laughed. "As soon as possible. I plan to see the countess settled, and then ride out and find my lady. I'm eager to bring her back here to be with me while this cruel plague haunts the country."

"The circlet will be done this evening," the craftsman promised.

Adrien paid the man without haggling over the price. In London or Winchester, it would have been considered low. He imagined that Joanna would love the circlet, and he suddenly pined to see her. She would enjoy Gariston with its high, strong walls and beautiful interior details. She would enjoy the warmth inside those walls from the huge hearths, and she would enjoy Sir Thackery as well, he was certain.

He had brought the countess safely here, as he had been commanded. By himself, taking shortcuts through more narrow trails, he could return to Winchester before Joanna had a chance to leave and convince her that she must come with him to wait out the plague here. Her father would forgive them both for not seeking his leave since time was so important. Adrien had been feeling a growing anxiety ever since he had seen the friars with their burden of dead, and he wanted to make sure Joanna was far from the congestion of Winchester. Perhaps she had already left for her father's estates, and perhaps not. She had not to leave for several days, since she had to see that the last of the queen's offspring and belongings were packed and gone before seeing to herself.

He would attend Sir Thackery's hunt tomorrow and assure himself that Danielle was settled and in good hands and that the fortress was well supplied, then depart the following morning with the dawn.

With that decision made, he found his mood lightened. He continued on his walk through the courtyard, and was not surprised to find Danielle holding her own manner of court with a number of young squires and men-at-arms. Somehow, she had managed to join in a training session for tournament jousting, and she laughed with delight as she balanced a heavy lance while seated upon her mare.

"You're extraordinary, milady, but the thing will burden you to the ground in but minutes!" came a warning cry. "Give it over, Danni."

It was Daylin, his own squire, who rushed forward to take the long, heavy shaft from her before it became too heavy. The girl smiled again, then spoke softly to all those around her, and a loud cheer went up for the new countess. She looked up suddenly, almost as if she had sensed that he was there, and a defensive tilt immediately came to her chin. She slipped from her mare, handing the reins to Daylin, then hurriedly left the group and headed for the east tower, ignoring Adrien as if she hadn't seen him.

Dear God, but she could irk him.

He followed behind her, whistling.

Once inside the hall she stopped and spun around. "What is it, milord? Do you feel that I falsely hope to gain the loyalty of Gariston's forces?"

"On the contrary, you seem to be doing just fine. The perfect lady."

She didn't seem to be surprised, merely wary. "Ah. So I can be the perfect lady. Is this your way of apologizing?"

He shook his head. "No, milady. You deserved exactly what you got from me. You will always get exactly what you deserve."

"Really? Well, perhaps you will be so good as to tell me, milord, just when you are leaving Gariston?"

"Actually, Countess, I am leaving at dawn the day after tomorrow." A look of such surprise and pleasure touched her features that he added quickly, "I have decided that I cannot leave matters to others—I am going back for Joanna. I will bring her here to reside until the king frees me from looking after his French ward. Pray God, lady," he said wearily, "tell me that you do not seek to fight me on this!"

"I adore Joanna," she said gravely. "She will always be welcome." She turned about and left him, seeking her own chambers.

They remained civil to one another that evening as they dined with Sir Thackery, Lady Jeanette, and Monteine. Danielle was charming as she assured the elderly steward that she was anxious to attend the hunt and meet the castle's birds.

She was weary, though, and retired quickly. Her emerald eyes assured Adrien it was his company that wearied her most. Adrien and Sir Thackery enjoyed a game of chess, which ended in a stalemate.

When he was climbing the stairs to go to sleep that night, Adrien encountered Monteine coming out of Danielle's chamber. The girl was pretty with dark sable hair and eyes to match—small, slim, and somewhat anxious.

"Milord!" she said quickly.

"Monteine."

She still blocked his way. "I—" she began.

"Yes?"

"Please," she said worriedly, "you mustn't be so angry with the countess. She is young and delicate, and lost a great deal in life with the death of her mother. She grew up in France, watching the destruction the English caused. I beg you, she does not mean—"

"She means every word she says to me, and she is about as delicate as the boars we will hunt tomorrow. She knows what to expect each time she crosses me, and that is the greatest kindness I can give her. Now, if you will excuse me, I am very weary."

He started to pass by her.

"Milord!" Monteine called again.

He paused. Her breasts were heaving, her hands folded nervously before her. She moistened her lips and stood very close, and he wondered if she might not be trying to offer him favors in return for his ignoring the wild streak in the countess.

"Aye?" he said.

"I wish—that you would not be so angry. If there were some way to ease your spirit . . ."

"The countess and I will have to learn to get along, Monteine, and we must manage that on our own," he told her. "Good night, Monteine," he said, and started up the stairs to the third floor.

He felt her eyes watching him as he walked, and he was certain that there had been more that she had wanted to say.

In the morning, Danielle was mounted along with her women, Sir Thackery, Daylin, and another young castle guard when Adrien came down. Mark was saddled and awaiting him this morning, along with a fine young falcon. He saw that Danielle was gloved and that she stroked the belly of a peregrine falcon that perched upon her arm, speaking softly to the bird. She greeted him politely enough with Sir Thackery before them, and then had her mare fall in step with Daylin's mount as their party started out for the forest.

The day was beautiful, the air clear. It wasn't long before they came upon a pond where waterfowl flocked. A pheasant suddenly started into the air and Danielle released her bird. They all watched as the magnificent creature burst gracefully into the air, bringing down the bird. The hunt was on.

Later, they rode hard across an open field. Adrien realized that Danielle enjoyed riding at great bursts of speed far more than she actually cared for hunting. She crossed a field ahead of him, then disappeared in a copse of trees. Suddenly a scream riddled the air and panic seized Adrien. He raced after her, his heart pounding furiously.

She was upon the ground and her beautiful bay mare was flat upon it, too. Adrien leapt from his horse, hurrying to Danielle. He hunched down before her and reached for her carefully, afraid that she had broken every limb. But she was already sitting up and not even noticing that he touched her, for her eyes were focused on her mare, Star, who had fallen, and lay flat . . .

"She threw you?" he asked.

She shook her head wildly. "Adrien . . . she was startled. Oh, God, Adrien, there!"

He looked where she pointed, past the mare, and saw a tree just beyond the fallen animal, where a corpse hung. It was bloated, pathetic. Crows had picked at the eyes. It appeared that an old hermit, suffering the agonies of the plague, had cast his own belt around his throat, jumped from the tree, and hanged himself. The horrible sight had startled the mare, and both Danielle and her horse had gone down.

"Jesus!" he whispered, crossing himself. He stood. "He's dead, Danielle—he's been dead a long time."

"I know," she said, but her face was ashen. She allowed him to help her up.

"Are you hurt?"

She shook her head. He cupped her chin, forcing her to look away from the corpse.

"Are you sure?"

"Aye."

Sir Thackery burst upon the scene then. He, too, saw the corpse, and crossed himself. "We'll get the fellow down. My lady . . . ah, Countess, you at least seem well. The mare will have to be put down."

"What? No, oh, no!" she whispered suddenly. She freed herself from Adrien's touch and knelt by the horse's head. Adrien sighed, kneeling down by the horse himself and discovering that a sharp branch had torn straight into the mare's inner right hind leg.

Daylin had reached them by then. "Ah, lady! She'll have to be put down. She won't be able to walk again," he said.

Tears stung her eyes. She blinked them back furiously and looked at Adrien. For once, there was nothing in that emerald gaze but pleading. "Please, Adrien, is there nothing at all you can do?"

"Danielle—"

"No, you cannot kill her!" she cried then, reaching for him, her fingers curling into his tunic and shirt. "Please, please, you cannot! Help me, Adrien, don't let them kill her!"

She loved her horse, but he realized as well that she was trying very hard not to see the dead man. She had already learned bitter lessons about the ravages of the plague, and he realized that fighting for her horse now was a means of fighting back against a horror that none of them could control.

He sighed deeply, looking at the horse, then at her. They all looked at one another—far better than seeing the long-dead corpse. "I can try to rig a stand for her and there are roots you can use to make poultices for her injury, but you'll have to dress the wound several times a day, *day after day,* and even then, she might not make it."

"But we can try!" Danielle whispered. Her lips were trembling. "Please!"

He nodded, and looked up at the men surrounding them, all of them staring at him in silent reproach as if he had gone daft.

"Don't stare at me, Daylin!" he snapped to his squire. "We've got work to do. We must create a litter."

"For a horse—milord?" Daylin said incredulously.

"For a horse!"

"Danielle, I don't want you near the poor fellow in the tree. Get away until the body is cleared," Adrien insisted.

"I've had the plague already and survived," she said softly. But she met his eyes, and apparently decided on obedience under the circumstances. She did as he bid her. One of Gariston's foot soldiers, Martin Nesmith, told Adrien that he'd had the plague as a child and would cut down the body which had so startled the mare.

When the body had been removed, Adrien turned his mind to the horse.

More of Gariston's men-at-arms were summoned to the task of moving her, which took all afternoon. At the end of their efforts, they were all drenched with sweat, but the mare had been returned to the stables where she was supported in rigging created out of oak building stakes and one of Sir Thackery's old battle tents. Danielle had listened to his every word when he had told her how to mix a poultice for the wound, and she followed his instructions to the letter.

"Three to four times a day, milady, you must tend to this!" he warned her. "Forget but once and the wound may fester, do you understand?"

Wide-eyed and pale, she nodded.

By then it was late—he was weary and covered in mud and hay. And he was still intending to ride out in the morning. He left her in the stables, asked Sir Thackery to see that he was brought a bath and hot water, and drank a large goblet of good English ale as he waited for the servants to fulfill his request.

"This is quite incredible, Laird MacLachlan," Sir Thackery said, shaking his head. "The poor girl has seen so much death, yet we will all see more of it, I fear. I pray that at least her mare can live, but sweet Jesu, sir! I have not seen such a thing before!"

Adrien lifted a hand. "The mare has a chance. And I have never seen Danielle quite so . . . eager."

"Ah, well, she loves the creature!" Sir Thackery told him. "The mare was a gift to her from the king of France."

Adrien's ale soured a bit on his tongue. He stood, setting his chalice down, and reminded himself sternly that he was going for Joanna in the morning and was not going to be responsible for Danielle much longer.

"I am returning to Winchester on personal business, leaving with the dawn, Sir Thackery, but I will return as soon as I am able."

"I will guard the lady in your absence, milord!"

"Ah, my thanks! And Sir Thackery, will you please be so good as to ready a guest chamber for the Lady Joanna? She will be returning with me."

"The Lady Joanna!" Sir Thackery seemed surprised.

"Is there something wrong?"

"No. Of course not, milord. It's just that . . ."

"What?"

Sir Thackery cleared his throat. "Well, the king sent messengers ahead of the countess and yourself, milord. Private word for my eyes alone, of course, but the king wrote that—"

"Wrote that what?"

Sir Thackery seemed truly uneasy now. "The king's message suggested that you and the countess would become betrothed before you left here on the king's business once again."

Adrien was silent for a moment. "Even kings may be wrong upon occasion," he said firmly.

"I was to show you the wonders of the place, milord. If I have failed—"

"You have failed at nothing!" came a cry from the doorway. Both men turned, startled. Danielle stood there, very tall and straight. She entered the room, looking from Adrien to Sir Thackery. "Sir Thackery, you mustn't press Laird MacLachlan, for he has made other plans for his life. Pray, sir, isn't that so?"

"But the king's command—" Sir Thackery stuttered.

"I try to obey the king in all things," Adrien said evenly, "but as the countess is so quick to assure you, I have made other plans. I bid you both good night."

He bowed deeply to them and hurried upstairs. The servants had left him a hip tub deep with steaming water. He eased himself into it. Water and steam rushed around him and he gave himself over to the pleasure of it, closing his eyes.

A moment later, his eyes popped open. He wasn't alone. He tensed, staring at the doorway. Danielle had followed him.

"What?" he moaned, reaching for his towel and soaking it as he dragged it atop himself in the tub. He closed his eyes, rubbing his forehead, for he had acquired a splitting headache all of a sudden. All he needed was Danielle at his bath. Alarmingly, he could feel his body responding to her feminine presence.

"I came to thank you," she said quietly.

His eyes opened with surprise, and he leaned back again, carefully covered and watching her. "Aye?"

"For my horse."

He lifted a hand in the air. "We have seen a lot of sorry sights. If the mare can live, I will be glad of it. I cannot, however, promise that she will."

"But she has a chance."

"Aye."

She moistened her lips. "I am grateful, and in your debt."

"If you are in my debt, then consider obeying me upon occasion," he said, but tonight, there was little bite to his words. His countess had her own sense of honor, he thought. He liked that about her, and he felt some of his anger abating. "Take good care of her," he said.

"You are still going for Joanna in the morning?"

"Aye."

She smiled, the beautiful smile he had only seen her give others before. "God speed you then, Adrien. I will be anxious to see your lady."

He nodded and admitted, "She is quite fond of you."

She stood a bit awkwardly for a moment, then said, "Good night, good journey, Adrien, and thank you again."

"Good night, Danielle," he told her.

She turned and left him. A moment later, he smiled. He was actually acquiring a fondness for the little temptress.

Maybe there could be peace between them after all.

But later that night, he tossed in the grip of a deadly nightmare. He knew that he dreamed, but could not awaken. He was caught in a tumultuous battle. Trumpets sounded, steel clashed, horses screamed, and men cried out in anguish. And there she was. In the midst of it. Walking barefoot through the battlefield, her ebony hair streaming down her back, caught in the winds of war. The battlefield, he knew somehow, was in France. And she walked determinedly through a field of blood, avoiding the flashes of steel that came her way.

He awoke with a start, soaked in sweat, swearing at himself that he could become so seized by a nightmare. He rose, paced the floor, drank deeply from a bottle of wine, and lay back down. But he could not sleep. He lay awake until the first cock crowed.

He wondered what had disturbed him so that he should have such a violent dream. Then he realized that he was worried. The horse he sought to save, the mare she loved so very much, had been a gift—not just from a Frenchman, but from the French *king*.

Chapter 7

In all honesty, Danielle admitted to herself, living in Gariston was pleasant. Sir Thackery was wonderfully old and wrinkled and kind, and anxious that she should be pleased with everything. Monteine and Lady Jeanette were pleased with the fortress, as was Dr. Coutin, who tended to think most places not in France to be entirely barbaric. Though his chief concern was his countess, he was quickly seeing to the aches and ailments and injuries of all the people.

Adrien had not been gone two days when Danielle came to the stable to see Star and discovered Monteine there, shaking her head with amazement at the mare's journey to recovery. "Milord MacLachlan is really quite amazing," she murmured. "You should make peace with him."

Danielle shrugged. He'd saved her horse; she was grateful.

"He is a powerful knight, milady, and he will hurt you if you cross him. He's very strong, a valued warrior—favored by the king."

"Monteine," Danielle said wryly, stroking Star's nose, "you are the one who has always reminded me that the English—such as Adrien!—are the enemy."

Monteine nodded. "Aye, but—"

"You don't know the half of what he has done!" Danielle said softly, remembering the anguish and humiliation of being dragged over his knee. "I am grateful for what he has done for Star, but I'm afraid he remains the enemy." She felt a twinge of guilt. Except for his fury against her, he could be decent and intriguing at times. But she couldn't forgive him because she couldn't allow herself to forget her mother's death. Lenore had been everything to her, and Lenore had made her vow to remember Philip. "I must always fight him," she added softly.

"Listen to me, Danielle, please," Monteine begged. "Once, you know, you used to listen to the things I taught you."

"Monteine—"

"The entire court is speaking of a marriage between you."

"There will be no marriage."

"Danielle, it would not be the worst thing in the world. He is young and vital, and very handsome."

Danielle smiled, setting her hands on her hips as she stared at Monteine.

"There will be no marriage—he has assured me so."

"Then you are both fools!" Monteine said wearily.

"I must one day return to Aville, and then, if I choose, I will marry a French noble."

"Danielle, you are a ward of the English king! Kings will have their way. You must take care, and be more courteous to Laird MacLachlan."

"I should take care?" she demanded, her temper suddenly flaring. "He blamed me for his own carelessness in that wretched saddle episode!"

"Danielle, it was not carelessness when he was nearly killed because of the loosened girth on his saddle."

"I'm telling you," Danielle began angrily, "I did not do anything—"

"But I did," Monteine interrupted quickly, her cheeks flushed. "I undid his girth. I was anxious to hurt an English knight, any English knight."

Danielle stared at Monteine, dumbfounded. She bit her lip, realizing that Adrien hadn't been at all foolish. He had known that his girth had been tampered with, and, of course, he would blame her . . .

"Monteine—"

"I'm so sorry. You must tell him, of course," Monteine said, swallowing hard. "Oh, Danni, I'm sorry, I do love you, you know! I don't want you blamed, I—"

"Monteine! You have every good reason to want to hurt an Englishman! The English destroyed your family, they left you with nothing, anyone can understand that!" Danielle said, adding slowly, "What I can't understand is . . . why have your feelings changed? Why this confession?"

"He is not the Englishman to hurt," Monteine said gravely. "I have watched him closely since we began the journey here. He has power and sway with the king, gained through both his strength and his wisdom. He is chivalrous—"

"Hmmph!" Danielle protested, barely looking up from the dressing she was changing on Star's limb. Chivalrous, indeed! Dragging her over his knee! But no one knew about that, because it was too humiliating a tale to tell. Still, she was about to tell Monteine that Laird MacLachlan was capable of being extremely rude, when she was suddenly hailed by a masculine voice. "Milady!"

She and Monteine turned to see that Daylin had entered the stables. "The Lady Joanna has arrived with a small escort!"

Danielle patted the clean dressing on her mare's injured leg and stood, looking over Star's haunches at Daylin, a puzzled frown knitting her brow. "But Adrien just went for her—"

"Joanna came by way of the old Roman road, as we did. Adrien rode alone, and cut through the forests. They missed one another, I am afraid. But Lady Joanna is here, and Sir Thackery has brought her into the hall. She is anxious to see you."

Danielle hurried from the stables to the hall where Joanna sat by the fire with Sir Thackery. Joanna rose, smiled, and reached out to Danielle who hurried to her, accepting her hug, then pulled away. Joanna seemed very warm.

"Are you well, milady?" Danielle asked anxiously.

Joanna shrugged. "A sore throat. And I am tired, I think.

The queen has so very many children! Assisting her to pack for them all from place to place is often difficult! But I'm here, now, and tell me truthfully, Danielle, is it all right? Do you mind that I am here?''

"I am delighted that you are here!"

Sir Thackery cleared his throat. "I will leave you ladies to your court gossip and be about my business!" he said, bowing as he left them.

"What a dear, sweet, old creature," Joanna said.

"I am quite fond of him already," Danielle agreed. "But I am so glad to see *you!*"

"Well, I tried very hard not to leave you alone with that ill-tempered knight of mine!" Joanna told her.

"He is nearly human when you are about!" Danielle admitted, wrinkling her nose.

Joanna grew somber. "The king wants a match between you and Adrien. I wouldn't hurt you, Danielle. You don't mind that Adrien and I are so determined that we will wed?"

"Oh, good Lord! No! I shall be the first to cheer when you exchange your vows. Your beloved is the thorn of my life!"

"Ah, Danni, he is not so bad!"

"You love him—therefore, you are blind!" she said, yet did so lightly. He had saved her horse. "And, of course," she added, "he loves you."

Joanna didn't answer that.

"Joanna, he did bring about the fall of Aville, so it's difficult for me to see him kindly. He can be a dragon, not that I want a monster for you—rather you than me!"

Joanna laughed. "Not such a dragon! Ah, Danni, if you could but understand what it feels like when he looks at me sometimes, when he touches me . . . sorry, never mind, I am wandering. I wish he were here! I'm longing to see him. But anyway . . . Danielle! You look happy here. Gariston agrees with you."

"I do like it here. It's almost as nice as—"

"Aville?"

"Aville is my home."

"This is your home as well."

"Indeed, my father's home. I heard such wonderful tales about him! Gariston is as warm and good as I always heard my father was. You will love it here as well, I'm certain."

"Oh, surely I will. I am only sorry that Adrien and I missed one another, and that he is out there riding into danger for nothing. Danni, everyone is fleeing the cities! Death is everywhere."

"I know!" Danielle said, remembering the friars with their wagonloads of dead, and the poor wretched hermit. "But we've no sickness at Gariston."

"Not here," Joanna agreed. "Danni, could you show me to my quarters? The days have been hectic. I am very tired, and if you'll excuse, I could sleep until supper."

"Of course!" Danielle called out for one of the servants. Amy, one of the kitchen maids, appeared. "Is the other tower readied?"

"Aye, milady. I will summon a maid to escort the Lady Joanna—"

"Nay, Amy, I will see to her myself."

She started to walk Joanna across the hall, but even as they walked, Joanna suddenly sagged against her. "Oh, Danni! I am even more weary than I thought! I can scarce stand!"

Danielle caught Joanna, calling out for help. Simms, one of the strong men who handled the heavy carcasses for the cooks, lumbered in and awaited further instructions.

"Simms, please, take her straight to my chamber—I think that is best," Danielle commanded quickly, and followed along behind. When Joanna was laid out on her bed, she ordered Simms to bring a cloth and fresh, cool water and to send for Doctor Coutin. Simms left to do as he was told, and Danielle sat by Joanna, touching her forehead.

She had been warm before. Now she burned.

Simms returned with the water and stood in the doorway, his dark eyes now deep and wide with alarm.

"Bring the water, please!" Danielle said.

"I've touched her!" Simms moaned.

"Aye, so bring the water!"

Simms just stood there and Danielle hurried to snatch the water and cloth from him. She sat at Joanna's side again and bathed her forehead and arms, her heart sinking.

She understood the terror Simms had felt.

They had thought themselves safe. Now the plague had come to them at last.

Doctor Coutin came and studied his patient.

"The Black Death?" Danielle said.

"Aye, milady. I am sorry. I'll do what I can, but as you know, there is so little that I can do . . ." He hesitated, clearing his throat. "Lady Joanna did not bring it. The cook, your man from Aville, fell ill earlier. He died just moments ago, milady."

"Oh, sweet Jesu!" Danielle whispered, and crossed herself.

"Those in the fortress are panicking, for the plague attacks so swiftly and is so merciless! Danielle, there are many falling sick, and I must attend to them. I pray you, you must help Lady Joanna."

"Aye, I would not leave her! I will help her, stay with her," Danielle assured him.

Joanna's condition deteriorated rapidly, and while Danielle attended to her, she heard with horror what was happening throughout the castle. A groom dropped to the ground while walking across the courtyard; one hour later he was dead. Farmers, craftsmen, one after another, fell.

By darkness, there were three more deaths.

The next few days would be the worst, Doctor Coutin advised her. He knew well, for, like Danielle, he had survived the sickness himself and seen Aville through it. "Sometimes death is all but instant. Usually, those who will die do so within two to five days. Let's pray God that most of our people will have the will and the faith and the strength to make their way through it."

By the following morning, Sir Thackery and Monteine had both been taken ill.

The household had gone mad, it seemed. When Danielle

tried to summon help from the kitchen, she found the maid-servants there dancing with the grooms, many of them only half-dressed. She stared at them all in shock, and when Swen, one of the young grooms, saw her, he gave pause, but only for a minute.

"Death is coming, lady. Take what you will of life, because death is coming now."

"Death will pass some by!" she cried out. "I have seen it come before, and some will survive! I need help with those who have fallen ill—"

Molly, one of the kitchen maids, her bodice fallen, her breasts completely exposed, giggled. "Some will die, some will live, lady." Then a sob escaped her. "The boils! They form on me already! Oh, God, oh, God!"

"Doctor Coutin will lance them if you quit acting like a lunatic!" Danielle cried. She remembered Doctor Coutin's words—the people had to have faith and strength for any of them to survive. Sir Thackery was ill; Doctor Coutin was busy throughout the fortress. She was countess here, and somehow, she had to force them all back to their senses.

The girl continued to laugh and cry. All around her, Danielle could hear the hysteria rising. Men had come in from the fields, men-at-arms mingled with the farmhands. It was only morning, and the whole of the kitchen reeked with the smell of spilled ale. Some had drunk themselves into stupors and lay where they had fallen. The others were ready to continue their mad, music-less dance, as if they could race their way into oblivion.

Swen the groom was grabbing for Molly's half-naked form, and Molly was squealing again—this time with laughter. Danielle leapt upon the huge oak preparation table amidst half-kneaded dough, decaying meat, and drying vegetables. Tears of frustrated anger filled her eyes. If MacLachlan had been here now, none of them would have dared behave so badly, even if the grim reaper himself were whispering in their ears.

A cast iron pot lay upon the table and she clutched it up and gave Swen a sound knock upon the head with it. He slumped to the floor, rubbing his head, staring up at her, dazed. The sound of it seemed to echo about the room, and to her amazement, the maddened revelers suddenly went still.

"You may act like fools and give up all hope of life yourselves, but I will not allow my friends to die! Molly, get to a bed. Swen, if you would fondle her so, help her to it. Get wet clothes and cool her down. Some of you start cleaning up. Those who are sick, may the Virgin Mother pray for you. Those not afflicted must help. Now, get out of my way!"

She hopped down and left the kitchen, going to the well for the cold water she had come for. When she came to the kitchen, she saw that some of the servants had sullenly decided to obey her. "Doctor Coutin will come as soon as he can to attend to all of you."

"Doctors can not save us from the Black Death!" Swen told her sadly.

She spun around. "Then a priest will come, and speed you on your journey to heaven or hell! By God! Can't you all at least fight to live?" she demanded.

Blank stares followed her as she hurried away from them all, wearily aware that what could be done here, she would be doing herself with little able assistance.

With Lady Jeanette and a few servants left to help, she and Doctor Coutin moved from sickbed to sickbed, trying to do what could be done. She summoned all the barbers from the town—those who could still stand—to see that the victims' boils were lanced. At Doctor Coutin's orders, Danielle worked very hard to keep the afflicted cool, bathing foreheads, throats, hands, chests, backs.

Black crosses were drawn in ash all around the walls of the fortress.

By the fifth night, the death toll within the walls of the town had risen to fifty. Miraculously, though, some began to recover.

Joanna continued to breathe, to fight for life, and Danielle hoped that since she had made it thus far, she had the will and strength to survive. She sat by her bed throughout another long day, keeping her body as cool as she could.

By the sixth morning since the Black Death had come to Gariston, Danielle could barely move. She'd had no sleep. She knelt down by Joanna's bed, her fingers entwined with Joanna's. She closed her eyes, and she must have dozed.

When she opened her eyes again, she saw that she wasn't alone with Joanna anymore.

Adrien MacLachlan had returned.

Chapter 8

He seemed incredibly tall and strong as he stood by the bedside, staring down at Joanna, so beautiful now, so very frail and fragile with her dark lashes sweeping her ashen cheeks. He seemed indomitable, a tower of power, life, and health, his shoulders broad beneath the magenta sweep of his mantle, his thighs sturdy as oak. In the pale light of the early dawn, even his rich red-gold hair seemed dark. His features were taut and drawn, his eyes like a mirror of death itself.

Danielle's fingers were still entwined with Joanna's. Then Danielle realized why agony filled Adrien's eyes.

Joanna had given up the fight at last. Danielle no longer needed to cool her from the fever. Joanna lay cold now, her fingers like ice. The fever had left her, along with the warmth of life.

Danielle had no chance to react, for Adrien MacLachlan let out a cry of grief, falling to his knees as well. He reached for Joanna, cradling her dead form in his arms, bowing his head over her.

Danielle struggled to her feet, backing away. She ached for Joanna herself, but she had been living in a nightmare between life and death for a very long time. She remained numbed, for

Adrien's grief was so very terrible and intimate. It was as if he hadn't even noticed her yet, and she wanted very badly to slip away. Still, she couldn't move. The seconds began to pass, and then the minutes ticked away, and still, Adrien embraced his dead lover. And finally, tears started to trickle down Danielle's cheeks, damp and silent, and they seemed to break her from her paralysis. She started to slip quietly from the room, but Adrien suddenly reached out, his fingers curling around her wrist. He stood, and his tormented, glittering eyes met hers.

"You have stayed with her all this time?"

His voice was hoarse, pained, different.

"With her, with some of the others."

"With no help?"

"So many are stricken. There aren't many left to help. And I love Joanna. I tried very hard to save her," Danielle whispered. "I swear to you—"

She was startled when he suddenly pulled her close, picked her up, and sat on a bedside chair with her in his arms. He held her gently, rocking slightly as he stared at Joanna again, giving comfort, taking comfort.

"Poor lass, you are quite something," he murmured. "The servants fled and dying, and you doing it all."

She didn't want his sympathy. She had been fighting too hard to betray any weakness now. "Doctor Coutin never deserted me," she whispered. "Nor Milady Jeanette."

Despite her resolve, tears rose to her eyes. She couldn't seem to stop them, but it didn't seem so bad. She had never wanted to cry in front of him, never, but his own cheeks were damp, his grief was so terrible. She was weary, bone weary from head to toe, dazed and numbed still. It felt good to be held, for the moment. It was good to rest, and feel that she passed a burden from her own shoulders to his.

He held her another moment, then stood, setting her upon her feet. "Things have settled somewhat. I understand you beat a groom upon the head."

"I didn't *beat* him, I merely gave him one good crack."

She was startled when the ghost of a smile touched Adrien's lips. "Still, milady, there is much to be done here, and I'll not watch these people lie idle waiting to die. They had no right to let you do so much.''

He strode from the room angrily and came down the steps. A number of the servants were in the hall, some slumped upon the floor, a few gaming with dice.

Adrien walked into the midst of them with a fury and energy that seemed to send off sparks of fire. Swen was the first to feel his wrath. The groom was sprawled by the hearth and Adrien clutched him by the shoulders, dragging him to his feet.

"Tragedy strikes and you lie about as if you were a beaten dog!"

"Death comes for us, milord! What matter?" Swen demanded.

Adrien drew his sword and there was a collective inhalation of breath as he touched its lethal tip to Swen's throat. Others who had been lying about quickly rose.

"What does it matter? You seem healthy as yet, lad. Be about your business and help with this pathetic siege of fever or else I will hasten you to your own grave this very minute!"

"Aye, milord, aye!" Swen cried.

Adrien looked around the hall. "Sweet Jesu, you lie here with your dead! By God, man, get litters!" He strode across to where a few of the men-at-arms had come to lie and wait. They rose, backing away from Adrien's wrath. "Get litters, now!" he commanded, "You men, dig a pit far outside the gate and see these poor wretches are burned and buried. Any man knows this—the dead must be taken away. They cause more disease by their poor demises! Do it, now. You—!" he cried suddenly, stopping a man called Robin Sentell, a stonemason. "You!" he said again. "You will begin work on a tomb for—for the Lady Joanna. She will lie within the crypt of the chapel, do you hear me?"

"Aye, milord, I will get to work immediately!" Robin promised.

"A hundred lashes to the next man to fear the plague with such fervor that he will not aid his fellow. Seek to dance with the Devil again and by God, I swear it, you will stand beside him before dusk!" Adrien's eyes, glittering with a hellfire promise, swept the room. Men and women stumbled upon one another to hasten to their work.

Danielle stood on the landing of the stairs, watching as the household guiltily went to order at Adrien's commands. Lady Jeanette came to stand behind her, setting her hands on Danielle's shoulders.

Adrien came up the stairs again, pausing before the two of them. "Sir Thackery?" he asked Lady Jeanette.

"He lives, milord. Fighting on."

Adrien's gaze flicked down to Danielle. The fury in them was gone. The pain was back. "Monteine?" he asked her.

"She fights as well."

He nodded. "Leave me be then, with my Lady Joanna," he said, and stepped by into Danielle's room, where Joanna lay in death. He closed the door, and he was alone with the woman he had loved.

Lady Jeanette and Danielle stood there for several seconds after the door had closed, then Lady Jeanette sighed softly. "Order is restored, milady. God will fight for the others now. You must sleep."

"I've nowhere—"

"Laird MacLachlan's chamber upstairs will do for now," Lady Jeanette said briskly. "Sleep, and perhaps when you awaken . . ."

The guest chamber was nearly as magnificent as her own. She allowed Jeanette to lead her to the massive bed, pull down the covers, and see her into it. Jeanette gave her wine; she drank the full goblet, relishing the burning that seared her throat and helped to numb her pain. But no matter what the tempest in her heart and soul, sheer exhaustion seized her when her head touched the down pillow. She slept.

It seemed she slept forever, and she was finally roused by a clinking sound nearby. She blinked, thinking it was night, for there was candlelight near her and a fire burning in the hearth. Her stomach growled, and she realized that she hadn't eaten. Then all the horror that sleep had erased returned and she remembered that Joanna and many others were dead. She sat up slowly, frowning. Adrien was there, his great length slumped in a chair before a table by the hearth. The clinking sound she had heard had been his wine goblet falling against it time and again. A carafe was by his hand, nearly empty now, and Danielle was quite certain it had been full when Adrien began drinking. A beautifully designed golden circlet for a lady's hair lay before him as well, and he fingered it as he sat there drinking and staring into the fire.

She slipped from the bed, watching him, once again feeling that she intruded. She wanted to escape the room, but even as she moved, he looked up and his brooding eyes fell upon her. Then he pointed at her sternly. "You should have been away. You should not have stayed."

"I had to stay."

"I would have sent you away."

"With no need. I survived the plague when my mother died. I don't believe that I can sicken to it again."

"Thank God," he murmured, but his voice had an emptiness—and a slur—to it.

He handled the delicate gold piece before him again. "Imagine I had intended to defy the king!" he said softly.

"She loved you very much," Danielle heard herself offer.

"I should have been with her," he brooded darkly.

"You were trying to be with her," Danielle reminded him.

He suddenly crooked a finger at her. "Come here."

She shook her head, afraid of his mood. She had never seen anything quite like it. He seemed to blame himself for Joanna's death, and his bitterness and pain and self-incrimination were bitter.

With an impatient oath, he stood and walked to her. She hadn't the strength at the moment to escape him but he meant her no harm. He merely ran a finger down her cheek and eyed her thoughtfully once again. "You are not quite so wretched a young shrew as I had thought," he told her.

"Indeed!" she murmured, amazed that a certain saltiness could come back into her tone then. "Milord, such compliments from your lips will cause me to faint when I have endured so very much."

"And managed so very much on your own," he mused, and paused a moment. "Thank you. For what you did for her."

"You needn't thank me!" she whispered. "I cared for her too."

"Then thank you for the words you have said to me. The assurances of her love. How ironic. Coming from you now."

"What do you mean?" Nervously, she drew away from him. She hugged her arms around herself, suddenly very aware of his sheer masculine strength and power.

He shrugged, walking to the fire. His movement was unsteady. She had never seen him over-imbibe before.

"I would have been back sooner," he told her. "The king's messenger waylaid me. Even while death rages, the king manipulates us all! The messenger told me Edward sternly forbade my marriage to Joanna. His mind is set. How strange. It seems that he is obsessed with you, my little pet. He does not want you on your own. He is quick to talk of your beauty and riches, then quick to rage against you." He turned and stared at her. "You know, I think, perhaps, he was a bit bewitched by your mother. Easy to see why."

"You mean the king?"

"Aye, the king. Lenore was very beautiful. I have never seen a more beautiful woman. Unless . . ." he broke off, staring at her again, then shrugging once more. He went back for more wine, then drank down the goblet in a swallow. "Anyway, I've been informed that you were to be married within the month to an old Dane, Lord Andreson, if we—you and I—were not betrothed as he wished."

"Lord Andreson!" she gasped. He was at least sixty, gaunt as a twig, stooped, and gout-ridden. He spent most of his time in Denmark, for he was kin to the Danish nobility. He was a horrible person, mean, cantankerous, and lecherous.

"Denmark is a beautiful country," Adrien mused. "I have been there for many tournaments. It is wet and cold, though."

"What difference would it make whether I was forced to wed a Danish knight or an English one?" she countered brashly. Dear God, even she could see the difference, but there was a point to be made. "I am French, milord."

"Milady—I would think the answer quite obvious."

"Oh? Because you are a bit younger? You would make a more palatable husband and father?"

He arched his brow at that, but shook his head. "Andreson is childless, and quite anxious to be a father. To have you, he'd give the king title to lands that have been in Danish hands since the Viking invasions. But he intends to live in Denmark, and is anxious to keep you there as well since you are so very young and so temptingly lovely. You might never see your precious Aville again. And besides—I, at least, don't drool."

She ignored that. "But I am a countess. Aville is mine by right!"

He didn't seem to hear her, continuing ruefully, "And I admit, once, I had thought of such a threat with amusement. I would have been well rid of you. Denmark would be a good, safe place for you. Far, far away."

"Go to hell, Adrien. I'd be safe and far away if I were back in Aville! The king cannot force me to wed and go to Denmark!" she insisted. But she was afraid. Edward considered himself the law, especially where his children or wards were concerned. She knew that priests could be bribed, and she'd heard stories about noblewomen being brought to their own weddings bound and gagged and thrown over the shoulders of determined, land-hungry knights. If such things happened at the whim of noblemen, what might happen when a king was determined to have his way?

"We must fight him. I won't be threatened and I will never agree to the king's wretched schemes!" she said, trying very hard to convince herself that she could fight Edward. "I have family across the Channel," she reminded Adrien. "I can escape England and get help from my French cousins."

"I'm sure, milady, that those very facts are why the king. is so determined you remain strictly beneath his thumb," he murmured, staring into the fire. "Joanna is gone," he said, "so it simply doesn't matter anymore. Nothing matters anymore. Except that you cared for her, so now, I am in your debt."

"I cared for her because she was my friend. You don't owe me anything. If you feel you're in my debt, tell the king to leave me be and let me go home to Aville!'' Danielle told him, her voice rising with desperation.

He didn't answer her. He continued to stare into the fire.

"Adrien?"

To her amazement, his eyes closed. He stood for a moment, wavered, then suddenly slumped to the floor. She gasped, staring at him in astonishment.

The wine! she thought. The fool was drunk. He had imbibed the whole of the carafe, sitting there in his grief. He had thought that it would wash away the pain . . .

She walked toward him, nudging him with her toe. He didn't move. She fell to her knees by his side. "Adrien!" she whispered softly, and she placed a hand on his arm.

He was burning. She wrenched her hand away. He wasn't drunk; he was sick.

"Oh, God!" she cried out. She leapt to her feet, fully aware that she could never manage to drag his weight into his bed. She had to have help.

She ran to the door, threw it open, and tore down the stairs to the great hall. She paused there, looking around.

The place was immaculate. No bodies littered the floor or table or chairs. The hall had been swept; fresh rushes had been laid. A bright fire burned at the hearth. Daylin sat before the fire, polishing a shield.

"Daylin, please, I need you."

Frowning, he set the shield aside and followed her up the two flights. At the doorway, he paused just briefly, then rushed to his lord. Even Daylin struggled with Adrien's muscled weight and Danielle hurried forward to assist him. Moments later they had Adrien laid out and half stripped. Danielle asked Daylin for the coldest water he could find, and to bring Doctor Coutin. Daylin paused just a moment, then obeyed her.

They bathed Adrien together. She was surprised to find herself trembling sometimes when she smoothed the cloth over the hardness of his muscles.

When Doctor Coutin came, she left him by his new patient, and stood by the window with Daylin, who told her that she had been sleeping two days, and much had happened in that time. Sir Thackery and Monteine were on the way to recovery. Molly had survived as well, though many died.

Messengers had arrived from Winchester early that morning; the disease was abating.

"Milady," Doctor Coutin called.

She came quickly to his side.

"It is the same as with the others. I have done what I can. Now we wait. The fever must be fought, as you know."

Danielle nodded.

"I will serve him," Daylin said. "Milady, you need not."

"I have done this often," Danielle argued, surprised that she did so. "I will tend to him," she insisted.

"I will be here as well, to do as you say," Daylin promised her, and she realized, looking at him, that they were both determined that Adrien MacLachlan would not die. Daylin loved his master. She wondered about her own passionate resolve not to let him perish. Perhaps she simply could not stand the thought of letting the plague best her again.

This time, she was not alone. As Adrien's fever soared, Daylin helped her, and Lady Jeanette, freed from some of her own efforts as her other patients began to recover, came and kept the great body of Laird MacLachlan cooled as well.

Still, Danielle discovered that she could not allow others to care for Adrien. She nursed him diligently, amazed to discover that she prayed for him fiercely as well. She didn't know why. If he survived, she told herself, he would once again become a thorn in her side.

Two days passed. He slipped in and out of consciousness. His gold eyes pierced into her when she would lift his head to give him water. "Go away!" he growled to her once. "You could still be in danger."

"I'm not in danger. I told you, I've had the plague."

"I am ordering you—"

"And what will you do to me now, milord?" she taunted. "You cannot drag me over your knee!"

"If I live, I will do so!" he promised.

But his threats, at the moment, were idle, for his eyes closed. He had lost consciousness again.

On the fifth day, he raved. He talked to someone called Carlin, and swore that he would never surrender, that he would hold the family name sacred. "If I fall, I will stand. I'll not fail you, sire, in battle or joust. I swear it!" He fell silent again, and still. Then later, the length of him constricted, and he next cried out his dead lady's name. "Joanna, forgive me. Sweet Jesu, my lady, forgive me!"

He began to shake convulsively.

She all but crawled atop him, trying to still his fierce trembling. "Don't you dare die on me, you wretched knave!" she told him. His eyes opened, wild, truly a flame against the gray pallor of his face. "Coward!" she charged him, close to tears. "Ah, the brave Laird MacLachlan, the Scots lad to bring down a French castle! The shadows of illness touch him, and he surrenders!"

She was truly startled when he suddenly gripped her shoulders with an incredible strength, a force that nearly caused her to cry out. He spoke fiercely in a language she didn't understand, and she thought it must have been his native Gaelic.

His hold upon her eased; he fell back. His eyes closed. He inhaled and exhaled deeply, and slept again. Shaking herself, Danielle eased down to his side. She heard a soft sound behind her and turned. Daylin had come just inside the doorway and stood there almost as pale as his stricken laird, watching.

"What did he say? Do you know?" Danielle asked him.

Daylin nodded. "He said, 'Never beg mercy, never surrender, not even to death'."

That night, Adrien was so still that she thought she had lost him. A strangled sob tore from her throat, then she gasped, for one eye opened upon her and she realized that he was still alive, that he was breathing easily; his fever had broken. He lay in the bed weak and spent, but alive.

"You!" he whispered, trying to point a finger at her. "I told you to go."

Daylin came behind her. "Milord!" he cried happily. "You have beaten it, sir. Sweet Jesu, but I knew that you would!"

Danielle backed away. "I'll see about getting you something to eat," she told Adrien, and hurried out.

When she returned, having told the kitchen servants that some broth must be brought to Count MacLachlan, the door was bolted from inside. Daylin opened it a crack and told her that Adrien was bathing. Danielle went back to her own chamber.

It had been cleaned, the sheets washed, the room aired. The scent of death was gone. The pain of it was not. She lay down on her bed and dozed. When she awoke, Lady Jeanette was there, a tray awaited her, and servants had brought a bath with steaming water as well.

The luxury of bathing was wonderful. She doused her hair and remained in the hip tub until the water had grown cold. She dressed, and ate fresh bread with sweet butter, meat, and cheese. When she was done, she found that she could not stay away from her patient any longer, and she hurried back upstairs.

Adrien lay in bed, bathed, refreshed, his chest still naked, his head up on a pillow. He was but a day away from the height of his fever, but that day had given him back the full faculties of his mind. His face remained ashen, but against the white linen sheets, his shoulders again seemed very bronzed, and powerful. He had surely lost some weight, and the illness had cost him tremendous energy, but already, the spark of vitality had returned.

He spoke to Daylin, giving orders in a low, husky voice, wincing upon occasion. Weakness, she realized, was a tremendous burden for him.

Daylin winked to her and left the room. She came near the bed cautiously.

"I told you to go away," he said. His voice was still hoarse and weak. Only his eyes retained their fierce glitter—vibrant, alive, the first full power of life to return.

"I did not choose to go away. I am countess here," she reminded him.

"Obedience does not seem to be among your virtues."

"I don't think of obedience as a virtue, milord, but rather as a requirement forced upon women by men who want something from them."

His eyes closed, but she thought that the slight curl of a smile touched his lips.

"I haven't the strength at the moment to joust with you, my lady. But virtue or requirement, I imagine we will have to discuss the matter of obedience soon enough."

Danielle frowned, quickly growing worried. Even when he smiled, he did so in a weary manner. Something was different about him now.

He had survived; Joanna had not. And as the fever had ebbed and left him once again with a clear mind, he had remembered burying the woman he had loved. There was a numbness about him. He didn't give a damn about much anymore, and didn't intend to battle her.

"Why?" she asked, frowning.

He winced, trying to sit up before answering her. But before he could speak, there was a tapping on the door. It opened a crack, and Daylin looked in. With a gesture, Adrien bid him enter. Gariston's young priest, Father Adair, and another man, a stranger to Danielle, entered the room.

"Ah, Sir George!" Adrien said, startled and frowning. "What in God's name are you doing here? There's plague here, man! Ask the good father there—we've crosses all about the fortress to warn away the unwary—"

"Adrien MacLachlan!" said the newcomer, a tall, well-built man with iron-gray hair, warm brown eyes, and a pleasant face. "And my lady!" he added, turning swiftly to bow to Danielle. "I'm one such as you are yourself now, a survivor of the wretched scourge. I do not fear to tread among it."

Adrien arched a brow very high. "But why, sir, have you come here?"

"I come in the king's service," Sir George said. "He grows anxious. News of Lady Joanna's death has reached him, and he sends you his deepest sympathy."

Adrien inclined his head. "Tell him I thank him for his sympathy."

Sir George nodded. "But many have died. Whole villages have perished. The king reminds you that, even in his sorrow and yours, he must lead his country."

''Sir George, just what is it that our mighty sovereign wants from me?'' Adrien asked flatly.

Sir George grinned from ear to ear. ''Adrien! I practice my diplomacy with the great care and tact, and you—''

''We both know the king wants something. What is it?''

Sir George hesitated. ''The matter of the countess must be resolved,'' he said at last.

Danielle gasped, staring from Sir George to Adrien once again. ''He has barely escaped the clutches of the Black Death!'' Danielle said, ''And you come here and—''

''Ah, my lady! Such concern. It is applaudable!'' Sir George said, pleased as he looked at Adrien.

''She isn't concerned, she's horrified,'' Adrien said bluntly. He leaned back and closed his eyes. He exhaled, a weary action, not opening his eyes again.

Danielle came to Adrien's bed and stood staring down at him, feeling tremors shake through her. She had sat here night after night, praying for him, doing all in her power to help him. But Adrien didn't give a damn about anything at the moment. He had buried Joanna. The future meant nothing to him.

''Adrien, you told me you were in my debt!'' she whispered.

His eyes opened upon her dispassionately. It was obvious that he had used his strength, and grown exhausted. ''I am in your debt, little fool!'' he whispered softly. ''I am not doing anything to hurt you. Can't you understand that? Appease Edward now, milady, and you will have years of freedom.''

''At what cost at the end of those years?'' she whispered frantically in return.

''You will not spend them in Denmark, married to a sick, cantankerous old man,'' he replied.

She started to turn away—to use what power she could and simply flee the room, but Adrien reached out, his fingers curling firmly around her wrist with a startling power and strength. She could scarcely move, much less flee.

''I am, as always, Sir George, the king's servant. His wish is my command,'' Adrien said with a touch of irony.

''Then—''

''Indeed, I agree to the betrothal.''

"But I—" Danielle began.

"We can attend to the matter at a convenient time," Adrien interrupted her.

"Now, my lord, is quite convenient," Sir George said.

"Now?" Adrien said. "I remind you, Sir George, I am lying on what was very nearly my deathbed!"

"No matter, it is a legal and spiritual matter, and though ceremony and pageantry are nice, they are not necessary. Father Joseph will bind you both spiritually as well as legally. I stand as witness for the king—and yourself, of course—and the Lady Jeanette for the countess. I have taken the liberty of providing the betrothal ring, and we can begin as soon as Lady Jeanette can be summoned. I shall call her myself." He bowed to Adrien and exited the room.

Danielle tried to wrench free from Adrien's grasp and she nearly shrieked out loud when he put more pressure upon her wrist. He might be half dead, but he could still crush her every bone.

"You promised me once you'd not agree to this!" she told him, leaning down and whispering to him alone.

"It's a betrothal, not a marriage," he told her.

"They are all but one and the same!" she hissed.

"Do you want me to leave you to the king's mercy?" he asked her. "You little fool! Trust me, Sir George has come here with all necessary legal papers. You will be the bride of the Dane, Sir Andreson, by proxy within the hour if you do not agree to this."

She bit into her lower lip, wildly fighting tears. Edward! It seemed that he wished to ruin her life.

"Edward can't—he can't—"

"You little fool. He can. Damn you, I'm doing this for you! Don't you understand?"

She understood; she understood all too well. Edward! She would do his will, or pay a terrible price. But she didn't want to be indebted to Adrien, and she definitely didn't want to be betrothed to him. He would never love her, never want her; the hostilities between them went far too deep, and now, he mourned Joanna as well. His heart was deadened.

''I hate the king!'' she whispered miserably. ''I cannot win—''

''But,'' Adrien told her softly, his eyes closed in weariness, ''you can gain what you want most.''

''Which is—''

''Aville,'' he said simply.

''What do you mean?''

''Safely betrothed to me, the king will not interfere if I allow you to return to Aville.''

She inhaled on a gasp. ''Do you promise? Swear on your knight's honor?''

''Aye. Milady, I pay my debts.''

''You are not in my debt!''

''You worked hard to save my life.''

''I'm sure you would have been wretchedly strong enough to live without my help!''

''Such words of affection will truly bind us forever,'' he assured her with soft irony. The young priest was watching them with a worried frown. Daylin was pretending not to notice their vehemently whispered conversation.

''Don't lie to me, Adrien! Will you really let me go to Aville?''

Adrien strained hard to garner the strength to come even closer to her. ''I owe you for Joanna, and for myself. Take care with what I offer you, for I will swear to send you to Aville, but you will not create a schism there between the people and their overlord, Edward of England. Keep your word and your honor with me, and I will do so with you. I swear it. By God, and on Lady Joanna's soul.''

''When may I go?'' she asked.

''As soon as I manage to give you safe escort.''

He fell back, exhausted, but his hold upon her wrist remained as tight as an iron shackle. It didn't matter. She didn't intend to leave.

She stood very stiff and straight, silent. When Sir George returned and Lady Jeanette and the priest began to drone on about the sanctity and commitment of a betrothal, she didn't utter a single word of protest.

Later, when all the words had been said, when the legal documents had been signed and sealed, she escaped at last. In her room she stood dazed. She suddenly felt the coldness of the simple gold ring Adrien had slipped upon her finger. It was too large for her, but oddly, it felt tight. As tight as the vise his fingers had twined around her wrist. As tight as the ropes that seemed to wind and knot around her throat, encompass her heart.

It didn't matter, she told herself.

She had obeyed the king's wishes, Adrien's command. She had sold her soul!

But she had gained . . .

Aville.

In the weeks that followed, Danielle was very careful to keep her distance from Adrien.

He scarcely noticed. A darkness had fallen over him, and he preferred to be alone. His recovery came quickly enough, and when it did, he spent countless hours in the courtyard, working with his horses, with his sword, with lances, and with his armor. Sir Thackery recovered more slowly, and Danielle realized after a while that Adrien had only been waiting for Sir Thackery to become well enough to take over the management of Gariston once again before leaving it himself.

Most of the countryside had been ravished by the plague. Nearly half of those living in the southern counties of England had died, and the Black Death had taken its toll elsewhere as well. Farm animals roamed wild, fields fell to waste. It seemed a time of waiting for them all.

Upon occasion, Danielle thought that Adrien lost his look of brooding darkness and watched her, yet with what thoughts she didn't know. He was longing to leave himself, she learned from Daylin. He wanted to go back to the rugged border lands, his father's home. He had recovered from the sickness, but something inside him had not come through so well, and some-how, Danielle understood. Still, he said nothing about her leaving, and held back on his own preparations to ride north.

But one night he finally sent Daylin to summon her to the great hall and she hurried down, wary and anxious.

He stood before the great hearth, hands folded behind his back. He turned and watched her for a long moment.

"It's time, my lady, that you may go to Aville. You may begin your journey tomorrow."

She moistened her lips. "Tomorrow?"

He nodded gravely, still watching her intently. "There are things you must know. The King of France has died," he said very softly.

"Philip!" she gasped.

He nodded. She swallowed hard. She was sorry; he had been so kind to her. But it had been years since she had seen him.

"His son, Jean, has been crowned, and when you return, you will visit Jean and honor him as his subject beneath our own overlord, Edward. You will, however, continue to hold Aville as Edward's rightfully inherited property."

"Aye, milord!" she cried, inclining her head to hide the excitement in her eyes. It had been so very long. It had been a different world . . .

Her world. Her home, where Lenore had lived. Where she had given a vow to protect and honor a different king . . .

Philip was dead.

But his son would now rule. Her vow to her mother to honor and protect the house of Valois would not change.

Traitorous thoughts! But Adrien was keeping his promise.

"I will, milord, attend to our French interests as you command," she said evenly.

"I will be going on to Scotland for some time," he told her.

"God speed your journey, milord."

"God hang me—as long as he keeps me away from you, isn't that right?" he inquired.

She gasped softly, but he waved a hand in the air dismissively. "Never mind. It doesn't matter. Lady Jeanette, it seems, has formed an attachment for Sir Thackery, and will remain here, aiding in his recovery. Dr. Coutin has determined to remain here as well. Monteine travels with you, along with a number of my men whom I have chosen to advise you and watch over you. You will have a safe journey, I am certain, for I don't believe that all the demons in hell could waylay you now."

"Perhaps not, milord. I bid you good night, and goodbye," she said.

Yet when she would have hurried by him, she found her wrist caught in his grasp, just as it had been on the occasion of their betrothal. She looked from the powerful bronzed hand to his face, willing herself to be still, and wait.

She felt the gold sweep of his eyes move over her. "Do not betray me!" he warned her. "Heed me well, Danielle. Keep your honor and your promises to me, as I keep mine to you. Break trust in me, my lady, and God help you. Do you understand?"

She nodded, not trusting herself to meet his eyes. A tightness rose in her throat. For a moment, she could scarcely breathe.

She could not wait to run away from him.

And yet . . .

She already felt the strangest anguish that he would not be near. A breathlessness touched her. Her heart pounded too fiercely. She needed to escape!

"Godspeed your journey!" she gasped.

And she tore from his hold, running up the stairs.

He had already left the next morning when she bid her fond farewell to Sir Thackery and rode out from Gariston. It hurt to leave, yet with Adrien already gone, Gariston itself seemed empty, and she couldn't understand the feeling.

She turned her eyes, and heart, toward France, amazed at how very hard it was to leave England. She had once thought that all she wanted to do was go home, but somehow, it now felt as if she were leaving home once again.

Aville! she told herself. It was where her loyalties must lie.

She would make it her home again.

Part II

. . . go the spoils.

Chapter 9

Adrien sat upon one of the high, rugged craigs near his family's ancient manor house, watching idly as a great flock of sheep were hurried along by two young girls and a pair of barking dogs. He saw them go, then laid back upon the cool length of the rock beneath him and stared up at the sun even as he felt the coolness of the breeze.

He had not come here immediately after Joanna's death as he had intended. A recklessness had seized him in those days, and he had found himself journeying across Europe, into Hainault, Bruges, Ghent, and even down into Bavaria. He joined any tournament, and for months, fought with such raw determination that he could not be bested. He did not lose a contest.

But Sir George had found him at a victory banquet in Flanders where he had been very drunk. And Sir George had informed him that the king was ordering him to stay alive with all his limbs intact. Adrien had said that he wanted to go to Scotland; if he still wanted to do so, it was time. In the morning, sober, he had begun his journey to the windswept fields of rock and heather his father had called his own.

He had been glad to come home, and it had been a strange experience. There was no land that he loved as he loved this rocky place, no place else on earth where tufts of grass grew so tenaciously, in so many different colors, where the wind could blow cold one minute, then offer a touch of warmth the next. He loved the hills, the raw rock, the lochs, the rugged beauty. He had been gone so long he hadn't known he had missed it. He had left here as a boy and returned a man, and there had been much that he wanted done. The MacLachlan manor he had once thought so huge and fine was decaying and small. He brought masons in to enlarge and repair it, bought more sheep to add to his flocks, enticed more craftsmen into his village. All this he did with a certain fervor, trying to forget the plague, the ostentatious court of the king, the death of Joanna, his betrothal to Danielle. He settled clan disputes, chose more young men to train at arms, and continued to work hard at his own strength and expertise, for he knew that he would not stay home forever. It seemed a waiting period for him, though he did not know what he waited for.

For some time he wallowed in the pain of Joanna's death, but in the end, he forced himself to realize that part of his pain was guilt. He had determined again and again that they would wed, yet he had let the time pass. He had been glad to be her lover, yet he had not been eager to tie himself down. He had cared for her, and deeply. But not deeply enough.

In time, he forgave himself, just as he knew that she would have forgiven him. Indeed, she had understood him better than he had himself, all that time. For many months, he mourned Joanna in abstinence. But even after he had come to peace with himself and taken a number of lovers, he found that no one could still the restlessness within him. And one night, in the warm, cozy cottage of a goldsmith's widowed daughter, he found himself staring into the fire that burned in her hearth and wondering what he was missing. The fire seemed to leap with a number of colors—blues, reds, and greens—and he frowned. To his amazement, he realized the green of the flame had reminded him of Danielle, of the extraordinary color of her eyes.

It wasn't that he hadn't thought of her before, or even often. He had accepted the king's commands regarding their betrothal for two reasons, the first being that at that time, it simply hadn't mattered to whom he had been betrothed, a witch or a warthog, since he could not marry Joanna. And secondly, he had cared for Danielle. He hadn't quite understood the feeling, but all the time he had longed to switch her, he had admired her as well. In the horror and trauma of the plague, she had behaved with wisdom and compassion, and he could not forget burning with his fever, but knowing that she was by his side. He had agreed on the betrothal to give her something in return—the gift of her homeland. He had known the fierce craving to see his own. He had understood her need.

No matter where he had been, he had kept a tight enough rein on Aville, or so he thought. His main determination had been that she stir up no trouble for Edward, and from every report that reached him, she had been all but angelic, never defying the English rule in Gascon, but managing as well to entertain her Valois kin with great tact and diplomacy. He had written to her a few times, praying that she was well and happy. Her letters, in return, had prayed that he was well and enjoying the north. She was, of course, hoping that he would stay exactly where he was.

Oddly enough, it had been in that darkened room with the goldsmith's widowed daughter that he had sat up suddenly, mindless of the young woman who half raised herself at his side, curious at what had started him so. It had just been the green flicker of blaze in the flame, the one that reminded him of Danielle's eyes. He remembered thinking of the day when he'd spoken to her about Lenore, telling her that he had never seen such a beautiful woman . . .

Unless that might be the woman Danielle was destined to become. He hadn't told her such a thing, of course. She had been far too aware of her own power as it was, swaying men with the beauty of her smile. She had, in fact, swayed him. Angered him, made him laugh. Her pride had been so tremendous, her stubborn streak long enough to rival the length of any road in England. Yet in certain things, her generosity had been almost as great.

In the goldsmith's widowed daughter's bed, Adrien suddenly longed to see Danielle.

"Adrien, me fine laird . . ."

Hearing the woman's whisper in the darkness, he had turned and felt her touch, and found his release. The widow was an experienced lover, eager to please him, but he had felt again a sense of restlessness and disappointment. Something was missing. Something he had almost touched once.

Something he yearned to find again.

He thought about that now as he lay upon his rock, and the sheep and the goats—and life—slipped on by. He had been here a long time now. The plague that had killed Joanna had been over for five years. He had regained his strength and agility at combat, and he had spoken the old language, come close to his king, become the MacLachlan, head of his clan. But though Scotland and the border regions remained an area on constant alert, peace and prosperity flowed in these lands now. He could not ignore the fact that he was King Edward's champion. He had been knighted by King Edward, and upon their return to England after the fall of Calais, Edward had honored him further by bringing him in as one of the twenty-six founding members of the Order of the Garter.

Upon his betrothal to Danielle, he had also received all the titles and wealth the king had promised. He had been created Earl of Glenwood, and he ranked among the wealthiest men in England and Scotland

He owed his service to Edward.

He was startled, particularly with this thought in mind, to blink, and see Sir George—still straight and tall in the saddle with his gray head bare, staring down at him from atop his great roan destrier. Adrien leapt up, smiling, glad to see the old knight. "Alas! Are the English at war again with the Scots? Do my eyes deceive me? What brings you so far north?"

"You, my rash young lad! Have you buried yourself so deeply among the rocks and the sheep that you have forgotten the world?"

"Mine is a world I rather like!" Adrien assured him. "But

come, please, to my home, share my ale—and tell me about the world as you know it!''

Sir George had come with a company of men. Adrien left them among his own men-at-arms to find food and quarters for the night and brought Sir George into his home where they sat to dinner in the richly carved great hall. They talked idly at first; then, when they had finished their food, they sat before the fire, drinking, and George looked around and let out a long, deep sigh. '' 'Tis a fine place here, Adrien. You look young and well and rested. You've recovered power and good health, you look stronger than ever. These wild men up here have kept you in good form.''

"Don't forget, I am one of these wild men, as you call them, and they taught me all about form when I was a boy," Adrien reminded him.

Sir George smiled, nodding. Then he grew serious. "The king seeks your service, Adrien. He invades Normandy, and is up in arms against the French."

"When is he not?"

"He wants Aville secured."

Adrien started and leaned forward, frowning. "Aville *is* secure. Is there some new trouble?"

Sir George lifted his hands. "In Aville? You do have men there, right?"

"Aye. Daylin. Richard Huntington, Giles Reeves, more. They have reported nothing ill."

"No ill. Aville is a very center of chivalry. Musicians, poets, and artists abound. English knights seek invitations to the countess's hall—just as do the French—among them, the lady's own Valois relations."

"What danger can the girl be?"

"Girl?" Sir George said with amazement, then smiled. "You have been hiding away too long, my good young laird! The Lady Danielle is quite fully grown—well past marriageable age. Men across Europe speak of her beauty. Indeed, knights and nobles from all of France come to her door."

Adrien was startled by the rush of anger that seized him.

"What are you saying? That she schemes with the French?" he demanded curtly.

"Nay, she entertains her kin, as you have allowed her to do, as is courteous and proper. But as King Jean and our own Edward veer toward a serious clash, the situation grows dangerous. It's time for you to enter my world, Adrien."

Adrien sat back, disturbed by the feel of fire that rippled through his body. He was anxious to be there in Aville— immediately.

"We will ride with the dawn," Adrien promised.

"Good. The Prince of Wales gathers his forces to sail for Bordeaux to put down a rebellion. He will be glad to discover that you have entered into the king's service again. There is just one other matter," Sir George said hesitantly.

"And that is?"

"There is a rumor that . . ."

"Pray, go on," Adrien said, growing aggravated.

"There is one particular young nobleman in the house of Valois who is frequently in your lady's court. There are those who believe that the two are anxious to find a way to set aside Danielle's betrothal so that they may be man and wife themselves."

It seemed as if something had exploded in his head. Sweet Jesu, but he had been a blind idiot. Perhaps it had been just, five years ago, to reward Danielle with her freedom—but to let this much time go by while he wallowed in self-pity had been sheer stupidity. Edward had trusted him. And he had allowed Danielle the freedom to court her French kin, and to become a danger to Edward himself.

"The betrothal will not be set aside!" he swore angrily. He stood, pacing to the fire to stare at the blaze. It snapped— red and gold, blue—and green in its depths. He didn't quite understand his own anger when he realized it was directed at her. What had he expected from her? She had wanted freedom desperately, she had never claimed to be anything but *French*. He had once brought about the fall of Aville, and she had never forgotten, nor forgiven, that fact. It was not without some logic that she might decide she was in love with a nobleman from the house of Valois.

It was not without logic!

But he had given her the gift of freedom and Aville with one warning—not to betray him or King Edward.

Damnation, but he would kill any man who had so much as thought to touch her!

"So!" said Sir George, pleased. "If you are quite resolved to the marriage, perhaps we should send ahead—"

"No, Sir George, I think not. I am not a man anxious for much ceremony, nor am I interested in offering the lady—or her kin—warning that I am on my way. We have long been betrothed. A marriage service on the night of my arrival will suffice. As I wish to leave very early, Sir George, I will bid you good night now."

He turned and left his friend in the hall, his temper simmering at fever pitch as he climbed the stairs to his chamber on the second floor. He entered into it, strode to the window, threw it open, and felt the brisk night wind on his face. Damn her! So time had gone by. Still! He had warned her not to betray him in Aville! By God, he had warned her!

It was time to take what was his.

It was an unbelievably beautiful day in early fall. The sun shone brilliantly, creating a vivid reflection on the water in the garden pond. Danielle sat upon a carved stone chair, idly drawing patterns in the water, laughing with delight as Simon de Valois, Comte Montejoie, strummed lightly upon the strings of a lute and tried valiantly to sing a love song. His voice was too deep, too hoarse for the tender ballad, and after a moment he laughed and then began to sing her a more bawdy song, one to which his voice seemed infinitely more suited.

It was nice out here today. She was certain that Edward's English and Gascon knights who resided in her home were still near—watching from the archer's slits inside the tower walls, probably—but she felt as if she had achieved a little bit of privacy, and such moments were sweet.

Not that she had ever cowered beneath any of the watchful eyes that always seemed to be upon her. She had ridden out where and when she pleased, and she had made every move she chose to make honestly and boldly.

Nothing that she had done made her in the least uneasy.

The world around her did.

There was trouble in the north. The Count of Armagnac was stirring up rebellion in lands Edward claimed as his own. The count was acting with the blessing of King Jean, who was determined to expel English dominance from all of France. Danielle was uneasily aware that her peaceful years here were coming to an end. The men in her own fortress would scurry to their different sides.

And she would be caught in the middle.

Not in the middle, she thought unhappily, for she had made a vow to her dying mother, and a death vow was sacred.

She had been back at Aville a long time now. She had grown here, matured here. She *ruled* here now, and she did so very well. She was proud to remember Lenore's ways, and make every effort to be as just. Life had a wonderful, familiar pattern to it. Mondays were for accounting, Tuesdays she oversaw the training of men within the castle walls, Wednesdays she supervised the making of soap and candles and other necessities. Thursdays she held court for all complaints among her people, Fridays, she greeted travellers, encouraging the arrival of priests and pilgrims, jugglers, dancers, musicians, and all artisans. Saturdays she received a report on the supplies in the fortress and the county, and on Sunday, the Sabbath, she attended Mass in the chapel and ordered the people to observe God's day of rest. There were fairs in between, holy days. And there were times when the people forgot for just a few hours how Christian they had become, and lifted maypoles, or danced around bonfires.

When she had first come home, she had dreaded the possibility that Adrien would arrive any day and seize control from her. But as the time had passed by, she had realized with a peculiarly heavy heart that—except for a terse message upon occasion—he had forgotten her. But then, of course, she had been very careful to see that there was no reason for him to find concern with Aville. The three guardians he had sent to watch out for her were absolutely charming—Daylin, she thought with a small smile, had become very loyal to her. Richard Huntington was just a year or so older than Daylin, with bright blue eyes, a body like an ox, and a willingness to be charmed. Giles Reeves was a stern old Scotsman, straight as an arrow, bald as a buzzard, and wary—but always ready to listen to reason. From the beginning, she had taken care to ask them about everything she wanted to do. She had just made sure that she managed to get the answers she desired. As Doctor Coutin remained with her and tensions seldom eased in the area where land could be instantly disputed between the English king and the French king—or the Pretender, as Edward insisted on calling Jean—she could usually explain things in such a manner that she managed to have her way. She was the countess; she didn't accept commands, but allowed advice. Throughout Aville, people obeyed her and sought to please her, and she often thought that in the wretched tug-of-war between the kings that had devastated so much of the countryside, she must always try to keep her people from harm. She was responsible for their welfare.

As countess, however, and a descendant of the house of Valois, she had insisted from the beginning that the fortress be a place where all were welcome. Aville had gained something of a reputation across Europe for its patronage of the arts. She welcomed everyone—artists, musicians, craftsmen, and nobility—including all those from the house of Valois. She had entertained King Jean and the dauphin, Charles. Simon, Count Montejoie, her distant cousin, had come to visit with King Jean, and a pleasant relationship had grown swiftly between them. Simon was six years her senior and very handsome with light blue eyes, auburn hair, a lean, defined face, and a quick, willing smile. He was trained to arms, tall and lean but solidly muscled. He enjoyed all forms of entertainment, laughed with her over the antics of jugglers, puppeteers, and singers, and advised her as well on defense strategems for a fortress such as her own. She had done a great deal of reading herself on sieges and defenses, determined that Aville would never fall again. Despite the plague which had killed nearly half the population of Europe, the rich fields of Aville had yielded abundant crops year after year and careful management of time and labor had kept her portions high, the fortress rich. Years ago, she'd brought in stonemasons and built a second wall around the fortress to prevent the tunneling that had brought about the collapse of the structure so many years ago. Aville would not fall easily again to any man.

Sometimes she wondered if she was building to prevent capture by the English king or the French king, and sometimes she even wondered a little nervously what Adrien would think of her building and expenditures. Nominally, he remained her guardian. She was certain that Edward had expected that they would have taken their betrothal the next step to marriage by now, as she was actually well past the age when most young women were expected to fulfill the obligations of a wife. But Adrien had lost Joanna, and though she had heard humiliating rumors about his various affairs across the Christian world, he seemed to have no desire for a wife. Or to have *her* for a wife. His heart had died with Joanna; he had meant it when he said that it was for her freedom that he had agreed to the betrothal.

But the betrothal still stood, and so, as Adrien failed to appear with the passing of time, she had spent years wondering how her ties to him might be broken. He could have no interest in her now; indeed, she was certain that he had forgotten all about her—even if he had not forgotten the revenues that their betrothal had brought him.

She wished that she could forget him. His reputation had grown larger than life. He had become the terror of the joust, and had reportedly not lost in a single contest. Giles wrote to him constantly, advising Adrien about what went on in Aville. Apparently Giles received more letters from him than she did, because he would say upon the occasion, "The earl would not approve, I do not think." She would have to smile and explain why what she did was right, all the while thinking somewhat rebelliously that the earl would not be *the earl* if he had not set his hand upon her and her property! But none of that really mattered, because Adrien stayed where he was, and she led her life exactly as she chose.

"Milady, I think that I have lost you. I have been singing the most decadent lyrics imaginable and you have not blinked an eye!" Simon declared.

She smiled slowly, leaning back against the masonry of the pond. "Decadent lyrics? For shame, Simon!" Simon was charming, and she truly enjoyed flirting with him. She couldn't help wondering what it would be like to be free—and in love. Really, truly, deeply in love.

He set the lute aside and sank down beside her. "I bemoan the fact," he whispered, "that lyrics are all that I may have of decadence!"

"Simon—"

"I love you, you know, Danielle," he told her, lifting her hand, and brushing the back of it with a kiss.

This had been coming, she thought, and she could only blame herself because she had enjoyed Simon so very much. She did care for him deeply—he stirred laughter and deep emotions within her. But he wanted more—just as he wanted Aville. She wondered then if she hadn't sometimes been glad of her betrothal. It had kept her from committing herself elsewhere and she liked being countess here in her own right. Husbands tended to enjoy being lords of their domains—and of their wives.

"Danielle," he said, his voice a whisper as he looked around, even though they were very much alone in the garden. "Danielle, I have ridden with the Count of Armagnac. We have stirred up rebellion in Languedoc, raided deep into Gascony."

She gasped, pressing a finger to his lips. "Don't tell me this!" she begged him.

He caught her hand again. "Danielle! You know that your love and loyalty belong to King Jean and the French."

"I know that Edward is strong, and you must be quiet."

"There is no one near us. And I trust my life with you."

"Simon—"

"Hear me out! I love you, I have since the day we met. Your betrothal is a mockery. King Jean can gain the help of the Church and declare it null and void."

"On what grounds?"

"I don't know, but trust me—lawyers and clerics can find grounds when they are needed."

"Simon, this is dangerous!"

"Just say that you won't betray me!"

"You know I'd never betray you!" she promised swiftly, aware then that there were footsteps on the garden path at last, and someone was coming.

"Danielle, please!" Simon said. "I must talk to you."

"This is dangerous, you risk so much—"

"I'll risk my life, I swear, here and now, if you won't at least talk with me in private! Please, I beg you! Tomorrow, let's plan a hunt, and we can manage to ride ahead and share a few more moments' privacy."

"Simon—" she began, but Giles Reeves chose that moment to come upon them, his eyes quite stern, his bald pate shining in the sunlight.

"Ah, my lady! There you are." As if he had not known! she thought with some amusement.

"Indeed, Giles, did you need me?"

"Aye, lady. The accountant is uncertain what payment we promised the bear-keeper who entertained in the courtyard last night. He thinks the fellow is out to cheat us, and wishes you to settle the matter."

"Ah!" Danielle said. She came quickly to her feet, assisted by Giles. But when she stood, Simon took her hand and bowed low over it, kissing it. Giles appeared ready to burst, but there was nothing amiss in the chivalrous way Simon treated her. He was a member of King Jean's Order of the Star, a French equivalent to the English Order of the Garter.

"I shall be riding out this afternoon, milady," Simon told her. "But I am eager to accept your invitation for the morning."

"Invitation, sir?" Giles said suspiciously.

"A hunt," Danielle heard herself explain swiftly. "The game is rich in the forest beyond the river. Simon has been telling me that the deer are plentiful."

Giles frowned. "Hunting has been rich indeed, my lady! You're well aware that the wretched Count of Armagnac raids more and more deeply into Gascon territory! There are areas nearby where the people are in terror. A small hunting party might appear to be easy prey."

"Ah, Giles! Who would dare cause me trouble?" she asked. "No Englishman would harm me, and no Frenchman, as I am kin to the house of Valois." She touched his cheek with a smile. "Adieu then, Simon. 'Til tomorrow."

He bowed and left her with Giles.

"That one will cause trouble," Giles said.

"Giles! He is a chivalrous knight, a member of the Order of the Star!"

"The French mimic his grace of England, Edward, in all things," Giles said disdainfully.

Danielle smiled. "Giles, the French are quick to say that the Order of the Garter is only the Order of the Garter because Edward's mistress, the Countess of Salisbury, could not keep her garter upon her person as she danced. What is the motto, Giles? *Honi soit qui mal y pense!* Evil to him who thinks evil of it!" She laughed softly.

"The Earl of Glenwood is a member of that most noble order, my lady! They place honor above all else, fight with great loyalty, care for knights who have become impoverished, who can no longer care for themselves!"

"So noble!" she agreed, trying to conceal a smile. King Edward himself was a member of the order he had founded. And she wasn't sure at all what sense of nobility had caused him to create the Order of the *Garter* when he did have so gentle, loyal, and noble a queen!

"You have been away from home too long, milady," Giles said sadly.

She started to tell him that she *was* home, but hesitated. Life could be so strange. Sometimes she longed to return to Gariston, to see Sir Thackery again, hold his old hands, sit with him before the fire.

"Perhaps I miss England at times," she told him, smiling. "But our life here is good, isn't it?"

Today, Giles didn't agree. "Milady, I don't think you understand all that is happening around you. Comte Armagnac is in open rebellion—King Jean claims he works on his own, but all know he works for the French King!"

"Pretender?" Danielle suggested with some amusement.

Giles sniffed. "The men beneath the Count of Armagnac behave as heathens!"

"All men behave as heathens in war."

"They burn houses, slay men, seize the women."

"Giles, I will be hunting with some of the finest trained men in the country. Aville is stronger than it has ever been, sure to stand against a force such as Armagnac's—if he were to dare to accost me! No ill will come to me, Giles, I promise you!" She gave him a quick kiss on the cheek and left him, hurrying in.

She smiled as she left him. There was always a diplomatic way to do as she chose. She wouldn't want to hurt Sir Giles under any circumstances.

But she was countess here.

And she was going to be the one to rule in a place that was hers by right.

A strange tremor raced along her spine, and was gone. She wondered at her sudden sense of fear. Giles had made her uneasy, that was all. No one would dare waylay her. She had to go hunting tomorrow, she had to try to understand just what Simon was doing, and she had to try very hard to persuade him from any danger. She didn't know quite what her feelings for him were, but at the very least, he was a friend, and she didn't want him hurt.

Leaves rustled suddenly as the wind changed direction. She looked about her, and felt a sense that the world was changing once again as well, that she must be wary of . . .

Of . . . something.

She laughed aloud impatiently, lifted her chin, and enjoyed the feel of the breeze.

The weather was beautiful; her home was beautiful.

She smiled to herself, and hurried once again toward the hall.

Chapter 10

There wasn't really a problem with the accountant. Giles had merely thought that she had spent a bit too much time with the handsome young Frenchman. Danielle passed through the great hall to the stairs, making her way to the master's chambers at the end of the hallway on the second level. When she came into the room and closed the door behind her, she paused. This had been Lenore's room, and little had changed since her mother's death. The massive canopied bed stood in the center of the rear wall; the tapestried spread and draperies remained the same. The room was a rectangle, with chairs and rugs before the fire, a stand for wine and goblets, a table for whatever work there was to be done. When she had come from Gariston, she'd had a separate privy added to the far wall, and a dressing hall. A very expensive looking-glass in a richly-carved frame stood next to the washstand near the fire. A line of books sat upon a small table by the bed, a curious mixture of material, for she loved romantic tales of deeds and daring that flourished in France and the Italian states and even in England, just as she was fascinated by texts on building, history, weapons, horses, and animal husbandry. She walked across the room, lying down atop her bed, selecting a book on poetry and unrequited love.

There was a light tapping on her door and she heard her name called. It was Monteine. Danielle rose, opening the door quickly with a smile that faded as she saw Monteine's worried frown.

"What is it?"

"Giles has told me you are going to ride out tomorrow," Monteine said.

Danielle arched a brow. "Monteine, I am an excellent horse-woman."

"I am really worried," Monteine said, the frown remaining upon her pretty face. "These raids that have been going on into Gascony . . the so-called noble knights riding with the comte have cruelly raped the women and beaten and slaughtered the men."

"Surely that is rumor! I can't believe that they would all behave so brutally," Danielle said. "They would not attack here, and if any man did so, the fortress can now withstand a massive force."

"Danielle, that is the point. The fortress is protected. That is why you should stay within it!"

"I am riding with trained knights—"

"With Simon!" Monteine hissed.

"I am deeply distressed" Danielle said, "that you have so little faith in me!"

"You have managed the castle with grace, justice, and wisdom," Monteine said. "Your parents would be proud."

"Thank you."

"But you simply do not realize . . ."

"What?"

"That you are quite a staggering prize."

"Monteine, surely—"

"Please, listen to me. You know the ways of the world. Were you a rotting old crone of eighty, men would seek your hand because you have created a magnificent property that is coveted."

"I am betrothed, remember?"

Monteine sniffed. "I remember, but do you?" she demanded

unhappily. "Covetous men can seek ways to break a betrothal. And you must be careful."

"I am simply going hunting with a good friend, and I will be safe with him."

Monteine turned unhappily. She shivered. "My bones are aching!" she warned.

Danielle grinned as Monteine left, then realized that she was shivering herself. She drew a soft mantle around her shoulders and went to the fire and stoked it. The flames burned more brightly. She still shivered.

They took no birds of prey with them when they rode out, for they were armed with bows and arrows, intent on taking down deer or boar. It was a day like the last had been, with a beautiful sun riding in a powder blue sky. There were ten in their party as Giles had insisted there might be danger.

But riding hard across the fields, Danielle didn't feel it. Star was nearly twenty years old now, but remained a wonderful horse, as fleet and agile as she had ever been. Simon's destrier was heavier and slower, and Danielle had always loved a race— and always loved to win. She led them all on a merry chase into the woods, with just Simon behind her as she entered into a sheltered trail where the world seemed green, covered by the thick branches of tall trees above.

"It's glorious, isn't it?" Danielle said as Simon caught up with her. He didn't seem terribly pleased that it had taken him so long to catch her, and he didn't respond to her mood. "Danielle, we must talk," he told her.

"Yes, Simon, I am worried about you. You know that I care deeply for you. But—"

"Hear me out, milady. Jean is a good king, a good man, deeply loved here. Edward is a treacherous bastard forever reaching out his grasping hands for France!"

"For his own lands!" Danielle said softly, surprising herself with her defense of the English king.

"Jean is going to see that Edward is expelled from all these lands. Ah, lady! Do not go down with the English. King Jean loves you, as his father loved your lady mother. He is your kin. Break the bonds that hold you now to an unworthy enemy!'' he said, his voice husky and trembling. ''Bear in mind, lady, that no man loves you more deeply than I!''

Her heart seemed to catch within her throat, his words were spoken with such fervor. He was so charming, so earnest, so courteous, deferring to her in all things.

She closed her eyes. She was afraid, but not for herself. She was afraid that war was coming again, and she was afraid that men would die.

''Simon! I know King Edward. You mustn't underestimate his power here, or his determination.''

''And you must realize that you are a part of his strength. But Aville is yours, those people are yours! Where your heart lies, Aville will follow!''

''Simon—''

''Danielle, I seek nothing from you. I am a rich man, a titled man. I would love you all of my life.''

''Simon, you are dear to me. I admire you, I enjoy your company, you have been the best friend I could find. But I must think—''

''Think with your heart! And remember this,'' he added anxiously, ''I would never hurt you, but time grows short—''

''Danielle!''

Her name was shouted vehemently from down the trail. Startled, she swirled Star around in time to see Daylin come speeding toward them. ''Riders are coming, armored and armed, bearing down on us. Turn, milady, and race for your life back to Aville!''

''Riders? From where?'' Danielle demanded as she quickly edged Star out of the copse of trees and saw what Daylin had seen. Over the hill, but coming swiftly toward their position, were perhaps a dozen mounted men. The ground seemed to tremble beneath them. Indeed, they wore battle armor. But they wore plain tunics and mantles atop their armor, with no crests, no badges or banners to identify themselves or their families— or even their nationality.

"Danielle, I beg you!" Daylin cried. *"You* must keep your-self safe."

"I will ride with my lady and protect her to my death!" Simon cried. "He's right. Danielle, come now, I beg of you!"

She hesitated. If she rode away, she left her men, not nearly so well armed, to face this strange force of riders.

"Go!" Simon cried, and he cracked a hand upon Star's rump, causing the mare to rear and then plummet back to the earth at a wild run.

Danielle ducked down flat against Star's shoulder and neck, all but flying into the field. The riders saw her and swerved. She bent low to race again, but just before she did, she saw that a second wave of men came over the hill, fast on the heels of the first.

She nudged Star hard. The ground thundered and rumbled beneath her. Behind her, she heart shouts, cries, and a tremen-dous clash of steel as her own people sped out to meet the attackers. She looked around her, anxious to see Simon at her side.

But he wasn't there.

Her heart seemed to congeal in her chest. She reined in, swirling Star about to search for him, afraid he had been injured and lay dying. She had come far enough away that she could not see clearly anymore. The knights and men-at-arms fought a distance back from her, perhaps a hundred feet.

Someone had come upon Simon! she thought, and her heart ached with fear. She told herself that he was a brave and well-trained knight, and could probably best any wretched thief or rebel raider.

Then she saw that some of the riders had seen her pause, and she knew her own danger. She turned to race into the forest once again even as three broke from the melee to come charging after her.

She would not be caught by any such wretches, she deter-mined, not when such good men fought to save her life. She tore into the forest trail, ignoring the branches that whipped against her. The green shadows brought darkness all around

her. She slowed her pace, making her way through the tightening trail. She reined in, barely daring to breathe.

They were almost upon her. She slowed Star to a walk and
stood dead still, her heart pounding.

She listened.

Someone was coming from her left. Someone else came
from her right. If she could just remain still, they would cross
in the shadows before her, never seeing her.

Then Star sneezed. The sound, in the forest, seemed as loud
as an explosion, pinpointing her exact location.

Desperate, Danielle slipped quickly from Star's back and
hurried into the dense growth. She ran hard until she couldn't
catch her breath and her lungs were burning, and then she
paused.

The two riders had come upon one another, and apparently
they had *not* been hunting her together. She held dead still
as she heard shouts and grunts—and heavy clashes of steel.
Someone was defending her, giving her time to run deeper into
the forest.

She started along the trail again, knowing that she couldn't
run forever. She kept running ahead, and suddenly burst into
a clearing with a cottage. She paused, her heart thundering.
The place had fallen into complete disrepair. It was dark and
empty. The door hung askew.

She looked behind her and heard rustling in the trees. She
paused another moment, but the rustling continued.

She ran swiftly across the copse, and into the cottage.

It was black as ink within. She leaned against the wall,
blinking, trying to adjust to the darkness. It was a one-room
dwelling, hearth to the far left, tattered, decaying bed to the
right. She cautiously took a step and paused, her heart pounding
as she heard the squeal of mice racing about. She swallowed
and came around the bed and just as she did, she inhaled sharply
and held her breath, ducking to the ground.

Someone else was in the cottage. Someone who had entered
cautiously, silently, footfalls and movements unbelievably
light.

How long, she wondered, before she was discovered?

She carried a small hunting knife in a slender sheath at her calf, and she started to finger it. It was not much of a weapon against an armed knight—she would have to be very close to use it.

It could too easily be taken away.

Flat against the floor, she suddenly saw the farm tools leaning against the wall. There lay a spade, an axe, a scythe. The last, she might not manage to wield at all, for it would be too long at such close quarters, and the spade might not offer enough of a menace. But the axe held promise. It had been some time since she had picked up a weapon, but now she was in real danger.

She could hear breathing, she was certain. The slow, sure, heavy pounding of a heart. Her pursuer was close, so very close upon her.

The footsteps were now coming around the end of the tattered bed. In a matter of seconds, he would be upon her.

She reached for the axe, curling her fingers around its handle. She waited. The footsteps came around the corner. She would have one good chance.

She leapt to her feet, crying out with a mighty lunge as she swung her heavy weapon.

In the shadows, she saw only a towering figure. He was quick and agile, for he leapt back from the lethal swerve of her blade. A sword shone in the darkness, striking the axe with a power that sent it shuddering from her hands. For only a second she stood stunned, then she leaped atop the bed to escape across it. She all but flew back to the ground, racing for the door. She cast herself out into the green coolness of the copse, only to feel him upon her again, arms reaching out, fingers closing around her shoulder.

She shrieked and started to run again, but the fingers closed around the material of her tunic, pulling her back. She lost her balance and fell. Face down in a rich tuft of grass, she quickly drew her small knife from its sheath. When she found herself rolled to face her attacker as he straddled her, she was ready.

She screamed and aimed her knife for the man's throat, praying for a weakness there. It did not touch him at all—his gauntleted hand waylaid her thrust, the crush of his fingers threatening to break her wrist.

The knife fell from her fingers as he stared down at her, and she stared up at him.

He wore a coat of mail. Atop it was a tunic with a heraldic emblem blazoned across it.

A lion above three leopards.

He wore a helmet and face plate as well, but she could see his eyes. Golden eyes she had long remembered. Staring down at her now with their blazing, warning glitter. Powerful eyes, taunting eyes, passionate eyes, and at the moment, furious eyes . . .

He sat back on his haunches. Her wrist was freed as he lifted his helm from his head. Thick red-gold hair, damp from its containment in the helmet, sprang about his face. A face she knew. Bronze, rugged, handsome—harsh. Small lines etched now around the eyes. The fullness of his mouth was taut, formed into a grim white line. She felt herself beginning to tremble, even as she stared up at him, even as she felt his touch.

"MacLachlan!" she cried out.

"Aye, indeed, lady!" he said, his voice deep, harsh. "Tell me, did you know my name before or after you tried to slash my throat?" he demanded.

She gasped, a hand instinctively flying for his cheek at the insult. But he caught her hand before she could strike, his fingers curling around her own. "How dare you!" she cried, her voice trembling. "You could have called out, you could have said my name, your name—!" She broke off, gasping for breath. Dear God, but her heart continued to pound; she couldn't draw enough air into her lungs.

"I did call your name," he told her.

She shook her head. She hadn't heard a thing. Dear God, it had been so long since she had seen him. Once, she had been his enemy, and would gladly admit to her deeds. But he was no longer the familiar antagonist she so readily met in battle, but a powerful stranger. One she knew to grant no quarter once he had judged her guilty.

Her eyes narrowed. "If you called my name, I did not hear

you. I was scared to death—how could I expect to see you? How can you be here? They were rebels coming for us, attacking us, I know that—''

''We rode in behind them, milady,'' he said, still watching her. She had never felt his eyes so intently upon her, felt their piercing power as they raked over her. They brought a warmth with them, like the gold of their fire. He studied her as if she were a new weapon, a painting, a tapestry, something he had not seen before.

Then she realized that although his face had grown more taut and lean, he had not changed much since their last meeting. But she had.

She felt herself trembling again, and she wasn't sure why. ''But there was someone else in the woods—''

''A man thought to accost you there. I convinced him otherwise.''

''Daylin, Simon, the others—''

''One man has a broken arm, there are a few minor injuries, but we lost no men. Five of the rebels were killed—the rest took flight when they saw us arrive behind them.''

She exhaled on a long breath. Oh, thank God, none of her people had died!

''Then you arrived at a most opportune time, my lord.''

''No, milady, I arrived because of the known danger threatening English holdings here. Which God knows, you should have seen as well!''

Anger streaked through her, and she forgot that she lay beneath him. ''Don't you think you can come in here chastising and giving orders! You have ignored Aville these many years and I have managed exceptionally well.''

''Until today.''

''I was not doing so badly!''

''You are the one flat on your back, milady.''

''Perhaps then, you would be so good as to allow me to rise?''

He paused, and she could hear the grating of his teeth. But he rose, offering a hand down to her. When she stood, she realized her disarray. Her hair streamed out about her with bits of tree and grass entwined within it. Her rich, fur-trimmed habit was torn and ragged. She smoothed her hands over it nonetheless, trying to summon her dignity.

"I'm still at a loss, milord. After all this time, you have come here now, today. You couldn't have come knowing that I might need assistance at this exact moment!"

"Nay, lady, indeed, that was indeed God's own rare opportunity," he replied, still staring at her. She felt the fire of his eyes, felt their full and very thorough assessment. Despite herself, she felt a flush rising to her cheeks. Warmth rushed through her.

"Then—"

"Alas, milady, I have come to take charge," he informed her gravely.

"Of what?" she asked cautiously, eyes narrowing. She had controlled things quite well, or so she thought!

"Of you," he said flatly. "And Aville, of course."

"But the king must see that I have—"

"The king has sent me," he snapped.

Enraged and offended, she retorted without thinking. "Perhaps another king can return you!"

Such rash, foolish words! She wished instantly, of course, that she could take them back.

She could not, of course. She wondered wretchedly where her mind had gone, how he had managed to strip all sense and wisdom from her in a matter of seconds.

He arched a brow, watching her for a moment, a slight curl to his lip.

"I did not mean that as it sounded," she said, keeping her eyes steady on his.

"Perhaps not," he murmured softly. "But then again, perhaps it is time for you to start to take great care, milady. And perhaps I made a mistake ever allowing you to come here."

"I have done nothing wrong, and everything right," she assured him.

He continued as if he hadn't heard her. "Perhaps I have come just in time."

"Perhaps," she suggested softly, "you must understand my position. Perhaps you are not welcome here!"

"Ah, but, *perhaps,* my lady, you will feel differently after
tonight."

"What is tonight?" she asked him cautiously.

He hadn't heard her and didn't reply. He was already walking
past her, heading for the massive war horse that awaited him.
She turned and stared after him.

"What is tonight?" she cried again.

He didn't even pause, but replied impatiently, his back to
her.

"Our wedding."

The world seemed to spin in green all around her. She never
fainted, never passed out! Only once before in her life had she
ever felt this way. Long ago. When . . .

He had mentioned their betrothal.

But then Joanna had died, and what he'd had of a heart had
died, and she'd been free all these years, and now . . .

He was back.

"What?" she demanded.

He turned back to her. "Danielle, we have been betrothed
many years. Surely you have not forgotten. There was a reason
for our betrothal—good reason, for England. I've most certainly
given you time to mature. Too much time. And surely, you
didn't expect to remain betrothed indefinitely?"

She was silent, staring at him, the blood drained from her
face.

He swore impatiently beneath his breath, then said, "Danielle, the time has come. There will be a wedding tonight."

"A wedding!" she cried. "Tonight! Because the king commands it! At the king's pleasure—"

"And mine, as well, I imagine," he interrupted, a soft taunt
to his words, a slight smile of amusement still upon his lips.

She was startled that he could seem so amused—and unop-
posed to the concept of a real marriage. She stood with her
hands upon her hips, furious. He had come to take charge. She
meant nothing to him. She was a pretty plaything, that was all,
now that he had decided to take charge.

She had done well! She cherished her independence, and,
admittedly, her power. *Take control of Aville—and the countess*

there! It seemed the king had commanded, and his earl had jumped to obey.

Walking swiftly, angrily, she started by Adrien and his destrier, certain she would find Star in the woods.

"A wedding tonight!" she lashed out, passing him. "In a pig's eye!"

She suddenly felt a hand firmly upon her arm, and she was swung around back to face him. He plucked her up from the ground as if she were weightless, setting her atop his stallion before she could so much as begin to protest or fight.

Gold eyes glittered upon her. "Indeed, milady. In a pig's eye or no, the king's pleasure or my own. There will be a wedding tonight. I swear it."

"Don't threaten me, Adrien!" she warned him.

He shook his head, the laughter gone, his lean, hard, handsome face quite solemn.

"Not a threat, Danielle. A vow," he told her. "And countess, I assure you, I keep my vows."

Before she could protest again, he leapt up behind her, his arms came around her.

And a wall of shimmering red fire seemed to sweep within her.

Chapter 11

Adrien had come with twelve men—six knights attended by their squires. All of them, Danielle noted, were well armed and armored, and on good horses.

They were experienced men, ready for battle.

A few wore plain tunics, while others wore their coats-of-arms upon them, as did Adrien. He had come riding John this time, a huge bay with feathered fetlocks and a long mane. The horse, like its rider, was clad for war, with plate armor around its massive chest and over its haunches and a narrow face plate with eye holes over its large face. Adrien's blazon with its lion and leopards skirted around the horse, just as it was drawn upon his own chest, brilliant crimson against a field of gold.

Adrien rode with Danielle straight back to Aville. Other members of his party and hers had already returned. Guards lined the parapets, watching and waiting, calling out that the countess and Laird MacLachlan had returned. Cheers rose, and Danielle flushed slightly to realize that they were for her safety, which she had taken so for granted.

Inside the courtyard Adrien dismounted swiftly, reached up, and set her down. Then he turned to clasp Daylin, who greeted him enthusiastically. Sir Giles was next to welcome him, and

Danielle stood very still, feeling the breeze lift her hair as she watched. The greetings went on, Doctor Coutin welcoming Adrien next, Lady Jeanette, and even Monteine flushing happily at his arrival. Her own men from Aville were eager to applaud him and his men on their swift assistance during the assault.

She felt as if she were being watched, so she turned. Simon was standing some distance from her, by his horse, staring her way with a look of pained anxiety that tore at her heart. She tried to offer him an encouraging smile, but it faded and her heart began to thud when she discovered that Adrien was watching her again. He was listening to one of her own men-at-arms, but as he towered over the shorter fellow, his eyes easily touched hers over the man's head.

"Daylin, Giles—Doctor Coutin, if you will—I've need of your expertise in the hall," Adrien said, his eyes still just touching hers. "Milady!" he called, "perhaps you would be good enough to see to the quartering and feeding of my men and their horses. They have ridden a long way."

He turned away from her, leaving his mount with one of the grooms and heading straight for the doors to the great hall in the keep. Daylin, Giles, and Doctor Coutin followed him. She almost gasped out a protest, wondering how he could be so sure of exactly where he was going.

But he had been here before, she remembered. He knew Aville. He had been here after he tunneled his way beneath the fortress walls and allowed King Edward to seize the place from Lenore.

She seethed inwardly, but spun around, smiling to the men as they doffed their helmets and waited patiently in the courtyard. "Welcome to Aville," she said lightly, and turned to Sir Ragnor, one of the men of Aville who had *long* served her family. "Would you please see them to the chambers in the north wall and have their horses stabled and fed? I shall see that the hall is readied for so large a group this evening," she said, offering Sir Ragnor a sweet smile and heading for the hall herself. She had just come into the entrance when someone stepped from the shadows of a tapestried alcove, accosting her quietly. Simon stood behind her, his face gray and taut.

"What is going on?" he asked. "How has MacLachlan come to be here today?"

"I'm still not exactly sure," she said, aware that MacLachlan was in the great hall, perhaps a hundred feet from where they stood in the stone entry to the keep. She lowered her voice to a soft whisper. "He's come with Prince Edward because of the trouble here," she told him.

"My love, we must speak!" he insisted.

"Not now!" She was still completely unnerved by Adrien's arrival and she was afraid for Simon, especially if he was acting with the rebels who had brought about such massive damage in King Edward's fief.

"When?" Simon persisted.

"Later."

"Tonight!" he promised her, and suddenly slipped away, back out the door to the keep. As Danielle came into the hall, she saw that Adrien was by the mantel, an arm leaned upon it. He had stripped off his outer tunic and armor and wore a simple shirt of linen over form-hugging trousers and knee-high soft leather boots. His gaze, even as she entered, fell upon her, and she was certain that he had heard her whispering in the entry. Rem, head of the household servants, had served wine and platters of bread and cheese and dried meat. Adrien held a goblet as he watched her, and when she entered, he spoke casually, halting their conversation as if he didn't trust her to hear what was being said. "Gentlemen, if you will please see to matters now as we have agreed . . . ?" he said, his eyes upon her rather than on the men.

"Indeed, milord!" Giles said, leaping to his feet from his place at the table. Daylin, his eyes upon Danielle as well, followed. Doctor Coutin bowed to Adrien, and then to Danielle. "I will see to any injuries among our men," he said, and departed with the two others. Danielle was uneasy as they left, for she found herself alone in the hall with Adrien. For all its vast size, the hall did not seem big enough.

Once again, his gaze seemed to impale her, penetrate her. The color of his eyes matched the hue of the fire in the hearth, unnerving her still further.

"It has been a long time," he said after a moment.

"Indeed. A very long time."

"And you are still determined to wage war with me?"

He left the hearth and strode toward her. Danielle walked around the great table to put its bulk between them. "The French and the English always seem to be at war."

"This is English territory."

"That, as well, always seems to have been in dispute."

"There is no dispute on the matter," he said with assurance. "Though I agree, the French and English are forever at war. You, milady, have waged battle against me. Let me see if I recall. Pepper in my wine. Honey in my boots. A loosened saddle that all but killed me."

"I didn't loosen the saddle."

It was obvious he still didn't believe her.

"And I stayed at your side while you nearly perished of the plague," she reminded him.

"I have not forgotten. I pay—"

"Yes, you pay your debts."

"I've done so here," he murmured, his eyes reminding her that he had fulfilled his promise of giving her years of freedom.

Those years were up.

"But," he continued, "I have not been here long, and it already seems that you are ready to fly to battle once again."

"Indeed, my lord, you have not been here long," she told him smoothly. "You were elsewhere—as you saw fit. I've been here. I've cared for these people, worked for the betterment of the fortress and all Aville. You have come here today and walked in as if you have ruled here all your life. Throwing out commands and orders!"

He paused at the head of the table, refilling his wine glass. "True, but remiss. I rode here today, saved you from a pack of knaves, and *then* barked out dictates—my lady."

"No great harm might have come to me—"

"I'm not sure of your definition of harm, Danielle. But rest assured, those cutthroats would have killed every man with you to secure their intended prize. Doesn't that disturb you?"

''This is my home!'' she said angrily. ''And you are familiar with it only because you once caused it to fall in battle.''

He was still and silent for a moment, watching her. When he spoke, there was a deadly tone to his words. ''I *am* lord here, milady, make no mistake about it.''

''I have the right—''

''And I have the king's command.''

''Ah, yes! The king gave you property, riches, and titles—and you haven't married me yet. You have been busy elsewhere, but now Edward commands you to marry me. I may refuse to give my marriage vows.''

''You will not.''

''Oh?'' she inquired. ''And why not?''

''You will marry me, my lady, because we have the blessing of the Church, we have been legally betrothed for years, and you have done nothing to break the betrothal.''

''But—''

''And you will marry me because I will drag you to the altar bound and trussed, if need be. Because—''

''You wouldn't,'' she said with deep contempt.

''I would,'' he assured her.

''Because the king has commanded it?'' she taunted.

''Because I have determined to do it, milady.''

''Surely, you must. If you wish to remain an earl.''

He smiled very slowly with a mocking twist to his mouth that she didn't like. ''Danielle, there's so much that you cannot forget or forgive! Well, my lady, I can keep memory alive as well! The pranks you played before were one thing. Cross me now, lady, and it will be war indeed.''

A hot flush seemed to ignite within her once again as he spoke, and she tried to tell herself it was the challenge he brought into her life. Or the outrage and fury—how dared he think he could just take over so easily? But it was neither challenge nor outrage that created the wildfires within her. It was watching him. It was realizing that he had changed little, that he remained so striking and so compelling. She was fascinated, longing to reach out and touch a muscle-laden bronzed arm, touch the planes of his clean-shaven face. Her eyes lowered, falling upon his hands. His nails were blunt cut and clean upon very long, powerful fingers, deeply bronzed by the sun as well. She thought of those hands upon her, and of what marriage meant, and the world began to spin again.

Something inside her yearned for what Adrien MacLachlan could not give her. What he had given to Joanna, what he had buried with her. She didn't want her strength, position, nor her soul taken away by a man who would ride away again to serve a warring king, do whatever he chose, and return to make demands. Especially if that man was Adrien. She didn't want to feel the quickening of her heart and the pains of jealousy that would follow. She was not a possession to be used when convenient and then ignored as if she was nothing more than a prize on a shelf when he had no further use for her.

"I don't wish to marry—anyone," she said.

"How strange! Rumor abounds all throughout Europe that you are interested in Simon, Count Montejoie."

"Simon is a distant cousin and a good friend. I told you, I've no wish to marry."

"Well, milady," he said, and he sounded tired, "I'm afraid that you—and granted Aville and Gariston—are too rich a prize between warring nations to make such a choice."

"If you and the king would just leave me be—"

"Politics will not let you be, Danielle. And you are right. I was given the title of earl and made overlord of all the counties within Glenwood on the good faith that our marriage would take place eventually. I was born the son of a proud and noble— but impoverished—Scottish laird, and he taught me to fight for what was mine and not to let it go. I give up nothing that is mine."

"I am not *yours*."

"You have been, these many years."

"When we were betrothed," she reminded him, "you told me that you agreed to it because you felt you owed me. Because Edward threatened to marry me to Sir Andreson. You said that our betrothal would protect me from other things the king might have in mind. And you gave me my freedom. If you now think to renege—"

She broke off angrily, because he was laughing. "Ah, milady! I see why you haven't been champing at the bit to break the betrothal now. You were convinced that Joanna's death had stolen my senses, and that I would let this situation go on and on forever!"

"You set no time limit!"

"I offered you years of freedom. You have had them. And your freedom is now disturbing many good Englishmen and Gascons loyal to Edward, for there are constant disturbing rumors about a marriage between you and your noble Frenchman."

She was alarmed to feel a flush creeping to her cheeks. She had mused about Simon; she had cared for him. But she hadn't been guilty of any misdeeds and she was furious to realize that her flush made her appear guilty as original sin.

She inhaled and exhaled slowly, seeking patience so she could speak with dignity. "You must believe this, Adrien. You don't want to marry me, because I cannot make all the promises you would want from a wife."

"Danielle, trust me. It's amazing what one can do when necessary, I promise you."

"Right before my mother died, Laird MacLachlan, she begged me to love and honor her king. I gave my promise."

"Philip is dead," Adrien said flatly, "and your mother was with the King of England when he stood godfather to you. She agreed that you were to become his ward—she entrusted your future to him. He has entrusted it to me."

"My mother was probably given no choice. Whatever, sir, I made my vows to her. I don't wish to do any harm to Edward, and I have not done anything here that would hurt him or his cause, I swear it, but if you think that your words can make me despise my mother's family, you are wrong! I made a vow, and I will not fight against the house of Valois. If you think I can change that for you, you are mistaken."

He sighed with great exasperation. "King Edward was Philip's *first* cousin, and the English king still retains a closer familial relationship with Philip's son than do you."

"Then Edward should respect King Jean's position," Danielle said.

"And you should remember that these lands are not King Edward's through any feat of conquest, but that they belong to him strictly by an inheritance brought to him nearly two centuries ago through Eleanor of Aquitaine. And Danielle, you have also made another vow. To me. To wed. Is your word honorably binding, or isn't it? Do you seek to break one vow, and not the other?"

"I am not seeking to break any vow!"

"Then we will be married tonight."

"I am not ready to do so!"

"Then become so, for it will happen."

"Adrien, damn you!" she cried. "You have become even more arrogant, if possible!" she charged him.

"More determined, is all."

She cried out with aggravation, amazed and dismayed by the tears that sprang to her eyes. She turned her back on him, and was startled into a gasp when she felt his hands upon her shoulders, for she had not heard him cross the distance between them. She was further alarmed when he spoke, for his voice was husky and deep, and the warmth of his breath touched her ear with his words. "Danielle, I am sorry that this has taken you by such surprise. Surely you knew in your heart that this day must come, that I could not stay away forever."

"What a good pretense you were making of it then!" she charged in a whisper. She was trembling, and she tried to will herself to stop. Time seemed to wash away. She remembered their constant verbal battles, the death in his eyes when he had found Joanna. She even remembered the edge of tenderness he had offered her then, and she remembered touching him when he had come so close to perishing.

She didn't want to remember these things. She didn't want the tumult of having him near, and she didn't want to feel the frightening fire he could so easily create within her.

"Damn it, Danielle," he said, growing impatient. "I haven't come with the intent to hurt you—"

''Then delay the marriage!'' she pleaded, spinning around to face him. ''Give me time!''

He stared into her eyes for a long moment, and she barely dared breathe, hoping that he would agree. Then he shook his head slowly. ''I can't delay this, Danielle,'' he said with finality, and she felt a chill, for she realized that no matter how she argued, the matter was closed.

''Then—'' she began, breaking off because she had to take a huge gulp of air.

''Then what?'' he asked, eyes narrowing.

''I'll agree, I'll give you the vows. I'll do so angelically, sir, without the least protest. If you just give me time . . . after.''

''Time after?'' he repeated, a brow arched high.

She nodded, furious that she was finding it so difficult to speak, and that he was tormenting her into finding the right words when he must surely understand already!

''I've never—'' she began, then broke off again. She wanted to be dignified, but she couldn't keep her eyes on his. She lowered her lashes and her head. ''The concept of marriage . . .'' She breathed deeply and tried again. ''Of intimacy is not a familiar one for me. Do you—understand?''

''Oh, indeed,'' he said. She wanted to kick him. He sounded amused at her distress. He wasn't going to give in to anything at all.

''Damn you—'' she began furiously, but his grip upon her shoulders tightened and he lifted her chin, forcing her to meet his gaze.

''Fine, Danielle. The marriage will take place tonight. I'll give you time. I will not promise how much, for I'm not sure how much I have to give.''

There was a warning in his voice; she didn't care. She had bought a concession, and any time seemed precious now.

It was true that Adrien knew the fortress of Aville from the inside out—though Danielle had made changes in it from the time he had last been here.

Rem had shown him to a room upstairs that was big and

spacious—and near the master's quarters at the end of the hallway. It had been Danielle's when she was a girl, he had been informed, but many other guests had stayed in it since then, he was certain. It was pleasantly appointed, but little that had been Danielle's remained, other than an interesting collection of books that sat atop a small carved table by the bedside. For the moment, it was his room; his trunks lined the wall, his mantle was hooked upon a peg, his armor was laid out on the table, gauntlets and bascinet at his side.

He sat by the roaring fire, glad to sip more wine and ease his weary body. He had ridden so hard to come here, only to find himself in a constant sweat each time he realized just how timely his arrival had been. Losing Aville would have been a strategic and political disaster.

And losing Danielle . . .

He clenched and unclenched a fist, trying to ease some of the tension from his body. She had matured from a beautiful girl into a voluptuous and stunning woman. She was more fiercely independent than ever, as prickly as a wild rose, but in her he could still see the passion of the girl he had known with the healing hands, proud spirit, and undying courage.

He lifted his wine glass and spoke softly and honestly to the fire. ''Most tempting, I admit, is the urge to strip the lady naked and taste and touch and feel every lush inch of her being . . .''

He'd been warned. He'd even known that she was becoming an uncanny beauty; he had felt her power to entice. He'd seen her flirt with other men, until they were ready to give their lives should she lift a finger. Somehow, he still hadn't imagined that she could mature into a creature quite so stunning, both innocent in her beauty and somehow incredibly sensual as well. Her eyes were gemstones, her hair a sweep as sleek and shiny as a raven's wing. In his life, he'd not seen a more seductive woman. Ever. She was like her mother, and even though he'd been very young when he'd been called upon to join in Lenore's escort to London, he'd been impressed by both her beauty and elegance. Danielle was taller than Lenore, as slim, yet more voluptuous. She had a far wilder streak, too, and she lacked her mother's elegance and dignity, though the seeds of it were sown within her. There was a subtle sensuality about Danielle that enhanced her perfection, something in her eyes, her voice, her movement—a passion that simmered beneath the surface, incredibly tantalizing.

He leaned back, realizing he'd been an idiot, and thinking about Joanna. He had been her first lover, while she had been his first maiden. He had known it, and had been tender and careful. Their first time together had been fulfilling and sweet; she had wanted him, she had been determined to defy heaven and hell, her father and the king, to be with him. She had sworn she scarcely felt the pain, that she had been dying for him with such fever that the heat had swept away all pain. He had come to terms with her death, aware that his memory of her was sweet; it was the guilt he felt that hurt. If he had just loved her with the same passion and determination she had given him, they both might have been far away from the ravages of the plague. Then again, they had been in the king's service, and there might not have been a way to change fate at all.

Now Danielle wanted him to wait. Never.

He realized that he had come here at first through sheer outrage—no one was going to take what was his, and certainly not the liege men of a foreign king. Now that he had come, he would ensure his holdings. Aville—and Danielle. It was almost frightening how passionately he wanted her.

It was an ironic situation. He had spent his life attracted to women, and finding that they were equally attracted to him in turn. It was certainly a slap to his pride to realize that while he lusted after her, she wanted no part of him whatever.

Then there was the matter of Simon . . .

As he sat musing, there came a tapping at his door. He rose and opened it to find Daylin, Giles, and Richard Huntington waiting to speak with him, their eyes grave. He opened the door fully with no further word, bringing the trio into his chambers.

"I found the man you wounded and left in the woods, Adrien," Richard told him. "I brought him back."

"Discreetly?"

FREE BOOK CERTIFICATE

Yes! Please send me 4 Kensington Choice (the best of Zebra and Pinnacle Books) Historical Romances without cost or obligation (worth up to $24.96). As a Kensington Choice subscriber, I will then receive 4 brand-new romances to preview each month for 10 days FREE. I can return any books I decide not to keep and owe nothing. The publisher's prices for Kensington Choice romances range from $4.99-$6.99, but as a preferred subscriber I will get these books for only $4.20 per book or $16.80 for all four titles. There is no minimum number of books to buy and I may cancel my subscription at any time, plus there is no additional charge for postage and handling. No matter what I decide to do, my first 4 books are mine to keep, absolutely FREE!

Name _____

Address _____ Apt._____

City _____ State _____ Zip _____

Telephone (___) _____

Signature _____

(If under 18, parent or guardian must sign)

Subscription subject to acceptance. Terms and prices subject to change.

KF0498

We have 4 FREE BOOKS for you
as your introduction to
KENSINGTON CHOICE!
To get your FREE BOOKS, worth
up to $24.96, mail the card below.

4 BESTSELLING HISTORICAL ROMANCES BY YOUR FAVORITE AUTHORS CAN BE YOURS, FREE!

Kensington Choice brings you historical romances by your favorite bestselling authors including Janelle Taylor, Shannon Drake, Rosanne Bittner, Jo Beverley, and Georgina Gentry, just to name a few! Each book is filled with passion, adventure and the excitement of bygone times!

To introduce you to this great club which is part of Zebra Home Subscription Service, we'd like to send you your first 4 bestselling historical romances, absolutely free! And once you get these 4 free books to savor at home, we'll rush you the next 4 brand-new books at the lowest prices available, as soon as they are published.

The way the club works is that after your initial FREE shipment, you will get our 4 newest bestselling historical romances delivered to your doorstep each month at the preferred subscriber's rate of only $4.20 per book, a savings of up to $8.16 per month (since these titles sell in bookstores for $4.99-$6.99)! All books are sent on a 10-day free examination basis and there is no minimum number of books to buy. (And no charge for shipping.) Plus as a regular subscriber, you'll receive our FREE monthly newsletter, *Zebra/Pinnacle Romance News*, which features author profiles, subscriber benefits, book previews and more!

So start today by returning the FREE BOOK CERTIFICATE provided. We'll send you 4 FREE BOOKS with no further obligation: A FREE gift offering you hours of reading pleasure with no obligation...how can you lose?

"Aye, discreetly, and lodged him in the cellar room beneath the far tower."

"How bad are his injuries? Will he live?" Adrien asked.

"Doctor Coutin tends to his wounds now. We promised him the best possible physician would try to save his life if he would speakly frankly about the raid."

"Was he also promised asylum in England?" Adrien asked.

Daylin nodded. "Aye, Adrien, as you instructed us, though it was scarcely necessary. He was afraid enough after he battled you this afternoon. He thought we had come to finish him off with all the methods of torture we could imagine."

"Was I right?" Adrien asked Daylin.

Daylin nodded after a moment. "So says this fellow. They rode with the troops in rebellion against Edward, and were told not to harm Simon, Count Montjoie. They were told to take their orders from him once the Countess d'Aville had been taken. They were to take no other prisoners."

"Aye, milord!" old Giles said, shaking his head sadly. "I had a bad feeling about it all, I did, but not even I imagined that young Simon might be involved in a plot against the countess!"

"Do we seize Simon now?" Daylin asked.

Adrien shook his head. "He assumes that the raiders from his failed plot have either fled or died. He'll not know that we suspect him, and he might try to get to Danielle once again. I'd like to know if King Jean is backing him or not, and that is something we might discover if we wait. Let him remain here as a guest—and witness the ceremony tonight. We do want all the witnesses we can have!" he added softly.

"Aye, Laird Adrien!" Daylin said, the sound of his voice suddenly passionate. "It is good, sir, to serve you once again!"

"Restored to good health in body and mind—passionate, cunning!" Richard added.

Adrien arched a brow, and Richard backed away a step. "Forgive me. It's been damned rough here at times, Adrien, what with the enemy all around, taking care at every word, watching the countess."

"Losing control of the countess," Daylin admitted sheepishly.

"Aye, we've needed you," Giles said. "Well and strong in spirit again, and that's what the lads mean."

Adrien smiled. "Thank you. I am here now, and my fellows, if passion and anger restore the spirit, then I am assuredly restored, and I thank you for your service and your great loyalty under the odds! Go now, to your leisure. You've nothing to do for the evening, other than to enjoy the meal—and the festivities."

"Shouldn't we be watching for the countess, for Simon—?" Daylin began to ask worriedly.

"Nay," Adrien said. "Not tonight, lads."

"But—" Richard said.

"I will be watching," Adrien told them. "Aye, I will be watching!"

By the late afternoon he had bathed and dressed for the evening, minus all armor and accoutrements of war other than his sword. He had been to see his prisoner himself, and to listen to the man's confession. He had assured the terrified man once again that no harm would befall him if he had confessed truthfully. When he was finished, Adrien was convinced that Simon had been involved with the planning of the event, and that he had been determined to spirit Danielle far away. He had come chillingly close. Whether Danielle was completely innocent or not, he did not know. But that afternoon, she had fled like a demon to the cottage, and when she hadn't known who he was, she had fought him desperately enough in the woods to convince any man that she faced an enemy. But then again, maybe she had known who he was; she had always considered *him* to be an enemy . . .

How could she have known at this point? He had been gone too many years; she'd had her freedom far too long.

He had arranged for the ceremony to take place in the chapel at the west wall at sunset. Father Josef, the plump priest here, was a Gascon brought in by Edward when Danielle had come to England years before. He was still very loyal to the English king, or so Giles had assured Adrien. Among his men was a young scholar who had studied for the priesthood before being drawn back to secular life at his older brother's death, and Adrien was certain that Darin would warn him if anything was amiss in the ceremony. Despite his promise to give his bride time, he would be much happier when the night's legalities at least were completed.

With that thought in mind, he came to the keep, leaving the great hall to the bustle of servants who prepared for the wedding feast to follow the ceremony, and walked up the stairs. He stopped by his own room briefly for a package sent by Joan, Prince Edward's wife, as a gift to his bride. He knew its contents—a sheer white nightdress of the softest spun silk. Hardly useful under the circumstances, but . . .

He strode the distance to her door, the door to the master's chambers, at the end of the hallway. Somewhat immersed in thought, he didn't knock, but pressed open the door before calling her name. "Danielle—"

He broke off. She was seated in a wooden hip tub, elegantly carved, secured with gold-plated steel bands. It stood close to her fire, and she had apparently been quite comfortable in it. Her hair had been washed, and she had combed it out wet, and it now lay with its great length damp and falling back over the rim of the tub and onto the white fur pelt that stretched out behind it.

She was outraged to see him, hugging her knees quickly to her chest as her green eyes sizzled a gemlike stare upon him. "I had not thought Scotland to rival Gascony in many matters of courtesy, but I had believed that men all across the Christian world were chivalrous enough to knock before opening doors to the domains of others."

"The domain is mine," he informed her curtly.

"Mine—"

"Mine. I am letting you borrow it—for the *time* being," he reminded her.

She was hugging her knees more tightly to her, but she

couldn't hide the long elegance of her legs, or the full swell of her breasts.

He wished he'd knocked. His groin ached; he was rising like a banner.

And he had promised her time . . .

"Adrien, please, what are you doing here?" she cried out, and he was perversely pleased to have her as unnerved as he was.

He walked to her bed with its rich canopy and tapestried spread. He drew open the leather satchel, displaying the beautiful, sheer garment beneath. Her eyes lit upon it, her breath caught.

"A gift from the Princess of Wales, Edward's wife Joan, Fair Maid of Kent," he told her curtly. Then he tossed a small glass vial of dark fluid upon the bed. "A *gift* from me as well."

"Which is . . . ?" she questioned warily.

"Chicken blood."

She stared at him blankly.

"To be dotted upon the bed," he told her, "before morning comes."

Crimson flooded every visible inch of her, enhancing the emerald of her eyes and shimmering blue-black beauty of her hair. "Thank you," she managed to say coolly. "Now, my laird, if you please? My water grows cold."

He meant to walk out of the door; he didn't quite manage to do so. He strode to the tub, and down upon one knee by her side. The ache to reach out and stroke the ivory clarity of her flesh was almost unbearable.

The ache in his groin was worse. In God's name, if he didn't get the hell out quickly . . .

"Adrien, get out!" The tension in his features must have been a warning to her, for she amended the command quickly. "Please, get out!"

But he didn't. He reached out, stroking a drop of water from her upper arm, becoming aware that she was trembling where she sat like a cornered rabbit. "I promised to give you time. I never promised to stay out of the master's chambers, or to pretend that I didn't gain a wife along with Aville."

Despite her discomfort and unease, her eyes narrowed sharply. "Aville remains mine."

"You gain more than I do as it is, Countess. I become count here, but you, milady, are now marrying an earl."

She stared at him boldly. "You are only an earl because Edward gave you the title when *I* agreed to become betrothed to you."

"Countess, anything I have gained from you, I have earned! I fear that I have had a much easier time of it dealing with armed enemies!"

She swallowed suddenly, eyes closing briefly, and he was stricken with the misery that seemed to fill her. "Adrien, I am not stone, not a wall, not a fortress or a keep! You have spun my world around in a matter of hours, and now you taunt me here. You find fault with me, while considering me to be nothing more than the woman who came along with the fortress. Well, sir, quite bluntly, it was my understanding that while you were mourning Joanna, you bedded half the women in England, Scotland, and the Continent. Forgive me if I—who have done nothing but listen to poets and musicians—bear a certain reticence regarding you!"

He hadn't wanted to smile, and certainly did not give in, for at that moment, he would have traded every title and all the land he owned just to possess her. But though she quivered beneath his eyes, she hadn't lost a bit of her own fire, and though he was determined not to retreat quickly and at her command, he had decided that he would leave. He arched a brow to her. *"Half* of the women in all Scotland, England, and the Continent? Surely not!" He rose then and walked to the door. He frowned as he turned back to her. "Surely, it was not more than . . . a *third?"* He exited, closing the door behind him quickly. Just as he had suspected, something slammed against it. The soap, he imagined. He opened the door again quickly, just peeking his head in. "Be ready with those vows, Countess. Dusk falls within the hour. I will await you in the hall, and we'll go to the chapel together."

She swore, and threw a shoe next. It had lain a little distance from the tub and she'd had to reach to get it, displaying the full, firm, roundness of her breasts. Her nipples were tantalizingly large, rouge, and pebble-tipped. From the water growing cold, he wondered?

He closed the door again before the shoe could hit him and he leaned against it, listening to her swear at him.

Ah, well, she could curse him no more than he could curse himself. She still had her time.

And he had a raw, hungry agony twisting through him, haunting him, tormenting him.

He left the doorway and hurried downstairs, staring into the fire there. Rem came upon him, offering him another goblet of their finest wine. He thanked Rem, and drank deeply.

A while later, he was aware that she had come down the stairs. She had dressed in elegant blue for the night. The soft sleeves of her undergown fell in long folds down her arms; the royal blue of her tunic, richly embroidered with blue thread at the bodice, hugged her breasts, then fell in a soft flow as well. A veil of blue mist swept down over her hair from a gold filigree headpiece, beautiful in its simplicity.

She didn't look his way, but strode toward the table—where the wine waited. She poured herself a goblet, drank down the contents quickly, and poured another. He watched as she swallowed that one down and began to pour a third. He strode across the room to her, taking the carafe and the goblet from her and setting them down firmly.

"Just how drunk, milady, do you feel you need to be to take these vows?"

"Very," she assured him solemnly, reaching for her goblet again. He held it away from her.

"Alas! I'm afraid I cannot allow you to fall flat on your face in the middle of the proceedings."

"One more!" she whispered, and added with both dignity and disdain, "I have been drinking this wine all my life. I fear that I could not possibly drink enough to fall flat on my face."

"Let's take no chances, eh?" he suggested. Holding her arm, he spun her around, walking with her from the hall.

"Most brides demand some ceremony with such an affair. A gown, a jewel, flowers."

"Most brides intend to sleep with their husbands," he reminded her politely.

"Who will act as my guardian here?" she asked quickly, swiftly veering from the dangerous path she had taken.

"Doctor Coutin, in the name of Edward III."

They had come out of the hall. Out of the courtyard, Danielle's people waited—carpenters, masons, farmers, maids, men-at-arms and their ladies. A cheer went up, and flowers were thrown.

All the flowers Danielle might have wanted.

She had been bred and raised to her station, Adrien was glad to see, for she instinctively responded to those who had given her their fealty, taking flowers from little barefoot girls, thanking her well-wishers sincerely. They reached the chapel where Doctor Coutin took her hand to walk her to the altar where Father Josef waited. The wine, he thought, had helped her; her eyes were glazed. When they fell upon her cousin Simon, who stood as tense as steel in a side pew with Lady Jeanette, Monteine, and others of the household, her lashes fell.

But not before Adrien had seen her gaze of abject misery. A scalding streak of jealousy ripped through him. Simon would quickly come to his reckoning. As to Danielle, if she had betrayed him . . .

Father Josef was droning on. Doctor Coutin said all the proper words on the king's behalf. Adrien gave his vows quickly.

Danielle seemed to choke over each word she said.

But it didn't matter; she spoke her vows, and without coercion, and in front of a goodly number of witnesses. The ceremony ended; Father Josef instructed him to take his bride in a kiss.

It was all that he was going to get. And Simon was watching. Adrien wanted the Frenchman to see that he was well aware of his wife's attributes.

He drew her into his arms, cupped her nape with his hand, and forced her mouth to surrender to his. His mouth crushed down upon her lips and parted them. His tongue thrust within and he tasted the sweet mint she had chewed. Her fingers clasped the loose sleeves of the shirt he wore beneath his tunic,

hard, protesting. He didn't ease his hold, or his kiss, raking her
mouth again and again with his tongue, exploring, delving
deeper and deeper into the sweet, seductive warmth of the kiss
she had not chosen to give. She was fire in his arms, angry,
and wild, agonizingly sweet to touch and taste, to hold and
crush against him. To feel. Her hair cascaded like black silk
over his fingers, entangling them, like the softest ebony
webs . . .

When he released her, she staggered and nearly fell. Her
eyes were brilliantly green as they clashed with his, offering
a furious reproach as he steadied her. She gasped for breath;
her lips were damp, swollen.

He wanted her all the more . . .

But the two of them were suddenly parted as well-wishers
sprang forward. Monteine and Lady Jeanette kissed him, his
men rushed forward to pummel his back or shake his hand.
From the corner of his eye, he could see that Danielle fared
much the same—his knights, her men-at-arms. Others rushed
forward, all offering brief kisses on the cheeks, a few on the
lips.

Then there was Simon. The crush in the church had taken
Adrien far from Danielle, but he was close enough to see
Simon take her into his arms. And he saw the way Simon
kissed her . . .

It wasn't as long as his first kiss for his bride, perhaps not
as dramatic or passionate, but it was too damned intimate.
Adrien felt as if all the fires of hell arose within him. He wanted
to kill the Frenchman.

Before he could reach Danielle again, the two had parted.
But he had seen them talking, whispering words they had not
wanted others to hear.

Just what were they planning?

Simon disappeared into the crowded courtyard when Adrien
came to claim his bride, pale now as she accepted the hand he
offered her to return to the hall. She didn't glance his way as
they walked together.

The great table had been set to accommodate the crowd,
with an ell added to each side. He took his place with Danielle

at the head of it while his men and her ladies were seated according to their rank and position. A musician already played a lute in the center created by the ells of the two added tables. Food, elegantly displayed, was set out in abundance—peacocks with their feathers spread, pheasant and other fowl, a huge boar with his lips formed into a snarl, a multitude of fish, fresh water eels, deer.

At his side, Danielle sat, pale and still. She didn't touch a bite; she barely sipped her wine. She seemed glad not to have to speak to him since they were continually approached by those who wished them God's blessing and a fertile union.

The hour grew late. Danielle leapt up at last, spinning around to tell him softly, "My lord, this contest, like all others, has been yours. I am in agony. My head is splitting. I must go to bed. To—to sleep."

He rose with her. "I have not taken this contest, my lady. It is scarcely a draw. Since you are intending to go to bed— to sleep." She ignored him and turned to leave. Apparently, she hadn't attended many weddings because she seemed truly stunned when she discovered that her ladies had been waiting for her to rise. They captured her arms to lead her, laughing and shouting, up the stairs. A few moments later he found himself so taken by his men, and brought upstairs to his guest chamber where they stripped him and decked him in a fur-lined robe before rushing him on to the master's chamber to meet his bride.

Her flesh seemed as white as the sheer fabric that barely covered her. The nightdress was elegant in itself but upon her, it all but had life of its own. Sweeping, soft, hugging her breasts, clinging to her hips, leaving just a hint of the rouge of her nipples, the raven's silk of the black triangle at the apex of her thighs. Her hair was free, brushed to an exotic gloss, spilling over the snow white gown and her own ashen countenance.

She had surely brought an ache to the groin of every able-bodied man in the room.

Including Simon. Indeed, the wretch was there, in the crowd, a forced smile upon his lips, anger in his eyes.

A wild cheer went up as Adrien and Danielle were thrown

together. He swept his cumbersome robe around them both, fighting the intoxication of the feel of her soft flesh and the fullness of her breasts as he shouted out, "Enough, friends! Leave us be now!"

"To bed, to bed!" called a drunken knight.

"Out!" he commanded again, and good-naturedly, the knight gave way, turning with a groan to exit the bedchamber. The others began to follow him, until one by one, the merrymakers were gone.

The door shut behind them.

Danielle slipped from his hold instantly, hurrying across the room to hug her arms against her chest as she stared back at him with wild eyes. "I fulfilled my part of this!" she whispered huskily. "Please, Adrien, now you keep your promise. Go!"

For a moment, he could not. The fire added to the see-through quality of the gown.

Tears touched her eyes. "Adrien, you promised!"

For a moment, she sounded like the child he had once protected. He believed in her innocence.

He bowed deeply to her, pretending that she wasn't awakening every bit of desire in his system. "Good night then, my lady wife."

He strode to the door, saw to it that the hall had emptied, and left her room, slipping quickly into his own. There, he ground his temple between his fists and swore loudly, damning himself.

If she hadn't been so naive, so frightened, so innocent! If he hadn't seen the dampness in her eyes . . .

He swore again, grabbed a carafe of wine, and sat before the fire, not bothering with a goblet at all.

He longed for sleep and he knew it would not come. Next best, he longed for a drunken stupor.

But neither would that come.

And still, he should have been sleeping long before he heard the creak in the hallway, and then the hushed whispering by her door. He bolted up, listening. The whispering had gone silent. Her door had opened, and closed . . .

* * *

"Danielle! Danni, quick!"

She had nearly dozed when she heard the whisper. She knew it was Simon, and she leapt up, her heart thundering in fear.

He had been so wretched at the wedding, in anguish when he had kissed her and wished her well, vowing his undying love for her once again. She hadn't been able to stand his pain, and found herself telling him that although she had agreed to marry, she was not going to be a wife in truth.

She should never, never have whispered such a thing, she realized, because Simon was here now. At her door.

She leapt up and opened it as quickly as possible, anxious to shush him even as she desperately prayed that Adrien had not been aroused. Simon stood in the hall, his sword belted to his waist, his eyes warily on the door to the guest chamber down the hall. He strode into Danielle's room before she could stop him.

"Simon—!"

He brought a finger to his lips as he looked about, striding to the bed and drawing the draperies from it. He sighed with relief when he realized they were really alone.

"Simon, you've got to get out of here!" she said desperately.

"Danielle, we cannot let this happen," he told her urgently. "If your marriage has not been consummated, we can still do something to annul it. We'll go now. I'll take you to King Jean—he'll manage something. We will have Aville back, we'll—"

"Simon, hush! For the love of God, hush! I have always honored my mother's family, but Aville is a part of Edward's holdings! Don't you understand? Most of the people here are very loyal to him—they know what happened the last time they fought him. They need the English here, they need the trade, the income from the alliance. Simon—"

"Oh, God, Danielle, but I love you!" He suddenly sounded as if he was choking. And just as suddenly, she found herself caught up in his arms, crushed in his embrace. His lips were warm and pressing upon hers and his hands . . . his hands were on her arms, her shoulders, her breasts, gliding over the sheer fabric of the white bridal nightdress. She tried to twist from his kiss, both stunned and afraid.

"Simon . . ." she protested against his lips.

Just as the door flew open.

Simon had not heeded her warning, but now he spun away from her, drawing his sword with lightning speed.

Adrien had come. He was still clad in nothing but the fur-trimmed robe—and naked steel, for he, too, carried his sword. His eyes were fire, his features as hard and cold as ice.

"If you touch my wife again, Comte, I will cut your foolish head from your body," he advised calmly.

"The lady has been meant for me!" Simon cried out and lunged for Adrien.

"No!" Danielle shrieked, jumping forward, foolishly hoping to come between them. Adrien caught her by the arm and sent her flying back out of the line of their battle. She fell against the wall near the hearth, slipping down to the floor. Dazed, she struggled to her feet, desperate to stop the men somehow.

But the battle was frighteningly brief. There was but one clash of steel, and then Simon's sword clattered from his hand and skidded across the floor to the open doors.

Heavy footsteps were heard in the hall as two of Adrien's men came hurrying to find out what was causing the noise. Adrien clutched Simon by his sleeve, dragging him out to the hall.

Danielle found her feet and came racing after him, terrified for Simon and desperate to explain to Adrien that nothing had happened. But as she reached Adrien, she saw the extent of his anger. Tension blazed from every muscle, as well as from the glittering gold of his eyes. Still she dared to touch his shoulder, but he didn't seem to feel it. She gripped his arm hard, tugging until he turned to face her at last.

"Adrien, please, you have to listen—"

"I'll deal with you, madam, when I've done with your lover," he snapped.

"Wait, Adrien—" she began, but could say nothing more.

He caught her mercilessly by both shoulders and thrust her back into the room.

She felt his eyes, hard with fury. She moistened her lips, knowing that she had to plead now and plead eloquently if she was to save Simon. But before she could move or speak, he slammed the door in her face.

Chapter 12

She'd been insane, she thought, trying to reach him. She spun from the door, staring into the fire as she felt the chill of fear sweep around her. What was she going to do? She needed time to think, to get a hold upon her fear.

No! No! What she needed to do was to pray that the door would remain closed upon her forever, that the miracle of an escape would suddenly show itself . . .

What a coward she was! What about Simon? She had to help him.

But the door had barely closed before it thundered open again. Her hand flew to her chest, as if trying to still her heart from beating itself to death.

Hands on hips, he filled the doorway. She stared at him for what seemed an eternity, and yet no time at all. He strode into the room, slamming the door behind him with a vengeance.

Simon! she reminded herself.

"What—what have you done?" she demanded, trying to remain still and straight, to keep her voice strong and a pretense of courage about her. "What are you—going to do?" Despite herself, she faltered.

"I should kill you!" he hissed softly, his voice disturbingly quiet. "Wrap my fingers around your neck and strangle you. But then, I would cost myself a wife. At the very least, I should beat you until you scream for mercy."

"I'm not afraid of you!" she told him, eyes narrowing. But she *was* afraid; her heart still hammered and she could scarcely draw breath. "You'll not threaten me, and you will answer me! What have you done to Simon? If you've harmed him—"

She broke off because he was striding toward her with such swift menace that she couldn't move until he was almost upon her. A gasp tore from her throat and she tried to run. She hadn't a prayer. His fingers curled into her hair and over her arm and he wrenched her back around to face him with such a force that she lost her breath. Both his hands fell tight upon her shoulders as he snapped her straight. Her head fell back, her eyes rose to meet his, and she wanted to cower despite all her most stalwart pretenses. She had never seen him so angry, not even that day in the woods when he had been convinced she had nearly killed him by loosening the girth on his saddle.

She didn't know whether to scream or weep. His fingers were brutal. "Let go of me!" she cried out, trying with all her strength to wrench free. "Arrogant, domineering, wretched, grasping Englishman!"

"Scotsman," was his brief reply. He lifted her from her feet and threw her down upon the bed. Her sheer silk nightdress snagged beneath her. Her legs were bared, she was naked from the waist down. Delicate ties had broken at the bodice, exposing her breasts. Winded, she gasped for breath and tried to rise, tried to hold the flimsy fabric together. She made it up to her elbows, but then fell back and met the dark fury of his features. A wild panic seized her. He remained far more than half naked himself, for the fur-trimmed robe had fallen open and she was painfully aware of the many things she had noted about him before; the bronzed strength of his shoulders and arms, the expanse of his chest, the hard, lean contours of his belly. She was painfully aware of what she had not noted before as well: the shaft of his sex rose long and hard against her flesh. She drew her eyes back to his as he leaned over her. She tried swiftly and desperately to shove against him, but he moved so

quickly, with such raw fury, that he seemed completely heedless
of her. She felt his hand upon the slim length of her legs. He
caught her knees, parted them, and eased his weight between
them. She tried again to strike out. The fingers of his left hand
vised around her wrists, pinning them just above her head. The
fingers of his right hand lightly brushed her cheek, his knuckles
stroked down her throat, over the bared mount of her breast.
She inhaled raggedly, afraid, yet achingly aware of that touch.
Desperate to fight it for the alarming sensation it aroused.

His eyes, alight with a shimmering glitter of pure flame, tore
into hers.

"Poor, bloody, sweet innocent!" he hissed. "Time! Give
you time! Time to welcome your French lover to your room
just feet away from my own door!"

"You're wrong!" she cried. "You don't understand—"

"I full well understand his hands upon your breast, his lips
upon your mouth. I wasn't the one to plead *time* because of
any innocence!"

"God, I could kill you!" he cried furiously. "Nothing wrong
with his lips devouring you?"

"I tell you, you mustn't hurt him. I swear, you don't understand—"

"No. *You* don't understand!" he told her flatly, and any
further words she might have spoken were swept away as she
cried out, stunned. His free hand had swept lower, over her
belly, onto her mount. Between her thighs, touching, stroking,
probing . . . a violent shiver seized her as she felt the tremendous intimacy of his touch. It seemed that something like fire
burned there now. And she knew his intent.

"Wait!" she gasped, straining to free herself, but his grip
upon her wrists was merciless, the bulk of his body far too
hard and heavy to budge. His face was suddenly very close to
hers, his eyes all but scorching her. His taunting whisper was
almost a caress against her lips. "Wait?" he inquired. "For
that French bastard to come before me again?"

"No—" she protested with a strangled scream, for he had
meant then to wait for nothing. The fullness of his sex thrust
into her like a knife. The pain seemed to sear through her body.

She shuddered with it and surged against him, insane to free herself from the invasion, but she managed only to wrap herself more fully around him. To bring him more completely inside her, to a point where he would split her in twain. It didn't occur to her that he had driven very hard and then gone dead still—until she realized that her hands were free. They lay upon his shoulders as her nails curled into his flesh.

His fingers wove into the hair at her nape. His eyes blazed into hers. "Sweet Jesu!" he exclaimed softly. It seemed that surprise had caused his anger to ease, just when she was longing to strangle him.

"Adrien!" she gasped, barely keeping the word from being a sob, longing to plead with him but not allowing herself the luxury of begging any small mercy.

"I cannot go back," he said flatly.

She opened her lips to speak; they were caught by his. His kiss all but consumed her. His tongue swept, hard and passionately, deep into her mouth, her throat. Molten steel rushed throughout her limbs, radiating from between her thighs. She could hear or feel the pulse of his heart, or hers, and it was as if drums pounded in her head. She could not twist away, only feel, and the intimate sensations were both brutal and oddly delicious, mesmerizing, so engulfing that he was moving again before she realized it. Searing sensation remained; the agony faded. His lips parted from hers, touched them again. His hand stroked her cheek, her breast. A whisper of tantalizing flame licked over her, inside her, a hint of something mercurial and as excruciatingly sweet as the pain had been intense. She could not fight him; she could only cling to him, ride out the wildness of the storm, and feel strange whispers of promised pleasure within the red mist that had been pain. She became increasingly aware of him, the corded muscles of his body straining, the fluid movement of him, hard, graceful, reckless, relentless . . . swift . . . plunging into her again and again until she was all but numbed. She gripped his shoulders as if she held on for life, and burrowed her face into his neck. The whole of his body gave a massive shudder; he held taut and still above her, then moved once again, a groan tearing from his lips as a tidal wave of liquid fire washed from his body into hers.

She felt a trembling deep inside her. She wanted with all her heart to throw him off, free herself of the invasion, and yet she wanted to touch the satin sheen of his rippling flesh, to feel his kiss again. She wanted to run away as far as she could get. But she realized she would never escape the longing to feel him again, touch him, have him demand so much from her . . .

He had gone still, but he had not withdrawn. She closed her eyes, silent for once, and fought the tears that sprang beneath her lids.

"Look at me," he commanded.

She wanted to do anything but.

But knowing him, she was afraid he would pry open her eyelids to have his way. She opened her eyes defiantly and found him staring down intently at her once again.

"You're killing me!" she charged him in a furious, accusing whisper.

To her amazement, he suddenly smiled. "You won't die," he told her. "But I might well have killed you had I stepped into this room a minute later!"

"You are still mistaken, you bastard Englis—Scotsman!" she seethed, willing herself not to cry. "You must realize that Simon and I weren't *lovers*—"

"But what might have been?" he demanded harshly. "It is difficult to feel guilt about taking your wife's innocence too recklessly when she is pleading for another man. Thank God, milady, you did not become lovers. At least now I don't feel quite so tempted to strangle you."

"Or beat me?"

"It's quite legal by *French* law for a man to beat his wife," he reminded her. "That is a matter I may well muse on for a while . . ."

She gritted her teeth, trying to shove against him. He caught her hands. His words had been spoken lightly enough, but his eyes narrowed in warning. "As I said, Countess, had I come in but a few moments later—"

"You would have found me alone!" she interrupted. "I'd not have allowed things to go further under the circumstances."

"Under the circumstances that I arrived here today?"

"Under the circumstances that I did not, nor did I ever intend to, betray the betrothal," she said. "Which I'm quite sure you have done on many an occasion!"

He smiled again. "I am a decade older than you, milady. And I fear I was not destined to live as a monk."

"Perhaps I was not destined to live as a nun!"

His smile faded and she was deeply sorry she had spoken.

"You should thank God then, Danielle, that you have chosen to do so until now!" he warned.

She felt her cheeks go pale, and once again, she longed with all her heart to throw him from her. It was intolerable that she had to remain caught beneath him after an act of such intimacy. He was so heedless of his nakedness beneath the robe, of his sprawl atop her. She felt the heat where his body touched her, felt the coolness of the air where it did not. A massive wealth of tears rose behind her eyes once again and she fought them furiously. She could not help but think of all the chivalrous, romantic tales she had read. Simon had loved her. Other men had been enamored of her. But she was married to Adrien, and her wedding night had become an explosion of fury, a familiar stranger sprawled atop her. His was a warrior's body, a knight's form, sharpened and honed to perfection like the blade he carried, magnificent in some ways . . . imprisoning in others!

She swallowed hard, blinking back the tears. "You promised me time. You . . . you had no right!"

He rolled to her side at last, then rose, his robe still about him yet open as he walked to the fire, hunched down, and sparked the flame with an iron poker. Danielle tried to fold the remnants of her nightdress about her, inching back on the pillows as he stood again, staring into the flames. "I had every right," he told her flatly.

"But you had promised—"

"Time. But time ran out this evening when I discovered that your lover—all right, your very close male friend-nearly-lover!—was guilty of treachery in more ways than one. And

I warned you, Danielle. I warned you long ago that I would give no quarter if you did not keep your word of honor.''

"But—"

"Danielle, you little fool! Didn't it occur to you that it was strange your *friend* was so determined to have a hunt on the same day that raiders rode down upon you?"

She gasped, sitting up to stare at him, forgetting her dishevelment. "You're wrong! Simon wouldn't have tricked me so—"

"Simon did trick you so."

"How can you be so certain?"

"Because I sent Daylin and your own Ragnor back to find the raider I battled in the woods. He was half dead and in agony. In exchange for Doctor Coutin's care and the chance to live, he was more than willing to tell us what we wished to know."

"If you tortured a confession out of the fellow—"

"Madame, I tell you in truth—I have never tortured a soul upon this earth."

She bit into her lower lip. "Other than me!"

His brow rose, his lip curved into a slight smile.

"What did you do with Simon?" she asked him.

He was still for so long that her deepest fear rose to her breast. Terrified that he had summarily executed the Frenchman, she found herself leaping from the bed. Scarcely aware of the soreness that still wracked her body, she catapulted for him. Her fingers wound into fists and she slammed them against his chest. "Damn you, Adrien—"

He caught her wrists, and her eyes widened as he dragged her hard against him. She had attacked with an insane aggression. Now she was on the defensive, painfully aware of him again. The thick, crisp auburn hair upon his chest teased her breasts. The tautness of his belly and hips ground against her. The hardness grew palpably against her even as she stood crushed against him, her cheeks flaming, her eyes as wide and glistening as those of a doe caught in firelight.

"Adrien—" she began, moistening her lips.

His eyes impaled her. "Simon is alive," he told her angrily.

"But you plan on slaying him—"

"An execution might be in order."

"Because he was my friend—"

"Because he meant to kidnap you from Aville, enjoy the very delights you have discovered tonight, rape you if you didn't come willingly into his arms, and bring you and Aville over to the domain of Jean of France. Ah, not so horrid a thought! Is that what you are thinking, milady?"

"Adrien, stop it! You judge without proof—"

"Proof! Do you think me a fool?"

"Perhaps he loved me, wanted me! You mustn't judge Simon so harshly—"

"Damn you!" he roared with such anger that she fell silent. His voice shook as he warned, "Milady, common sense should warn you that for his sake as well as your own, you should keep Simon out of this bedroom for the rest of the night."

"But you must tell me—"

"You must let it suffice to know that I have not skewered him through with my sword. Sweet Jesu, don't press this further or I might be tempted to run out and do just that!"

She kept quiet, afraid he might carry out his threat. They were married, and he had caught Simon with his hands on her in their bedroom. Any man would say that he had a right to his fury.

He did not release her. She knew that she dared not mention Simon's name again. She stared up at Adrien finding it difficult to breathe, wishing to be left alone to gather back some shreds of dignity. She inched her chin up and told him, "You have bested Si—your adversary, and you have had your vengeance upon me. Please, I beg you, if you would just please go now . . . ?" she whispered.

"Vengeance?" he inquired, and seemed amused once again. "Any bride spends a night such as this!"

"Nay, sir! You know that you owe me an apology—"

"Never, milady, will I apologize for making love to my own wife!" he told her, eyes narrowed, a spark of warning to his voice.

Her lashes lowered. "You didn't—make love. You were furious."

"For that, Danielle, I am sorry. But it is done now, and perhaps it is well that this all came to so explosive a point, for I was not pleased with your arrangement."

"I was not pleased with your demands, nor the king's!"

"Ah, but I am delighted that the king's pleasure and mine coincide so completely!" he assured her. He suddenly swept her up and into his arms and she gasped, palms pressing against his chest once again as he carried her back to the bed. He laid her down upon it and tiny flames leaped through her as she felt the golden heat of his eyes once again, and knew his intent.

"Adrien, please—" she protested on a broken whisper. "This is—agony."

"Nay, milady, it will not be so again. Don't seek to dissuade me—I will not be dissuaded. But this time, Danielle, I will make love, I will strive to be gentle, tender but passionate . . . perfect," he promised very softly. A deft movement with his hands split what remained of her silk gown, and she felt a whisper of cool air sweep over her body. She twisted her head to the side, wishing she could curl away from the man who now lay by her side, propped up on an elbow. "Lie still!" he whispered.

"I—cannot."

"Ah, Danielle!" he said, his voice still soft, and oddly whimsical. "You—who do not surrender! Do you beg mercy of me now?"

Aye! the word shrieked within her mind. But he was only teasing her, taunting. He would not let her go tonight. She knew that full well.

Her head snapped back. Her eyes met his. "Never. Damn you!" she cried.

He smiled. His hand cupped her cheek, his lips found hers once again. She wouldn't allow the kiss, she determined. She would refuse to succumb to his demand.

But his kiss didn't demand. His lips just feathered over hers, the tip of his tongue teased as lightly as a butterfly's wing. She gasped for a breath while her heart beat in fury. Only then did his mouth cover hers, sensually, the stroke of his tongue filling her mouth slowly.

His hand moved . . . over her breast, cupping and cradling the weight of it. He massaged her nipple with his palm. Amazingly, she felt that touch like a streak of lightning all the way inside her, and down . . . down to a deep warmth that now began to spread with a-strange, exotic sense of urgency between her thighs. She tried to stir again, to turn from him. His lips broke from hers. His weight shifted down her body. His mouth closed over her breast, his tongue stroking the nipple. She swallowed back a cry, her fingers falling into his hair, tugging upon it. He could not be budged, and the sweeping sensations began to swirl, hot and honeyed throughout her. Dear God, but she would fight them—she would not fall prey to this knight who had ridden back into her life only to seize upon everything . . .

Even upon her heart.

''Nay!'' she cried out, but he would not be stopped. His body eased further down upon hers. She tried to escape him by inching upward, yet only managed to serve his purpose once again, for now his gold and auburn head lay at the juncture of her thighs, parted by his weight and body, and she was powerless to stop him when his most intimate kiss came even there—slow, lazy, relentless. Excruciating. Touching, tasting, exploring . . .

A cry escaped her lips. She twisted, writhed, swore, threatened, and gasped. She shoved his shoulders, tore at his hair. Then, with another gasp, she ceased to fight, stunned by the sensations overwhelming her. Then she gasped out a ragged breath and began writhing, undulating, her fingers tearing into the bedcovers. Sweet hunger raged through her, soaring, eclipsing all but an aching desire to fulfil the erotic promise that licked and teased at her, flesh and soul. She strained against him, felt the hot, wet sensation that at last exploded into an anguished pleasure that shot through her again and again until she thought she would die.

Then he was atop her and within her again. She could bear no more, she thought, pleasure or pain. Tears stung her eyes as she braced against him stiffly, alarmed by the volatile ecstasy that had burst upon her.

"Hold me, lady. By God, cease to fight me, cease to fight me!"

His arms were around her as he moved within her again. He was slow, careful. Waiting. She felt no pain at all. The sweetness, the hunger that she had thought so sated, grew once again. She didn't want to allow it; she writhed to avoid his thrust, but she couldn't fight the onslaught of longing. Incredulously, she realized that she was rising to meet him, to feel him deeper and deeper inside herself . . .

The magic began, the liquid fire starting where his body joined so intimately with hers and sweeping through the length of her again. She clung to him as he had commanded, gasping for each breath. Slowly, his rhythm grew faster, harder. His pace built, his thrusts deepened, and he began to move like the winds of a winter storm. He held her firmly to his desire, stroking the swiftly rising fire he had created within her. He swept into her as fiercely as a tempest, and the spiral of desire rose and rose until she was crying out, desperate to reach that sweet intoxication once again.

The sensation burst within her. All of her body seemed touched by the violent explosion. She shuddered and shuddered again, barely aware of him as the world seemed to shatter to a velvety blackness scattered with stars. Tiny convulsions rippled through her again and again while she pressed her face hard against his slick, muscled chest, fingers digging into his arms.

Then she was aware of her own breath. Of him sliding away from her. The pleasure had been all but unbearable. It left her shaken.

Afraid. Embarrassed.

"Danielle?" He reached for her, drawing her against him. He had the strength to do so, no matter how she stiffened at his touch. She kept her head bowed and her lashes down. She was surprised and unnerved by the tenderness in his touch as he smoothed back her hair.

"Was it agony?" he asked.

"No," she admitted curtly.

"Ah. Well, then—was it wonderful beyond all words?"

"No!" she cried out, lying with deep mortification.

But his husky laughter assured her that he knew she had suffered no pain.

"Alas, I fear I have failed you. But you needn't fret. I shall simply have to keep trying until I get things . . . perfect."

She met his eyes in alarm. "You've not failed me in any way. You were—stupendous!" she snapped out.

But he smiled again, lowering his head to hers. "You are too kind, and I am so very delighted. You will therefore not mind the act of consummation once again!"

She groaned softly, too dazed to find any way to win against him tonight. She was alarmed at how quickly she had fallen prey to him. Not to his strength, which she could not best, but to his powers of seduction and persuasion. She had never imagined feeling this . . . this passion, this desperate longing.

"If you would only let me be!" she whispered. "I tell you, I cannot, I cannot move, I cannot feel, I cannot—" She paused, aware that he was staring at her, waiting. "I cannot do this thing again!"

He didn't laugh. He was very serious, his knuckles brushing her cheeks. His lip curled just slightly. "And I tell you, my lady, you can, and you will. I am still seeking to be perfect."

"You have been perfect enough."

"Alas, you fight me so, it's hard to tell."

"Surely, no knight has ever been more perfect."

"What sweet flattery! If only there was a touch of truth behind it!"

"Adrien, I swear—"

"Nay, lady, *I* swear. You are my wife, you can and will make love with me yet again. When tonight is over, you will never forget that we are legally wed, before God, and man and wife in all ways. I'll not let you protest . . ."

* * *

When dawn broke, she slept at last. And in the end, he'd had his way, as usual.

She'd not managed a single protest.

Nor would she ever, ever forget that she was married, nor her first night as Laird MacLachlan's bride.

Chapter 13

When Danielle awoke, she did so from a deep fog. Colors around her seemed muted. She could only half open her eyes and she was only aware of things very close to her—the sheets beneath her, her pillow, the fast-fading trail of light that caught dust motes in the air above the bed as it reflected from the archer's slit across the room.

She shifted, and found the simple movement difficult, shifted again, and realized she was sore from head to toe. The night came blazing back at her then, waking her fully, snapping her mercilessly from the fog. She ignored her aches and leapt out of bed, then streaked across the room for water to douse her face, then her body. She nearly dumped the entire pitcher and bowl atop herself, then stood shivering in the room, for the fire was dying. After a moment, she started back to life again as she wondered just how late it was. Shadows should be filling the corners of the room once again, *and just where was Adrien and what had he done with poor Simon?*

She frantically dragged clothing from her trunk and dressed, then started to comb out her hair but gave up when she found that her fingers were shaking and her hair was in a hopeless mass of tangles. She threw her comb down with an oath, turned to leave, but hesitated, her eyes on her bed. The covers and sheets were twisted and tangled, nearly wrenched from the bed. They carried proof that her marriage had been consummated, and not from chicken blood. Her fingers wound into her palms and she felt herself trembling again and longing to shake Adrien until he begged for mercy. Once he had allowed Edward to seize Aville. Now, he had laid claim to the fortress. And to her.

And he had Simon. At his mercy.

She hurried from her room and down the stairs to the great hall. Rem was there, aligning goblets and trenchers upon the table. There were far fewer than there had been last night, for now that their wedding feast had been celebrated, only the immediate household—increased somewhat by Adrien's arrival—would dine in the hall. "My lady!" he said and beamed with pleasure as he saw her. He was a gentle man, tall and very slim, sometimes appearing to be little more than a long bag of bones. She'd known him all her life, and he seemed as much a part of Aville as the stones of its walls.

"We were not to disturb you," he told her. "The earl is not due to return until dusk, but my lady, you must be hungry. May I get you something to eat?"

"No, thank you, I'm not hungry. Rem, can you tell me where Laird MacLachlan has gone?"

"To the field with the men. They are at archery practice."

"Thank you, Rem," she said, and turned to leave him. She hurried out into the courtyard and saw that the gates were open, the bridge down. Her people were busy about their lives again— craftsmen at their stalls, young girls watching flocks of squabbling ducks, housemaids carrying wine pails, coopers at their crafts. She was greeted with calls of "Milady!" as she passed through, a number of bows, and, she thought, smiles, for everyone seemed to want to grin at the mere thought of a wedding night. She gritted her teeth, acknowledging the greetings with nods and smiles.

She strode into the stables, telling the young groom who

dropped his hay-spreading task to serve her that she could fend for herself. She didn't take time to bother with a saddle. She slipped a bridle over Star's nose, looped her gown so that she could leap up on the mare astride, and rode out of the stable quickly. A guard from atop the parapet called out to her, but she ignored him, riding hard across the field where targets were kept for archery practice.

Horses grazed at a distance from the men, who were aligned on foot. Daylin stood at one end of the grouping next to Ragnor, while Adrien strode along the list of men, dropping a word here or there, a suggestion, a comment. He came to a youth who had missed the center of the target entirely. The young man apologized profusely for his error, but Adrien clapped him upon the back and warned, "Steady nerves are needed here, lad. Pay no heed to what is around you, keep your eye firm upon the target, so." He took the long bow from the man, deftly drew an arrow, paused a split second, and let the missile fly.

To Danielle's great irritation, the arrow found its mark with exacting precision. Adrien returned the bow to the youth and ordered him to try again, warning him to concentrate.

The arrow found its mark and cheers went up among the men.

Amidst the noise, Adrien turned and saw her. His features were unfathomable, his gold gaze dispassionate, but she was certain he was annoyed she had come here. He called to Daylin, who then saw Danielle as well, nodded, and called out to the next man to draw his bow. Adrien strode to Danielle, reaching up without pause to draw her down from Star.

"It's not proper for you to be riding bareback and astride," he told her irritably.

"I ride so frequently."

"Not, milady, in the future."

She was beginning to wish she had not come; she felt flushed at his nearness. She eased a foot away from him, stroked Star's nose, not looking at him, and said with quiet determination,

"You will not walk into my life after such an absence, sir, and think to instruct me *in your ways* at this late date!"

"Nay, Thibald!" Daylin was crying to one of the young men of Aville. " 'Tis like the earl said, lad, concentration!"

Without really thinking—just determined to put some distance between herself and Adrien for a moment's respite—Danielle started forward to the line.

"Danielle! Get back here, you could be hurt!" Adrien called after her, but she ignored him and came to Thibald, taking his long bow and an arrow just as Adrien had done moments before with the other young man. "I agree that it's in the concentration, Thibald," she told him. "In battle, you cannot be aware of the confusion around you, only of your target." She prayed she would not falter as she studied her target, then let her arrow fly. God was with her! Her arrow arced and flew beautifully. But then, she had studied in the household of a king's son, with the finest masters available. She felt a satisfied smile curl her lips as her arrow struck the target with the same precision as Adrien's. The men applauded her. She smiled and thanked them, twisting about to acknowledge each man, pausing when she saw that Adrien watched her with his arms folded across his chest and no look of surprise. He had expected her to hit the target with perfect aim, and had merely waited impatiently for her to perform before the men.

"A contest!" someone cried out suddenly. "A contest between our lord and lady!"

He hadn't been expecting that! Danielle thought with pleasure, and he didn't seem pleased with the prospect. But to her surprise, he shrugged, unfolded his arms, and came forward, accepting a bow and a quiver of arrows from Daylin while more arrows were brought forward for Danielle. Men sprang forward to clear the target, using a small piece of charcoal to narrow in smaller segments for a contest between such experienced contestants. Then Adrien and Danielle stood side by side, close, as the others retreated.

"Begin!" Richard Huntington called cheerfully, having determined he was the master of the game.

Danielle looked to Adrien. He bowed slightly to her. "Ladies first. Though, under the circumstances,'' he added quite softly, ''I do use the term quite generously.''

She smiled, ignoring the taunt, and took aim with her first arrow. It fell very close to the dead center of the target and she was immediately cheered.

''What a wondrous accomplishment for a wife!'' Adrien said, drawing his bow, taking aim himself. ''Imagine, had you been born a poor peasant lass, your husband might have come in from a wretched day in the fields seeking his supper, but alas! He would find his good wife ready to shoot arrows for him instead!''

''But, sir, I was not born poor, but rather to rule a castle. Which it appears I do well enough, for even in such a skill as this, I am your equal, sir.''

He let his arrow fly. Like hers, it landed almost dead center, just a breath from her own. Once again, the men cheered.

''Milady!'' Richard encouraged her.

She slipped an arrow from the quiver and drew her bow.

''Alas, milady,'' Adrien mused, ''born a rich countess, and still, born not to rule a castle, but serve the lord who, as destiny's son, was born to rule *her!*''

She let her arrow fly. To her own amazement, it struck the target between the arrows there already. Gasps were heard again; she had surprised even herself. It had been an incredible shot. Another round of cheers and applause went up, along with warnings to Adrien. ''Ah, milord! 'Tis impossible!''

Danielle smiled sweetly. ''Alas, milord. Whatever I was born, there is no lord alive who will rule me.''

He smiled slowly in return, gold eyes sparkling with fire. ''That's to be seen, isn't it, my love?'' he inquired politely. Then he raised his voice and cried out with assurance to his men, ''Nothing, my good fellows, is impossible!''

His eyes remained on Danielle while he drew his bow-string and set his arrow. Then he turned to the target.

Seconds seemed like eternity.

His arrow flew . . .

And split hers straight down the middle. Sir Richard cried

out in delight, other men rushed forward to stare at the target with disbelief.

Danielle didn't believe it herself, but as the others milled around, all staring at the target, she felt Adrien's smug and self-satisfied gaze upon her once again.

"So?" he said softly.

"So, milord," she replied politely, "had this been battle— and had you been my target—you'd not have been able to strike back, because it wouldn't have mattered that I had pierced your heart just a bit to the side of dead center!"

He was smiling, mockingly she thought. "I was not referring to the contest. I was wondering why you had come here. Did you miss me? Have I been gone too long from our marital bed?"

The blood drained from her face. "An eternity, my lord, would not be too long."

"Oh, milady! I don't suppose it would be chivalrous to denounce you as a complete liar—"

"What has ever been chivalrous in your manner to me?" she cried.

"Indeed! Fine. Then, my lady, you are a liar."

"Adrien, for the love of God, I demand to know what you have done with Simon!"

"Ah!" He arched a brow, studying her, a smile playing at the corner of his lip once again. "Simon . . . ah, yes! Simon, the young man guilty of plotting treason against King Edward whom I discovered fondling my all-but-naked bride last night, right?"

"Damn you, Adrien, he isn't English, so his plotting against an English king would not be treason."

"So he did plot to seize Edward's holdings?"

"I did not say that! Adrien, you will tell me, now!"

The smile faded from his lips and his gaze was sharp. "Perhaps, lady, you should quit making demands. I've not forgotten how I discovered the two of you together. You might want to beg my forgiveness and mercy for the event—for, I assure you, young Simon was quick to do so."

She paled still further. "What—what did you do to him?"

"Nothing, my lady. Nothing at all. I needed to do nothing for him to realize that he must beg my pardon, and beg for his life as well."

He turned away from her, striding for Star. When he reached the mare, he threw the reins over the horse's neck and gave her a swat on the rump, sending her to race home across the field. Close on Adrien's heels, Danielle demanded, "Why did you do that? Am I to walk home? Is that some bizarre punishment?"

He wheeled on her. "Punishment? Nay, lady. I've missed you in the few short hours we've been apart, and would have you ride with me, that is all."

"Don't mock me, Adrien, you've not missed me at all, you've been playing war games. You don't intend to let me ride astride Star—that is all!"

He didn't respond, but called out to his men. "Lads, we've finished here for the day—darkness comes quickly!" He whistled and his well-trained mount—Matthew today—obediently trotted toward him. He set Danielle atop the animal's back quickly, then leapt up behind her. She sat as stiffly as stone, gritting her teeth against the constricting feel of the arms that came around her. He nudged his mount with his heels, and they moved ahead of the others at a slow lope. Night was indeed coming quickly. The very last pale pink rays of the sun rested on the stone walls, and the castle of Aville shone as if it were created of marble.

Adrien reined Matthew to a walk. Danielle was startled when he spoke to her, his voice surprisingly husky and soft. "It is always to be a contest, then, milady? If so, remember, you have long been forewarned. Take care, for I do not lose in battle or in games."

"But I very nearly won," she told him. "And you should take care as well, milord, for I do not give in, in life or in games."

"Whether you admit defeat or not, Danielle, I am the victor."

She sighed softly. "Do you speak of the archery contest—or Aville? Is there no state of compromise?"

"Compromise!" he repeated, and laughed. "With you, my

love? I doubt it,. But at least you've quit haunting me regarding your—friend. You enjoy a fight, because you're always determined you'll win. You've forgotten Simon again—as you did in the thrill of nearly besting me at archery.''

She hadn't realized that she had leaned against him until she stiffened angrily, trying to sit straight and away from him. He laughed, and drew her back.

''Adrien, no more games—''

''All right,'' he said flatly, ''no more games. Your Simon is a wealthy man. I have sent him with an escort to Prince Edward, who will see to it that he is sent to England and held for ransom.''

''But—''

''He remains in full possession of his head, heart, limbs, and so on, if that is your next question.''

''Adrien—''

''That will be enough on Simon,'' he said firmly.

She bit into her lower lip, and remained silent. When they returned to the hall, she fled from him as soon as he had eased her to the ground. She hurried on into the keep, restless and unnerved and anxious to accept the wine Rem offered her as she entered the great hall.

Within minutes, Adrien entered behind her, followed by his close retainers. It seemed to add insult to injury to see that her own companions, Lady Jeanette and Monteine, entered into the hall with Adrien's newly arrived men, chatting and laughing.

Danielle hadn't eaten in so long that the wine seemed to bypass her stomach and soar straight to her head and swim there as Adrien took his place beside her and the meal progressed. His men spoke glowingly of their astonishment that she should be such an accomplished archer. She tried to respond to their compliments, to eat, to forget the feel of Adrien so close beside her, but she could not forget. This had been her hall, and he was making it his. As soon as the meal ended, she escaped upstairs.

Her room had been cleaned. The fire burned brightly; fresh,

cool linen sheets lay on the bed. She paced before the fire, watching the door. Adrien didn't come.

At last, she undressed and dug through her belongings until she could find the least alluring nightdress she had, a linen shift with full, long sleeves and a high throat, fine for cold nights. She stumbled into the gown, afraid that Adrien would come while she dressed. He did not.

At length, exhausted, she crawled into bed. She would never sleep, she thought.

She dozed almost immediately.

She awoke with a start to find gold eyes burning into her own. The breadth of his bare shoulders glistened in the firelight as he straddled her, watching her intently.

"Don't fight me at every turn!" he warned. "I have no wish to cause you pain, but I will hurt you if you do."

She felt hot tears burn behind her eyes. She was tired, the world seemed blurry; the entire room shimmered with the gold of the fire, and of his eyes.

"Perhaps, my lord, I will hurt *you*," she said stubbornly.

"Don't fight me," he said again.

"I cannot help being what I am!" she whispered.

"Cease to hate me, then."

"I don't hate you," she admitted on a strangled breath.

She was startled by the tender smile that curled his lip. "Ah! With such sweet words of encouragement, lady, I could fall forever beneath your gentle spell!"

"Adrien—" she began, protesting the mockery.

But his smile faded; he mocked her no more. "No contests, no battles tonight!" he said, and she wasn't sure if he demanded, or perhaps pleaded, that it might be so.

It didn't matter. She was in no mood for battle herself. And when his lips touched hers, she felt the warmth of them spread throughout her, and she longed for the feel of him. She might have been wearing armor rather than the linen gown, and it wouldn't have mattered in the least. Her clothing was too quickly shed . . .

Without a fight.

* * *

In the days that followed, Adrien spent the vast majority of his time in the field.

She often watched from the parapets as the men practiced with various weapons—swords, lances, maces, battle axes, and even crossbows. The crossbows had evolved into very powerful weapons that needed windlasses with pulleys and cords to bend them, and still, a bowman had to have a great deal of strength. The men trained to use them were well aware that the power of their weapons came with a danger—they had a much slower rate of fire than the longbow. Each crossbowman was joined by a second as he practiced his particular art of war, and the second man's function was merely to carry a large shield to protect them both while reloading. Adrien, she knew from listening to the men talk, was intensely concerned that all men under his command be aware of the importance of the shield-bearers. Military strategists across Europe had determined that the renowned Genoese crossbowmen had failed so miserably at Crécy, falling to the English, because their shields had been left behind.

Men always trained; in feudal society, the men who lived off the land or within the village owed their lord a certain amount of service, just as the lord—or lady—owed her people protection. And seeking to make their fortunes, young men often worked very hard, but seldom with such vigor as they worked now. At first, after the incident at the archery field and the very sore point between them regarding Simon, Danielle determined to keep clear of Adrien. She watched the men from a distance. But her curiosity was growing, as was her unease.

Adrien had chosen to keep his own distance from her—during daylight hours. He was already up and about in the morning when she awoke. He spent the day with his men, with the smiths and sometimes the masons. When it was dark he came into the great hall for supper, and though he was as courteous to her as any code of chivalry might require, he also managed to avoid her questions. He was usually called out of the hall once again on business after the meal, perhaps to see to a lame destrier, the care of weapons, the smith's work. She tried several times to wait up for him, but once he came to her at night, he had no patience for her questions, and whether she had been awake or asleep, the nights ended the same. If she managed to remain awake, she tried very hard to talk, but his eyes would be like the hungry, yellow-gold eyes of a wolf, and he too quickly silenced her. If she slept when he came, she would never have the chance to voice her questions at all, because he would arouse her as he woke her with the most gentle touches, feather-like strokes with his fingertips, a whisper of sensation against her until she became aware she was in his arms, thoroughly seduced before the conscious desire to protest could slip into her mind. The one time she managed to lie awake and demand to know his real and immediate purpose in Aville, he answered with a sigh and a note of impatience. "Danielle, what purpose? It was time that we should marry, time that I should claim Aville."

"There was no reason to claim Aville. I made no trouble for Edward."

"You entertained his enemies."

"His enemies remain my family."

"Then it was time to claim you."

"Aville remains mine, and my family remains welcome here."

He was instantly over her, eyes glowing with anger in the firelight. "Will you entertain them all as you did Simon?"

Her lashes swept her cheeks. Mention of Simon's name was enough to ignite his temper, which in turn enraged Danielle, since Adrien had done whatever he damn well pleased during the years of his absence. "Adrien, many a young woman might have forgotten a coerced vow such as I made, and embraced a French lord. If you look at the situation through my eyes, I owed nothing to a man I had not seen in years!"

"But you have seen me now," he reminded her.

"And if Simon were free, he'd visit us both as well!" she declared fiercely.

"Leave be with the mention of Simon!" he warned.

"You brought up the name, milord."

He eased away from her, left the bed, and walked across to the arrow slit. Suddenly chilled in the expanse of the bed, she pulled the covers over her and watched the way the light played on his muscles. He seemed to glow in copper and bronze, from the richness of his hair down to the power of his thighs and calves. She hugged her knees to her chest, furious that her heart was thundering. She admitted then, to herself, that he was an extraordinary knight, sculpted to perfection. If he were never to demand her touch again, she would be in anguish. But even as he stood there, thinking thoughts he'd no desire to share with her, she wondered if he wasn't pondering what his marriage might have been had only Joanna lived—sweet, beautiful, docile in every way, and on his side in every venture. He had loved Joanna. He would not have deserted her with every dawn, and come back only in the darkness of the night. And he would have talked to her, shared his world with her . . .

He turned suddenly, found her watching him. His features were dark and hard and brooding, and he scowled. "Danielle, it's late. Go to sleep."

"Go to sleep!" she repeated. "Do you think you can dictate to me regarding everything? You do, you think you're king, that you can walk in, seize all that you see! Well, sir, I am not to be claimed! I am not—"

She gasped, rigid as stone, for he moved back across the room as swiftly as a cat in the night. He crawled in beside her, sweeping her into his embrace, his arms warm as he pulled her down on her pillow. "Fine, milady, as you wish it, as you will. Lie awake. Don't sleep. But if you're not tired enough to sleep perhaps . . ."

"I am exhausted!" she cried.

He laughed, and his arms remained tightly around her as he cradled her against him. "Sleep then," he told her. "I am weary of battle."

"How amazing, for you seek it constantly."

"*I* seek it? You, my love, would fight me unto death!"

"I am honest with you! While you—"

"Grow weary. This fight may go on, lady, if it must, but at another time!"

She didn't reply. She remained still, barely breathing, feeling the warmth of his body against her own.

And she was both amazed and alarmed by the simple pleasure she felt when his arms were so comfortably, so naturally, around her. He held her determinedly against him as she closed her eyes. She breathed in the masculine scent of him, and lay secure.

But once again, he'd told her nothing . . .

Chapter 14

The next day she determined to try to listen to the men during the sessions. They practiced with their swords in the courtyard, and she found endless reasons to pass them by—at a safe distance, so she thought. But Adrien was well aware that she was watching him. As she crossed the courtyard with a book of Latin poems to return to the chapel—it being perhaps the sixth time she had managed to pass by the men—she was stopped. She was amazed to find that Adrien had quite suddenly sprung before her, his exceptionally fine sword, fashioned in Toledo, in his hand—the point of it aimed at her throat. For a moment, alarm swept through her, then anger, and she lifted her chin furiously. "What is this new game, milord?"

He didn't answer her, but spoke to the assembled men. "My good fellows, I'm quite certain my lady has kept quiet out of courtesy to me, lord of the fortress here, her mentor in all things, but since she has watched these proceedings so determinedly, I am certain she finds something amiss in the training." He smiled, gold eyes gleaming. The point of his sword moved with absolute precision, clipping one tiny hook from her bodice.

She swung around. "Indeed, sirs! The Earl of Glenwood is

woefully remiss, for he teaches you to threaten an unarmed lady!''

"Aye, milady!" came a cry.

"He's a knave!" offered Daylin, teasingly. "Take him, milady!" Daylin tossed her his sword. She swept it up deftly and swung on Adrien, grateful that Daylin's weapon was a good one—he was, after all, one of her husband's right-hand men. Yet again, Daylin's weapon would serve her well, for it had been fashioned for a lighter man, and was not so heavy as Adrien's Toledo steel.

She saw the light in Adrien's eyes, and knew he had carefully provoked this battle. She had fallen prey to his challenge just as he had planned. No matter. She was ready for it. She held perfectly still and calm, forcing him to take the offensive. He played without his full strength, she knew well, but again, she had learned her early lessons in the household of a prince, and she was good with a sword. "Don't be frightened by massive, unwieldy bulk and strengh!" she called to the men, ducking and spinning and slipping with an agile bound upon a water trough to avoid one of Adrien's blows.

"Unwieldy?" He paused, indignant.

"Graceless!" she said, wrinkling her nose.

"Ah!" To her alarm, he was too quickly upon the trough beside her. She leapt down again, parrying blow after blow as he stalked her with single purpose. She managed to spin around behind him, rolling beneath his form and sword, but he was too quickly back around to face her. With a lightning-quick flick of her sword, she caught his cheek, drawing a tiny drop of blood. A cheer went up along with good-natured laughter among the men. Adrien's gold-glowing eyes touched hers, and he smiled slowly himself. "Well done," he applauded.

She inclined her head graciously. "Speed can take down the strongest man!" she said.

"Alas, but strength can and will take down the swiftest woman!" he replied. He struck a blow, one that seemed nothing but a silver flash in the air. The strength behind it was such that her weapon was wrenched from her hands.

And she knew. He had played with her all the while.

But she had put up a damned good fight.

"I could have beaten most men," she told him very softly.

"Most men, not me," he replied.

"There is a little blood on your cheek."

"Only because I allowed it."

"It is only a little blood because I did not choose to draw more," she informed him.

He arched a brow; she decided to make a speedy exit. She spun around and collected her book from the man who had taken it from her. "Good day, good effort!" she called to the men, and they chorused "Milady!" as she passed them by, head high, as she hurried for the chapel.

The following morning, she woke to the strange sound of explosions. She jumped out of bed, grabbing only her sheet, to race to the archer's slit and look to the courtyard below. A crowd had gathered, but nothing seemed to be amiss. Danielle could see Adrien's red-gold head below her. He was casually dressed in shirt, short tunic, and form-hugging breeches, so he had not yet gotten ready for the grueling cavalry training he had planned for the day. For the moment, it seemed the men were at play. Adrien was handling a long stick, which he aimed toward a target set upon the wall. He carried a wick from which a little spark of fire seemed to glow, and he set it against the stick. Once again, the sound of an explosion seemed to shatter all around them. Danielle jumped back, gasping. Adrien looked up and saw her there, and grinned. Devilishly, she thought. "Come down!" he told her. Then, "Never mind—I'll come up."

A bit breathlessly, she backed away from the window. She made a dash for a trunk, but had just begun to choose clothing when he came into the room. The still-smoking stick was in his hand, a contraption partially made of wood and partially of metal.

"It's a gun," he told her, and his smile remained devilish. "Come closer. Come see."

She'd heard of such things—they far predated her birth. She'd even seen huge iron balls and cannons made of metal, but she'd never seen anything at all like this very small weapon.

Curious she came forward, studying the creation in his hand. "Made by one of your own blacksmiths," he said.

"Timothy? He's very inventive. He's been working on cannons to be set upon parapets near the drawbridge," she said.

"And working hard with gunpowder."

"Four parts saltpeter, one part carbon, one part sulphur," she said by rote.

"Umm," he murmured. "I should have known you'd be well-versed in weaponry. One day, I imagine, such little creations will make mockery of all our armor, the plates and the mail, and no man's skill will matter against such a force. At the moment, however, any weapon which requires gunpowder for its use remains volatile and dangerous."

"Were you thinking about taking these—into battle?" she asked.

"Ah! You are interested in my battle plans, aren't you?" he said softly. The gun had ceased to smoke and he set it down upon the table.

"What an amazing comment from a man who has managed to evade my every question."

"I don't evade. I'm not ready to discuss the matter."

"If you're going to show me a weapon, I am naturally going to ask you about it."

"Umm," he murmured. "Indeed, it is volatile and dangerous—but no more than you, my love, I do imagine."

"And what does that mean?" she inquired. He sat upon the bed and she found herself drawing the sheet more tightly around her shoulders. He laughed, leaned down upon an elbow, and patted the space before him. "Come here, and I'll show you."

"It's morning," she said indignantly. "And very—light."

"The light is something I'll enjoy. Come!" he grinned. "Your master has summoned, my lady wife. Alas! There are parts within him which most earnestly desire your presence!"

There was a wicked gleam in his eyes as he teased her. He knew that she could not bear such references. "Dear Master!" she taunted in return. "Be advised regarding just what you should do with wayward parts!" She turned regally, heading for the door, wondering if she dared stalk out into the hall clad in a sheet.

But she was certain she would not reach the hall, and she did not. In seconds he had swept her up, and the wild feel of tension and heat in his touch and gaze were enough to awaken the fires within her. She found herself back beside him on the bed, shivering as he unwrapped the folds of the sheet. She felt suddenly shy despite her nights of marriage, for brilliant streaks of daylight poured in upon her flesh. She stared up at him, then closed her eyes as she felt the seductive brush of his fingers sweep over her. Other than quivering, she lay perfectly still. He ceased to touch her. After a moment, she opened her eyes. He smiled suddenly. "Danielle, it occurs to me that you are not at all disturbed by actually making love—you are merely appalled that you may be forced to admit that you enjoy it."

"Oh!" she gasped, and slammed against his chest, furious now that he lay against her fully clothed while she felt so vulnerable and naked beneath the casual splay of his leg and arm. She shoved against him but his grin deepened, and she tried again to strike out. He caught her wrists and lay more fully atop her. "Volatile, and dangerous," he teased.

"Very!" she promised.

"Ah, then let the danger come!" he whispered softly. "I am willing to risk it for the wealth of fire and beauty that come as its fair price!"

Again, just as her fury crested, he had spoken soft words that somehow tempered and twisted the emotion. His hold upon her eased—he kissed her forehead, her throat, and at last, her lips. He fumbled swiftly with his breeches, and she was speared with sudden, searing heat just as his tongue delved deep into her mouth. Daylight rippled all around them, and she thought that he was right; she didn't find him a monster, did not at all despise his touch . . . only her own swift reaction to it. Yet that morning when their passion had been sated, she lay awake beside him as she seldom did at night, and realized that her feeling for him was becoming more intense. She was far too glad of him beside her in what had been her bed. She was fascinated when she lay against his chest and felt his heartbeat, the deep sound of his breathing. She loved his warmth, the feel of his bare flesh against her, his arms around her, or a leg draped here, a hand lain there, while they slept. Adrien had never left her unaffected. Once upon a time, she had convinced herself she hated him deeply; she could want him just as passionately now.

He had married her because the king had commanded it. He had achieved greater power and a higher title, she reminded herself. And she should not become too enamored of his presence because he would ride away again to honor his obligations to the liege lord who had given him such riches—through her.

She felt his eyes upon her as she lay against him. His arm looped possessively about her waist. He rose on an elbow and stared down at her with a curious glitter in his eyes. "Ah, Danielle, what I would not give to read that ever-calculating mind of yours!"

She tried to roll away from him, but he held her tight. She tried then to pry his arm away, but he did not intend to budge. When she heard his soft laughter, she ceased her efforts and stiffened indignantly.

"What would you give? A fortune in gold? A county, your earldom? One of your horses, perhaps?"

"One of my horses? Matthew, Mark, Luke, or John? Why, never, lady—they serve so well!"

"And each of them is of more importance than one wife who is not so well-trained and cannot be ridden so well?"

"On the contrary, lady, you are beyond a doubt the best ride a lord could desire."

She colored from head to toe—that hadn't been at all what she had meant, but leave it to him to twist her words! She tried again to escape him, but failed in her efforts, other than to amuse him. She lowered her head and bit hard into one of his restraining hands, and was satisfied to hear a sharp cry of surprise. She started to smile, but her smile faded and her teeth eased their hold when his palm landed with a firm crack upon her bare backside. She shoved at him with such force and fury that he actually gave ground to her, falling to his back as she crawled atop him. "How dare you, how dare you!" she raged, only to discover him laughing again, reaching for her. She very, very quickly discovered her mistake, for he rose slightly and quickly and she was impaled upon him, captured in a glorious new rise of passion as his hands held her hips and guided them. Swift shudders riddled through her. She closed her eyes, seeking to fight the hunger that swirled within her with each rise and plunge, but then she was drawn down, rolled beneath him. He withdrew from her and she was stunned, left aching, yet her desire burned ever brighter as he captured her mouth, her throat, her breasts with his lips and tongue and the erotic brush of his teeth. He moved against her, the caress of his lips and fingers brushing ever lower against her body, creating a maelstrom within her. His touch became achingly intimate until she shrieked out. He rose above her, and the second he swept within her again, it seemed as if the world ignited and exploded with force of gunpowder, and only the stars left to twinkle down upon her.

The sensation ebbed. He eased his weight from her. She felt the coolness of the room and realized how easily she had been seduced, how very much she wanted him. She swung her legs over the bed, ready to bolt from it, needing to escape him. But again, his hand was on her arm, drawing her back down, and his features were duly puzzled when he leaned over her and demanded, ''What in God's name have I done now?''

''Other than being a tyrant?'' she inquired stubbornly.

''Other than!''

Her lashes fell. ''Adrien, will you just let me be? Please, you may feel free to gloat alone. You have won again. You never lose, in battle or game!''

She didn't open her eyes; she felt him watching her as long moments passed, then felt him rise. He adjusted his clothing. She heard him take the gun and stride to the door. But curiously, he paused there. ''Ah, but my lady, you are so mistaken. I have been nearly bested now so many times in these skirmishes that I am left all but defenseless!''

She opened her eyes with surprise, twisting to see him go. But it was too late. He had uttered his strange words, then departed swiftly and silently, and all that she could do was lie there and ponder them . . .

That afternoon, the men practiced out in the field again, this time on horseback with blunted lances against *quintains,* pivoted arms with targets on one end and weights on the opposite ends. When a man rode and struck at the target with his lance, he had to duck quickly—or be unseated by the force of the weighted arm. From the parapets, Danielle watched as Adrien shouted out orders, as the men laughed when one of their number failed, as Adrien saw to it that the man tried again and again, until he triumphed over the quintain. Even as they remained at their practice, she saw a group of four armed knights moving in upon the field from the southern road, their leader carrying the banner of the noble they served—Edward, Prince of Wales. The horsemen approached Adrien and he accepted a sealed document from the man with the banner.

Far across the field, Adrien looked up, as if some instinct had warned him that she was watching. Despite the distance, she was certain she could feel the fire of his eyes. At last, he turned. Her breath caught, and she realized that he had indeed been in such rigorous training for a reason. The letter had been a summons. He had known damned well that it would come. He might have come here to claim her, but he had also come to create a larger fighting force with the men from Aville. He intended to bring her people with him to do battle for the English prince.

She hurried from the parapets and rushed back to the keep. In the hall she told Rem that she had suddenly been taken very ill, that she could not come down to dinner that evening. She fled from the hall.

She was not going to dine with any representatives from Edward, and she didn't give a damn if Adrien was humiliated by her absence or not. She didn't trust herself to try to speak with him in front of others tonight.

Monteine came, and seemed to believe that she was ill, she was so pale. She rubbed oil into Danielle's forehead, ordered a steaming bath, washed her hair with rosewater. Danielle thanked her, then asked to be left to sleep and told Monteine that she must inform Adrien that she had a devastating headache and would not be down.

Darkness fell. She sat in a chair before the hearth, watched the flames, and hated him for taking her people away to fight and possibly die for Edward, the King of England. He had no right to do so! Gain their trust, and pit them in battle against the house of Valois. He had come just to leave, just to take her people, while making sure that he left a strong enough English force behind to assure that there would be no action against English rule in Gascony here.

Her temper flamed with the heat of the fire. After a while she rose and paced in front of the hearth, and it was then that the door opened and closed so softly that she didn't hear it, didn't hear him as he came into the room and watched her pace like a cat.

She turned at last and froze as she saw him there, his features rugged and tense, eyes narrowed and angry. "You don't appear to be ill—my love."

"Oh, but you're mistaken. I swear that I am sick. Sick to death of treacherous Scotsmen!"

"There has never been anything treacherous about me, Danielle. I am sworn to Edward III of England, in the service of the Prince of Wales."

"And you don't care if you rip France to pieces in his service!"

"Hardly France. We battle those who rebelled."

"All this time, you have known that you would come, take what you wanted, and leave! You have forced men into your service, and you haven't given a damn where their own loyalties might lie!"

"I'm their count, lord here, and their loyalty is to me."

"They are *my* people."

"And you are my wife, and damn you, lady, but your loyalty is to me as well!"

"You have no right—"

"The campaign will not be long."

"Pray God that it may last forever!"

His eyes narrowed. "Pray God, lady, that I do not fall, for the prince, though he loves you like a brother, so he tells me, does not trust you. If you are left a widow, there might be dire consequences indeed, my lady."

"Dire consequences, indeed, for by God, I'll not be a pawn to the dictates of your kind any longer! I would place my fate in my own hands, and perhaps it is you, sir, who should pray God, because you are mistaken. Aville is mine, and I may not be here if and when you return!"

They were the wrong words. She instantly regretted them, and her reckless fury, for he stared at her with such icy anger that her breath caught. He strode for her then with movements so swift and menacing that she cried out even before he reached her. His fingers gripped brutally into her arms and he shook her, forcing her head to fall back, her eyes to meet his.

"Ah, Danielle!" he warned, voice deep, shaking, and it seemed he waged an awful battle with himself not to strangle her. "You have just sealed your fate!"

She gasped as he spun around with her, lifting her, tossing her down upon the bed. She sprang up quickly, gasping for air again, tears springing to her eyes. She would fight him. God, yes, tonight, she would not be seduced! She would hate him with her very last breath.

But he didn't intend to touch her again. He was already striding angrily from the room.

She had just sealed her fate . . .

She leapt up, running after him. The door slammed before she could reach it. She fell against it, but it would not give.

"Adrien!" she cried out, her voice rising in panic. "Adrien! Adrien, please . . ." she whispered.

But Adrien didn't hear her.

Adrien was gone.

She slammed her fists against the door. She called his name. She banged again, and again.

No one was coming. Ah, she was lady here! She had ruled wisely and well. But he had come. And he was lord. And those who had loved her so dearly now obeyed and honored him.

She kicked the door furiously. It shuddered, but did not budge. Her toe was in agony.

She began to pace, and time passed. She felt as if she walked the room forever, planning what she would say to him if he returned, then plunging into despair and fear again as she wondered just what he could do to her. Leave her locked here within these four walls for days, weeks, months? Have her sent to England, trussed and gagged?

The questions taunted her mercilessly, but at last, she wore herelf to exhaustion and she sat upon the rug before the fire, seeking warmth since she felt so very cold. She stretched out, laying her head down upon the soft white fur. She couldn't start crying. She wouldn't stop. And she couldn't admit that having to face the truth of Adrien's steadfast loyalty where Edward was concerned seemed all the more bitter because he had made her care.

She stared at the fire, and her eyes began to close.

When Adrian returned to the room, his heart first seemed to skip a beat, then stop, for she was not there. Not pacing, not on the bed, not in the chair, and not by any arrow slit, looking out into the freedom of the night. But then his eyes fell to the fur rug before the hearth, and he saw her there. He paused in the doorway, for the candles in the room had burned low in their brass holders, and the only light in came from the fire. The rug was white, her nightdress was white, and her hair was a contrast of striking sleek ebony against it, sweeping over her shoulders, tendrils falling over her hips and buttocks, long locks sweeping in waves over the fur itself. Time seemed to stand still, with only the crackling sound of the fire to surround him, its warmth to beckon to him. And Danielle . . .

He closed the door and came into the room, striding to the fire to stand over her, anguish seeming to rip through him from limbs and loin and heart into his soul. Sweet Jesu! He had not imagined this knifing turmoil when he had come here, that he could feel himself entangled into such knots with her, that the passion and anger and even tenderness she could evoke would rival any other emotion he'd ever felt. He had loved Joanna, but he had never felt this fever, never the haunting pain, and *damn* her, never the fear! Never before in his life had he remained in his great hall until no one else stirred, until even the wolves in the forest had fallen silent, staring into flames and wondering *just what in God's name to do.* Never.

He hunched down beside her, felt the tightening within, the pain of muscles clenching, the thunder of his heart. If she had tried to tempt him, had created some exotic fantasy, she could not have awakened a fiercer hunger and thirst and anguish than she did just by lying here, simply sleeping. The flames created a flickering light that delicately pierced the white linen of her gown, outlining her breasts and hips, dipping into the contours of her waist. Fabric fell from her right shoulder, baring perfect flesh all the way down to the mound of her breast, leaving just the hint of the rose-peaked nipple, inviting a man's touch. Strands of ebony hair were all that clothed her where the gown fell free. Where she had curled her knees up, the gown had fallen away as well. A wickedly long, shapely length of leg and thigh were visible, hauntingly seductive.

Raven-black lashes fell in a soft sweep over her cheeks, alabaster touched with gold in the firelight. He was not dismayed to want her the way he did, with all the fire and life within him. Fate had made her legally his wife. A night's treachery had made her so in all ways. The force of his own passions had made her his lover. He had buried Joanna and known nothing but guilt; he had come here thinking that he had buried emotion as well, that strength and power and *possessions* were what mattered in life now. He had meant to have her simply because she had been destined to be his. He had never realized that though he might take her, she would be the one to actually *have* him.

She called him a tyrant; he had commanded many things. He had touched her, touched her again . . . but it seemed that he could never touch deep within her. She remained his enemy, sworn to a vow made when she was a child far too young to know or understand . . .

Sworn against him.

But it couldn't be.

He reached out at last, smoothing a strand of hair from her

face. She awoke, her dark lashes rising above emerald eyes. She stared at him for a moment, then rose quickly to her knees, breathless suddenly as she sat back upon her heels, barely a foot from where he hunched down beside her.

"Adrien!" she whispered. Studying her, he realized that she was glad that he had come, that she had been awaiting him. Aye. She might not ever beg mercy, but tonight she probably meant to seduce him from his anger. She knew what he had the power to do, and she had hastily threatened him. She had to know that he might well send her to England as a prisoner.

He forced a wall to close around his heart. He could not be seduced.

"Come!" he told her suddenly, his voice so rough that for a moment, he saw a hint of alarm in her eyes. That was as it had to be. He caught her hands, and drew her heedlessly to her feet, and all but dragged her across the room. He paused just briefly to take one of her mantles from the hook by the door and sweep it around her.

"Adrien, what are you doing?" she demanded.

He didn't reply.

"This is insane!" she told him as he led her down the stairs. He still ignored her, his hold upon her implacable as he led her through the still and empty hall and out into the chill night air in the courtyard. She shivered fiercely. "Adrien! Damn you—!" she gasped, panting. She cried out suddenly, and he realized with a certain remorse that he had taken her out barefoot. But he couldn't stop, and he damned well couldn't afford to offer her apologies now. He lifted her up into his arms to continue his long strides toward the chapel. He paused for a moment to seize a torch from the outer wall before entering into the dark interior.

"Adrien, before God—" she protested.

"Indeed, lady, before God!" he agreed, setting her upon the ground once again. In the eerie light cast by the torch's wavering glow, statuary of virgins and saints seemed to move. Danielle pulled back, but he gripped her wrist more tightly, leading the way down to the altar, and then to the left of it, where a wide stairway led down to the crypt.

"Adrien!" she cried furiously, struggling fiercely to escape his hold. Her voice had a note of desperate pleading. He ignored it. The torch brightened the way as they moved into the cool, pitch-darkness of the crypt. Once there, he set the flaming torch into a niche in the wall, and it illuminated most of the realm of the dead.

The temperature here, deep in the earth, helped preserve the bodies. To one side lay the simple shelving where the dead nobility and gentry of Aville decayed slowly within their shrouds upon beds of stone and marble. Throughout the crypt were elegant tombs made for those who could afford them.

"Adrien!" she cried again, desperately trying to free herself. He let her go. To his amazement, she went tearing for the stairway to escape the crypt. He flew after her and captured her with an arm around her waist, spinning her back into the center of the crypt. He met her eyes. They were wild. To his amazement, he realized that he had inadvertently discovered his wife's Achilles' heel: she was afraid of the crypt, of the bodies in their shrouds. He hadn't meant to terrify her in such a way, but maybe it was best that she be terrified of something.

"You're afraid!"

"No . . ."

"Liar!"

"Why are we here?" she cried out.

"Why are you afraid?"

"I'm not!"

"Why, damn you!"

"I came after my mother died . . . the doors were closed by accident." She paused, moistening her lips. "I was locked in here in the dark for hours . . ."

"Ah," he murmured, and started to walk by her, deep in thought.

"Adrien, don't leave me, don't lock me in here!" she cried out.

He spun back to her. She was white as a sheet, her beautiful features fragile and delicate against the ebony of her hair and the green of her eyes. He didn't dare show her compassion, but he'd never had any intention of leaving her. He strode back to her, an arm around her waist, and she cried out as he drew her over to her mother's tomb, in the center of the crypt. She struggled against him again, slamming her fists wildly against his chest. "You will not leave me here—"

Once again, a wave of remorse swept over him as her head fell back. She tried so desperately, always, to hide her fear and emotion from him.

He shook her, determined to force her from the raging fear that had assailed her. "I've not come to leave you here!" he told her. "What kind of a monster do you think I am? Never mind!" he said wryly. "It is just that you are so damned fond of vows." He took her hand again. She resisted but he ignored her, laying her hand palm down, fingers splayed, upon her mother's tomb. "Here lies Lenore. Now, you'll give me a vow. Swear. Swear on her grave that you will not run from Aville while I am gone, that you will await me, your husband. Swear that you will not welcome my enemies, that you will hold this place in my name for its rightful overlord, Edward of England."

"Adrien . . ." she began in protest, but her voice was weak.

"Swear it!" he interrupted harshly.

"Oh, damn you! I swear it!" she cried at last. Then a sob suddenly shuddered through her and she cast her face against his chest, hiding from the scent and feel and touch of decay and death.

Sweet Jesu, but the little things that she could do! Had she held a knife against his throat, he would have forgotten and forgiven at that moment. He swept her up into his arms once again, grabbed the torch to lead the way up the steps, and carried her from the crypt. He strode swiftly from the chapel, fitting the torch back into the sconce on the wall outside it. He brought Danielle back across the courtyard once again. They entered the keep, and she still lay silent, curled within his arms as they crossed the hall and climbed the stairs. In their room he set her in one of the huge tapestried chairs before the fire. He poured wine from a carafe on a nearby table into a goblet and brought it to her. Her fingers closed around the goblet. "Sip it!" he commanded, and as she did so, he knelt upon one knee and took a small, very cold foot into his hands, rubbing it until the warmth of life seemed to sweep back into it again.

"How did you know?" she whispered to him suddenly. "How could you have known?"

He looked up at her, a small frown knitting his brow. "Know—what?" She didn't answer, but sipped the wine again, and he sighed softly. "Ah, that you were afraid of the crypt?"

Her lashes, lowered.

Afraid was not a word she liked, he thought, and he smiled. "I didn't know that you were *uneasy* in the crypt. Had I known, I wouldn't have brought you there."

"Really?" she asked, and she looked up frowning. Her eyes were so bright on his. Her lips were the color of a rose against the pale marble of her face. They trembled slightly as she spoke. "But what else might you have done to—"

"I don't know. I didn't know that I intended to force a vow from you until I came into this room," he admitted flatly.

She stared at him, sipped the wine once more, then passed the goblet to him. He took a long swallow himself, and was glad, for it did take away the chill of the night. "You did give me your word," he reminded her softly. "You made a vow."

She stood and walked across the room, hanging her mantle back on the hook, her head slightly bowed. She hesitated there, then walked back to the fire, staring into the flames before she turned back to him. "I gave my word," she admitted after a moment. "I'm not so very sure that you needed it. I threatened you because I was angry. But where would I have gone? What rebellion did I stir up before you came? What will be different here now when you leave?"

"Danielle, you did threaten me. There's the small matter of Simon, and indeed, if you desired, you could run to the French king."

"I love Aville. I was not a part of Simon's schemes, whether you believe me or not."

"Danielle, you threatened to be gone."

"I've never lied to you, in all these years. You know I cannot break a certain loyalty I feel I owe to the Valois kings of France! I have sworn to you that I will not leave, and that I

will hold Aville in your name for you and your king. I never
meant to threaten you. It's just that I am weary of this constant
tug of war—not just between you and me!—but between
Edward and the house of Valois, my countrymen against my
countrymen. So many dead on the battlefields, so many
wounded, maimed, dying cruel deaths long after the fights have
been waged. And you are to ride away . . .''

As her voice trailed off, she lifted her shoulders and turned
her back on him.

He strode across the room to her, spinning her around to
face him again. ''Could it be that you fear for me, milady?''
He couldn't quite keep the taunt from his voice, and he damned
himself for it.

She kept her head down and would not look at him.

''Perhaps I fear what will happen to me if you fall, and I
am left to the whim of kings once again. God knows what King
Edward might plan next. You have already warned me he
intends something dire.''

''But I never fall, lady, in battle or game or life.''

''No man is immune—you said so yourself when you were
showing me the gun.''

''I said that one day gunpowder might well make all our
armor, chain and plate, obsolete. That lies far in the future,
lady. Far beyond any battles here. And at this point, we are
doing nothing but retaliating against those who cruelly raided
Edward's territory. I am not at great risk—other than that risk
which threatens me here.''

''How can I threaten you?'' she whispered.

''You hold yourself, and Aville.''

''Even if you were to lose both, what difference would it
make? You are the Earl of Glenwood, laird in your far northern
country. You have come here by order of the king—''

''I have come here because you and Aville are mine, and
because I give up nothing that is mine,'' he told her.

''Then you have it, for fair or foul. You have wrenched your
promises of Aville—and myself!—from me!''

The argument could go on, he thought, circles within circles.

She had made a promise to him, but she had made the deathbed vow to her mother as well, and no words he could say now would change her mind. The night was slipping away. The dawn would come so quickly. Despite the tenseness in her body he engulfed her in his arms, drawing her closely against him, chin atop her head as he whispered "And once again, Countess, you have gained freedom. The fortress is yours once again, and yours alone, from the great walls surrounding it to this room and the bed within it."

"Held in your name!" she reminded him, her words muffled against his chest, and he didn't know if there was a bitter twist to them or not.

"Held in my name!" he agreed, then shuddered fiercely as he held her. "But by God, lady, I am not gone as yet!" He fell to his knees there upon the fur before the fire, bearing her down with him. He caught the sweetness of her lips, easing her down upon the softness that seemed to engulf them both, along with the red-gold heat of the fire. The shining ebony darkness of her hair splayed out over the whiteness of the fur, entangling him as he held and caressed her, his love-making passionate, aggressive. Slender, silken fingers touched his cheeks, dug into his shoulders, stroked over his back. Her lips, liquid, her tongue, a touch of fire, brushed his flesh. Climax threatened him; he withdrew from her and began again, lips upon hers, down the length of her body, intimate, mercurial. He spread her thighs, his caress still slow, merciless. He heard her whispers, heard her cry his name, he felt her touch, and knew that it would never leave his heart. He came to her again at last, and the world exploded into shimmering flames, his body searing into hers. He eased from her, savoring her beauty upon the fur, and when her eyes touched his again, he took her into his arms. "Hold all in my name!" he warned her vehemently. She didn't reply, but curled against him, and as the fire continued to lap and burn its golden, warming glow, they slept.

* * *

When Danielle awoke, the fire had all but died. She shivered, but realized that the tapestry from the bed had been wrapped around her.

Still, the room seemed so chill, so empty.

And then she knew. Adrien was gone.

Chapter 15

The days seemed to pass peacefully enough at Aville. The circle of life turned, with peasants working the fields and tending their sheep and cattle and chickens while masons repaired walls. Women bore children, the old sickened and died, the sun rose in the morning and set at night.

But every time a traveler came by Aville, each time a pilgrim en route to a shrine, a juggler, a poet, a cleric, or other passed by, Danielle found herself in turmoil. The news visitors brought was alarming. Adrien had said that Prince Edward's forces were determined to put down rebellion in the English king's ducal lands. The situation seemed to be growing far worse. The English were amassing in great force. The French king meant to expel them. They didn't plan to leave.

Danielle had learned that war killed with more than weapons. Invading armies levelled crops and decimated livestock. Whether friend or foe, an army was deadly to the land. Men and horses needed to be fed. Strategically, armies often swept the land barren to see to it that their enemies starved. Sometimes, the victors of a battle were decent—and merely pillaged the villages they took. Sometimes, men were tortured, women were raped, and children were left to be orphans. Such was war, and such was life for lesser men when kings became greedy.

It was bad enough to worry about the country and the people, but her turmoil was inner as well, for despite herself, she missed her husband. In his absence, it seemed that life went on as normal, for Aville was like a well-oiled wheel, as it had been for years and years. Her mother had made it so, she had made it so—and Adrien had made it even more so. For even though he was gone, his strength could be felt in the subtle changes he had made to the fortifications, and in those he had left behind to guard it. Aville, though border land, had long been claimed by the English kings. And since her mother had long ago lost her battle with Edward, the people had gained a greater loyalty to the English king. If there was ever to be war within the walls, the English might well win.

She prayed each morning that a miracle might occur to make King Jean of France and Edward of England reach an arrangement.

And she prayed each day, even as she damned him, that her husband would return.

She despised the fact that she missed him. She felt his absence in the cold at night. She lay awake remembering his wry comments, his smile, and the way his eyes looked sometimes when they fell upon her. Aye, she lay awake far too long and far too late in the darkness, wishing she could feel his warmth and his touch. Yet day by day, she forced herself to appear tranquil. Aville was hers, it remained hers, it would always be hers. With or without him.

He had been gone several weeks. She was sitting in the great hall, listening to one of the masons explain an extension to the parapets which would give them a far greater view of the countryside, when Daylin appeared with the news that a party carrying the banner of Comte Langlois, one of King Jean's able supporters, was approaching. She accompanied Daylin to the parapets and watched where Sir Giles stood like a stern sentinel as the Frenchmen approached. The comte was riding with five other men, a small party of horsemen, and they displayed their colors in the peaceable manner of a diplomatic delegation.

"Do we welcome them?" Daylin asked her.

"What else can we do?" she replied. "They have obviously come to talk, and no more. Jean is the King of France."

"Danielle," Daylin reminded her softly, "we are in a precarious situation. Edward battles rebellion and claims to be King of France himself—"

"The Plantagenets have been claiming to be kings of France for decades now—they think it gives them the right to do what they will here."

"Surely, King Edward does have some right."

Danielle looked down for a moment, fighting a great wave of nausea. She had seen this coming; she hated it. Edward didn't have the right because he'd been born to be the king across the Channel. Why couldn't Edward be content with England? And why did it seem that the French kings were always eager to taunt the English kings, claiming France to be far greater and more important a country to rule than the tiny, backward island property of England? She felt as if she were viciously tugged two ways and she suddenly wished God would reach down and strike both kings with a lightning bolt.

"I cannot refuse to see an emissary of King Jean," she said simply. She stared at the two men sternly. "You know it as well as I do!"

The gates were opened; Danielle stood at the entry to the great hall surrounded by her own and Adrien's men as the comte and his party rode in. She had heard of Langlois before, from Simon and King Jean, but she'd not met the man. He was tall and well-built with dark, searing eyes, dark hair, and a perfectly manicured mustache. He dismounted and approached her, bowing deeply before her.

"M'lady! I confess to hearing wild tales regarding your beauty but none come so much as close to the truth. It is my greatest pleasure to be here, having been sent by our sovereign, King Jean of France. He has sent you a roll of silk, recently arrived from Persia, and a sword of Toledo steel for your husband, as King Jean has heard he favors such weapons."

"How very kind. I hope that my distant cousin, Jean of France, is well."

"Indeed, he is so."

"Comte Langlois, you are surely aware that my husband rides in the service of Prince Edward right now, but he would welcome you as I do. Will you join us for our evening meal?"

"With the greatest pleasure."

"Come into the great hall and enjoy the wine from our vineyards. It is exceptional."

"So I have heard," Langlois said pleasantly.

As she turned to enter the hall, she realized that Daylin flanked her tightly and Sir Giles walked closely behind their guest.

"He's come to cause trouble!" Daylin whispered.

Langlois heard him, but appeared not to take offense. "No, he has not come to cause trouble!" he whispered softly as well. Daylin flushed, and Danielle could not help but smile. "I have come in peace to remind the countess—"

"And what of the earl?" Sir Giles asked gruffly.

Langlois smiled. "Indeed, to remind the earl and the countess that Aville has always been friends with France, for though we are split into counties and duchies, France is our mother country. That is all."

In the great hall, wine was served as Langlois displayed the fine, shimmering silver silk King Jean had sent for her and the handsome sword, for her husband. Danielle sat in a chair by the hearth and Langlois stood some distance away at the table by the wine decanter. While Danielle touched the silk and commented appreciatively on its beauty, Sir Giles approached the mantel, leaned low to the fire, and whispered to her.

"You must not accept it!"

"I am to refuse a gift from the French king?"

"A bribe! And Edward claims to be King of France."

"Giles, I cannot appear to be rude. I must accept these gifts. And one could hardly be bribed by a roll of silk or even a magnificent sword."

She rose then, taking the handsomely fashioned sword from the French soldier who offered it to her. "My cousin, King

Jean, is thoughtful and generous. I thank him for thinking of us, but Comte Langlois, I must remind you that my husband is a Scotsman who—''

''Who, alas, rides for Prince Edward, when so many of the Scots have embraced the French with love over the centuries! But he is King Edward's champion, and so his marriage to you was arranged. He is one Scot who must certainly come to appreciate all that is French.''

She smiled graciously. ''Comte, it's quite true that over the years the Scots and French have often bonded together—against the English. But my husband is overlord of lands in England as well as Scotland, so he understands the trials of Scotsmen, Englishmen, and, as we live now at Aville, Frenchmen as well.''

''Edward of England seeks the French throne.''

''I don't know the workings in the minds of kings, Comte Langlois. I pray that Edward and my cousin, Jean, find a peaceful solution—cousins themselves.''

Langlois stared at her, then at Sir Giles to her one side, and Daylin at her other. He smiled boldly. ''Sirs, I promise you this, I've not come to stir up trouble, merely to offer King Jean's friendship. May I tell the king—the true and rightful King Jean of France—that you, milady, remain, at heart, his subject?''

''You may tell him that I love him as I did his father, and pray for his continued good health. I hold this place—Laird MacLachlan and I hold Aville together, sir, and we both pray for peace and prosperity for all the people of France.''

''If Laird MacLachlan rides with the English prince, he rides with danger. I pray, lady, that he survives to enjoy his great bounty.''

''I pray for his health and welfare daily, sir.''

Langlois appeared pleased, and she wasn't certain why. She had been very careful to state that she was one with Adrien's will, and she had been just as careful not to make a statement of sworn loyalty to either sovereign. Not even Sir Giles seemed to take offense at her words.

Supper was served; Langlois remained charming throughout. Yet, toward the end of the meal, he leaned slightly toward her.

"If you ever have need of my services, milady, leave word at the Twisted Tree Tavern. The Twisted Tree Tavern, do not forget. I cannot come here again. For King Jean, I would serve you in any way, as I know you would risk any danger were his life at stake."

He turned from her, and she almost wondered if she had imagined the words, so quickly was he engaged in conversation with Sir Giles to his right.

Her heart thundered. She broke a piece of bread but could not swallow it down.

Despite the late hour, Comte Langlois and his men departed when the meal was done.

She stood by the gates with Sir Giles and Daylin after saying farewell.

"Aye, and best they're gone!" Sir Giles said.

"Now, Sir Giles, we must learn to live together, since the situation never seems to change," Danielle said wearily.

"He came for something," Daylin said.

"He came to find out if Danielle would betray her husband and King Edward should the French king ask her to open these gates," Sir Giles said, and he turned to Danielle, his light blue eyes warm with pleasure. "But our lady put him in his place!"

"I wish they would all be done with battle," Danielle said in reply. "But . . . aye. He came to see which way the wind blew here."

"Perhaps we should have turned a cold shoulder to the Comte Langlois and his party. After all, Comte Armagnac ransacks the countryside, ravaging, pillaging, murdering . . . and it seems ever more likely that King Jean stands behind him."

"I will not believe that King Jean encourages wanton destruction and cold-blooded murder!" Danielle protested. "And that is all supposition. We've not heard from Adrien—"she began, but broke off, because Daylin's cheeks were growing red. He was a young man now, handsome, full grown, but he still blushed quickly, and gave away his secrets far too easily.

"You have heard from Adrien!" she said, fighting hard to control her temper and the hurt that welled in her.

"A messenger arrived from the front a few days ago, but with very little to say," Sir Giles said quickly.

"So little that no one informed me?"

"You'd not have been happy, my lady."

"I'd not have been happy, so Adrien said I wasn't to be given the truth! Well, now I demand it. What is the truth?"

Daylin shrugged uncomfortably. "Unless an agreement is soon reached, there will likely be an all-out, terrible battle. Prince Edward is amassing more and more Englishmen on the Normandy shore. Jean, in turn, is enlarging his armies. So you see, the messenger really brought littlle news that we did not already suspect."

"Whatever news a messenger brings, I must be told."

Daylin was silent, and she realized that Adrien had sent word she wasn't to be told anything.

Upstairs, she paced her room, looking from the fur before the hearth to the fire that blazed within it. She sat down on the fur and hugged her arms around her knees, remembering how Adrien had found her sleeping there and how he had dragged her to the crypt and wrung vows from her. Even though she steamed with new fury now since he did not trust her with the least information, she wished with all her heart that she could simply make a vow to him, and honor it. Even if Edward was wrong, as she believed in her heart.

Would there ever be peace between England and France? Or between herself and her husband?

Damning both kings, she closed her eyes and wished that she could hate Adrien. It would be far easier to hate him than to want him.

At length, she stretched before the fire and slept.

In the days that followed, she was watchful, lest another messenger should arrive from Adrien or Prince Edward's army and she not be apprised. But no one appeared.

It was almost a week later, while she was in the great hall going over accounts, that Monteine appeared with a tall, handsome priest anxious to speak with her. She dismissed the accountant when she saw that the priest wished to see her alone. Monteine started to protest, but Danielle firmly pressed her to leave them alone after introducing her to Father Paul of Valois.

"Ah, thank you!" the young priest said, taking a long swallow of the wine she had given him. They sat before the fire and he leaned forward to speak with her.

"I am, my lady, distant kin to our good King Jean, as you are yourself. And I am heartily worried about the events taking place in our country."

"War ravages," she agreed.

"The greed of the English is never ending."

"Father, King Edward's mother was French," she reminded him. "It seems he feels he has an equal right to the throne."

He waved a hand in the air, not about to accept such a reminder with patience.

"In fact, Father," she murmured, disturbed to be remembering Adrien's observation, "the kings are more closely related to one another than we are to Jean—as more distant relations."

"Your mother met defeat at Edward's hands. She accepted marriage with an Englishman, but she remained true to the house of Valois throughout her life. By God, lady, you are her daughter! Would you so dishonor her by doing less?"

Danielle sipped her wine, stalling, as she stared at him. "Father, would you have me betray the man to whom I am legally wed in God's own eyes?"

He sighed. "Never, my lady. But you needn't betray your husband if you were to warn King Jean if the English had a design upon him, if you knew when a battle was to take place, if you could help to save his very life. We can't control the great forces of the armies—men will battle men, and one leader will be a victor while the other tastes defeat. But if King Jean can just be warned of the greatest dangers, he can hope to cling to life and liberty, and perhaps save all of France."

"What exactly do you want from me?"

"Fair warning if his life is at risk. You will know how to make contact when necessary, I am certain."

"I don't know much, Father. I am here—the armies are elsewhere."

"Your husband will surely warn of the danger if a massive battle is to take place."

She lowered her head, suddenly wishing with all her heart that she didn't have to be in such a position. But she had given her mother a vow to honor the French king. To honor France.

"Naturally, if King Jean's life were threatened . . ." she murmured. Then she stared at him. "I am caught in the crossfire, Father. I can swear to you that I'll do my best to get warning to King Jean if I know of English attempts upon him, but I can do so only once. Once, and that is all."

"Once will be enough."

Father Paul stood. "A vow before Christ now, my child. You must use what you learn to protect our rightful king. Bless you—you will sit with your mother among the saints one day, lady."

She rose with him, praying that she wouldn't sit among the saints because her husband or Edward would be determined to have her head for being a traitor.

Monteine swept back into the room, carrying a tray with lamb stew and fresh bread. Father Paul thanked her and praised the food as he ate, then spoke casually of books, musicians, and the stars. When he finished the last morsel and seemed about to be on his way, Danielle invited him to stay the night. He thanked her but told her it was early still, and he intended to ride for several more hours before sleeping beneath the stars.

When he had gone, Monteine looked after him suspiciously, though Danielle didn't understand why; the priest had been nothing but polite and casual while Monteine was with them.

"A very handsome man to be a priest," Monteine commented dryly.

"Monteine, the priesthood is a vocation," Danielle reminded her.

Monteine sniffed. "Indeed. The priesthood is a place for younger sons when great men have wives who bear a surplus of sons."

Danielle shrugged. "I don't understand your point. Father Paul is a handsome man, and perhaps you're right—he *was* a rich man's younger son and was given little choice."

"I don't think he's really a priest."

"Oh, Monteine!"

"He looked at you quite . . . strangely."

Danielle sighed again. "He must be a priest, and you're being ridiculous. I mean—"

"What?"

"Well, priests make a vow of celibacy, but . . ."

"But we all know that even the men who serve the pope have mistresses and bastards."

"What difference does it make? If men of God falter, who are we to judge? Besides, the fact that the man is good-looking does not make him guilty of . . . of . . ."

"Lechery," Monteine provided. "Well, if he is not guilty . . ."

"Yes?"

Monteine grinned suddenly. "Then he should be, for surely, it would be quite a waste if some fair lass were not to enjoy such a man."

Danielle threw up her arms in exasperation. "Monteine, you're suspicious of him, while thinking that he looks so charming that he should sin. I'm worried about you. I think we've waited far too long to find you a proper husband."

Monteine smiled. "Ah, Danielle, I'm not a richly-landed heiress! I'll tend to my own situation, thank you. Shall I call the accountant back?"

"Yes, please."

Monteine smiled, and left Danielle.

That night, Monteine spent endless hours pacing in her room, wishing she might have heard more of what the priest had said to Danielle.

Once, Danielle would have readily told her everything. No more. And that disturbed Monteine. Even more than the priest.

And once, she admitted to herself, she would have readily done anything to hurt the English cause—or any Englishman, for that matter.

But now, she felt a deep, unsettling fear. King Edward was powerful, his men were powerful, and worse, they were determined. And Adrien MacLachlan had his own particular brand of power and prowess—and justice and mercy. The young Scotsman had stayed his sword against Simon when he might well have skewered the man through with no one to blame him. He had dealt justly with Danielle at every turn. There was just one thing to fear: that he might be betrayed again. For if he were . . .

She trembled, wondering what she should do.

She had never had such an uneasy feeling. The priest had been . . . no true priest.

She quit pacing at last, left her room, and quietly slipped down the stairs. It was very late, but she knew that one of Adrien's men would be on guard in the great hall throughout the night. At all times, men-at-arms walked the parapets and guarded the walled village of Aville, but with Adrien's absence, there was always a man on guard in the great hall as well. She wondered if Danielle knew.

Tonight, it was Daylin.

He sat in a chair before the fire, somewhat sprawled. Monteine thought that he slept. What if she was making a terrible mistake? Perhaps she was wrong. She felt foolish, standing in the great hall in her nightgown and bare feet with the fire burning against the shadows of the wee hours while even their guardian slept!

She turned about, ready to race back up the stairs.

"Monteine? What is it?"

She froze, and held dead still. A minute later, she realized that he stood behind her. She felt his hands on her shoulders, and he turned her slowly around to face him.

"Nothing, I . . ."

"It's not nothing. What's wrong?" He smiled as he spoke, and smoothed back a strand of her hair. "How strange! I've never seen you like this. All these years we've known one another, and I've never seen your hair down and so pretty, so wild . . ."

She felt warm, captured by his gaze. Speechless. She needed to draw away, murmur some excuse, return to her room.

"The priest was so strange!" she heard herself babble. She

gathered her wits about her. "Oh, Daylin, I'm worried. A priest came this afternoon—"

"Priests, monks, and pilgrims travel our way often," he said carefully.

"I know. But this priest insisted on an audience with Danielle—I knew when I came back that Danielle was uneasy. The priest was fine, composed, and spoke easily about many things, but while I was gone, I think he asked her for something. I think he wanted something."

"Did she intend to give it?" Daylin demanded.

"She was unhappy, so I don't know." Monteine said and sighed as his eyes searched hers. "You see, he said that he was kin to the house of Valois. I shouldn't have come to you. I'm just so worried . . ."

Daylin nodded slowly. "These are dangerous times."

"What will you do?"

Daylin arched a brow. "I'm not sure yet—I'll speak with Sir Giles. But you needn't worry. Adrien is not really so far away. He has often said that he would come home if he didn't feel it was important to be ready and to keep their numbers intact and powerful as they battled Armagnac. If there's really a problem . . ."

He shrugged.

"Then?" Monteine whispered.

"Then he will come back."

The houses were burning, the dead and dying lay strewn about like broken tinder. Armagnac's men struck swiftly, decimating the peasant villages, stealing what poor treasures they could find, then fleeing with fierce speed. Today, however, Adrien's men had been given a warning of the attack, and they had ridden to the village in time to prevent mass slaughter.

From the hill crest above the valley, he had let out a blood-chilling war cry and thundered down upon the attackers, his sword swinging. They battled the attackers, who did not retreat quickly, with little mercy, his fury fueled as he saw lads little more than children among the dead.

One of Armagnac's men came rushing from a burning house, ready to leap atop his horse and escape. He saw Adrien bearing down on him and stopped to fight, attacking with a battle axe. Adrien urged Luke hard forward, leaping from the horse, ducking the swing of the axe, and rising to slice the man from throat to gullet. He fell. As Adrien turned, he heard a woman screaming and shrieking, pointing to a horseman riding toward the forest with a young woman thrown over his horse's haunches. Adrien whistled for Luke, mounted, and raced after the abductor. The man turned and saw him in pursuit. Pausing, he dropped the girl on the path and raced onward. Adrien reined in, wishing that someone had seen him and followed, but no one had. He couldn't pursue the man; he stopped for the girl, hoping that her bones hadn't been shattered or her head crushed in the fall.

He dismounted and helped her up. She was young and pretty, and unhurt. She looked up at him with dark, adoring eyes. "Thank you, thank you, my lord."

"You're not hurt?"

"No."

"Then all is well."

"You saved my life."

"Perhaps just your honor."

"It is yours, my lord," she told him gravely.

"Well," he murmured, "I don't ask such a payment. Come, let me bring you back to your mother."

She slipped her arms around his neck and he carried her back to Luke. They rode to the village, where he set her down to wild cheers and the teary-eyed gratitude of her mother.

"Terese is all I have, my lord," the woman told him. "I would do anything for you. You only need ask."

"Please, you are loyal to Edward as your duke. It is my duty to protect you." He smiled as he spoke, removing any hint of rebuke from his words. Many of his men joined him and he called out orders about helping with the wounded and the dead. He dismounted from Luke, and as he did so, he was surprised to see Sir George riding toward him with Michael, one of the young men he had trained and left behind to guard Aville.

As they came closer, he saw that Michael's tunic was muddied, and red with blood. His heart quickened with fear. Aville was a great prize, and could sway the entire balance of battle. Had the wily French Jean found a way to seize it? Aville could stand—should stand—against any assault. The only way it could fall was from within.

He strode quickly toward the men as they approached. "Is something wrong?" he demanded, reaching up to help Michael from his mount. "Where are you injured, boy, and how badly? Woman!" he shouted suddenly, turning back to Terese's mother. "Get me help for this man, quickly."

Michael winced. " 'Tis not mortal, my lord, though I bleed like a pig!"

"Aville—"

"All is well at Aville—I've only a strange story to tell."

The woman had come to his side, Terese with her. They worked quickly and well together, Terese fetching water, her mother removing Michael's tunic and shirt, and the two of them bathing the long slash on his chest.

"I will be anxious to hear it," Adrien said, then raised a hand. "Bring him to the house yonder. I will be right along."

He asked Sir George to see that the fires were extinguished as soon as possible, that the wounded were all cared for—and the dead buried. Then he followed those who had carried Michael twenty feet to the small house with the thatched roof.

The house was empty; Terese told him the owner had been the first to die. Michael had been helped to a rope bed, where he lay on a heavy comforter, his wound poulticed and bandaged. Adrien thanked the women and sent them away, then sat beside Michael, alone.

"Tell me what has happened."

"First, my lord, Comte Langlois arrived with a small party, bearing gifts."

"For Danielle?"

"Silk for her, a sword for you. Sir Giles said to assure you that they were not alone for so much as a heartbeat; the countess was polite and firm, stating that you held Aville together, but that you were with Prince Edward and she heartily wished the fighting would stop.''

Adrien arched a brow, dismayed at the pleasure he felt simply because Danielle had remembered a vow to him.

"Then . . . ?''

"Then the priest came.''

"The priest?''

"He claimed he was Father Paul de Valois. The countess agreed to speak with him in private. He departed quickly, but her woman, Monteine, felt distressed by his visit and came to Daylin, who ordered me to follow the man. I did so, only to encounter him in an old hermit's cottage deep in the woods, where he was meeting with others. I did not learn their whole purpose, but neither did they learn mine. I believe they were all to travel to different parts of the country, watch King Edward's forces, and discover where King Jean might find weaknesses among Edward's holdings. I was seen, and attacked. I did fight back, my lord, and I gave a good accounting of myself, I swear I did. But I pretended I was dead when I fell over my horse . . . and had the good beast race like the wind out of there! I looked as hard as I could for your position, and most luckily stumbled among Englishmen with Prince Edward's men. I knew my wound was not so severe as it seemed, and so insisted I be sent straight to you.''

Adrien closed his eyes, clenching his teeth. It felt as if the blazing roar of a brush fire was hurtling through his limbs; the heat that settled over him was painful. She had sworn to uphold Aville for him, but she had carried on a secret conversation with one of King Jean's spies.

He walked away from Michael's bedside, his back to the man. He remembered her terror in the crypt, her vulnerability, and her eyes when they touched his. He thought of the nights he had lain awake wanting her.

And he thought what a fool he had been to fall in love with her.

He stiffened his shoulders. Battle was coming, fierce as a storm, inevitable. He didn't dare leave her at Aville.

"Could you find this cottage again?'' he asked Michael.

"Aye, my lord."

"Then, as soon as you are able—"

"I'm able when you are, my lord—"

"Rest through the day. We'll ride by night."

"For the priest?"

"Aye," he said, and added with a deadly calm he did not feel, "and for my wife."

Three nights later, Danielle awoke in raw panic at the sound of her door being burst open in a fury. Wood struck against stone and shuddered and groaned as if it would splinter into a thousand pieces.

The sudden noise caused her to leap up. She stood by the side of her bed, groggy and terrified, trying to remember where in the room she might find a weapon. What had happened? Had all the men been seized or killed? How could someone burst in upon her?

The sword! King Jean's gift to Adrien lay by the bedside. The light was dim, as the fire in her hearth was dying, but she quickly hunched down and ran her fingers over the floor to retrieve the sword. She stood again, holding the weapon before her as she had been taught so long ago.

She blinked, for a towering figure filled the door frame, as menacing as any form she had ever seen. Cast against the dim light of the hallway, he was an imposing silhouette; hands on hips, he stood like an angry Zeus, ready to shatter the earth with thunder.

Yet she recognized the shape and form . . .

"Adrien?" she whispered, relief flooding through her.

"Oh, aye. It's Adrien."

The tone of his voice brought tension racing back to her muscles. She'd been about to lower the sword.

She held it more tightly.

He stepped into the room, and the door slammed closed behind him.

Chapter 16

He walked to the hearth, taking the poker and prodding the half-hearted fire back to life. Sparks flew and sizzled. He hunched down, adding a log, and flames leapt up again, illuminating his face. His expression was grave and frighteningly dispassionate. He turned back to her; she hadn't moved a muscle. "So . . ." he murmured, striding toward her, "you would take up arms against me now?"

He was not in full armor, but wore a coat of mail beneath the tunic that bore his MacLachlan crest. His Toledo blade was encased in a sheath at his side.

His tunic had been ripped—or slashed—at a point by his shoulder. His boots were muddied, and spatters of mud—and blood—were dotted upon the rest of him as well.

He strode toward her, stopping perhaps ten feet away, his eyes scanning her with a lack of emotion that unnerved her. He removed his gauntlets, and set them on the trunk at the foot of the bed, his cool gaze never leaving her. "Are you going to put the sword down?" he demanded.

She found her voice at last. "That depends. Are you going to tell me why you've come in here like an executioner?"

"Maybe you're to be executed."

Her heart skipped a beat. Surely he couldn't be serious.

"Then I'll keep the sword, Laird MacLachlan, and you may go down with me."

"Put it down, my love, before I decide to beat you black and blue."

"Ah, indeed, let me relinquish my last defense so that you can strike me unimpeded!"

"Fine. Let me wrest it from you so I can be angrier than I am now!"

She was startled when he drew his own weapon. She backed away from him in fright, fury, and confusion. What in God's name had caused this?

She held her weapon out defensively, aware of his power, yet feeling she had no choice. She countered his first angry swings, leaping on the bed, scurrying across the room. He followed her relentlessly and she realized that though she was holding her own, he was methodically letting her exhaust herself until he came in for the . . .

Kill.

She was finally backed against the wall. His steel met hers with such force that she thought the bones in her hand would shatter. She couldn't hold the sword, and it fell in front of the fire.

Adrien was but two feet away. He brought the tip of his sword to her throat. She stared at him, wondering if he had gone mad.

Yet his anger remained controlled, absolutely dispassionate. He sheathed his sword and reached for her arm, wrenching her around to stand before the hearth. "Pack," he said simply.

Her heart took flight. "Pack. That is it? Pack? You come in like an avenging angel, dictate and threaten—"

"I'll do more than threaten in a minute. Pack, and quickly! A few garments will be sufficient, since I do not intend to travel heavily laden."

She shook her head, so furious she could feel tears welling in her eyes. "Where are we going? What have I done that you should treat me so callously?"

"What have you done?" He arched a brow, leaning against the mantel.

"Yes, that's what I asked! Have you gone daft? Have you been hit in the helmet by a broadsword one time too many?"

She saw the tick of his pulse at his temple and bit lightly into her lower lip, fearing a greater violence.

But he spoke very softly. "Is that what you think, my love? That I have become a fool?"

"In God's name, I don't know what you're talking about!" she cried.

"Ah, well, I will refresh your memory regarding your activities since I departed. First, there would be an emissary from King Jean."

"And I should have refused him admission to Aville? He brought a gift for you as well."

"A weapon for you to use against me. But I believe that visit was merely superficial . . . your Comte Langlois came to see the defenses and strengths of Aville. But as to the matter of the priest . . ."

"Now I am not to admit priests to Aville?"

He took a single step toward her. "Nay, my lady, you are not. Not when the priest is merely a rebel in a cassock, a wolf in sheep's clothing."

She felt as if the breath had been swept from her. She shook her head slightly. "But I didn't—"

"Oh, but you did. Actually, he was an admirable fellow. He didn't wish to give away any information. But under the duress of my sword point at his throat, he confessed that you'd sworn to aid King Jean."

She felt as if her heart sank and dissolved within her. She shook her head. It was the truth, and not the truth. She stared at the fire. "I did not know the man was not a priest—I told him only that I would do what I could to see that King Jean lived!" She looked to Adrien, her gaze sweeping over his muddied and blood-stained clothing. "So . . . he was an admirable fellow, fighting for his king—as you fight for yours. Is he dead?"

He stared at her in turn. ''Does his life matter so much to you?''

''Yes—as you said, he was an admirable fellow.''

''Handsome and daring,'' Adrien agreed.

''Did you kill him?''

''Pack,'' Adrien said.

''I'll not make a move until you answer me.''

''You'll do what I say, and I say we're leaving.''

''No, I'm not. I wish to stay here. You may fight your battles, rape the countryside, and leave all laid waste for the common folk who must simply try to survive and make a living and feed their families!''

''My lady, you may dress and pack, or I will take you from here naked and with nothing. I do not give a damn, but since your 'priest' was part of a rebel conspiracy determined to take this place from within, you'll not be trusted here. I mean what I say.''

''Adrien, I am innocent!'' she protested.

But he had turned away and was striding for the door.

''Adrien!''

He paused there, looking back. She gritted her teeth and forced herself to remain still. ''You've no right to do this! I have been honest with you. You know all there is to know of my life. Aye, I would do what I could to see that King Jean was not killed. But I said no more than that to anyone. I am innocent of any treachery or plotting!''

''You admit guilt while telling me you're innocent. It doesn't matter. Danielle, you cannot stay here now. You are far too big a temptation for the house of Valois.''

''Where do you think you're taking me?''

''With me.''

''To—''

''Prince Edward has forces manning the Castle de Renoncourt now as his armies battle the rebels in the surrounding countryside. For now, you will come with me there.''

''I won't go! You've judged me unfairly.''

''You will leave, my lady.''

''To be with you when you act like a vicious fool? Never!''

"My dear *wife,* you will be with me."

"If you touch me, so help me God, I will scream so loudly that every man in the castle will hear my cries."

He bowed to her mockingly. "Every man in the castle will then envy me all the more, my lady. Scream loudly enough, and given the mood of some of these fellows, Prince Edward will be able to charge for the entertainment. You haven't long, Danielle, so if you want any belongings with you, you must pack them."

"I will not go."

"You will."

She turned away from him and sat at the foot of the bed, hands folded primly before her. He ignored her and exited the room, slamming the door behind him.

Her mind raced. How had he known of the priest? Had he killed the poor fellow? Monteine had been right—their visitor had not been a man with a vocation for the cross! But she was innocent of any wrongdoing, and damned nonetheless.

It made no sense. He would have heard of the visit of Comte Langlois easily—his men probably sent reports daily. It had not mattered to her, because she had felt very righteous in everything she had done. So they had told him that a priest had come, but . . .

Many priests came, and monks, and nuns, and merchants and others, on pilgrimages or traveling to visit relatives in distant places. What had alerted anyone to that particular priest?

She stared at the flames, feeling their warmth, but she was still cold. Time was passing, and quickly, but she wasn't going to agree to leave. Not to sit with the English army while her country was torn asunder.

She stood at last, sparks of anger filling her, and walked before the fire. Damn them all. Damn Adrien.

There was a tapping at her door then. Not Adrien, she knew that. He didn't knock.

The tapping came again. The door cracked open. "Danielle?" Monteine said softly. Danielle didn't move but Monteine stepped hesitantly into the room. "You didn't pack yet? Laird MacLachlan is nearly ready to leave again, so Daylin has told me. I thought I'd get some things together for you—if you hadn't managed to do so yet yourself. I understand that Adrien is determined to have you nearer to him, since he must be gone so long.''

Danielle spun around, arching a brow. ''Is that what he has said?''

''Yes.''

''And that's what you believe?''

''Well . . .'' Monteine shrugged miserably. ''In all honesty, Sir Giles, Daylin, and I heard . . . heard your sword battle. And unless that is a new way of greeting one another lovingly . . .''

Danielle crossed her arms over her chest and sat at the foot of the bed. ''I'm not going anywhere.''

''Danielle, he will make you.''

''Then he will have to do so.''

Monteine looked exceptionally unhappy. ''Well, I will pack a small saddle bag so you will have a few of your own belongings—just in case. Danielle, you must be reasonable. These are dangerous times. Aville is a great prize, and so are you. I saw the way that man looked at you. I knew that he was no priest. He intended to return here, bringing others pretending to be holy men. Then they would have learned how to open the various gates . . .''

''How do you know all this?'' Danielle asked her sharply.

''I—I've heard the men talking,'' Monteine stuttered out. She looked away from Danielle and started moving about the room, collecting clothing, brushes, and other articles to pack in a large leather satchel.

''And you think I'm so foolish I wouldn't have realized it if a plot was afoot?''

''No . . . of course you would have seen, in time. But,'' Monteine insisted, ''I did know, from the beginning, that Paul de Valois was no priest! He was far too sensual a man.''

''*Was*! So Adrien did kill him,'' Danielle muttered bitterly.

''No . . . no, he didn't. There was a skirmish at a cottage deep in the woods where the men met. A number of the conspirators were killed, but our own Michael assured me that any man who set down his arms and accepted imprisonment in

England would be allowed to live. Danielle, you are wearing nothing but a thin white linen gown. I'm truly afraid that Adrien does not mean to relent.''

''I will not go—'' Danielle began, but she swung around even as she spoke, for her door, which had been slightly ajar, had thundered open again. Adrien was back. He had bathed and changed. His armor was gone; he wore a fresh tunic and a warm wool cloak, tossed back over his shoulders. His boots had been cleaned. His hair remained damp from a washing; even his cheeks were freshly shaved. She looked away from him quickly, wondering how her heart and body could be so traitorous, for he looked magnificent. Though she wanted so desperately to despise him, all she yearned to do was lie against him.

''Monteine, are the countess's things ready?'' he demanded, staring hard at Danielle.

''Aye, Laird MacLachlan.''

Daylin was behind him. He stepped into the room, and— cheeks flushed, not looking at Danielle—he picked up the satchel Monteine had packed and left the room.

Monteine fled like a rabbit behind him.

Danielle stood and backed away from Adrien toward the fire. ''Adrien, I will not go willingly.''

''Then, my lady, you may begin screaming now.''

Long strides brought him to her, and before she managed to deliver a single blow against his chest, she was swept up like a sack of grain and tossed over his shoulder.

She had thought she would scream, but she did not. She was far more humiliated than she imagined she might be. She tried to look about as she struggled against her husband's back while he took the stairs at a wicked speed. No one was about.

Yet he had not come alone. As they reached the courtyard, she saw with a sinking heart that Sir George, along with other of his men-at-arms, waited on horseback—eight of them, she counted quickly. The night was briskly chilly, her hair was a long, wild tangle that kept blinding her, her feet were bare, her nightgown thin.

She was set atop Adrien's war horse. She swept the long

cascade of her hair back so she could see, and balanced herself quickly rather than tumble from the horse.

"My lady," Sir George said gravely at her side.

"Sir George," she acknowledged courteously.

The dear old fellow looked quite distressed. "You must be cold. Let me offer my cloak—" he began.

But Adrien leapt up behind Danielle then. "Ah, Sir George, a gallant gesture, but no, thank you. This is how my wife has chosen to ride."

"Indeed, you see I did not know I was leaving before the dawn until Laird MacLachlan swept me off my feet."

"Indeed. She inspires a man to be ever so romantic," Adrien murmured irritably. "Daylin! Open the gates! We ride!" he commanded.

The ride was cold, hard, and long. Adrien intended to make the fifty or so miles that separated them from Prince Edward's camp by nightfall.

She rued her stubbornness soon after they left; despite his body at her back and his arms around her, she was freezing. Her feet were scratched by long grasses and branches, and she knew that Adrien must have been very angry to let her suffer so for so long.

When they at last stopped to water the horses for the first time, she was afraid she wouldn't be able to stand. But it didn't matter. He lifted her from the horse and carried her to a rock by the stream where they'd stopped, and from the deep pockets of his cloak, he produced a pair of her shoes. He slipped them on her feet and she didn't protest, nor did she say a word when he took off his cloak and set it around her shoulders.

Then he walked away from her.

Sir George brought her water and offered her their breakfast fare of bread, smoked fish, and cheese, but she wasn't hungry. He stayed with her, talking politely about the beauty of the day. She responded courteously in return, then asked him, "Monteine was not even to come with us?"

"Apparently not—not for now, my lady."

"Sir Giles and Daylin are staying behind?"

"They know Aville very well."

"And will loyally guard my property—for their master!"

"My lady—"

"My apologies, Sir George. You had nothing to do with any of this."

She rose and walked away from him, to the stream. A few minutes later, she felt Adrien behind her. "You know, you might have allowed me to bring Star," she said. "Your horse will be worn out, carrying the two of us."

She was surprised to feel him hesitate. "I would not have allowed you to bring Star under any circumstance."

"Because she was a gift to me from Philip of France? He is dead now—it is his son who battles Edward."

"I would not have allowed you to bring her because she means a great deal to you and I wouldn't have her seized if there were a shortage of horses."

She spun around to look at him, but he had turned away. "Come, Danielle."

She gritted her teeth, hating his tone. It was stupid to fight him in every small battle. She still couldn't bear his autocratic manner, and she refused to move. Ahead of her, he paused, bowed deeply, walked back to her with controlled anger, and swept her off her feet.

She didn't eat until late afternoon. When they began to ride again after that, she was appalled to realize that she was going to be sick. She whispered Adrien's name, afraid that she wouldn't find the words to warn him in time, but he saw her face and quickly reined in. He helped her from the horse, and when he would have helped her further, she broke free and ran from him, into the brush by the side of the trail. They still rode parallel to a stream, and she hurried to it, anxious to douse herself with cold water. He found her there, and she was afraid for a minute that he was going to accuse her of feigning her illness to escape, but he didn't. He came to her, lifting her chin and studying her with a frown.

"I'm—all right. It must have been something I ate, perhaps the fish."

"We can rest a while—"

"No. I'm all right. Honestly. I feel fine now."

His knuckles brushed her cheek and his eyes seemed to sweep her with fresh fire. Her knees seemed weak and she was afraid that she'd crumble there, before him. She lowered her lashes quickly, wishing with all her heart that she did not love him.

His hand lowered. He stepped away. "Then we will ride," he told her.

She was better; she didn't feel ill again the entire way. A few hours after sundown, she saw the vast village on the hill that Prince Edward had chosen to use as his base in the English ducal lands. The Castle de Renoncourt was a magnificent structure, commanding a view of the countryside for miles.

The town itself was not walled, but the castle was moated. The bridge was down and they crossed it, yet even as they entered the courtyard, Danielle was startled to see Prince Edward himself coming from the keep to meet them.

Prince Edward was a son and heir to make any father—or king—proud. He was magnificently tall, as the Plantagenets were famed to be, with thick honey-gold hair and flashing blue eyes. He was heavily-muscled, a mature man and a powerful warrior. Like all Plantagenets, he could be known for his excesses, but he had married Joan, known as the Maid of Kent, reputed to be one of the most beautiful women of their day. He could rage in fury like his father, and sometimes find mercy.

She realized that he had come out to welcome Adrien back, but also, to see her. She was afraid, she realized, yet far less unnerved by the prince than by her own husband.

"Adrien, no trouble along the way returning?" the prince demanded.

"Nay, my lord, none at all," Adrien said. He was about to dismount from Matthew, but before he could do so, Prince Edward came to stand by the horse's haunches and reached up for Danielle, taking her by the waist to lift her down. "Welcome, little sister," he said softly, kissing her cheek, then folding her against him. He drew away from her to study her. "My God, but it's been a long time since I've seen you, Danielle. Come into the hall here—we've warmed wine waiting, and hot cooked food after your long journey."

"Prince Edward, I'm afraid I'm not dressed for a formal occasion—" she began.

"A small supper," he interrupted, glancing over her head to Adrien, "just the three of us."

"As you wish it," Adrien said.

Prince Edward slipped an arm around her waist, leading her up the massive stone steps that led to the entry of the keep. Danielle remained aware that Adrien followed closely behind her.

They entered into a long, arched hallway where a number of guards were posted.

Welcome, he had told her, but she was certain there had been a warning in the words.

They entered the great hall, which was empty, as he had said. The prince did not release his hold upon her, but led her to a small table set before the hearth, pouring her warmed wine from a carafe. She accepted it, glad to feel the heat as her fingers curled around it.

"I'll take your cloak," he said.

"Nay!" she protested, but too late. The cloak was gone, and she stood before the fire in her thin linen nightgown. Edward arched a brow and looked at Adrien, who helped himself to wine at her side.

Adrien shrugged. "We left rather quickly."

"He swept me right out of bed, my lord, anxious to return to your service," Danielle said. She lifted her wine goblet. "He is a rogue," she murmured most pleasantly.

Adrien's keen eyes observed her as he lifted his goblet to her, saying pleasantly, "She is a witch, my lord. A siren, surely worthy—or deserving—of a rogue."

"Ah, a marriage made in heaven," Edward said and laughed softly. But he then addressed Danielle, his tone somber. "You weren't anxious to see me, my lady?"

"Indeed, it is with pleasure that I see you again," she replied, her lashes sweeping her cheeks. She meant the words. Edward, as his father's oldest son and heir, had already been a warrior, riding with his father, when she had come to live with the Plantagenets as the king's ward.

He had always been kind, ruffling her hair when he passed by, assuring her she would grow to be a great lady, saying some gentle word about her father. She was glad to see him; she liked him and admired him. She would like him even more if he would remain in England.

"Well, it is with pleasure that I see you—except that I also see what the fuss—and temptation—are all about. You have grown into an unrivaled beauty. I know that you honor my father—you were raised in his house, loved as one of the family. But you do have dangerous French relations, so it is best that, for the time being, you reside here at Castle de Renoncourt where you'll be safe while your husband rides to war. Many men might be tempted to risk much for the pleasure of your company. You do understand, don't you?"

She raised her eyes, meeting his. "I wish, my lord prince, that someone would understand that I am a very capable woman—"

"Too capable," Adrien commented softly.

"I can defend Aville."

"If you choose to defend it," Edward stated, and she realized that he trusted her no more than Adrien did.

"And if, my love, you were not as great a prize as the castle of Aville," Adrien said.

Edward smiled at her, refilling her wine goblet. "Therein lies much of the point, I'm afraid. Your Valois kin are most eager to bribe the pope into giving you an annulment from your marriage so you may be given to a Frenchman who would try to wrest Aville from the English! We will prevent that from happening. My father planned your union with Adrien, knowing his strength—necessary for such a task as holding Aville, and its countess, I do so imagine! Ah, but think back! I know that you must bear us all great affection. My father took you in like a daughter—you are like my little sister. I love you, as you honor me—and my father. I pray that you will enjoy the time you spend here."

He was sincere, she thought, but wary. Yet she was suddenly trembling, and very tired. Bone weary. It had been a long ride. She seemed to ache in every muscle.

"Thank you—you were always most kind. I beg you to

extend that kindness now and allow me to beg out of supper. I can scarcely stand.''

She was irritated to see that Edward looked over her head to Adrien, who must have nodded, because the prince then murmured, ''Indeed, let me have you escorted to Laird MacLachlan's quarters. We can talk more later. I see that you understand your own position clearly—and mine and my father's.''

''I will walk my wife to our rooms, my lord, if you will allow me to do so? I will return immediately,'' Adrien said.

''Indeed, Laird MacLachlan, you must escort your wife and show her the wonders and strengths of the castle. I will be awaiting your return.''

Adrien swept his cloak around Danielle's shoulders, and escorted her firmly out to the hallway.

''Your new home for the time being, my love!'' he whispered softly. ''A wonderful castle. Strong, well-built, with many conveniences.''

''And guards?'' she inquired angrily.

''And dungeons!'' he announced. ''Come along . . . there may even be a torture chamber about somewhere.''

''You are taking me to your rooms,'' she said. ''And I do stand condemned.''

He didn't laugh; he wasn't amused. His words sent chills racing along her spine.

''Aye, lady. You do stand condemned.''

Chapter 17

He moved her quickly through the long hallway. At its far end were stairs, and he caught her hand, drawing her behind him up to the second floor of the castle. They followed another long corridor down three doors where at last, at the third, he ushered her into large, pleasant chambers. There was an outer room with a table and a number of chairs; a young man was there, working by the fire, polishing pieces of Adrien's armor.

"My dear, meet Luke, youngest son of an armorer, serving now as my squire. Luke, my countess, Lady Danielle."

The young man, tall and lean with straw-blond hair and green eyes, leapt up, bowing deeply to her.

"We heard you were coming back tonight, my lord," Luke said. "There's a hot bath prepared by the fire in the bedroom. I believe everything is in readiness."

"Alas, the rooms look fine, Luke, but I must return to the prince for a time. My lady," he said wryly, eyes flashing as he looked at her, "make yourself at home."

He escorted her to the second door, leading into the main chamber with a large, carved wood bed, handsome chairs and trunks and wardrobes, and a big wooden hip tub. Water steamed from it.

"Enjoy yourself," he murmured. "Let the steam clear your throat—so you may scream loudly and clearly when I return."

With that he turned and left her, closing the door behind him. She wanted to throw something after him, but did not. She hurried to the tub, cast off her cloak, shoes, and ripped gown, and stepped into the delightfully hot water. She sank into it, heedless at first of all else.

A few seconds later, she heard the door open a crack, and she tensed. Had Adrien returned already?

A girl had come into the room—young, blond, pretty, and generously endowed. She smiled. "I am Terese, my lady. I've come to serve you."

"Thank you, Terese. But I'm very tired, and I can manage on my own."

But the girl walked into the room, going to the hearth. "I have more water here, my lady, lest your bath grow cold." She picked up her skirt to protect her hands as she looped her fingers around the pot of water bubbling on a tripod above the fire. She poured the water into the tub. Danielle managed to edge back just in time to keep from getting scalded. "Oh! By the Virgin Mary! I am so sorry!" Terese cried in distress.

"I'm fine—it's all right," Danielle said. "Please, if you'll just—"

"I'm so sorry. If you'll ease back again, I can wash your hair for you."

"I can manage—"

"It's so long. Like fire."

"Terese—"

"If I don't serve well, my lady, I will be cast out. And that wretched Comte Armagnac burned my village. I've nowhere to go."

She knelt by the back of the tub and began washing Danielle's hair. Her touch was light and assured, soothing. Danielle leaned back. Just when she had almost begun to doze under the gentle ministration, she felt a sharp tug on her hair.

"My lady! You were about to go under! To drown!"

She wasn't going to drown, but she was growing sorely aggravated. "I'm fine, thank you! She reached for the snowy linen towel by the tub and stood, wrapping herself in it. "Terese—"

"Sit by the fire, please, my lady, and I will brush out your hair. It is so dark and sleek, like sable."

"Terese, you must be tired—"

"Nay, lady. I like the night."

Something in her words made Danielle uncomfortable, but she allowed the girl to brush out her hair, and again she was startled by her expertise. While the fire dried her hair, Terese's nimble fingers brushed it to a sleek shine. "You're from here?" Danielle asked her.

"A village nearby. One that was nearly destroyed, and I with it."

"Ah, well, thank God you are safe."

"Aye, the earl saved me."

"Did he?" Danielle inquired.

"You cannot imagine, my lady, what cruelties are being inflicted upon the people! Men—butchered! Even little children are slain."

"I've heard. I'm so sorry, so deeply sorry."

"Are you?" Terese's touch was suddenly a little rough. "Rumor has it, my lady, that you have supported many of those who have ridden with Armagnac."

Danielle stood, swinging around to stare at the girl. "Rumor is wrong! I would never condone such behavior. You may leave, Terese."

The girl lowered her eyes, a slight smile playing at her lips. "Indeed, my lady. I will be in the antechamber. Please, call if you need me. I will be near. I am in my Lord MacLachlan's service."

Danielle was startled by the pain that enveloped her as she realized that the girl was not only denying her authority to dismiss her, she was hinting that she had become Adrien's mistress.

"Indeed? Well, then," she murmured, "if he requires your services, he will send for you."

Terese turned around and opened the door between the antechamber and bedroom.

Adrien stood there.

"My lord!" Terese murmured. "May I bring you something? Is there anything—"

He was staring past her, at Danielle. "That will be all, Terese," he said.

Terese stepped out—unhappily, Danielle thought. Adrien closed the door, his eyes on Danielle. He walked slowly into the room then, never taking his eyes from her as he removed his scabbard and sword, then drew his tunic over his head and stripped off his shirt. He wore tightly woven trousers that hugged his hips and legs, and his boots, and nothing more. She averted her eyes, wishing she didn't long to touch him, and that the searing pain of jealousy would cease playing havoc with her heart.

"Is Terese accustomed to staying here?" Danielle asked, trying to keep her tone casual as if the matter were of no importance to her.

"Does it matter?" he inquired.

"No," she lied. "How can it matter? You have made certain that it cannot. What you do makes no difference to me whatsoever. You wretchedly refuse to listen to anything I have to say, and trust any stranger over me. Naturally, however, if you'd like to keep company with Terese, I would appreciate it if you'd be so good as to leave me—"

"Indeed? So—you would go casting accusations my way when there is another man in your life every time I turn around, my lady. And, my love, what *you* do does matter to me. Incredibly so."

"You are referring to a priest?"

"The man was no priest."

"I didn't know that."

"You should have."

"You're being curt and cruel," she assured him, looking at him at last. She drew the linen towel more tightly around her. God, that her heart would not leap so! His chest was pure bronze in the firelight. Sleek as satin.

"You're a traitoress," he replied flatly, but walked toward her as he said so.

"Not to France."

He stood before her. "To me!" he stated vehemently. "By God, to me!"

She thought he meant to strike her, but he didn't. He reached for her, savagely drawing her into his arms. His fingers cupped her chin, tilted her head back. His mouth descended upon hers. She longed to fight. She felt the force and heat and liquid fire of his touch. Her lips parted to his onslaught, and the heat seemed to saturate her. Her fingers slid through his hair; she clung to him. His lips parted just slightly from hers.

"I'm not a fool—wanting you does not mean that I trust you!" he swore angrily. But his mouth lowered, and he kissed her again, kissed her and kissed her, as if he could not have enough of the taste of her.

Pride came to her and she twisted free from his lips, pressing furiously against his chest. "No! You cannot ignore what I say and think and feel and then expect that I will want you, have you!" she insisted. "I swear I will have no part of you!"

"I swear that you will!" he countered. "My lady, I have spent endless days at battle only to hear that I must fight and kill more men because you encourage them to treachery. You'll not tell me what you will and will not have!"

She let out a startled shriek as he lifted her with a swift and violent force and threw her upon the bed. Her towel was lost, entangled in his arms. He swore, wadding it, crushing it, savagely throwing it across the room and out of his way. Hands on his hips, he stared down at her, his pulse ticking madly against the veins in his throat. "You'll not play games with me, lady wife, by God, not when you are the cause of the tempest!"

"You will not trust me!" she cried in protest, inching up against the bed. "You will not trust me—"

"I spoke with the bloody priest!"

"I did not encourage anyone to treachery. You had no right to drag me from Aville. I kept my word to you!" she cried back, shaking but determined.

"Ah . . . I have taken you from your precious home!"

"You have judged me unfairly. You have condemned me when I am not guilty. You—"

"Enough, Danielle, enough!"

He spun around on her and strode to the hearth. He leaned against the mantel for a very long time.

Then he began to walk around the room, pinching out the candles. When the last was dimmed, he stood again before the fire in the dim light, his back to her. She hugged her knees to her chest, clenching her teeth, watching him. She didn't want to fight him. She just wanted to be with him. If he would just turn and force her into his arms . . .

But he didn't. He left the shadowy illumination of the fire. She heard him strip down in the darkness and slide into the bed beside her.

But he didn't touch her. He turned his back on her.

It seemed that a very long time passed. She was almost certain that he slept, when he shifted to his back, causing her to jump. "So I am at fault, Danielle? And you should be returned to Aville?"

"Yes," she said, keeping her distance.

"I am to believe that you mean to keep the vow I forced from you, and no matter what I hear to the contrary, you're true to the promises you made to me?"

"Yes."

"The king has a special soft spot in his heart for you, though God knows why—you have defied him often enough. But he doesn't trust you now, nor does his son."

"The king believes every word you say to him. He always has, though God knows why."

"Because I am honest and unwaveringly loyal?" he suggested dryly.

"I was loyal," she whispered. "I was loyal at Aville. It is my home. It's where I want to be."

"If only . . ." he murmured.

She could not see his face in the shadows, yet there seemed to be some whisper of belief. She didn't think she could bear the distance between them, the huskiness of his whisper. Yet neither could she accept his fury when she hadn't done anything.

As of yet! an inner voice taunted her.

"If only?" she queried softly.

"If only I could believe in you," he said. "If only you could hold Aville for me—and King Edward," he said very softly, and she waited for him to touch her.

He turned his back on her again.

He had dozed. He didn't think he'd ever manage to do so that night, but he had. Exhaustion could be a strong force, even against the furor in his heart and soul. Yet, wanting her as he had, he had fallen asleep at her side. A bloody miracle.

And so . . .

He first thought that he was imagining or dreaming her touch. Her fingertips, like butterfly's wings, over his shoulders, along the length of his spine. Her lips . . . at his nape, feverishly hot, delicate, erotic, moving down his back, over his shoulders, lower again . . .

He stayed very still, waiting, as angry as he was hungry, aware that he had hinted she might return to Aville if he could be convinced to trust her.

So she had her price.

Let her pay it.

And she did.

The tip of her tongue teased his bare flesh.

He could ignore her.

Would ignore her, he assured himself.

Except that . . .

Her lips and tongue continued to move. Stroked with tiny little laps that wickedly teased and awakened. Moved up and town, her fingertips caressing . . . her kisses eliciting a strip of liquid fire that burned across his flesh, into his limbs, straight to his groin. Then he felt the supple length of her body, warm as a balmy breeze, sultry as sin, as she moved more closely against him, her softly exotic kisses running the length of his shoulders again.

He could, and would, ignore her . . .

Her hands moved over his shoulderblades, onto his chest,

low down upon his abdomen, stroking, lower, lower, not quite low enough. He felt himself hardening, aching, hurting.

Be damned.

He turned, drawing her into his arms. Her body undulated against his, his fingers curled into the silky-clean seduction of her hair. She took him into her mouth, instinctively caressed him with her tongue. He cried out hoarsely, wrenched himself up and caught her by the waist, swiftly pinning her beneath him in the shadows. By God, indeed, she had her price, and if it had not been for that thought, he might have told her that there could be no other woman, ever, for him.

He took her with a searing, swift, force, scarcely able to contain himself until he felt her shudder beneath him before soaring to his own explosive climax. Exhaustion, satiation; and contentment filled him, and he drew her close, amazed, happy as he had never imagined, that she had come to him with such sweet hunger.

But then it seemed his mind snapped back and he remembered that he had teased her with the hint of a promise . . .

He lay still as she curled against him. Her voice, soft and young and innocent, teased his ear.

"Adrien?"

"My lady?"

"I . . . I did nothing. I swear it."

"Ah . . ."

"Please, bring me back to Aville."

The room was cast in shadow, yet he thought that he could see her beautiful face and the glitter in her emerald eyes.

He let her words play upon the air, as if he considered them.

Then he rolled to her, rested upon an elbow, and studied her lithe, supple form and luxurious hair in the shadows.

"Never," he said flatly.

"But—but you said—"

"You'll stay here, Danielle. And that is that."

She looked away from him, biting her lip as tears stung her eyes.

"Seducing me is not the same as earning my trust," he told

her. "You can't go home, Danielle. But may I say, as your husband, I was absolutely delighted."

"Oh, you may go right to hell."

"I could return the favor."

"Don't you touch me!" she cried, which was, of course, ludicrous, because she was powerless and he was touching her in many ways. Her head twisted to the side. "Don't you touch me! I mean it, Adrien, get away, don't . . . don't . . . you're a bastard, and I do not forgive you for this!"

Something within him hurt, for her voice was cold in a way he had not heard before.

"If only I could trust you!" he whispered.

She stared at him. "You could trust me! Please!" she cried, distressed. "You are hurting me."

He thought that his weight might be crushing her, and he eased himself to her side. She leapt up, finding the huge linen bath towel and wrapping herself in it.

He sighed and stood, then walked over to her. "Danielle, you can't go back to Aville. Not now." He dropped to one knee, reaching for her chin. "Danielle," he whispered softly, amazed to realize that his voice was growing husky, and that he wanted her again. Ached for her. He had been away too long.

She wrenched her face free from his touch, stood, and walked away.

"Don't you touch me!" she whispered vehemently again.

He stood, too, wishing he wasn't tempted to sweep her up and throw her down again. But the sun was rising—if he could make love to her just once again . . .

"I mean it, Adrien, don't touch me. I don't want you—I can't bear . . . I can't . . ."

"Make me believe in you," he said.

"Don't ever think to touch me!" she repeated.

He forced himself to shrug. "If that is your wish, my lady."

As if he weren't suffering the pain of hell's fire and damnation. As if his limbs were not coiled into knots of agony.

He turned away from her and began to dress.

He knew that she watched him. He didn't glance her way. He donned his pants, shirt, tunic, and boots, and swept his great cloak around his shoulders.

He walked to the door, opened and closed it.

And did not look back.

Chapter 18

Prince Edward and his forces were gone, riding the country-side—preparing to attack the French king, Danielle assumed. She chafed at being basically imprisoned, even though the Castle de Renoncourt was a fine facility and the surrounding land beautiful. She was allowed to ride, accompanied by two older knights, Gervais de Leon and Henry Latimere. From her first morning under guard at the castle, she studied her circumstances. One of the two knights was always near her, standing guard at the outer door. Terese did not seem to be in the castle, and Danielle was far more distressed than she was willing to admit to learn that the girl had accompanied Prince Edward's troops. Neither was her husband's squire about, having ridden to attend to Adrien's horses and armor.

Different servants brought her meals, tended her room, prepared baths, and came to collect her clothing for the laundry. Listening to servants' gossip outside her rooms one day, she heard that Prince Edward had ordered that she not be attended too often by any one servant, lest she manage to befriend anyone who would help her leave the castle.

The days seemed very long, the monotony maddening. She had never been good at needlepoint. She read, she rode, she waited. The food didn't agree with her, and she sometimes felt exhausted and ill. As more and more days went past, she grew more restless, and more angry. She'd never really done anything to Prince Edward—or to Adrien. They had no right to do this to her. Aville was her home, and she belonged there.

At night, as she tried to sleep, she was tortured by images of her husband and Terese, and she would lie awake, ruing the role of women in politics and society. It wasn't fair, none of it was fair. When she wasn't angry, she was afraid—afraid for Adrien, and afraid for the French.

While pacing one night, she realized that there was a small, semi-circular balcony off her room. She liked to stand there, watch the night sky and the stars, and pray that she wouldn't go mad with the waiting, that God would send her a solution.

God did. Leaning against the wall, she discovered that it opened, and a narrow, circular staircase led downward from the balcony to the courtyard below. It was dark, covered in spider webs, and at first, she was loath to go down it, but finally she lit a lamp and explored the old stone stairs. They led to a corner of the courtyard near the stables.

First, just to prove it possible, she decked herself in her long, hooded cloak and took a walk about the courtyard.

The next night, she walked into the village, where children fetched water from the well, fires burned in small cottages, and farmers and craftsmen rested after long days of work. She was elated to realize that no one knew she had left the castle.

She took numerous jaunts at night, all well within the town limits. She grew bolder, starting out earlier, and buying little pieces of jewelry from a silversmith who worked near the castle walls. One night, as she was about to walk away with a charming new brooch, he stopped her. "Countess?"

Startled that he was aware of her identity, she paused, glancing at him more carefully. He was perhaps fifty, a serious, slim man with long, delicate fingers, well suited to his craft. She didn't reply, praying that she had not been discovered beneath her hood by a fanatical follower of her husband or the prince who would feel obliged to find one of the men and tell him about her nocturnal jaunts. But the man leaned forward. "If you ever wish to go further than the village, you only need ask my help.''

She froze for a moment, aware that she had found a loyal follower of King Jean. For a long moment she stared at him as he stared at her. With a strange ache in her heart, she wondered if she shouldn't just accept his offer—and flee this place, and the husband who had so completely forgotten her—and seek refuge with King Jean, a man who recognized her rights to her own home. But no matter how furious she was with Adrien, she didn't want to run away. She wanted him to realize that she hadn't attempted treason against him, and she fantasized a charming picture of her husband on his knees before her, abjectly apologizing for ever having doubted her.

She watched the man, shaking her head slowly but smiling as well so that he wouldn't fear the fact that he'd given himself away. ''I must remain a guest of Prince Edward. But it is good to know, friend, that you are here.''

He indicated the silver bauble she had just purchased. ''If you need help, send it to me through my boy, Yves. He works in the kitchen.''

''Thank you,'' she told him.

''To serve you would be my greatest pleasure.''

She thanked him again, and hurried away.

Three nights later, she crept down the stairway at night again. It seemed that Adrien and the prince's forces had been gone forever. She was sick, uneasy, and restless, and it wouldn't be quite so bad if she could just go home. Monteine wrote to her, as did Sir Giles and Daylin, and she wrote in turn. But she longed to be in Aville with them.

As she exited the secret door out of the stairway, she paused in fear, flattening herself against the wall as she saw a group of three armored horsemen who had just ridden into the courtyard. She started to hurry back into the stairway, but then paused, hiding in the shadows, listening as they began to speak. None of them noticed her, and their words were brash and freely stated.

''What a way to end the war, eh? Seize the French king himself, and if his people want him back, they can pay for all our arms and forces for his return!'' said one young knight, dismounting from his horse.

"Aye,'' said a companion, "but how do we find him in the midst of battle?''

"It's possible,'' said a third man, whose tunic showed that he was from the English house of Percy. "But there's sound rumor that three nights from now, he's to be riding from field to field, rallying his forces. He'll have a small escort. If he can be ambushed by a small force . . .''

"Such as ourselves?'' inquired the first man.

"Aye, aye! And if we kill him in the contest, so much the better for our good King Edward, eh? And what a boon to us! We're sent here to see that the Countess d'Aville remains safe. We not only do such duty, but kidnap or kill the French king! The prince will reward us well!''

"As long as we're careful not to die!'' said the first young knight.

"What is life without risk?'' taunted the other.

Laughing, clapping one another on their shoulders, the men left their horses to a groom and headed into the castle keep.

Danielle could barely breathe. She remained where she was for long moments, flattened against the castle wall. She had sworn before Christ that she would do her best to help Jean if his life were threatened. Treason, her husband would say. But if she managed to warn Jean and save his life, then her part in this travesty might well be done. She had promised that she would help once, but only once. Her vow to her mother and her promise to the false priest would both be fulfilled. Perhaps she could then be the countess her husband desired.

Her husband. The man who had ridden away from her . . .

With his mistress following behind?

She turned and quickly followed the stairway back to her room, afraid that someone would be calling on her that night— to see to her welfare. She had scarcely reached her balcony before she heard a tapping on the door, and Henry calling to her. She quickly sped across the room and opened the door. He stood there, one of the knights from below behind him.

"Yes?'' she inquired.

He bowed. "We've just come to see if there's anything you need, my lady."

She shook her head, staring at the knight behind Henry.

"Sir Ragwald, my lady."

She studied the young man. "Have you come from my husband?"

"No, my lady."

"Oh?"

"From Prince Edward, my lady."

"Oh, I see."

He went down on a knee before her, his head bowed. "If there's any way I can serve you, my lady . . ."

"Thank you. There nothing I need. Good evening."

She closed the door to her rooms and began to pace. After a while, she took her silver brooch from her cloak and started out into the hallway. Now, only Henry stood guard. "I've found myself famished, and need wine as well. Could you send for the kitchen lad?"

"Of course, my lady."

Henry bowed and left her in the hallway. He turned a corner—but returned very quickly. "I've sent a maid, my lady."

"You're too kind," she said. Smiling, she went back into her room. She found paper and a quill and set about writing a hasty letter to Comte Langlois. Worried that the letter might be seized, she didn't address it, explain the danger, or sign it. She wrote about her own situation, signing herself as a loyalist bound to a man who served the English king.

There was a tap on her door and she hastily folded her letter, then opened the door. Henry was there with the lad, Yves. He had a tray for her. As he set it on a table before the fire in the outer room, he cast a glance her way. She dropped the silver brooch in his hand. Henry remained in the hallway. Danielle watched him carefully as she whispered, "Tell your father this must reach Comte Langlois. Someone can find him through the Twisted Tree Tavern. Will your father know the place?"

"Aye, my lady. It's no more than an hour's ride from here, if the ride is hard."

"My thanks."

"Nay, lady, our thanks!" the lad whispered quickly. Pocketing the brooch and her letter, he quickly left the room.

That night, she lay awake in more torment than ever. What if Yves were caught? He might be tortured, killed. What if the father failed her? And just what had she written in the letter? Enough to entice Comte Langlois to come to her aid? Yes, definitely. She had hinted that she was unhappy, desperate to see him. Had she promised him anything? No, surely not . . .

The following day, her stomach was in knots. She paced endlessly, worrying herself into a frazzle. But that night, Yves returned to her room, bringing wine. He left her a letter in return.

Nervously, she ripped it open. Comte Langlois had written in return: *The Twisted Tree Tavern, tomorrow night, an hour after sunset. Your obedient servant, L.*

She exhaled and lay down, suddenly drained. Tomorrow night she was going to have to slip down the stairs, find her way to the tavern, speak with Langlois or have him bring her to King Jean—then slip back into the castle!

Could it be done?

She left the castle that night and hurried to the place by the wall where the silversmith worked. He was there, working very late by firelight.

"The Twisted Tree Tavern, my lady, is not hard to reach."

"On foot?" she queried softly.

He smiled. "There will be a horse in the copse beyond the courtyard. Yves will be there, and ride with you part way."

She nodded, her mouth too dry for words.

"Laird MacLachlan!" A voice hailed him.

The riding had been hard as they chased the French army, searching for the battleground to make a stand. Adrien was tired, muddy, and worn as he gave his squire instructions on caring for his horses. He'd had an exhausting day, having led men into heavy skirmishing with a band of French scouts.

He looked up as David Chesney, a slim young man seeking

knighthood and his fortune in Prince Edward's army, called to him from the back of his muscled gray gelding.

"Aye, David!" he returned.

David slipped quickly from his horse. "Laird MacLachlan," he said again, and seemed suddenly nervous. He looked around to see if anyone was near them.

"David, what is it?"

David came close to him. "Rumor, my lord."

"Rumor?" David had been with him at Aville, and he was instantly wary. Danielle had been quick to capture the hearts of many men.

"Some of the men were boasting when they returned to the Castle de Renoncourt. Prince Edward had sent them, to ascertain that all was well with the castle and with . . ."

"My countess," Adrien finished for him. "And?"

"They were boasting—they had planned to try to capture or kill King Jean."

"Aye?"

David lowered his voice. "One of the laundresses who has ridden with us received word from her brother that there are many traitors at the castle. And they are in contact with your countess. And though I don't know that she is involved, there is to be a meeting to warn the king—"

"Where?" Adrien demanded.

"The Twisted Tree Tavern, Laird MacLachlan. I can lead you there—"

"Nay, nay, my friend."

"I can't believe that she could betray our kind, my lord. She is watched carefully in the castle. Henry is a good man, and would not let her escape him. He and Gervais are very careful, one of them always at her door. She can't escape the castle."

"I wish I could believe that."

"How could she—"

"I don't know. But if there is a way, my lady has found it."

"I'll ride with you, my lord."

"Nay, David. I'd have no one with me."

David cleared his throat. "Laird MacLachlan, I don't condemn her. She is beautiful, loyal—"

Adrien arched a brow.

"She is French, my lord."

"She was raised by Edward."

"But you must understand the lady feels a loyalty—"

"I understand that she can be hanged or beheaded," Adrien said curtly. "Does anyone know—"

"Only my brother, and the laundress, and she . . . she sleeps with me. My brother Donald is very happy in your service, and wants no other place. And the laundress is loyal and discreet."

"If God is with me, I will find her, and once I do so, I'll have her sent from France—and temptation."

"God will need to be with you, for the tavern is a den of thieves, my lord."

"David, if you would serve me, see that no one follows me. If my wife is to be found in the act of treachery, pray God that I find her on my own."

"My lord, you mustn't judge her too harshly—"

"I'm not judging at all. I am chilled to the bone, and at the moment, have no plan other than to attempt to save her life! For if Prince Edward were to discover her betraying his father now . . ." His voice trailed off.

He *was* chilled to the bone. Amazing, when he was so angry that he could scarcely see for the fire that seemed to blaze within his eyes . . .

Damn her. A thousand times over. If anything were to happen to her . . .

He didn't dare think. He needed to cling to his anger. It was the only way to save her. From herself.

Danielle reached the tavern and dismounted quickly, surveying the place, shivering. She was already unnerved. She had seen some of the men searching the wall at the base of the keep that afternoon. Were they looking for her secret door? Did someone know that she could come and go like a wraith in the night?

She could hear masculine laughter even as she approached the doorway. She pulled her hood lower over her head, thinking she'd lost her mind. This once, she would give King Jean a warning. And then she would be absolved from the promise she had given her mother all those years ago. She would return to the castle de Renoncourt and bide her time peacefully while she waited. Good God, the kings could not fight one another forever!

Get in, give your message, get out! she told herself, and so she pushed open the door and surveyed the room, hoping that Langlois was already there and that she could be quickly on her way.

A young woman with dark hair, rouged cheeks, and monstrous breasts laughed and wiggled her way through the tables carrying tankards of ale.

And the clientele!

Enough to make the Devil himself shiver. A more scurvy lot she had never seen, all in shadows, and nearly all clad in dark, face-concealing hoods. The few faces she could see gave fair warning that the place was inhabited by the worst kinds of criminals, men who bore the scars and eyeless sockets of many a back-alley battle. Where was Langlois?

Just when she was ready to turn and flee, she saw him rise from the back of the room and quickly come toward her. He was wearing a dark, hooded cloak, but allowed the hood to fall back from his face as he came to her so that she might easily recognize him. "My lady, I have waited with such anxiety, you can't imagine. I shouldn't have had you come here at this time, but any place more respectable would have been highly dangerous, what with Edward's men prowling the countryside . . . come, I've a place where we can talk."

He pointed to the stairs. She instantly felt uneasy. What if she were caught here?

She'd never be caught here, she tried to assure herself. Adrien was the only one who might imagine that she would simply walk out of the castle by night and come to a haven for criminals with a warning for the French king.

And God alone knew where Adrien was.

She felt ill, completely sick at heart. She had sworn before that she hadn't betrayed him, and that had been the truth, and yet now . . .

Now she honored that first vow she had made, to her mother. Yet . . . if Adrien were to discover her now, if he were ever to find out about this escapade . . .

Best not to think about it.

Better to worry about Langlois. He seemed very different tonight from when she had first met him. He led her up the stairs, and down a darkened hallway, deep into the far back of the old building. There he pressed open a door to a room already alight with a candle's glow. A carafe of wine awaited on a table with a wedge of cheese and loaf of bread. A fire burned; the cover had been drawn down from the bed, which seemed to dominate the crude room. It had been arranged as if for a lover's tryst.

She stood, straight and regal, and waited. Comte Langlois entered behind her and leaned against the door.

"There was no need for so elaborate a set-up. I arranged this meeting that you might bring a message to the King of France. You will be amply rewarded."

"Ah, lady? How can you be so like ice, when I have risked life and limb to come here—to your rescue?"

"How so, sir?"

He slid the bolt, walked to her, and caught her hands, bowing as he held them, like the most gallant of knights in the most chivalric of times. "Alas, my lady, it has been said that there is all but open warfare between you—and the Scottish savage of King Edward's choosing."

Cold seemed to sweep along her spine. She longed to wrench her hands free.

"I wrote to you because—" Danielle began to Langlois.

"Ah, lady, if there is no consummation of your vows, then you are free, and the good French king can bring matters before the pope."

"Perhaps there are matters we can discuss at a later date. But this matter must be settled first. Perhaps it would be best if you escorted me to King Jean, and I gave him my information in person," she said. She felt a chill again. His dark eyes narrowed and took on a cunning and very determined glitter. "Comte, I don't intend to offend you." she went on. "You are surely a worthy nobleman, but there are matters at stake of greater importance than myself and Aville."

"But think of it, lady," Langlois interrupted, his voice grating now. "King Jean would be pleased. We go to the French king with our love an accomplished thing, and a marriage can thus be surely arranged—and you are free from that savage, heathen lout! Lady, you led me to believe in your summons that there would be great reward for me if I were to help you. I will have that reward. Now, dear sweet beauty! Since there is nothing at all between you and the savage—"

"Comte, I have a message for King Jean! Think of his anger—"

"Think of his pleasure that you may be claimed by a Frenchman rather than that arrogant Scottish bastard!"

She stared at him, growing outraged with him and furious with herself. "No!"

She pushed impatiently past him, and for a moment, she prevailed. Langlois fell back. But when she would have kept moving toward the door, he suddenly caught her shoulders and wrenched her back before him. He was angry now, dark eyes glowing. "I had meant to be gentle, to seduce you," he said, and as she stared at him incredulously, he began to rattle on about being a loyal servant of the French king, but in dire need of riches—such as those offered by Aville. He meant to make them lovers, there and then.

She swore something, she wasn't even sure just what. And she kicked him, hard, in the groin, knowing that she had to take any advantage to escape.

He cried out; she shot past him. But his fingers snagged into the fullness of her cloak and she went down with a hard thud in a tangle of coarse brown wool, and then he was on top of her, speaking his wretched intent. "Dear lady, I had meant to have this done upon a bed, but if the floor be your choice . . ."

Chapter 19

In the hallway, Adrien's fury reached a deadly peak and he cast his shoulder against the door, breaking it down. He stepped into the room to see Danielle struggling on the floor while Langlois tried somewhat ineptly to subdue her. A few seconds more, and the man might have done the deed. Adrien's instinct clamored to slay Langlois, and spray the blood from his jugular vein across the room. But Langlois was a French noble, not a common cutthroat, and Adrien forced himself to an icy calmness.

Danielle was holding her own, for Langlois, so intent in his pursuit he'd not heard Adrien arrive, was arguing with her. "Sweet Jesu, milady, by God, will you just be still! I'd not hurt you, if you'd just let me touch you—"

Then Langlois saw him, and broke off. Danielle, amazed that he had suddenly ceased his attack, looked up. Her face went decidedly ashen as she stared at Adrien.

He'd never felt this way. Never. As if his blood burned with such a fever it would explode. The very thought of Langlois touching her . . .

What spell had she cast on him that he could feel such wretched fire, loving her, wanting her, wanting to strangle her,

and like a fool, aching for her despite the fact that she most
obviously set this up, telling Langlois lies, to arrange this meeting . . . ?

He struggled for control and forced his attention to Langlois.

"Touch her, my good man, but once again," he warned,
"and I shall sever that protrusion of your lower body that
makes you act like such a fool before I lop off your head!"
He set his sword against Langlois's throat. The comte rose.

"Now you, Danielle," Adrien commanded, carefully keeping his focus on Langlois.

"How—" Danielle began in whisper. "How long were you
standing there?"

He didn't glance at her, didn't want to see her emerald eyes.
"Long enough."

"And you let him maul me so—"

"You seemed to be doing fine on your own. In fact, I was
not at all sure you desired a rescue, since you were so intent
on this assignation."

"Aye!" cried Langlois. "Indeed, I am the man to come to
the lady's rescue, and indeed, my lady, you needn't fear now.
Who is this lout? Be aware this house is filled with men loyal
to the French king, men who will mow down this English
knave!"

"Call them," Adrien suggested softly. It didn't matter.
Someone had heard the disturbance; help for Langlois was
coming. A fat man came waddling into the room, followed by
two large men armed with knives.

"Do you need assistance, milord?" the fat man demanded
of Langlois.

"Indeed!" Langlois cried wryly. Adrien granted him a certain courage and a sense of bravado, for with Adrien's blade
against his throat, it seemed far more than obvious that he
needed assistance. Yet he still hoped to escape the night with
as little bloodshed as possible.

"I seek no trouble with you, and with the dead already upon
my conscience, I'd not add more corpses here!" he said. "I
don't intend to kill the comte, just leave with the lady—"

"She came to me to escape the English!" Langlois cried. "You will not leave with her—I mean to wed her—"

"Well, that, sir," Adrien said, feeling as if he were strangling on his ire, "cannot come about, for she has a husband."

"No true marriage—"

"True in every way." Adrien corrected, staring at Danielle then with pure fury. She had started this. She deserved whatever came her way. He would never let anyone touch her for any reason while he still drew breath, but there was no reason to let her know that at this moment. He almost smiled to Langlois. "I would be delighted to prove it, should the lady not be willing to admit it. A midwife can be called."

"But—" Langlois began.

"Alas!" Adrien said. Poor Langlois was honestly befuddled. Greedy, and an idiot to think he could wrest Aville from Adrien, but he was confused. "I am aware that the lady used her wiles upon you, milord comte. And she does so exceedingly well! Unless one knows her, of course. Which I do. You were duped, sir, and that is why you draw breath this very instant. She is charming, is she not? But as I've said, I know her well, and you, sir, should now be warned to beware of such devious and seductive beauty! I'll let you live today ... but if we meet again, sir, you die!"

Langlois stared at him and then gasped. They had never actually met, so it wasn't a great surprise that Langlois had not known him when he burst in. "MacLachlan!" he cried out.

"Indeed." Adrien inclined his head. "Ah, yes! I am that savage, heathen Scotsman. *Comte, c'est moi.*"

The comte seemed to weigh his chances for a moment, then cried out, "Take him!"

Foolish thought.

As one of the men came toward him, he but shifted his sword in a swinging arc. He halted the man, then felled him. He heard Danielle cry out.

"Seize him, fool!" Langlois shouted to the second man, who started forward, stared at Adrien's blade, and swiftly turned to escape. Langlois let out a strangled sound which was silenced when Adrien's swordpoint pressed against his throat again.

"Adieu, milord comte! I should kill you, but I will spill no more blood than necessary over this treachery. She did summon you."

He reached for Danielle, heedless of the brutality of his grasp as he pressed her out the door. He caught her hand then, aware that they must escape quickly, and that he must move like lightning. More men were coming.

"Get me a weapon!" she cried to him.

"Not while I draw breath, milady! It would fester in my back!"

"I never brought arms against you!"

"I beg to differ!"

"You've too many men to fight!" she cried. "You'll kill us both, unless you've men of your own waiting below."

"I came alone."

"Alone!" she cried in dismay.

"I try not to invite witnesses when I am hoping to prevent a rock-headed little wench from endangering herself while in the act of betraying the King of England—not to mention me!" She flushed; her eyes blazed against her taut features. "Get behind me. Close," he commanded furiously. "And if you even think to betray me here again, I swear before God, I'll live long enough to make you regret it!"

Would she betray him, even here, he wondered? Were filthy French cutthroats better than a Scotsman serving the King of England?

He didn't dare so much as glance at her again until they were free from this place—there were a half dozen men ready to do battle with him now. He reminded himself that speed was necessary, and he methodically and swiftly began to slash his way down the stairs, with her at his back. His saw a blade arcing and warned her to duck—then killed the man who had wielded the blade. At one point, she screamed—a warning, he wondered—or a simple reaction?

Matthew waited for them. Adrien didn't intend to give Danielle a chance to escape on horseback, so he whacked her mount's haunches, sending it flying into the night, certain the animal would find its way home. He threw her up on Matthew, and they began to race.

He was barely aware of the ride home, his temper remained so incensed. She protested at the stream; he was glad of the ice, glad that they both froze as he finished the trip to Aville.

Perhaps he would shrivel completely from such cold, and cease to want a woman who had betrayed him so.

The gates of Aville opened as they neared them and they rode quickly in, the gates closing behind them at an invisible command. He rode to the door that led to the manor keep. In the darkness, a groom stirred when called to take the stallion's reins and care for him.

Adrien leapt down swiftly, dragging Danielle down after him. She tried to elude him; he wasn't about to allow it.

Not tonight.

He dragged her into the hallway, and when she tried to pause—desperate, it seemed, to see someone—he dragged her onward.

"Upstairs, my lady!" he commanded, and when they reached the master's chambers, he released her at last, shoving her into the room where she stood like a statue, trembling, yet not moving. Defying him.

She looked longingly to the door. He wanted to shake her until her head rattled, press her skull between his hands until he could press some sense into her.

"No servants will attend you here tonight, milady," he told her, fighting for control. "When I discovered your foolish treachery, I saw to it that I could bring you back unseen. These are no longer games you play with me! You and your indignant protestations of innocence! This was treason, Danielle. The servants have been sent out for the night. Don't look to others for help."

"I look nowhere for help!"

"Nay, lady?" he queried.

She didn't respond, but her trembling increased.

"Get those things off!" he commanded. But she lifted her chin stubbornly, staring at him, ready for a fight.

"They are causing you to shiver," he snapped.

"I shall shiver if I choose."

It was all he could do to manage to stand still.

"Indeed," he replied. "You shall shiver, but because I choose—I want you to shiver in abject fear!" He took a step toward her and she must have been more unnerved than she appeared for she moved backward, emerald eyes on his, and cried out bitterly, "As you—command!"

He could hear her teeth grating as she dropped the cloak, and then began stripping away her soaked clothing. He grabbed the blanket from the bed, then waited as her clothing fell piece by piece. He locked his jaw, watching her, wondering why the icy water couldn't have done more to dampen his ardor for her. Her breasts seemed swollen, roundly enticing, her nipples hardened to rose peaks that would tempt a saint.

He tossed the blanket to her. She wrapped herself quickly in it. He let his own cloak fall and stood before the fire, again fighting his temper, and his desire.

She was dead still in her blanket, not moving, not saying a word in her defense.

"Sweet Jesu!" he swore soundly. "Edward does not deserve this hatred on your part!"

"I wished no harm to Edward. I don't hate him. I merely sought to warn King Jean—"

"King Jean is well aware there will be battle, and what aids the French king injures the English one! To help Jean, lady, you do great hurt to Edward!" He paused a moment, realizing himself just how dangerous a game they played. "My God! Do you know that heads have rolled, that necks have been broken, for far less than you attempted this night? Good Lord, I should strike you down, you little fool!"

But she stared at him defiantly still, and denied him. "You are Edward's lackey. You have gained everything through him."

"Including you?"

"Including my lands and titles!"

"Would that I had been deprived! And, aye, lady! I am his lackey, I am his man, and I warn you now, don't ever forget it again, or that you are my wife!"

Her chin went even higher. She spoke with dead calm. "Well,

sir, you came for me—I was duly stopped in my efforts. And I know that you will judge me and sentence me as you see fit—you condemned me when I was innocent. At least this time I am guilty of hoping to see King Jean live! But as you are in such a wretched mood, I am well aware that there's nothing else I can say to you this evening. I cannot apologize to you for what I meant to do, I have never lied to you about my loyalties or—emotions.''

He stared at her, amazed. After this, after this night, she thought that she would walk on by him. Did she think that she could command him not to touch her again, *after tonight?*

He stared at her as she walked across the room, heading for the door.

He let her reach it—almost.

"Oh, no, milady! You're not leaving tonight!" he assured her, and he strode past her, not touching her yet, but blocking the doorway.

She stepped back, still silent, lashes lowered. She didn't move; she didn't tremble. His temper snapped.

"I should flay you to within an inch of your life!"

"I had to—"

"Ah, yes, the hell with the English blood in you, you had that French vow to keep! Well, that somewhat explains why you would so wretchedly use the very king within whose household you were raised.''

"Then give me over to the king!" she cried. "Let's end this—"

"End it? We've barely just begun."

Words began to spill from her, angry words, taunting words. "Surely you are needed elsewhere. You are the king's champion. Have you no enemies to challenge tonight? No dragons to slay?"

"No dragons this evening for me, my pet. Just one for you. Me. Tell me, milady, just what did you write to that dolt, Langlois? You had taken no vows? No marriage was consummated?"

She flushed. "I merely said that I needed his assistance.''

Control, he warned himself. If he were to touch her now,

he might well break her. "You were willing to lie with him to reach the French king?" he inquired.

She shook her head, her face ashen. "You were there! You know that I was not—"

"Ah, yes, my love, thank God that I am aware you were not willing to give anything away—for free."

"How dare you—" she began furiously.

"How dare you ask?" he slashed back. "You seduced him with promises of your hand in marriage. Sweet Jesu, milady, but you speak of vows! I remember the vows you made to *me*, quite clearly, if you do not. Every vow."

He strode toward her.

Now.

Now he was going to touch her.

"I remember the vows!" she whispered. Her eyes were locked with his, liquid, wide, beautiful. Her hair was long and rich and radiant, cloaking her like the blanket. She backed away from him. He followed, until he had pinned her against the wall.

Control. Oh, God, his temper was soaring. His muscles wanted her, his body pulsed, his groin ached. Let her deny him now.

"Ah, milady," he murmured, watching the beat in the slender blue vein at her throat, "Do you know what astounds and dismays me most?"

"What?" she demanded warily, watching him, straining as close to the wall as humanly possible.

"That you could say that our marriage had not been consummated. Indeed," he taunted, thinking of the way he had found her with Simon, "I remember even that first night so very well!"

"Aye!" she cried, and raised her chin. "You threatened to prove to that rabble tonight that our marriage was real!" she accused him contemptuously. "You call yourself a knight! You speak of chivalry—"

"I seldom speak of chivalry. And I merely informed the fools that a midwife could be summoned to prove that you were no sweet, innocent lass!"

She gasped, horrified. "You would have had me—"

"I would have given nothing to those wretched fools, milady, even to prove to your too amorous but well besotted Frenchman that you are *legally* and in every way very much a wife—*my* wife. But there is something I do most earnestly intend to give to you!"

Her glittering eyes narrowed on his. His heart skipped a beat. "And what is that, milord tyrant?" she inquired coolly.

He smiled. "A jog to your memory, milady wife. I had not realized I had so failed in my husbandly duties that you could forget such a thing as the consummation of your marriage."

"Oh, you fail at nothing!" she cried out. "And my memory is just fine, I haven't forgotten a thing—"

No more. He would take no more. He reached for her blanket and wrenched it away from her with a fury. The desire in him burned with an all-but-crippling brutality as he surveyed her, his wife. He thought of the way Langlois had very nearly raped her—*when she had arranged the meeting with him.*

He didn't know exactly what she read in his eyes then—the anger, or the desire.

"No . . ." she whispered.

The last time they had met, she had furiously denied him—for not believing in her. And now . . .

Now she had proven them enemies. And he wanted her anyway. Wanted to touch and taste her, have her, caress her, drown within her. Her blanket was gone; her hair cloaked her perfect flesh, her breasts, even the curve of her hips, the slim length of her legs, the triangular shadow of hair at the apex of her thighs. Hunger filled him, undeniable, inexorable.

"Damn you," he told her, bracing her there.

She tried to wrench away. He would not allow it.

"You will remember who you are!" he cried to her.

"And to whom I belong?" she shouted back in angry protest.

"Aye, lady, indeed!"

He leaned to her, and kissed her. Found her lips, pressed within them, ravaged her lips and mouth with his tongue, and wanted more. Yet his lips broke briefly from hers.

"Please . . ."

He stood still, aching, tied in knots. "Ah, lady? Beg mercy, would you?" he inquired. And if she did, what then? Could he walk away from her now?

Never. It wouldn't matter if the king himself commanded him to do so.

But her eyes opened wide and furiously on his.

"Not in a—"

"In a pig's eye?" he suggested, using her term.

"You are the worst of knaves!" she cried out, "and I'll never beg anything of you!" She was suddenly struggling against him, pounding on his chest.

He captured her wrists with a grip of steel. She was silent, staring at him, her breasts rising and falling in the firelight. And he was both more furious than he had been in all his life, and more aroused. God, but he was in agony, and by God, she would heal him!

"Indeed, milady," he assured her, "tonight, by God, you will please me! For I want everything that I have remembered burned within my form and mind again and deeply, the hungers of so many nights appeased. Aye, please me. Ease away the rage. I demand it!"

He swept her up into his arms, heedless of the few steps that brought them to the bed. He fell ruthlessly with her into the cool softness. If she twisted, he did not know. If she fought, he fought harder. He found her lips, assaulted, tasted, caressed, savored, and demanded. He touched her, caressed the fullness of her breasts, her nipples, thighs, throat . . .

He rose above her, impatiently shedding his clothing. Her eyes were on his, huge, so green in the firelight. She didn't whisper a word of protest then, but neither did she reach out.

But she would.

He caught her hand, and brought it to his burning flesh. His muscles bunched and pulled and leaped in anticipation as he brought her fingertips down against his chest, then around the throbbing length of his manhood.

A shudder wracked through him. She almost jerked away. He held her to him.

"Lest you forget!" he whispered, and she trembled, yet didn't pull away again.

He pressed her down, easing his weight between her limbs, and when she cried out softly, he ignored her, capturing her knees and spreading them wide to his access and hunger. He kissed and teased the soft, silky flesh of her inner thigh, then moved against her, his caress a whisper of flame and liquid fire, his intent to mercilessly coerce and arouse . . .

Yet he was the one in torment, the taste and scent and feel of her infusing his blood, his every breath, the fury of his need. She writhed to escape, then writhed to come closer . . .

Enough, too much, never enough, more than he could bear. He rose above her, buried himself within her. Her eyes were upon him, and he wondered again that any woman could have so much power over him, filling his thoughts so constantly, tormenting him, yet taking such a place in his heart that he would gladly die for her, kill for her . . .

If any man ever touched her again . . .

He met her gaze.

"Lest you forget *me* . . ." he whispered.

She sobbed out, closing her eyes, reaching for him. And he embraced her, his arms as fierce as the thunder of his movement as he embedded himself again and again, as if thereby he could be with her forever.

He felt her surge against him, and in the following seconds, lost all conscious thought, violently shuddering against the crest of his own climax.

Yet even as he held her, his seed spilling into her, he called himself a fool. Ah, indeed, he had proved that she was his, his wife, his lover, his to seduce, his to arouse. He had made her respond to him, he had proven that he could do so.

And he had sold his own damned soul to her again. There was no one like her. She had been in his blood, in his life, haunting his soul and his senses forever.

But she would betray him again. And again. God knew, she was French. To the core.

And the real battle was about to commence. She was dangerous. To them both. He dared give no more, for she risked her life, and he would defend her to the end, yet both their heads might well roll.

His muscles constricted painfully.

And he rose.

He wanted to stay. Hold her throughout the night. But he dared not. Damn her, he dared not!

He found clothing in his trunk and dressed quickly. He didn't want to look at her, but he could see her even as he pretended to give his attention to the task of dressing. Her arms were crossed over her chest, her knees drawn together and up. Her dark hair splayed over the white sheets; her lashes swept her cheeks. Her features were marble, her flesh was ivory and perfect, and he ached just to touch her again . . .

He belted on his scabbard and sword.

And slammed his way out of the room.

Hearing the door, Danielle jumped and winced. And the tears that had burned beneath her eyelids suddenly sprang hotly into being.

What could she have done differently? How could she have changed her fate, indeed, changed what she was, her loyalties, her own sense of honor? If only he could understand.

What did they do now?

Where did they go from here?

She had wanted him so desperately. And she had had him at last, touched him, felt the violence, tenderness, hunger, and passion.

She had really loved him so very long. So long. And she'd missed him, wanted him, ached for . . .

Well, tonight she had had him.

And lost him. If only he would come back. What then? She could whisper the real truth. That she loved him. He wouldn't believe her, and it wouldn't matter. Not tonight.

Nay, not tonight . . .

She allowed herself the luxury of tears.

Part III

Chapter 20

Three weeks after Adrien left his wife at Aville, the armies at last clashed in the giant battle that had long been coming.

The Battle of Poitiers took place on September 19, 1356. King Edward was in England at the time; the campaign and battle were waged by his son, Prince Edward, known after as the Black Prince, for the color of his armor as he led his forces into the fray.

It was a splendid victory for the English; the French were soundly defeated. Adrien, being part of the mounted assault, had followed the archers onto the battlefield, riding Matthew and bearing down on his enemies with tremendous power and speed. He fought with his sword, a fallen mace when he was disarmed at one point, and with an opponent's battle-axe. The day's work was grim, and at one point, mired in a combination of blood and mud, the battle was so horrible that had he time to think, the horror would send him howling from the field. He did not have time to think. His enemies—strangers who raged at him with their own weapons—sought his death, and there was little to do but fight them in return.

As the French gave ground, he shouted to his men to encircle them. In the midst of the fighting, he realized that he and his men had the French king in their net, and so it was that King Jean of France became a prisoner of the English.

Adrien could admit to admiring the man, for he was a young king, courageous while he fought—and valiant in defeat. He was a striking fellow, a charming Valois, quick-witted as he was escorted to Prince Edward. "Ah, well, Laird MacLachlan, if I am to be taken, at least I am escorted by an in-law. How is my fair young cousin of Aville?"

"She is well, King Jean."

"Despite the machinations of men such as Langlois," King Jean muttered, smoothing his dark hair. He shrugged, smiling at Adrien as they rode. "Naturally, Laird MacLachlan, I am not a fool. I heard what happened at the tavern; Langlois was not so remiss as to fail to warn me that the countess had been trying to reach me. I can see where this might have been a matter of great marital tribulation for you."

"Frankly, I feared for her life should Edward discover her treason."

"Then he'll not discover it," Jean said shrewdly, and again, Adrien thought that he liked the man.

They came to the battlefield tent where Prince Edward awaited his royal prisoner. "Cousin!" Edward greeted Jean. "What a pleasure!"

"For you, surely," Jean said.

"You are a valued guest."

"What is my value going to be?"

"When he discovers that we have you, my father will be calculating the sum," Edward told him. He clapped a hand on Jean's back. "I can hardly ask you to drink to my great victory, but I will drink with you in commiseration, eh?"

Prince Edward remained joyous, which was natural. His victory had been complete, and around the campfires, men already noted that it was a battle so great it would go down throughout generations in song and story. Soldiers would study the tactics; kings would take note.

But though Adrien joined Edward in his celebration, he was anxious to see to his own men and his horses. Despite the sweetness of victory, there was a bitterness in his soul. He couldn't forget that his wife had so willingly risked her life to go to the Twisted Tree Tavern. And he couldn't believe that he loved her still, beyond sense and reason. He couldn't trust her. The danger she had threatened to the English royal house was over now, with the French army so soundly defeated and King Jean a prisoner, but he suddenly wanted her out of France. Perhaps it was the anger in the soul. She was at Aville now; he had left her there under guard, since he'd had time for little else with the armies in motion. But it galled him that she was there, for it seemed that she had achieved what she wanted through treachery. And she would soon learn of Jean's defeat, and God alone knew then if she would begin plotting for his freedom . . .

She wasn't going to stay at Aville. He'd been gone too long from England and Scotland. He wanted to return to his border lands, he realized. Home was a place where he could replenish his soul. And whether she found his rocky northern terrain barbaric or not, it seemed the ideal place for her.

He would bring her to Scotland, and leave her there while his temper cooled. Perhaps he could rid himself of his obsession for a wife who betrayed him at every turn. And if not, well, he would go to London. London was full of diversions.

Late that night, when Prince Edward was at last alone, Adrien returned to his battlefield tent and asked for permission to leave the field and return to Aville for his wife.

"I need you with me a while longer—there's much to settle here. Send to Aville and have her brought to the Channel. We'll meet up with her party there. Will that do?"

"If that's what you're granting me," Adrien said.

Edward smiled. "You needn't worry. She's not going to find a way to help King Jean escape."

Adrien arched a brow. "I'm glad you're so certain."

Edward laughed. "That is your fear, isn't it?"

"Perhaps . . ."

"I don't think she'll manage to free him from the tower, either."

"I'm not bringing her to London."

"To your English estates—"

"No. Home. To Scotland."

"Far, far away. But I'll require you to come back to London. My father will expect you—"

"I'll return to London after I've seen to affairs in Scotland."

"With the countess?"

"Doubtfully."

Edward smiled. "Perhaps some time in the barbaric wilds will be good for your fair damsel. But I imagine that my father will ask to see her, eventually."

"Perhaps. He has always held a tenderness for her, though why, I honestly can't imagine. She betrays him time and time again."

Edward shrugged. "Perhaps it's guilt, regarding Aville. Or perhaps it's in memory of his friendship with her father, or guilt for seizing her mother's property. Father can be a strange man."

"If he commands that I send for her, I will. But I'd like to take her home to Scotland now."

"As you wish."

News of the terrible defeat of the French army at Poitiers came quickly to Aville.

Though she'd had the run of her home once again, Danielle had known from the beginning that she wasn't to leave, and she was to be allowed no quarter should she attempt to do so. She was home, where she wanted to be, so she made no attempt to leave. But Sir Giles escorted her to her room every evening, and she didn't move a step outside the keep without Daylin or another of her husband's men behind her. Monteine was with her again, for which she was grateful, but she had awaited some word from Adrien or the front with a greater nervousness than ever. When word came, it was grim. It came first in the way of maimed, bloodied, and worn men, trying to make their way home. They were the enemy, defeated, but at Aville, as ordered by Adrien through the first messenger to reach the place, they were fed, their wounds were treated, and they were helped on their way.

News of the disaster wasn't given to Danielle, but to Sir Giles, and it was he who asked her to come into the great hall, and he who told her quietly that God be praised, Prince Edward had beaten the French, and King Jean was a prisoner of the English.

"And Adrien?"

"Laird MacLachlan emerged unscathed, my lady, noble warrior that he is."

She was shaking, first with relief for Adrien, then with sorrow for the French, and for Jean. She fled from the great hall and hurried upstairs. Flushed and nauseous, she lay down, worried. What would happen now?"

Within a few days Daylin came to her room to tell her that she must prepare—they were going to travel.

"Where?"

"To the Channel."

"And then?"

"And then I don't know, my lady. King Jean is to be taken to London. Many more French nobles have been taken for ransom, and they will become prisoners in the tower as well."

She felt very cold. Had Adrien disavowed her then? Was he seeking a divorce? Was she to be among the French prisoners in the tower?

She would have plagued Daylin for answers, except that she knew he had none. Monteine had questioned him ceaselessly, and he had angrily told her that he knew nothing. Monteine was nervous about what was to happen, and Danielle found herself becoming very afraid of the future.

The house of Valois was, for the time being, shattered, and so, if she had been frightened enough to try to run away, there would have been no one to help her. She hid her fear, involved herself in packing, and asked if she would be allowed to ride Star. She was. On the appointed day, she rode out without a murmur of protest, determined to keep her head high.

They rode to Calais, where they were met by one Sir Timothy Field, who was gracious in greeting and escorting her to spacious quarters in an old Norman castle. She was given one room, but it was huge, with a fireplace that stretched almost the length of one wall. A large canopied and draped bed sat on a dais in a far corner, while warming tapestries covered the narrow windows and numerous shelves of books lined the walls.

"I hope you will be comfortable," Sir Timothy said. He was an old knight, but his shoulders were as broad as an ox's and he was tall as an oak. "My family has lived here for generations, and we have done what we can for warmth and comfort."

She smiled at him and flashed a glance to Daylin, who stood to his side.

"I'm sure I'll be very comfortable. Am I to stay long?"

Sir Timothy looked at Daylin, arching a brow. He bowed to Danielle. "That, my lady, I cannot say. If you'll excuse me, I'll allow you to settle in."

Daylin followed him out; Monteine nearly tripped over herself to follow Daylin, and Danielle was left alone.

She soon discovered that her door was bolted. She wasn't a guest. She was a prisoner.

But she was tired, more tired than she could ever remember being. A manservant came to ask if she would like a bath, and she gladly accepted. The ride had been long and muddy. She had barely finished with the castle's elaborate brass hip tub when dinner was brought to her. After eating, she was still too tired to bang on the door and demand an explanation, so she curled up on the bed and slept.

Hours later, she awakened. There were no lamps or candles lit, and the fire in the huge hearth had died down. She moved the drapes and stepped barefoot from the bed, then walked to the fire, shivering. She sat down on the rug before it, stretching her hands out to feel its warmth.

"So, Adrien!" she mused to the fire. "What am I doing here, locked in this room in Calais? What have you planned for me, you . . . bastard!" she whispered, tears stinging her eyes. The future loomed bleak before her. Apparently, he couldn't be bothered with her anymore himself. She was simply to be escorted from place to place. Left behind, while he went about the business of being one of King Edward's great champions!

"You should burn in the fires of hell!" she whispered to the flames.

"How charming."

She was glad she was sitting. Hearing Adrien speak, his voice deep ice, was so startling she would have fallen had she been standing. She spun around on her haunches to see that he was seated in one of the huge leather chairs before the fire.

"Adrien!"

"My love," he acknowledged evenly. He sat comfortably back against the chair, studying her with eyes that glittered pure gold against the flames. He wore no armor, just tight breeches, shirt, tunic, and boots. His crest was embroidered in red upon the white tunic.

She rose, slowly and carefully, wanting the advantage of looking down at him. He didn't move, but continued to watch her gravely. Then he smiled with casual indifference. "So, you've missed me?" he inquired.

She ignored the taunt, swallowing hard as her stomach knotted. "What am I doing here in Calais?" she asked him.

"You are Sir Timothy's guest," he said flatly.

"I'm a prisoner. My door is bolted."

"Surely you can't be surprised at that."

"King Jean is a prisoner."

"Aye, and we intend that he should stay that way."

"What harm can I do—"

"I'm afraid to find out."

She fell silent, looking down at the thick bear rug. She looked back at him, fighting for control.

"What is to happen to the king?"

"Edward? Why, his people will honor him for this great victory."

"I meant Jean, and you know it."

"He will come to England and be a prisoner in the tower."

"Am I to be imprisoned in the tower as well?"

"No," Adrien told her. "You needn't worry so much about your King Jean. He will be a prisoner, yes, while the English await his ransom, but he will also be King Edward's guest. I sincerely doubt that he will suffer in the least."

"So . . . what is to happen to me?"

"You're leaving France."

She felt herself grow pale. "For London?"

"Scotland."

Scotland. His homeland. Far, far away from everything, and everyone. A barren wasteland.

Where she could be left.

"What about my father's English estate?" she murmured.

"I'll see to it."

"When do we leave?"

"In the morning. Early." He rose, and as he towered over her, she saw that his hair was still damp. He smelled cleanly of a pine-scented soap. He hadn't bathed here; she saw none of his belongings, and she felt a weakness in her knees as she thought that he had taken a room himself elsewhere. She was very tempted to throw herself at his feet and cry out to him that she had never meant to hurt him, that she was miserable, sorry for King Jean and France, and sorry for the two of them, because it seemed that their marriage had become a casualty of war.

She didn't throw herself at his feet. Or cry out. She stood very still, unnerved by the way he studied her.

"You should get some sleep. I hear you haven't been well," he said.

She shook her head. "I've been fine."

"Monteine has told Daylin that you're frequently sick."

"Monteine has no right discussing me with Daylin."

"They are both concerned about you."

"Then I am grateful for their concern, but I'm fine, and they shouldn't be discussing me." If he was leaving, she thought, he needed to leave. She didn't feel sick at the moment, she felt like bursting into tears. Everything had gone so very wrong. He sounded like a distant stranger when he spoke. It was tormenting to wonder where he was going when he left her to her comfortable prison.

He shrugged, still watching her with his golden eyes. "At least you are here. You didn't escape Aville."

"I didn't escape Aville because I had no desire to escape Aville. It is my home, and where I should be."

"Ah, so if you had been at Aville, you'd not have gone to the Twisted Tree Tavern?" he inquired, his head inclined slightly.

She sighed with exasperation. "I made a vow to my mother to honor the king—"

"Aye, lady, I'm aware of your wretched vow. But don't you think you fulfilled it long ago? Long enough so that you might now have kept a vow to me?"

She exhaled slowly, trying not to shake. "I made a promise to the priest that I'd save Jean's life if I could. The knights were threatening to kill him, Adrien."

"The priest was not a priest."

"I still promised to Christ to save King Jean's life if I could. That was all. And it is God's truth that I never knew the priest was not a priest. Had you just left me home at Aville—"

"Well, lady, you are going home now."

"Not *my* home—"

"Then you will make it so!" he interrupted sharply. "Sleep while you can," he told her, and stepping past her, he exited the room.

She heard the bolt slip into place.

Eventually she lay down and slept. And she awoke slowly, aware of warmth, and the soft brush of fingers against the bare flesh of her back. She inhaled, afraid to move at first—then momentarily afraid that some stranger had come upon her. But it wasn't a stranger, it was Adrien, and she knew he could touch lightly and seductively when he was so inclined. His hand had slipped beneath the hem of her nightgown, and he teased her awake, fingertips against her spine, circling her buttocks. His hand rounded her hip, drew her hard against his arousal. An arm slipped around her, holding her tight, and he caressed her breast as his lips pressed against the flesh of her shoulder and his manhood prodded against her until he slipped within . . .

A small sound escaped her at first, and she tried to hold very still. But it seemed so long since . . . and the feel of him was so good. Within minutes she was on fire, moving against him, slick, wanting, reaching. She escalated quickly to a sweet, soaring climax, and scarcely moved as she trembled with the aftermath. He remained behind her, and did not withdraw for a long time. She kept her back to him when he did so.

"There's nothing you want to say to me?" he inquired.

She wished he would not speak. She wished that the night could just be silent, and that they could lie together and forget the battles of the day.

"What would you have me say?" she whispered.

"Ah . . . well, Adrien, you do look well. No battle axes in your head? No, well, thank God for that. Christian charity alone might make you glad to see that I did not bleed my life's blood over your precious France."

"The French did not ask you to come from England to fight or die here."

He sighed, and she was aware that he stared up at the ceiling, worn and weary.

"I knew you would survive," she told him. Then she admitted very softly, "I prayed that you would survive."

"And why is that?"

"Christian charity."

"Ah . . . but there is nothing else you would say to me?" he inquired, and he turned toward her back once again, an arm around her, fingers gently upon her waist and breast.

"No!" she whispered.

She felt his head settle on the pillow. He held her, and stroked her. He didn't speak again, and neither did she. She barely breathed.

When he said he would start early, he meant it. Dawn had barely broken when they started across the Channel. The seas were not wild, but slightly rough. Danielle had been at his side as he spoke with the ship's captain when the motion became more than she could bear. She hurried aft, and was violently sick. Monteine brought her a cool, damp cloth and she cleaned her face, but as she thanked Monteine, she saw that Monteine had left her and Adrien had come to stand at her side. She flushed, looking over the water. "I'm sorry, I didn't mean to be rude to your English captain or disgrace you in any way. I don't know what this is; I admit that it seems as if it has gone on forever and forever. Most probably—"

"Danielle," he said, leaning against the oak-rimmed hull and studying her with a fair amount of amusement. "I had thought you were trying to shun me in some way, and now I see that you are truly naive."

"I don't know what you're talking about—"

"So it seems. And if I hadn't been with you last night, I'd not be so certain myself."

"I still don't—"

"You're not sick, my love. You're expecting a babe."

She sucked in her breath with surprise, and then she was angry because he was laughing at her. "You don't know!" she whispered. "You can't possibly know—"

"I can, and I do."

"Oh! And how many children have you fathered?"

His gold eyes glittered on hers. "None other, my lady," he said, and she felt a tremendous relief until he added, "That I know about." And with that, he walked away.

By afternoon, with the good winds that had made the Channel rough, they reached Dover. Adrien had no wish to stay overnight, and when their horses and belongings were unloaded, they immediately began riding.

That night they stayed at a tavern outside Winchester. Adrien spent much of the early evening in the public room, drinking with Daylin and the men-at-arms who accompanied them, Michael among them, but not Sir Giles, who had remained at Aville. Until late at night, Danielle could hear the men as their voices drifted up to her. They laughed, drank, gambled, told bawdy jokes, and played with the tavern wenches. Danielle tried to bury her head in her pillow. It did little good. Toward dawn, Adrien came up the stairs and into their room. He stumbled, slamming against the doorway as he came in. She heard him disrobe carelessly, then crawl in beside her. He reeked of good English ale. She had every right to fight him when he pulled her into his arms.

"Now you're a drunken wretched Scotsman," she told him, which amused him no end.

"Ah, but *your* drunken Scotsman, my love."

"Oh? And how often is that?" she whispered.

"As often as I desire."

She shook her head violently. "Nay, sir, you can't claim a wife that way. Drink with your comrades, whore with your friends, and then . . ."

"You," he informed her, rising above her, "are now being a pious French traitor. But you're my pious French traitor, God help me!"

"Adrien . . ." she protested, and tried to squirm from the bed; he dragged her back. He kissed her, stripped her, laved her breasts, her belly, her intimate flesh unbearably with liquid strokes. She couldn't remember why she had been protesting. She no longer cared.

In the morning, for once, she rose before him. When the tavernmaster banged on the door to tell him it was the hour he had asked to awaken, Adrien winced. He glanced at her from half-closed eyes and winced again. "My apologies, my love. Was I terribly rude?"

"No worse than customary," she informed him coolly, having already washed and dressed. He sat up in the bed, holding his head between his palms.

"Good God, it's been years and years since I've drunk so much . . ." he murmured. He glanced her way, hair tousled, eyes red. He groaned, and lay back. "What's that I smell?"

"Fish. The tavernmaster brought fresh fish and bread for our breakfast."

He groaned anew, closing his eyes. "Must you eat it?"

"It's quite delicious," she said. "Try some!" she added maliciously, coming toward the bed with her plate.

"Come near with that, and I shall thrash you."

"And risk your Scottish son?"

"You'll probably have a girl."

"I shall do so on purpose, if it will irk you."

To her surprise, he smiled, lying back, casting an arm over his forehead. "You're an evil woman," he told her, waving his arm in the air. "Out—get out of here with your fish!"

"Out—my door isn't bolted?"

"I beg of you, go downstairs and enjoy your meal with Monteine."

She hesitated, puzzled. "You're not afraid I'll run?" she asked softly. "We're still very close to Dover."

He leaned on an elbow and stared at her, the laughter gone from him. "If you run, I'll come after you. And I'll find you, wherever you may go."

He made no actual threat, but the sound of his voice was chilling, and she realized that whether he had been tender and passionate did not matter; he had not forgiven her. She was not to be trusted.

She fled from the room, and ate downstairs with Monteine. She was startled, moments later, to see that he had made a complete recovery. When he strode down the stairs, he was dressed in emblemed tunic, sword, and scabbard, and was impatient to be on his way, shouting orders even as he entered the public room.

It was a long, hard day. When they stopped that night at the manor of a friend, she tumbled into bed, exhausted, as soon as they had supped. She was aware of Adrien taking off her shoes, loosening her gown, removing it. And she thought that he watched her for a while, but she was too weary to know. She was aware of his warmth in the night, yet he was up when she awakened.

They didn't ride so hard again. He said that they would stop early the next afternoon.

"It will take us a long time to reach Scotland at this rate, Laird MacLachlan," Daylin warned.

"We can go no faster. I dare not risk Danielle and the babe," Adrien replied.

Danielle flushed, feeling everyone stare at her. Yet she was absurdly glad that he had noted her state of exhaustion, and that, simple courtesy though it might be, he offered her that much.

It did take them a long time to reach Scotland. But Danielle didn't mind the time, nor the ride.

Adrien did not forgive her, nor did she bow to him in any way, asking forgiveness. But they were together. They frequently rode apart, Adrien leading, then tending to the line of their men, goods, and baggage, and riding ahead again. They slept some nights in taverns and inns, and some were passed at the castles of his friends and acquaintances. And at night, no matter who he talked with, or how late he stayed awake—gaming, drinking, or talking by a fire—he always came to her before dawn. And she never tried to deny her pleasure in making love, or in simply being held through the night. They were man and wife, she thought, drifting off to sleep one night, in a way they had never been before.

And for weeks, it was all even better when they reached Scotland. She had charged him that his land would be barbaric; it was charming. The sprawling manor house, built of wood and stone, was warm and comfortable, furnished with beautifully carved pieces. The hall boasted a huge table with lion-clawed feet and huge, high-backed chairs. The master's chambers were warmer still, the bed covered in a tapestried blanket, the hearth huge, the walls lined with shelving that housed books and armor, Gaelic carvings, and swords from around the world. Off the master bedroom was a nursery, already furnished with a cradle that had been Adrien's, she was told.

The people were charming to her, welcoming her with a familiarity she hadn't known before, but that she found pleasant. The house sat on a loch, with the water just feet away, cool and crisp and beautiful. Through a series of channels, it reached all the way to the Irish Sea. The land rolled and weaved; in places it was greener than emerald, in others, mauve, and in others still, it was the color of the stone that seemed to be cast carelessly down upon it. The wind smelled sweetly, cleanly, of the cool, crisp water of the loch, and she found herself quickly entranced by the colors.

Her first night home, she wandered from the bedroom to the

attached nursery and stared at the cradle. She set her hand upon her abdomen, admitting that it had grown quite round. Even having been so constantly sick for so very long, she hadn't really believed she was going to have a baby, create another life. A child who would be a combination of herself and Adrien. It seemed such a special and unique thing to share.

As she stood there, for the first time, she felt movement. She cried out, startled, pleased.

"Danielle!"

She hadn't known he was in the house, but he was at her side instantly, hands on her shoulders as he turned her around to face him. "Danielle—"

"He moved!" she whispered.

The anxiety in his face fled to be replaced by a wide grin. "He? You told me it was going to be a girl."

"She moved."

He laughed softly and swept her up into his arms, carrying her back to the bedroom and laying her on the bed. He set his hand upon her stomach, waiting.

"He—she—moved. I swear it!" she whispered.

"Patience, my love. It's a virtue with which you don't seem very familiar."

She frowned at him, ready to argue. But the baby chose that moment to move again. She wondered if only she could feel it inside her womb, but then she saw his face, and for a moment, it was filled with simple wonder. "I'm glad I've brought you here," he murmured. "I'm glad my son will be born here."

"It's a girl," she protested for the sake of argument.

"My child," he amended.

There was a knock on the door; supper had been brought to them. They dined in the room, for it had grown late, and when they were done, Adrien undressed her and made love to her very gently, with a strange poignancy.

Over the following few days, he rode the estate with his Scottish steward. Danielle made a point of getting to know the servants in the manor, and the farmers, masons, and craftsmen in the village who also stood as men-at-arms to protect the castle against attack, should some border lord, Englishman or

Scot, decide to hunger for greater lands. She enjoyed the people, loved the sound of their speech, and was surprised to realize she was content. Evenings, she shared suppers with Adrien, who told her colorful tales about the great William Wallace and Robert the Bruce, while admitting unhappily that King David of Scotland, like King Jean of France, was a prisoner in Edward's tower. They argued over books, philosophy, and history. No matter what the argument, he was with her at night. Sometimes he made love very gently, and sometimes with a hungry, yearning, almost desperate passion.

They'd been there a week when she went down by the loch in the afternoon. She wore a simple linen dress, and at the water's edge, she stripped her stockings and shoes and waded in. It was cold, but delightful. She was there when he came to her just as night fell.

He sat on a rock by her side, chewing a blade of grass and watching the water. "You look very well here," he teased. "Your cheeks are flushed, your eyes are bright, and very lovely."

"Thank you," she murmured, emerging from the water. She sat on the embankment and drew her shift over her bare feet.

"You'll survive my heathen and barbaric lands?"

"They are wild and beautiful," she said.

"Treacherous as well—you must sometimes take care. Dangerous, wild, and beautiful—my land, and my wife," he murmured. Looking back out to the water he said, "I leave for London tomorrow."

"So soon? We've just come here—"

"*I* leave for London tomorrow," he repeated.

She stiffened. "And I am to stay behind?"

"Aye, my love."

She lowered her eyes, afraid for him to see the depths of her disappointment. London. Prince Edward and his troops would be in London. What of the peasant girl, Terese, always so willing to serve her husband? Her pride would not allow her to ask.

"So I am not to be trusted in London?" she inquired bitterly. "One would think the King of England would have enough men in London that I would not be such a danger. Edward said that I am not to come?''

Adrien stood, still staring out at the water. ''Nay, my lady. I have said that you're not to come.''

And he turned and walked away.

Chapter 21

Evening was coming—with it, a fierce chill in the north.

Danielle drew her knees to her chest, feeling the breeze by the loch. She didn't hate this place; she loved it. Loved it more, possibly, than any place she'd been before. Something about the colors of the land was especially beautiful to her. She loved the rock that jutted from the ground, the sweeping hills and plains, the crystal beauty of the loch as it stretched away into the sunset. She even liked the sound of the wolves howling at night. She just didn't like Adrien leaving her. She was the French wife who had betrayed him and the king. She'd provided a continental title and property, a rich income from that property, and now, she was about to give him an heir. And he was leaving again.

She put her palms to her cheeks and felt how her flesh burned. She stood, staring out at the water. He would never believe in her again, not while the house of Valois ruled France.

The lock seemed incredibly tempting. She waded out into it again, glad of the cold water that seemed to sluice right through her. She walked deeper, and when she could, she began to swim, desperate to ease her rage and frustration, jealousy and fear. She plunged beneath the surface, freezing, shaking, yet feeling a strange freedom and elation in the act.

"Danielle!"

She surfaced to realize that she had come a long way from shore. Adrien, minus his boots, sword, and scabbard, was thrashing into the water, then coming after her, swimming hard. Alarmed by the sound of his voice, she swam toward the shore, only to be caught up by him and dragged back to the embankment.

"What is it—?"

"Have you gone daft, lost your senses, lass?" he demanded angrily.

She stood before him, seriously shaking then, for she was out of the water and goosebumps had arisen all over her skin.

"I was swimming, Adrien, nothing more. Am I not free to swim?"

"You were swimming?" he repeated, golden eyes narrowed.

"I went swimming. I'm not to go to London. Am I not to go into the water? You forgot to tell me there would be no swimming!"

She was startled when he suddenly clasped her to him, his fingers threading into the hair as he cradled her against his chest. "Swimming. My lady, it's cold. And that water is far colder than any you knew in France. You'll catch your death."

He carried her into the manor house and to their bedroom, where he stood her before the fire, peeled her wet gown from her, and wrapped her in a warm wool blanket. He cast off his own damp tunic and breeches, then lifted her, and sat with her in a chair before the fire, just holding her. "You can't risk illness," he said, smoothing back her hair.

"Because of the bairn," she murmured, using the Scottish inflection. "I wasn't trying to hurt myself, or the baby."

He didn't say anything. She leaned against his chest, fighting the temptation to cry. She was going to miss this. She knew his chest so well. The muscle structure, the scars, everything about him. She stroked a finger down his cheek, seeing the way the fire reflected in his eyes. "Adrien . . . it was long ago now, but I can remember when my mother died—she was so fervent! She insisted that I acknowledge the king. She had been hurt so in war ... and maybe she felt that in surrendering Aville, she had betrayed her own people. I made a vow to her. I carried it out.''

He nodded. "You made vows to me."

"I didn't break them."

"That, my love, is certainly debatable."

"But," she said, "there is argument for my side, at least."

He smiled, and stroked her hair. "There will always be argument with you." He sighed after a moment. "It was all very strange ... I knew your mother, you know."

"Of course, I know. You caused Aville to fall. There's a great deal I might continue to hold against you."

He ignored the taunt. "She might have been a Valois and Edward's enemy, but she liked the king. Honestly. I don't know why she would tell you to fight foolishly against him."

"Adrien?"

"What?"

She looked up at his face, his beloved face, and stroked his chin, wondering how she had ever hated him. "I love you," she whispered.

He stared at her a long moment, gold eyes glittering a strange fire, yet giving nothing away. He caught her fingers and kissed them. "Do you?" he asked her softly. "Or are you simply such a beautiful seductress that you will have your way at any cost?"

She closed her eyes, furious that tears stung against her eyelids. She had confessed the truth, and gained nothing but more accusations. She started to shift against him, struggling to rise, but he held her closer. "Danielle, would that what you say is true! I cannot, will not, take you to court now. I want my child born here. I don't want you traveling anymore, and God knows, I want you far from temptation."

"I want you far from temptation as well!" she returned, still stiff and anxious to free herself. She might as well press against a brick wall. His arms did not relent.

"And what does that mean?"

"It means that I don't like a woman's lot in this world. You locked me in a castle while your mistress followed you off to war! And now you'll go to London—"

She broke off because he was laughing. She slammed a palm against his shoulder and he caught her wrist. "Sorry, sorry, my love. But could this mean ... if I kept a mistress, would you care?"

"I'll not answer you, and you can stop this game. I tell you that I love you and you call me a liar. Am I to cast myself at your feet with even greater humiliation while you laugh and ride away to join ..."

"To join whom?" he demanded, eyes sizzling.

"Edward!" she lied.

He sat back smiling, lifting a strand of her fire-dried hair, twirling it in his fingers. She snatched the lock back, and he smiled again. "I'm truly curious. With whom do you think I've dallied?"

"Leave me be, let me up—"

"Oh, my love, there are lots of things I mean to do with you tonight, but leaving you be and letting you up are not among them!"

"Damn you, Adrien—"

"Whom?" he demanded, holding her still, his eyes piercing into her.

"I don't know! How would I know? The king's court is full of women—"

"I've been at war."

"Camp followers go to war."

"Ah ... so you accuse me of a whore here or there?"

"Oh! Could we not discuss—"

"Whom specifically?"

"The girl, Terese, who informed me she meant to do your bidding."

He eased back in the chair, smiling broadly. Once again, she tried to leap up. Once again, she hadn't a prayer of escaping him.

"I am sorry. Perhaps I shouldn't be enjoying this quite so much, but I've spent so much time in pure torture wondering what your next mischief might be."

He caught her chin, forcing her to look up at him. "I never slept with Terese. She did follow the troops to battle, and I suppose she did let me know that she was available to serve me in any way. And she is a pretty young thing."

"Adrien—"

"I've never betrayed my marriage vows, Danielle. Never. Though there were times I admit that I wondered why I didn't."

He stood, lifting her, setting her on her feet, drawing the blanket from her and allowing it to fall on the sheep's wool rug before the fire. Darkness had fallen, and only the reds and golds of the flickering firelight bathed them both in their nudity. He slid his fingers into the hair at her nape, cradling her head, and kissed her. And when he was done with her lips, he kissed her shoulder blades and breasts. And as she began to tremble, he went down upon his knees, and his hands cupped the roundness of her belly, and he pressed his lips against her flesh, and his cheek against her, as if seeking a movement from his child. Her knees began to give, and she came down before him. His lips locked with hers once again, and kissing her, he eased her down before the flames. The fire seemed to dance upon their flesh. Each spot he caressed came alive, his kisses teased and tortured. Where flame danced, he touched and paused, then consumed her with his eyes, stroked again, kissed again. She began to writhe with wanting him until she could stand no more and she cried out his name. Yet when they were first sated, she felt a strange desperation, and it was she, not he, who began again. She could not make love tenderly enough, passionately enough . . . desperately enough. She wanted more and more. She wanted to keep him with her somehow, when he would be gone.

Sometime during the night, someone knocked to bring them supper. But they were both too absorbed. If they hungered, it was only for more of one another, for more intimate moments from which to create memories. Sometime, during the long hours before dawn, they slept on the lamb's wool.

With the dawn breaking, Adrien opened his eyes. She lay curled upon his chest, hair entwined around him, fingers laid delicately upon his flesh. He closed his eyes again, feeling her, and he realized it was going to kill him to leave her.

Perhaps he had meant to do so in hopes that she would learn she could not fight him and the English forever. But he knew now that he didn't want to bring her because he was afraid. He didn't know what the situation at court was going to be, but King Jean was there, an honored prisoner, and her old friend Simon was there, as well as Paul de Valois, all of whom were being held for ransom. If there was trouble at all in London . . .

God help them all.

He opened his eyes and allowed himself long moments of staring at her. She was her mother's daughter, beautiful beyond all measure, bold, thoughtful, caring, intelligent. She had said that she loved him . . .

He eased her from him, rose, and lifted her, laying her on their bed and covering her with the linen sheets and blanket. She barely stirred, and he smoothed her hair from her face, feeling a tightness within him for the passion they had shared, and a surge of protective tenderness as well. He loved her. He hadn't told her so yet. There was still something that gnawed painfully at his heart, still the fear. Time would pass. His child would be born. And pray God, there would be more time together, away from the battles of the world.

He dressed quietly, and when he was ready, he came to her again. He kissed her forehead, then her lips, and she slept on, exhausted. And at last, he forced himself to leave.

Adrien first arrived at court just in time to be sent with an army to Wales, to smash a revolt near the border. It wasn't a happy labor, for he felt a deep kinship with the Welsh. They fought for their identity often, as did the Scots. Edward, however, was making his presence firm; castles, the like of which had never been seen before, had been raised at English strongholds, and more were going up. The building was fascinating to watch, but Adrien was restless. He'd hoped to serve at court and return home. His child was due in late January or February, and he had hoped to be there for the event. As the months passed by, he was anxious as well, for it seemed that—now that he was to become a father—more and more of his friends were ready to tell him some dire story of misadventure, tales of infants born to die too soon, and stories of beautiful wives lost to childbirth.

When he finished fighting in Wales, there were more prisoners to be brought to the tower in London. Christmas passed as he returned to Edward's court, and he chafed at not being home. Every minute away from his wife became torment, despite the fact that life around Edward was anything but mundane. Each night, the nobles at court attended great banquets to which the English king brought David Bruce, King of Scotland, Jean, King of France, nobles from Scotland, France, and Wales, and his own courtiers. David and Jean were both young rulers and interesting men, and despite the fact that they were prisoners, the occasions were intriguing and pleasant. Adrien was customarily seated near David, by virtue of them both being Scotsmen. They talked passionately about Scottish history, religion, the people, highlanders and lowlanders.

Along with the royal guests, though, came others. Simon, Danielle's would-be lover, was among the French nobles often brought to banquets, as well as Paul de Valois, kin to Jean— and his wife. King Jean did not irk Adrien, nor, surprisingly, did Paul de Valois. However, Simon de Valois, Comte Montjoie, perhaps by virtue of the fact that Danielle might have thought herself in love with him once, irritated his temper beyond measure.

Simon was popular among his English captors, charming to the ladies of the English court who were not aware—nor did Simon admit—that he had been aligned with Count Armagnac, who had raped and pillaged without remorse. Simon was simply a prisoner of circumstance, in the English tower because he had fallen in love with the betrothed of another man. When he and Adrien met, they were cordial, as their positions and the court demanded. Adrien knew that Simon hated him with a vengeance. He felt the same.

It was rumored that Simon was having an affair with the

young wife of an old noble, a situation which occurred frequently enough when girls were married to grandfathers.

The poor young woman was in love with him, a sad situation apparent every time she sat at her place down the long banqueting hall. She was the daughter of an old friend who had been killed years ago fighting the French, and it hurt Adrien to see her in such pain. At such times, he was glad that Danielle wasn't with him. He wanted her nowhere near Simon, who seemed to watch him frequently as if he calculated some plot. Simon was an eloquent speaker. God only knew in what ways he might twist his situation if he were to speak with Danielle.

Simon lived in tower rooms separate from those of the King of France; King Edward didn't mind being a charming host to his prisoner, but he'd be damned if he'd have them plotting together while beneath his wing. As to the situation, King Edward was in exceptional humor, being 'host' to his two most troublesome enemies. He was as gleeful as a boy. Adrien wanted to go home. Edward promised him he might do so if the Welsh could behave throughout the month.

Mid-February, as they banqueted at court, a messenger arrived, speaking to the king. Adrien, several chairs to the left of the king—on the 'Scottish' side of the table—saw the king's expression change, his head lower. Edward indicated that the man should come to Adrien. For some reason, as he watched the messenger, Adrien felt his heart begin to pound, seeming to fly to his throat. News had come from the north. He was afraid it was going to be bad.

Yet, as the man neared him, he saw that the messenger smiled. ''I have come from the north, sir—''

''Danielle?'' Adrien interrupted anxiously.

''Does exceptionally well, Laird MacLachlan. As does your son, christened Adrien Robert last Saturday.''

Adrien didn't know he'd been standing until he sank back into his chair. Apparently the messenger had spoken loudly enough for many to hear, and a cheer went up around the table. Knights, nobles, ladies—and even royalty—raised their glasses to him.

His son. She'd meant to have a girl, to spite him. But he

wouldn't have cared. He'd never known such a strange sense of panic, simply praying that Danielle would be all right, with nothing else mattering.

Later that night, he went to the king, and was granted an audience. "Sire, the Welsh may remain subdued for months, or flare into battle any day. I've served long and hard, and I'm anxious to see my son—"

"Do you think, Laird MacLachlan, that I've seen all my offspring the moment they are swaddled. Nay, young man, I can tell you that I have not!"

"But—"

"Send for your wife, and your child. I am anxious to see them myself."

Adrien stared at Edward warily. "Sire, King Jean of France remains your prisoner here, and there are others—"

"Good God! We are in our tower, in our city." He was quiet for a moment. "I would like to see your wife, my ward, and the child."

"So you are commanding me to send for Danielle?"

"I am asking you to do so."

It was one and the same. "I'll send the messenger back immediately," Adrien said, and left him.

He left the king, and nodding to the attendants who lingered outside in the hallway, he started down the long corridor to his quarters. As he started to turn a corner, he noticed a sudden billowing of one of the curtains that enclosed an alcove. He paused, thinking that a pair of lovers met for a quick tryst, and he hesitated, thinking of a different way to go. He saw that a number of armed guards lined the hallway, and when he glanced back to the alcove, he could see a booted foot that extended beyond the curtain. Before he could turn around, he heard a female voice, whispering in French.

He knew the voice; it was the girl Terese, who had chosen to follow Prince Edward's army across the Channel. Curious little vixen. She continued to cast invitations his way upon occasion, so he wondered just how deeply she could be in love with the man behind the curtain.

The man spoke, and he felt himself tensing.

Simon. Simon de Valois, Comte Montejoie. Apparently, King Edward allowed his noble guests what entertainment they desired, because the guards would not have allowed the comte a tryst in the hallway without the king's permission.

Adrien walked on. He should be glad. The two were welcome to one another. Still . . .

Something about the meeting unnerved him.

Later, alone at night, awake and staring into the darkness, he missed his wife, and yearned to see his son—and was still strangely unhappy that they were to come to him, rather than that he should return to them.

In the midst of his ponderings, he heard a soft tapping on his door. Then a woman's whispered voice. "Laird MacLachlan!"

He rose, slipped a robe around his shoulders, and drew open the door. He arched a brow in surprise as he saw Terese standing there. "Aye, lass?"

She smiled tremulously. "May I come in?"

He arched his brow higher.

"I can't stand here in the hallway, Laird MacLachlan."

He stepped aside, and she entered. When he closed the door, she leaned against it, breathing heavily, staring at him. "Your wife is coming soon at the king's command."

"Aye?"

She smiled prettily, lifting her hands.

"These nights to come . . . they're perhaps the last chance that we'll have to . . ."

"To?" he inquired, stepping back.

She lowered her lashes over her eyes. "I cannot forget that you saved my life, Laird MacLachlan. I would serve you in any way. I would die for one night with you. Your wife is far away. I've heard that she is your enemy, and betrays you at every turn."

"And where do you hear this?"

"There was a man plotting against Edward and masquerading as a priest—that's why you brought her to Castle de Renoncourt. Everyone knew it. She hurts you. I would ease the pain. I would give you a night of pure bliss, I would love you simply, and without complications, ease your spirit, your soul, your body.''

A pretty speech. ''Really?'' he murmured.

''Your wife is a wicked vixen, my lord!''

He reached for her, taking her arms, setting her from the door. ''You're lovely, Terese, and that was a fine speech, but there is a problem.''

''Nay, my lord, I've no problem—'' she broke off, flushing. ''All I want is a brief time together. Just to please you.''

''I wonder if there isn't more,'' he murmured.

''Laird Adrien, you saved my life—''

''So live it well. Be careful of the friends you make. But the fact remains that there's a problem—''

''None that I cannot solve—''

''Nay, I've the problem. You see, I love my wife. Goodnight now, Terese, and be careful of wolves in the hallway.''

He spun her, around and prodded her gently back out into the hallway, then closed the door.

In the hallway, Terese stared at the door and fumed, feeling a spiraling jealousy of the Countess Danielle. The woman had property, titles, and she was adored and admired by the French and English. And Simon had loved her and . . .

Terese, with all her wiles, could not sway Adrien MacLachlan from her.

As she stared at the door in frustration, another man came along the hallway. It was MacLachlan's squire, Luke, the handsome young man she'd met first at the Castle de Renoncourt.

He laughed when he saw her.

''Oh, how dare you!'' she breathed angrily.

He leaned against the wall, watching her. ''You keep throwing yourself at him. When will you realize he is married to an angel, and he loves her.''

''She is a witch, and in time, he'll despise her.''

Luke shook his head. ''No, she is a beauty. There is something deep and real between them, and you can't change that.''

She lowered her head, unnerved by this young man. She

thought of the others she had met, the rich men, the great men, the nobles, all who flattered her—but wanted something from her. He didn't flatter her; he just stared at her with steady eyes.

"You will not have the earl, Laird MacLachlan," he told her steadily. "You cannot have such a great man."

"Can't I?" she demanded impertinently.

He smiled, setting his bundle on the floor before MacLachlan's door, and reaching for her. "You can have me."

She was about to slap him. How dare he? But his hold was firm and real. His eyes lit into hers with a real hunger, and his words, though blunt, were honest.

"Let go."

"You've lusted after him, I've lusted after you. But there is something I can offer," he said softly.

"What is that?" she queried, surprised to find herself breathless.

He was MacLachlan's squire. Young, unseasoned, untried. But with such a lord as his sponsor, he would become a knight. He could go to battle . . .

Return with great riches.

And he wanted her.

"I can marry you!" he said.

"Oh!" she cried softly, and she slipped into his arms.

Later, in his small, cramped apartment, she stared up at the ceiling and wondered if she should or shouldn't carry through with the promises she had made to another man. She rolled over, looking at the gold ring she'd been given earlier. Payment. Payment . . .

And now, she was to do her part.

No . . . She could not. Would not . . .

Yet she was afraid. Very afraid.

Chapter 22

Danielle had never known anything so cold as winter on the borderlands, though many of the household assured her that it could be far colder in the highlands.

Such a winter was a ridiculous time to have a baby, but as Maeve, the midwife, told her, bairns come when bairns choose, and that is the way of it.

She had missed Adrien more than she had even begun to imagine. He wrote to her about his campaign to Wales, and she wrote back, wishing him Godspeed, and telling him about the birth of kittens in the barn, how Star was growing far longer hair, and that she was certain that Daylin—who had remained with her—intended to ask his blessing to marry Monteine.

On the day that Adrien Robert MacLachlan was born, Monteine was with her. And though she had missed Adrien, by the time her pains began to come one upon the other, she wanted to strangle him for having put her in such a wretched position. Her labor lasted day and night; little Adrien did not appear until dawn. Until that time, she alternately spoke rationally with Monteine and Maeve, or came up with new and imaginative ways to torture Adrien. It was during those moments when Monteine told her that she blamed Adrien for far too much.

"It was I, Danielle, who caused the difficulty over the priest. Of course, he wasn't a priest, but—"

"What are you talking about?" Dripping with sweat despite the winter's cold, breathless and in agony, Danielle stared at Monteine.

"I went to Daylin about the priest. I was worried. Daylin went to Adrien. So you see—"

She stared at Monteine, her eyes narrowed. "First you rig his saddle so that I take a beating!"

"Danielle!" Monteine protested indignantly. "That was years and years ago! I was afraid—"

"Then you become his friend, his doting servant! Oh, you should hang in a gibbet with him! Ohh . . ."

"Aye, lady, good now, up and push and the wee bairn will be 'ere at last!"

And so it was; she was angry and she sat up with a hard push, and his little head popped into the world. She demanded to know what it was and Maeve calmly told her, "Scottish, lass, for his father, that I ken tell ye, but not until the wee bottom is oot ken I tell what sort of Scot! Now, once again . . ."

"A boy, me lady, a big, fine boy!"

She was suddenly crying, and Monteine rushed out to tell Daylin. Maeve cleaned the babe, cut his cord, and forced Danielle to push again to rid herself of the afterbirth. Danielle obeyed but barely noticed. She was awed by the babe in her arms, fascinated as he first began to nurse, amazed to find that he had ten fingers and ten toes, a cap of his father's blond hair, and eyes so blue they were like a summer's sky. Eyes changed, she reminded herself. Everyone said so, and since his thatch of wheat hair seemed to be his father's, it was possible still that his eyes would change to the color of a MacLachlan's as well. Perhaps not—perhaps they would have a green cast to them, who could tell? He was perfect in every way, and he could scream with an amazingly lusty cry . . .

Doubts and fears plagued her in the days to come; she loved him so much, she was terrified of losing him. She wouldn't

allow Daylin to bring a messenger from the field to go to
London with the news until the babe was christened, Monteine
and Daylin standing as godparents.

Then she began to wait, praying that Adrien would at long
last come home, and that they could be proud and pleased
together. She loved her home here—she was comfortable and
she enjoyed the people, settling disputes regarding sheep, cattle,
and even the weaving of cloth. They made delicious ale, and
she learned from Aran, who worked with the kegs, and in turn,
she did her best to teach them about storing fine French wines.
Katherine Mary, a stern matriarch, ruled the maids, while
Joshua acted as head of the household and Taylor as overall
steward. She drank with them to the baby's birth, and all hailed
the new heir. Life was full and rich, except that . . .

It was unbearable without Adrien. Thinking about him constantly, seeing him in little things the baby did. Wanting him.
Worrying, wondering.

The days passed, the winter eased, and as March came,
though some days were both blustery and cold, spring weather
began to break through as well. At the beginning of April, she
lay on a blanket on the rich, thick grass by the loch with
Monteine and Daylin nearby. She dozed with the baby by her
side and awakened to see Monteine scampering away in the
grass, laughing, cheeks rosy, with Daylin after her. The two
fell in the grass together and arose kissing. Monteine broke
away from him, saw that Danielle had awakened, flushed furiously, and hurried back to her and the baby, apologizing.

"Must you be so happy in front of me all the time?" Danielle
demanded. Monteine at first appeared dismayed, then realized
that Danielle was smiling.

"You must be happy as a lark, with this precious one!"
Monteine said, touching the baby.

"I am!" Danielle whispered. "Except that—"

"Someone's coming!" Daylin said. He moved toward the
blanket, always the defender, his hand going for the hilt of his
sword. But even as he stood by her and men from the fields
grouped around him, having heard the riders, Daylin relaxed, for
the riders coming carried King Edward's banner, and Danielle

quickly recognized Sir George. She rose, the babe, whom she called Robin rather than confuse him with his father, in her arms.

"Sir George!" she cried with pleasure. He was quickly off his horse, anxious to reach her, going to a knee and taking her hand, then reaching for the baby. "Ah, what a fine lad, a fine lad! What hair! The king himself would be jealous of such a golden mop!"

"Will his father approve?"

"His father is in ecstasy with the news of his birth, and the assurance that you are doing well—which I can see for myself. You look more radiant and beautiful than ever, my dear."

"You're kind, Sir George. But tell me, if Adrien is so pleased to have his son . . . where is he?"

His eyes fell upon the anxiety in her face and he answered very kindly. "The king still requires his great champion be near him."

"Oh!" she whispered. So he had sent Sir George. And now there would be more long, agonizing weeks while she waited and wondered . . .

"But he is so anxious, he surely would have bolted from the king's service, and the king himself, it seems, is anxious. I am to escort you to London—that is, if you can bear the journey."

"If I can bear the jouney . . . ?" she repeated.

"Aye, lady, with the bairn so young—though I can see he's a fine, healthy lad at that!"

"Sir George, we will ride at the break of dawn, if you and your men can bear the journey!"

Raymond, Comte Langlois, arrived at Dover via a Flemish ship. The captain was a fellow sympathetic to the French cause, furious that so much had been destroyed in the war with the English. His sailors were a scurvy lot, asking no question regarding the simply dressed but well-armed man who accompanied Langlois on the voyage.

Comte Langlois wore the heavy, cowled robe of a Franciscan

monk—a not-too-original disguise, he thought, but one that served his purpose. His education was such that he had little difficulty spending time with local clergy, nor in enticing a young priest to ride with him and his young 'cleric' to London. There, he met with King Edward's confessor, who allowed the French 'monk' time with his own sovereign. To the comte's great distress, King Jean, granted time to see him alone, was not pleased to see him, nor impressed with his disguise, or even the fact that he risked death to save him.

"Raymond, my dear comte, this is nothing but foolishness. You do risk our lives. King Edward has hundreds of men at his beck and call here, and though he wouldn't dare slay me in cold blood, if I were to perish in the midst of a chase, he could show his great sorrow and horror to the world."

"Mon Dieu! My liege! I walked in here—"

"As a man of God," Jean said impatiently. "Do I take your cloak, and leave you here? Are you so truly willing to give your life for me? For I daresay the English would have your head and display it upon London Bridge were they to discover you here. No, no, Comte, you are too eager for riches end rewards! I ride to battle when battle can be fought. I'll not be shot down like a dog by the English in their streets!"

"I had gold smuggled to Simon so that guards might be bribed. If I was served by traitors to your cause, sire, I will dice them into pieces, "

"Simon received the gold. If you've clear and quick passage across the Channel, take Simon and escape with him."

Langlois was deflated and unhappy. He meant to be the savior of the king, a true hero to the people. "Escapes have thus been managed before—"

"Of regular men. Not of kings. Simon is not so well-guarded. He is friends with many of his jailors, and he is free sometimes to walk the corridors and wall. Take Simon—he has been awaiting your arrival for a means to find a ship with a crew that will not betray him to the English."

"I have such a ship, sire!"

"Then take Simon, and when you return home, put your efforts into raising my ransom. My son rides the countryside—

you must do likewise. Then, Comte, I will honor you among the finest and most loyal of my nobles.''

Head down, Langlois left King Jean's apartments. He met the priest from Dover outside the door and murmured a blessing with the assurance that the king was well. They would move on to give comfort to Simon, Comte Montjoie.

Simon greeted Langlois joyfully. "Have you horses?" Simon demanded.

"I came with a priest. The horses are not adequate. With the gold I had smuggled to you through our countrymen—''

"Yes, I can arrange for good horses. Bring the priest here tonight. We will depart as two religious fellows who have done their duty to God and countrymen."

They continued to talk, working out the fine points of the escape. Langlois need only take care not to run into any of the enemy he had encountered in France.

"Who recognizes an enemy minus his armor and heraldic emblems?" Simon demanded.

"Adrien, Laird MacLachlan," Raymond spat out.

Simon tensed. "MacLachlan! I'd give my life to see him dead." He paused suddenly. "Maybe I'll not have to do so. Laird MacLachlan has been sent to Dover to prepare to launch an attack against Castle Cardineau. The men will be busy . . ." He looked at Langlois and smiled. "His wife is to meet him there.''

"His wife?" Langlois said, intrigued.

"What a blow to strike against him, and the English, were we to take the lady of Aville!''

The road was long, and Sir George constantly urged that they slow their pace. Danielle never wanted to stop for the night; she was far too eager to reach London.

She was touched when they at last reached the city, for King Edward and Queen Philippa had come out to welcome her with King Jean riding at Edward's side. She was tenderly greeted by both kings and even more so by the queen, who was quick to take Robin to cuddle and appraise him. Danielle was glad of the queen's care and listened eagerly to her every word, since the queen had borne the king so many children. "He's like his father, eh?" the king said to the queen, who looked at him strangely.

"Perhaps. But such blue eyes . . . !"

"Adrien's are hazel and mine are green," Danielle said. "Perhaps they'll change."

"Umm," the queen murmured.

"Where is Adrien?" Danielle asked.

"Ah, well, he's moved on to Dover, I'm afraid."

"Dover!" she gasped, dismayed.

"Don't fret, dear. He's waiting for you, gathering men and supplies. There has been a flare-up at Castle Cardineau, where I allowed Count Germaine to rule in my name! The petty upstart thinks to defy me. Nothing too serious. Adrien will handle it in a matter of days."

"Am I to go back to France with him?" she asked.

"No," Edward said bluntly. "But come tomorrow, you can ride down and meet him for a night together, show him his son. Then you'll wait in London with the queen and me for his return."

Looking down from his window in the building of the great Tower of London where esteemed prisoners resided, Simon saw Danielle in the courtyard with the queen. They were followed through the garden by her friend, Monteine, MacLachlan's man, Daylin, and a number of the queen's women. They laughed, smelled the flowers, enjoyed the warm day. The queen held the babe, and watching her, Simon felt a rush of fury that was painful. He'd like to take the child and smash it into a wall. Destroy the little rat before it could become a big one.

News traveled fast, even to the prisoners in the tower. Countess Danielle was to ride in the morning to meet her husband by the Channel. She'd be with him by the afternoon tomorrow. Watching Danielle smile at something the queen said, her eyes alight, Simon thought how he would best use his time, were she his wife, and he given but a night . . .

MacLachlan would be vulnerable. Simon smiled suddenly, remembering with an aching heart the last time he had seen Danielle. How fickle she'd become; she seemed so happy with her child. MacLachlan's child. She had forgotten him completely. Or had she? Would she ask to see him and King Jean before she left? He needed to see her. It would be the last little link in his plan.

She did visit with him, briefly. She stayed no more than five minutes. She took his hands, asked anxiously if he was well, and pulled away when he would have held her. "Don't begrudge me holding your hands, Danielle. Don't you remember how I loved you?"

"Oh, Simon, you'll leave here soon enough!" she assured him, and smiled. Her smile was like the sun. It brightened the gemlike beauty of her eyes. He felt his heart beating like thunder. "I've heard you've amused yourself quite well among the English damsels at court."

"Anything to forget the prize I desired most."

"I have to go, Simon. I knew you were here—I wanted to see that you were well. I have been to King Jean, and he was happy, playing chess with King David of Scotland. They were cheerfully plotting the downfall of King Edward, who I've been told, is amused by their conversations, joining in them at times."

"Edward thinks he is all-powerful—as does your husband, lady. But we all have an Achilles' heel."

"I suppose, Simon." She stepped forward and kissed his cheek, then carefully exited his room. The guard locked the door as she departed.

"Indeed, lady!" he said softly. "We all have an Achilles' heel."

Comte Langlois caught up with the girl, Terese, in his monastic robes. She didn't know him, and she seemed terrified that she had been watched by God, and judged by Satan, as he wrenched her from the hallway into an alcove. "You're Terese. You promised to help Simon de Valois. He's given you gold and jewels. Now you will earn your portion. Listen to me, you're a bright girl, you'll do as I say now. You'll have fresh horses just beyond the sally port this evening, by dusk. You'll wait with them until I appear."

The girl was pale, her teeth chattering. "Horses? Taking horses—"

"Good horses, from the stables."

"I meant to help, but I can't. I can't do this. What if I'm caught? I'll be hanged—"

He gripped her throat with both hands. They were huge, and his fingers encircled her neck, cutting off her words.

He gave her a shake, tightening his fingers until she gasped.

"You will do this!" he told her. "Or they won't need to hang you. I'll find you and slit your fair throat ear to ear. Are we understood, woman?"

She nodded, trembling with fear. He smiled. "Ah, there's a good girl. Bless you, child!"

Adrien paced the docks, anxiously waiting, barely aware of the activity around him as horses, food, arms, armor, and more were loaded into the many ships that would bring his contingent across the water. He damned the king a thousand times over as he paced. At last his wife was coming, and he was being sent to France. And though it was Edward who had asked that Danielle be brought to London, he was equally determined that she should not return to France with him, though Philippa had followed Edward to battle often enough.

Danielle was to see him, then he was to leave and she was to return to London.

And somehow, he thought, he was to bear it. Life, he realized, had been far more simple when he was ruled by ambition rather than love. He used to do the king's bidding with little thought; now he ached to demand that another man pick up the fight so he could be left alone to enjoy the fruits of his long years of loyalty and labor.

"My lord!"

He heard her voice. He swung around, and she was there.

She stood on the dock, dressed in blue, hair free and streaming down her back. And she was slim again, except that her breasts welled against her gown. She was more beautiful than ever, her eyes glittered, her face was flushed, she seemed to glow with the essence of her smile.

"My lady!" he whispered in return, and she uttered a cry and came running down the dock toward him. He captured her and held her to him and spun her around, delighted to see her, smell her clean scent, drown in her hair, the touch of her, the feel of her against him . . .

He eased her to the ground.

"We're to have but one night!" she whispered.

"Aye, but I'll not be long."

"So the king said."

"You're well?" he asked anxiously.

"Very."

"And the bairn?"

She smiled, for all his years at the English court and serving in France had not changed him from being a wild border laird. "Behind me," she said softly. "Monteine has him."

He gazed into her eyes, then hurried past her to Monteine, taking the baby from her and moving all the swaddling from his face. Danielle came to stand by him and was overjoyed to see the look of awe on his face as he studied his son. He glanced at her and she smiled, trembling with absolute pleasure.

He kept his son, reaching out to slip an arm around Danielle's shoulder. "Come. I have a room in the old tavern down the street."

They left Monteine and Daylin behind, hurrying to his quarters. Men frequently tried to stop him as they walked, asking him questions about arms or armor, horses, supplies. He answered every man's question quickly, "Keep at it, men. We must be ready to sail by the dawn!"

"Pity we can't leave now, Laird MacLachlan," one sailor told him. "The tide would be with us. But then, we've still supplies to be boarded.'' ''He bowed and hurried on with his cask of supplies.

''Come, let's hurry out of this sea of curious admirers or I'll not have you a second alone!'' Adrien murmured and hurried onward with Danielle along a long, low Norman building to a side door in a deep courtyard. He led her into his room, closing the door behind him, leaning against it, staring at her.

''Crude, I'm afraid. Drafty. The bed is wretched. The smoke spills in from the chimney. The place was convenient to the docks. And . . . I remembered a cradle for the baby.''

''Good!'' she whispered, and smiled, gazing toward him and their babe, tucked beneath his arm. ''He's sleeping.''

Adrien looked down at his son. ''Aye, that he is.'' He looked back to her. ''He's beautiful, he's wonderful. I'm grateful, and lass, I'm proud. And I thank God he's sleeping now!'' He strode across the room, setting Robin into the cradle, and then she was in his arms. She was stunned and amazed by the way he shook as he held her and kissed her. His fevered hunger swept into her like wildfire, aroused her like a wicked wind. She kissed him back, marveling at the taste of him after so much time, the feel of him, the heat in his muscles. She found herself half laughing and half sobbing as they fumbled in their attempts to remove one another's clothing.

''My God . . . I've ripped . . . something!'' Adrien said.

''Doesn't . . . matter. I'd rip more if I only had such strength!'' she replied. His lips fused with hers. He swept her up and bore her down on the bed. Then he began to kiss her, and kiss her everywhere, until she cried out.

He paused, rising above her.

''I wouldn't hurt you—'tis soon after the bairn—''

She shook her head. ''I asked!'' she whispered. ''Plenty of time has passed.''

He cupped the globe of her breast. ''Perhaps it was best that I was not with you.''

''No, oh, my lord, no . . . I can't tell you how I have missed you, needed you . . .'' She reached for him, drew her fingers down the side of his face, and then slowly along the length of his body. She reached for his sex, cradling it in her hands, drawing the length against her, to her.

He groaned, burying his face against her flesh. And he tried to be gentle, aware that he hurt her when he entered her, yet she clung to him with such ardor, telling him that he was a brief agony that she could not bear to live without. He had been too long without her. The first time was quick, and desperate. The second was slower; the third, they savored. The baby awoke then, squalling with hunger, and Adrien stroked his little back while Danielle nursed him, and they both marvelled again at the wonder of their creation. Adrien set his son back in the cradle and lay down beside her. He'd thought himself sated. She smiled at him, and he felt the surge of arousal once again. Damn the French. He kissed her. She wrapped her arms around him in return. "Adrien . . ."

As she whispered his name, the door suddenly slammed open. Adrien sprang up and back, stunned as men burst into the room. With a warrior's instinct, he set himself between his wife and babe, knowing that only deadly enemies would burst in on him so, damning himself and wondering where he had shed his scabbard in his hurry to be with his wife.

To his fury and dismay, he faced his enemies: Simon de Valois and Comte Langlois, each flanked by a burly swordsman.

"Now, messieurs, I have had the pleasure of spending some time with King Jean. I can't imagine that he has taught you two your manners," Adrien said.

"Simon," Langlois said, "we shall have to be more cordial when we cut him."

Adrien saw his sword then, just three feet away, beneath his cloak. He sprang for it, falling back by the bed. Danielle had partially risen, the covers clasped to her. She was pale and white, staring at Simon.

"Perhaps I'll die," Adrien said softly, "but we will meet in hell." He should have killed Simon long ago when he'd had the chance. Now, as they faced one another, Simon smiled and turned away, reaching back out in the alleyway to bring Monteine into the room. He held the blade of a long butcher's knife to her throat with such fierce menace that a slim trickle of blood began a slow drip down the length of her neck.

"Let her go!" Danielle shrieked, rising with the sheets around her. She suddenly raced across the room, attacking him. "Danielle!" Adrien roared, catapulting into motion to catch her and drag her back against him.

"Come to me, Danielle, come!" Simon called. "Come now, don't play games, and I'll let Monteine go. Don't worry about MacLachlan. He doesn't matter anymore. He'll learn soon enough that you managed to bribe the guard so I could escape!"

"What?" Danielle gasped.

Despite himself, Adrien had to see her eyes. He wrenched her around to stare at her. He felt a man moving behind him and he spun around, quick as the wind, and sliced through the man's chest. But when he started to turn again, aware of new danger at his back, he heard Danielle screaming.

But too late.

Langlois had managed to step in with determination and skill. He struck Adrien a stunning blow to the temple with the hilt of his sword. The pain was excruciating. He fought the fog that came with it, tried to feel the pain. It was fading, and there was nothing he could do . . .

Adrien stumbled . . . and fell.

It seemed he heard a keening on the wind . . .

"Come, Danielle, now, let's go, now!" Simon said.

Danielle gazed at Monteine, still in Simon's death grip. She looked at Adrien on the ground, wondering if he were dead or alive. She was desperate to go to him, terrified for her friend. She looked back to Simon, shaking her head in horror, fighting tears which would do her no good. "Come with you? Let her go, you rotten bastard—what are you trying to do, bring the English and French to all out bloody warfare again, strip the land, starve the people—"

"Shut up, Danielle!" Simon said.

"I'm not coming with you, Simon. You let Monteine go, and you leave me alone. My God, my baby—"

"The babe, aye, the babe. We should bring him. Cast him into the Channel," Langlois advised.

"No! I'll gouge your eyes out!" she cried.

Monteine, gasping against the knife at her throat, made a sound, and Danielle knew she couldn't fight Simon and Langlois at that moment. The two, together, were ruthless. One man lay dead by Adrien's hand, and Adrien might be . . . she didn't dare think, didn't dare!

"Let her go. Let Monteine go, to take my babe, and I'll come with you."

"The babe is the Scotsman's seed. He should die in the Channel. You're young. You can have many more babes."

"If you hurt my child, or Monteine, I'll scream until you're forced to kill me. Let Monteine go to tend the child, and I will walk out of here with you."

Simon looked at Langlois, who shrugged. "It will help matters if she comes quietly."

Simon thrust Monteine from him. Stumbling, she came forward to stand before the cradle, staring at Danielle with horror.

"It will be all right," Danielle said. "See to my lord, Adrien." She stared hard at Simon, then Langlois, then Simon again. "Adrien let you live when he might have killed you. And you, Comte Langlois! He could have severed your head. Could have, should have killed you, but he didn't!"

Simon turned to one of his men. "Quickly, roll Laird MacLachlan in a rug—we'll throw him in the Channel."

"No!" Danielle shouted furiously. She started hurrying the few feet to where Adrien lay, but Simon caught her, throwing her back, his eyes narrowed. "He's gone, lady, gone as I was gone, and you will learn my ways once again!"

She slapped him, hard enough to redden his cheek, and with such surprise and vigor that her nails caught his face. In a fury, he slapped her back. She slammed against the bedpost. Light blazed before her . . .

Then, perhaps mercifully, utter darkness.

Chapter 23

The cold of the water revived him—that and the burning sensation of the sea in his lungs.

How far had he fallen? He awoke in a black void in which he was drowning . . .

Drowning, yes, damn, he was drowning. He gave a furious kick, and began to rise, and he kicked again, willing himself not to inhale, to give way to temptation . . .

To die.

His face broke the surface. Night had come, and a Flemish ship was moving away, many feet from him. He was cast adrift, far adrift, in the rough waters of the Channel.

At first, he was disoriented, and he couldn't see the shore. He was tossed about by the waves; his head was pounding. The water was deep, and cold.

He found the shore and started to swim, too quickly at first. He might be miles from land; he couldn't tell how far. The waves washed over him, lifted him, threw him. The sea was rising to whitecaps.

Then he saw bonfires. They had been lit along the shore. With renewed vigor, he started swimming again. He got control. Smooth, slow strokes. Easy strokes. Strength-saving strokes, slow, sure, constant. His head ceased to ache, his arms were so sore. He floated, fighting the waves that sloshed over his face, the taste of the salt, the innate fear of what might be below him in the pitch dark. He had to reach the shore. By Christ and all the saints, he had to reach the shore.

He swam again . . .

Yet even his resolve might not have been enough if he hadn't seen the boats as he neared the coastline.

He closed his eyes, praying. He had to live. To kill Simon. To bring Danielle home. To tell her he believed in her. That he loved her. Simon had wanted him to die believing that his wife had betrayed him. He refused to die, and refused to believe that Danielle had done so. He wondered where his son was, and he opened his eyes, his energy suddenly restored in a fierce burst of desperation.

Cast in the firelight, he could see the cliffs. They appeared truly white, like angels' wings. He swam again, damning the shore, for it seemed that every time he neared it, a wave rose, and it was farther away.

"Adrien!"

At first he thought he imagined his name, that some siren summoned him from the depths of hell.

"MacLachlan, damn you, man, you can't be dead!"

He knew the voice, had heard it booming time and time again in battle, part of his life. Edward, the Black Prince, was no siren. The prince was out on the water . . . in the small boat that was now shooting toward him.

"Row, men!" Edward roared.

And a moment later, arms were reaching into the water. He was dragged aboard, naked and shivering. A blanket was thrown around him, a leather skin of warm ale was pressed into his hands. "Drink, my friend, warm yourself. Sweet Jesu, sir, how long did you stay out in that water?"

Amazingly, he discovered that the blanket and ale caused him to cease the jerking that had first seized him. He inhaled, exhaled, leaned back, and looked at the prince. "I don't know. Edward, by God, tell me what you know."

"Your wife's woman came shrieking out to the men preparing the ship that you were being cast into the sea while Danielle was being abducted. Meanwhile, that French girl, the one you saved from Armagnac's attack on her village, had gone and thrown herself on my mother's mercy, babbling some story about Comte Langlois threatening to kill her if she didn't provide horses for him to escape—with Simon de Valois. Don't worry, no ill befell the girl—she wants to marry your young armorer, by the way—the lad stood up for her, risking death himself. Anyway, I arrived as quickly as I could to discover your men lighting fires and searching the shoreline for you. Had we not found you soon, I'd have sailed without you. Comte Langlois apparently arrived from France to assist in an escape by Simon de Valois, and it's my assumption they'll have to head for the French coast and cast themselves upon the mercy of their ally, Comte Germaine of Cardineau. There, we will do battle."

After a moment, Adrien smiled. "You're a good prince to serve, Edward. You've saved my life, and you're ready to do battle for my wife."

Edward shrugged. "Well, friend, you've saved my skin a number of times. And as to your wife, well . . ."

"Aye?"

Edward shook his head, hunkering down in the small boat so the oarsmen wouldn't hear him. "Such a clever Scot's boy. I must go. Father has demanded that Comte Germaine be trounced from the castle, and I must go for Danielle. She is my sister."

"Aye, the king's ward."

Edward sighed, a slight twinkle in his eyes. "Haven't you figured it out yet? I don't mean that she is his ward. I mean that she is my sister." He sat back and bellowed out, "Row, men! We must reach the ship and sail the Channel. Quickly!"

Wrapped in the blanket, Adrien was able to see Monteine briefly before setting sail upon the ship for France. Cheers went up when he walked ashore; his men shouted out that it was a miracle, that he was blessed from above. "The saints preserve you, aye, they do, Laird MacLachlan!" came a cry, and then, a moment later, Monteine was rushing to him.

"Laird MacLachlan! I swear to you, Danielle had nothing to do with it! The bastard struck her, knocked her out, he's taken her—"

"It's all right, Monteine, we're going for her."

Daylin came up behind Monteine, grasping Adrien's shoulder, embracing him. "Thank God . . ."

"My son—" Adrien began.

"The babe is in the best of hands," Prince Edward assured him, pounding him on the back with such a wallop that he stumbled forward. "My mother has Robin."

The sea churned and churned; it seemed that the ship was tossed endlessly. Danielle lay in a tight little cabin in a state of sheer misery, desperately sick, and caring little. Adrien was dead. They had knocked him out and thrown him into the tempest of the night sea. She wanted to die herself.

Simon came into the cabin. He was handsomely dressed, yet she wondered that she had ever found him charming. His features did not seem so classically cut tonight; they were too slim, too narrow. He gripped the woodwork above the bunk and stared down at her.

"It may be hard at first. But we are French. You will forget him—"

"Forget that you murdered him?"

"Langlois struck the blow."

"And you ordered him tossed overboard."

"He was a knife in the side of France. Danielle . . ." He started to sit by her side.

"Touch me, and I will be sick."

"Oh, come now, you will grow accustomed to me again. You will remember how close we were, how we laughed—"

"Touch me, and I will be sick."

He touched her. She kept her promise. Swearing furiously, he rose and slammed out of the cabin.

Still wrapped in sheets, Danielle arrived in France and was dismayed to see the castle at Cardineau. The walls were high and thick and the fortress heavily manned. She didn't know if anyone would come for her, if anyone would care. If, by a miracle, Adrien had lived and if he tried to free her, it would take a seige.

She was brought to the highest tower at the northeastern section of the castle. There were no balconies here, no means of escape except for one circular stairway.

When she was brought in, she saw that a hot bath awaited her along with a trunk of clothing, perfumes, wine, bread, and a large carved bed. She sat on the floor, curled into a ball in her sheets, refusing to look at Simon.

''Danielle, you will see to yourself,'' he told her, ''or I will see to you.'' She didn't move, and he stepped toward her. She didn't want him touching her so she rose and told him, ''Get away from me, Simon, and I will rise and dress.''

''Do so then,'' he said firmly.

She stumbled to her feet and walked to the elegant copper-edged hip tub, the sheets still wrapped around her. Simon watched. She kept her back to him and said, ''Simon, if I led you to believe that I loved you before, I'm sorry. I am married to Adrien MacLachlan, and I love him, and if you think that you can force—''

''MacLachlan is dead,'' Simon said flatly.

''I'll not believe it until I see him dead,'' she said.

''He's in the Channel, food for fish, Danielle.''

Tears stung her eyes.''Then I'll never believe myself a widow.''

''Perhaps his carcass will wash up on the English shore!'' Simon snapped. ''It's no matter, Danielle. Your life with the English is over.''

She turned on him. ''There is war, Simon, but this isn't *English* and it isn't *French*. I am French, Simon, my people are French, but though there is war, some people remain decent, and some do not. I hate you. I see you for what you truly are. You were part of Comte Armagnac's forces when they were pillaging, raping, and murdering people in *France* in a bid to wrest power from Edward. My life will never be with you. You were shown mercy, and all you gave in turn was cruelty.''

"Get in the tub, Danielle, and wash his stench from you,"
Simon replied.

She tested the water, seeing that he was moving. She wondered if she had the strength to kill him. They would slay her
in return, of course, but she wasn't sure that it mattered. He
said that her husband was dead; she didn't know if her child
had survived or not. She'd rather die than be touched by the
butcher of her husband and son.

The water was cold, but a kettle bubbled above the fire in
the hearth. She walked around the tub, reaching for the kettle
of water over the fire to add to her bath. "Simon, you're gone
mad!" she told him. "Don't you understand? You murdered
the man I loved."

"Love is fickle, Danielle—that is what I understand."

She gasped, spinning around, because he had come to stand
next to her. He reached for her, intent on stripping away the
sheet and plunging her into the water.

She didn't actually plan her attack so much as she simply
fell into it. She lifted her arm to repel him, and sent the boiling
water sluicing over his midsection and groin.

Simon screamed in agony. Danielle realized what she had
done, and backed away in horror. Simon ripped at his clothing,
shouting for help. Guards burst into the room.

Danielle backed against the wall. For the moment, she was
ignored as Simon howled and more guards rushed in. Then he
was carried out, the men shouting for a surgeon. The door was
bolted. Shaking, she slid against the wall until she was on the
floor. She suddenly started sobbing, and then, just as suddenly,
she ceased. She refused to believe that Adrien was dead. She
rose, walked to the tub, washed in the tepid water, and found
clothing and dressed. She waited, praying.

No one came near her that night.

In the morning, the door burst open and Simon made an
enraged, barely controlled appearance. He moved slowly and
stiffly, and she realized that he was wrapped in bandages and
still in great pain.

Despite her anger at his entry, she forced herself to remain standing near the northeastern tower window. She stared at him and waited without betraying her fear.

''The English, my lady, have always excelled at the art of torture, but we French are craftsmen at the art as well. I've thought of many ways for you to begin to feel the pain you have wrought upon me.''

''If you're in pain, you brought it on yourself. I told you not to touch me.''

''Thumbscrews are wretchedly painful—I have seen them used. You could be chained to the wall in a dungeon far below, hung from the ceiling until your arms ripped from their sockets. Your eyes could be pierced with a burning stick, so hot that they exploded in your head . . . and yet you would live. Ah, you think there is no dungeon here? But there is, lady, there is! There are rooms and tunnels beneath this castle leading all the way to the sea, and I assure you, through the two centuries this castle has stood, many an enemy has been maimed, twisted, burned . . . and discarded without anyone being the wiser. I can't tell you the horrors that await the unwary below.

I will heal. Perhaps in no more than a week's time. I gave my most serious consideration to having you flayed until you were in such agony you could no longer scream. But, Danielle, your husband is dead, and you are going to be joined to me in holy matrimony. And I don't want a scarred, deformed wife. Therefore, you will await your just punishment until I am ready. And at that time, you will pay, because I will heap every degradation known upon you, and you will serve my needs because I will force you to do so.''

She turned from him, losing the facade of complete control she had longed to keep. She looked toward the window; if he healed, she would cast herself from the window.

''Danielle!'' Simon said softly. ''Look again. It is an archer's slit, no more. Not even your slim frame would fit through!''

She could starve herself until she was nothing but bones, she told herself, her dismay and desolation overwhelming.

Yet even as Simon stared at her, Comte Langlois and a tall, graying man she had never met burst into the room behind him. The man she didn't know paused, staring at her. He bowed deeply, assessing her, then spoke bitterly. "Countess! So you are the woman who causes men to act insanely! The great prize who pits warrior against warrior! Well, madam, I, Count Germaine and master of this castle, do not welcome you!" He turned furiously to stare at Simon. "MacLachlan is dead, or so you claimed!"

"He is dead—we threw him into the sea—" Simon protested.

"Well, the English have arrived, and—"

"The Prince Edward leads the forces!" Comte Langlois said.

"Look out the window, Comte Langlois, Simon de Valois, for beyond the gates you will see a man atop a giant bay, and it is MacLachlan."

Danielle cried out, and raced for the window.

The English forces had arrived, en masse. She could see them settling into position beyond the thick walls of the fortress. Armored horsemen and foot soldiers were at the fore; she could see siege equipment being hauled behind them, toward the walls.

And at the front of the line of horsemen, she saw a rider. On Adrien's great warhorse, Matthew. In Adrien's armor, in a tunic bearing Adrien's crest.

Simon wrenched her away from the window, throwing her back across the room as he stared out himself. "It's a trick. An impostor is wearing his clothing and armor, riding his horse. See, there is the Black Prince . . ."

Germaine said, "There is the Black Prince, conferring with the horseman in MacLachlan's armor! It is MacLachlan, I tell you. I have ridden with him into battle, and I know the way he rides a horse. I know his motions, and you two have brought ruin upon my castle!"

Simon was undisturbed by Germaine's anger. "Indeed, Count, you say you know MacLachlan because you rode with him. You chose to betray your English king and seize *his* castle. I have not brought ruin down upon you. MacLachlan was bringing an army against you before we ever came. In his place, the Black Prince has come. Be grateful for the men and arms I bring to you to hold this castle against him!"

As the three men argued fiercely, Danielle felt a rise of hope so sweet it was like a taste of ecstasy. She longed to dash back to the window and study the figure in her husband's accoutrements herself, but she could not do so while the three remained.

"There rides a messenger to the gates!" Langlois said.

"What is he shouting, can you hear?" Simon demanded.

"Yes, I can hear!" Germaine exclaimed. "He's saying that King Edward will grant me the noble death of beheading if I return the countess unharmed! Dammit, Simon, you will give the woman back!"

Germaine spun angrily on the other two. Simon looked at Danielle, and he must have seen the excitement in her eyes. "Now, sir . . ."

He stepped toward Germaine, setting a hand on his shoulder. Germaine opened his mouth to speak . . . but all that came out was a gasp. Danielle saw the reason. Simon had quickly, quietly, plunged a small dagger into the man's chest. Blood spilled over his tunic. He slipped to the floor, dead before the fall.

"And what of his men within these walls?" Langlois raged to Simon.

"His men—French men. They will fight for us. We must quit sniveling and answer the messenger with a rain of arrows from the parapets."

"What of Germaine?" Langlois demanded.

Simon stared at Danielle. "Leave her with the corpse for now. Let her see what death is like as he rots and the stench rises to her nostrils."

They started to the door.

Danielle rushed to the window. She could see the horseman, waiting with Prince Edward at the front of the forces. She studied him, his movements, the way he gestured. Then he lifted his visor and it seemed her heart stopped beating. It was Adrien.

She turned, too overjoyed to be prudent. "It is Adrien. And this time, he will kill you, Simon. Surrender to him—he knows the meaning of mercy, if you do not."

"Leave her! We've more important matters!" Langlois snapped.

But Simon strode back to Danielle, grasping a handful of her hair and wrenching her to him. "I'll survive, and you'll be mine, and I will relish every agonized scream from your lips . . ."

He threw her from him. She caught herself, finding her balance, and stood tall as she cried out defiantly, "No, Simon, *I* am going to survive! *Adrien* is going to survive."

Simon took an angry step toward her.

"The castle must be defended!" Langlois bellowed, and Simon at last turned his furious eyes from her and stamped out of the room. The door slammed, and a bolt fell into place. She stared after the men, exhilarated . . . and frightened. The walls here were high and thick. It was a formidable castle. A siege could take weeks . . .

Adrien had not had a reason to study the Castle Cardineau before, having never been called upon to put down revolt here. It was dismaying to study the fortress, and he did so with his jaw locked. The castle had three main towers, with no discernible breaches in the structure itself; beyond that, it was completely encircled by a thirty-foot wall, with a sally port and bridge, now tightly drawn.

A messenger had called down from the parapets with a reply to the demands given Germaine in the name of the King of England. The reply stated that the Englishman, Count Germaine, was dead, the castle was seized in the name of King Jean of France—and the Countess d'Aville had planned to escape England and return to her homeland.

Adrien knew that he had doubted Danielle for several terrible seconds when he had been struck and she had been seized. He didn't doubt her now. He would not do so, no matter what lies Simon and Langlois tried to tell. His heart ached. He prayed that she wouldn't fight too hard, and that she wouldn't be hurt. Whatever Simon did to her would be fleeting, and it would never change his love. He would, however, find a way to kill Simon. Or he would die.

"Don't fret, my friend," Edward told him. "We begin the attack now."

"Arrows can't penetrate stone," Adrien said, sliding his visor back into place. "I don't see a weakness in the walls."

"There are castle servants, loyal to my father, who have slipped out. We'll have plans drawn."

"Aye, we'll find a weakness!" Adrien agreed.

"Archers!" Edward bellowed.

With that, the attack began. Adrien had fought with Prince Edward for years, as had many of Edward's men, and they were good at what they did. They were able to communicate with little effort, and able to move an army efficiently with deadly results. Flaming arrows were sent arcing over the walls; they heard the screams of many of the defenders as they fell. After the initial volley, foot soldiers carried a ram against the drawn bridge that created the outer gate to the fortress. When Adrien saw that the defenders were readying with boiling oil to hurtle down on the attackers, he called the retreat; the minute the Englishmen were safely out of the way, the archers took up their posts again and another rain of death fell upon the castle.

So it went throughout the day. Attack, retreat, attack, retreat. They lost very few men.

But they came nowhere near to breaking the defenses of the castle.

Adrien paced the ground outside the walls that night, staring up at the castle, his muscles knotted with tension, his mind racing with anguish. With darkness fallen, where was Danielle? His love for her transcended anything Simon might do, but his rage and fear were becoming uncontrollable. How would he bear the time it would take to breach the walls, wondering constantly what Simon was doing to her.

"Laird MacLachlan!"

It was Sir George who approached him anxiously.

"Aye, Sir George, you've some news?"

Sir George smiled. "Not a way to breach the wall, Adrien, but a bit of good news. Your lady is well."

"Thank God!" Adrien breathed. "How do you know?"

"One of the kitchen lads who hauled bath water slipped to our side before the bridge was drawn. And there's more."

"Aye?"

Sir George's smile deepened. "She's well, and, er, in a chaste position—for the time, at least."

Adrien frowned, his heart leaping. "How do you know this? Simon's first act would have been rape."

"Yes, but apparently he decided to force himself when there was some boiling water about, and . . . well, he's not functioning at this time."

"What about Langlois? He was eager to annul our marriage and seize Danielle."

"Simon is a a Valois and outranks him, apparently."

Despite his fear and desolation, Adrien found himself staring up at the castle, pleased. "So she scalded his . . ."

"Yes, to put it bluntly, Adrien, that is the case."

Adrien started to laugh, then spun on Sir George. "Simon did not hurt her in retribution?"

"He intends to take his revenge at a proper time."

Adrien tensed, telling himself that he mustn't go mad and throw himself against the stones.

"We must breach those walls!" he exclaimed.

"Aye, Laird MacLachlan, we must!"

They left Danielle through the night with the corpse of Count Germaine. She had covered him with the linen from the bed, but she couldn't take her eyes from the sheet.

Flies were flocking into the tower room. Their droning was beginning to make her insane.

At dawn, she heard men shouting. A catapult was sending missiles over the walls, and in the courtyard, men were screaming as they were struck with burning, splintering wood. She watched, pleased, and didn't hear the door to her room open. She didn't know that Simon was behind her until he wrenched her around to face him. "Come, lady, we're going to the para-pets. We'll see what Prince Edward hurtles over the walls when you are in the firing range! Then, if you've any sense whatsoever, you'll say that you're here of your own free will and that you intend to marry me."

"I'll never say that."

"You know how adept I am with a knife. You'll speak, or die."

He threaded his fingers into her hair, wrenching her along. She had thought she could fight him, but the pain was excruciat-ing. He dragged her down the two flights of stairs to the ground floor, then out across the courtyard and up the steps that led to the parapets on the outer defenses. She heard shouting from the English, and the arrows that had been flying toward the castle ceased to fall. From where she stood, she could see the vast alignment of the English forces, Prince Edward and Adrien, always warriors, at the head.

Simon gripped her arm in a painful vise, making sure she was visible to the men. "Englishmen, see! The Lady Danielle of Aville! She stands here of her own choice! I say you are a false knight, you who wear the MacLachlan's colors. If the lady's husband lives, he should come forward, and she will tell him that she has come here by choice, is my mistress, and will be my wife as we reclaim our land for ourselves!" He finished shouting and added softly to his archers on the wall, "Be ready!"

Danielle watched as Adrien moved his horse closer to the wall. He lifted his visor. She heard Simon inhale sharply as he realized that Adrien had survived.

"Talk to him!" Simon raged. "Bring him closer to the wall, tell him you betrayed him with me, that you want to be with me—if he goes away, he won't die!"

She raised her voice. "Adrien! Come no closer—" she warned.

"Bitch!" Simon roared, and she felt the point of his knife cutting into her side. She wanted to live, Adrien was alive. And perhaps, there was even a way . . .

"Adrien! Leave this castle! How can you forget? Do you think that I can forget?"

She could see her husband's eyes, giving away so little to anyone else. But she also saw that he didn't believe she had betrayed him.

"Adrien MacLachlan! Don't you remember? *You were the one responsible for the fall of Aville! You* were the one. Remember *how* you were the one?"

"Now!" Simon cried. He wrenched Danielle back while his archers tried for Adrien.

But Matthew was swift, and Adrien was quickly beyond their range of fire.

Swearing, Simon dragged her back to her tower room.

"I told him what you wanted!" she proclaimed, facing him. He stared at her, then struck her across the face with a blow that sent her flying down on the bed. He stood over her. "Pray he goes away," he said. "Your time is coming."

The door slammed in his wake. The bolt slid home.

Adrien stood before Edward in the command tent. "Tunnels!"

"What?" Edward demanded.

"We tunneled into Aville. She was telling me that there is some kind of underground passage from the castle, and that to breach the walls, we must get inside them."

Edward, who'd been sitting on a camp chair, rose. "Send for that kitchen lad!" he commanded his men.

The lad came.

While arrows continued to fly and the battering ram was brought against the bridge, they began to plan. The boy knew about the dungeons and could point out what he knew of the maze beneath the castle. "They've tortured many a poor soul down there, aye, that they have, my liege prince!" the lad told Edward. "I've heard that they took corpses—noble corpses at times—straight to the sea so that they might disappear."

"I'll find the entrance. I'll take twenty men with me, no

light arms, no heavy armor. We'll get inside and get the bridge down," Adrien said.

"Perhaps you shouldn't—you'll be too hasty, Adrien, too involved—"

"I've done this before!" he told Edward softly. "At Aville. Keep up the appearance that our attack is purely frontal."

"Aye, that I'll do," Edward said. "Take the castle in my father's name, Adrien."

"Aye!"

"And, bring your wife safely from these walls!"

Adrien nodded, turned, and called out to Sir George to arrange for the men who would attend him. Daylin was quickly at his side, and Michael, from Aville. Others joined behind them.

They rode a direct route from the castle to the sea and there split up, exploring the cliffs and caves that let out at the sea. Daylin found the entry. "Here, Adrien, here!" he cried. Adrien rushed to where Daylin stood. He studied the opening in the cliff and told his men, "When the tide rises, this opening must flood. We'll move as quickly as possible through this area."

They entered into the cliff by the sea and began walking into a stone tunnel of darkness. Torches led the way.

The water began to rise as they walked.

Higher and higher.

To their waists . . .

To their chests . . .

Not a single man voiced his fear of being drowned. And then, they came upon a sharp turn, and higher ground. In a large, damp cavern area, they saw the corpses of a dozen men, mostly bones, chained to the walls . . . left to starve or drown or expire from the elements.

The men looked around in silence. "There's a tunnel," Adrien said, and they moved through it.

They walked another thirty minutes before coming to more corridors. "Spread out," Adrien ordered softly, and they did. He moved quickly himself, taking different paths that led to dead ends—rooms where others had been imprisoned. They came upon implements of torture—and more corpses. Each man looked grimly upon the death around him without flinching. They returned the central point to report on what they had seen.

"I believe I have found the right way," Michael told Adrien.

"Aye, and how are you certain?"

Michael, sodden and muddy, smiled, his teeth flashing white through the grime. "I can smell food. If we find the kitchens . . ."

"Aye, Michael, lad, lead the way."

Danielle stood at the window, watching the battle with a sinking heart. King Edward was tenacious; his son was even more so. But the castle was strong. And if the siege waged on, day after day, week after week . . .

Her door suddenly burst open. Simon stood there. He was white, and still.

She heard a roar of shouting and a clash of arms from the courtyard below, and she looked down to see that a melee had broken out. Men battled men with swords, maces, hammers, whatever was at hand.

The gates were opening; the bridge had been lowered. Her heart leapt to her throat. Adrien had understood her message.

"You should go below and lead your men into battle, Simon," she told him.

He shook his head. "You're not going back to him."

"Perhaps you should escape. Run, quickly, get away from here."

He shook his head again, looking at her. "I'm sorry, Danielle. It could have been so different. If you'd have married me before he came . . ."

His voice trailed. He was just staring at her. Then she realized he was holding his knife. His thumb was sliding over the hilt.

He started walking toward her.

"No!" she cried, aware he meant to stab her in the heart. He came closer and closer. She leapt over the bed, picking up the washbowl, hurtling it at his head. He followed her around the bed, and she stumbled over it again, screaming as she tripped over Germaine's corpse. She threw the sheet at Simon, and then a pillow, then a shoe, realizing that she was running out of missiles and was defenseless—and he was very, very good with a knife.

She tried to run past him, but he caught her arm. She struggled against him, spitting, clawing, trying to make him drop the knife.

He wrenched her around so that she tripped backwards and fell on the bed. He straddled her, pinning her with his weight. Then, with both hands, he raised his blade above her.

"Danielle . . ." he whispered.

She cast her arms before her, shrieking.

But when the knife would have fallen, he was suddenly wrenched away from her and thrown across the room. He crashed against a wall, then slid down it.

Adrien was staring down at her. He was muddy, hair askew, tunic torn. His eyes were fire. He reached for her, helping her up.

"Adrien . . ." she began softly, then she screamed anew, for she saw that Simon had rallied and was catapulting toward Adrien with the knife raised, aimed for the heart.

With a supple gesture, Adrien drew his blade.

And Simon impaled himself.

He fell slowly to the ground, staring at them both. Then his eyes glazed over and he was dead.

Danielle cast herself against her husband, sobbing with relief. He swept her up into his arms.

"Come, my love, let me take you from this place. Let me take you home . . . ah, lady, I meant—"

"Home, Laird MacLachlan, is France, England, Scotland— wherever you may be!" she told him. And she clung more tightly to him. "In your arms, sir, I am home."

And shaking with relief, he carried her from her place of imprisonment.

Chapter 24

Prince Edward, being young and a romantic himself—and also pleased that the castle had fallen so quickly—gave Adrien and Danielle immediate leave to go about their business. Adrien suggested that they go to Aville, but she was anxious to return to London.

"I can't bear being away from the baby, Adrien, even if he is with the world's most natural mother in the queen. I want to continue to nurse my own child, Adrien. It is very important to me."

"I understand," he told her, and he did. She didn't mention her discomfort, but her breasts were heavily swollen, and he was glad that she wanted to nurse their child rather than bring in a woman as so many of the nobility did. Once, Aville had been everything to her, just as having his way had been so vastly important to him—serving the English king in all matters. The world around them wouldn't change, but they had changed. The world being what it was, they still had many rocky roads ahead of them.

They headed immediately across the English Channel. With the sheer relief of being together, and sailing in one of Prince Edward's own ships, they were able to take the captain's cabin.

And there, as Adrien tried to cradle Danielle, she pulled away, intent upon staring at his face, touching him. He caught her hands, and said, "What is it, my love?"

"I'm in awe, and so grateful. I still can't believe that you're alive. I wanted to die myself. I know that they threw you into the sea . . ."

"And you know that I can swim. The water was cold, and snapped me back to consciousness. And we've many good friends. Monteine came out of the apartments screaming for help and the men quickly began to light fires and organize a search. And Terese—aye, the little wench with whom you so rudely assumed I amused myself—went to the queen, hysterical because she had been forced to help provide Simon and Comte Langlois with horses."

"If she helped save your life, I am eternally grateful to her."

He grinned. "She and my squire, Luke, wish to marry. She will be a busy young woman."

"And Monteine and Daylin are just waiting for a proper date to wed!" Danielle said, smiling. "But still, how were you able to—"

"Prince Edward departed London immediately following Terese's story, and was with my men as they scoured the coastline in small boats, looking for me. Prince Edward himself found me, swimming toward the shore."

"The Plantagenets are very involved in our lives, aren't they?" she inquired.

He started to answer her, then decided that trying to tell her just how involved the Plantagenets were should wait. "Aye, lady," was all he said.

She mused regretfully, "I can't understand what happened to Simon. I swear, he was not such a monster when I knew him before. Men become obsessed with who and what they are. I think he believed that as a Valois he was owed greater riches than he had accrued, and perhaps that worked on his mind. I tell you, Adrien, he became so evil, but he is not like most of the people. My people are good talented, hard-working, charming—"

"Danielle, my love, this thing between King Edward and

King Jean will not end, for Edward can be obsessed as well! I have many fine French allies. Your mother was one of the most beautiful, intelligent, and kind people anyone could know, and as you are French, my love, the likes of Simon could never convince me that the French are not among the world's finest people.''

She smiled, dazzled by his words.

"I was so afraid that Simon—'' he began.

"He never touched me!'' she said quickly. "And I never betrayed you.''

He shook his head. "I was never afraid that you had, and if he had touched you, I'd have only prayed that you survived his cruelty. Nothing would change my love. But did you really scald him?''

"Yes.''

"Having fought you many times myself, I should have known just how good you were. You were clever—but foolish. He might have hurt you terribly in retribution, and I was powerless at the time.''

"I wasn't incredibly clever—the water happened to be in my hand. And he was convinced that you were dead and that he would marry me—and find his retribution then. He didn't want his wife to be an ugly, scarred creature.''

"It is over now. And you mustn't feel sorrow. Danielle, believe me, Simon was plotting against Edward with Armagnac. He didn't care what he did to his own people. You didn't see his total disregard for life . . .''

"You have to understand, Adrien. I made a vow to my mother once, and it was sacred. But I believe that I fulfilled it, warning Jean when men meant to kill them.''

"Edward never gave anyone an order to attempt to kill King Jean.''

She nodded. "I was afraid that even if you could, you would never come for me!''

"I will always come for you. I hadn't even thought of the prospect of tunneling. If you hadn't said what you did about Aville, I might never have known about the structure. I was half mad, trying to reach you.''

"I knew there was something below because Simon kept telling me how I could be tortured in the tunnels, and how bodies had been dumped in the sea. Imagine! I hated you for so many years for what happened at Aville before I was born. And if it hadn't been for Aville, my mother never would have met Robert, my father."

It was the perfect time to tell her, but he couldn't bring himself to do it. Not yet. It was too dazzling just to be together, to know a love so deep and secure and unchanging. He couldn't bring himself to spoil the tenderness between them at the moment.

He held her against him instead, thinking that the right time would come. They'd be home in Scotland, or even Gariston, perhaps, on a cold winter's night before a roaring fire, and then . . .

Then he would tell her the truth. Not now. Now, he just meant to cherish her.

"It's over, Danielle. Langlois will lose his head, I'm afraid, but Prince Edward has offered mercy to those who only followed the orders of the nobles. And Simon is dead."

She shivered. "I don't want to talk about him any more. I just want you to hold me."

So he held her, and they made love, and it was more intimate than any time between them before, because they whispered words of their feelings along with their hunger.

They didn't pause for the night when they reached the English shore, but rode hard for the tower where the queen was residing. When they burst into Adrien's apartments, they found Queen Philippa there alone, rocking the baby.

She pressed a finger to her lips and lifted a hand, halting the two of them at the door when they would have walked forward.

"The news of another great victory through your sense of strategy has arrived before you, Laird MacLachlan. We're grateful, of course, to know that you serve us."

"I'd not have managed it without my wife," Adrien said.

The queen looked up and arched a brow, then looked down at Robin. He wasn't actually sleeping, but his eyes were very heavy. She was talking to the baby as she rocked him.

"So your father thinks that light thatch on your head is his!" the queen exclaimed, smiling down at the boy, who cooed in response. "He's apparently not seen that little mark on your bum, then, eh? Of course, then again, neither of your parents has probably had much occasion to stare upon the king's bum, and therefore wouldn't know that such a mark is hereditary. Now mind you, it's not that your mother bears much resemblance to the Plantagenets in the least—thank God for the small mercies that have upon occasion saved my pride!"

Adrien looked worriedly at Danielle, damning himself a thousand times over for not having told her the truth, but the last thing he would have imagined was the queen talking so matter-of-factly about the situation when they returned for their son! Danielle had adored her mother, and the legend of the English knight, Robert, she had believed to be her father.

Danielle was staring at the queen, her eyes wide, her face pale.

Philippa looked at Danielle and winked, rose quickly with the baby in her arms, and walked over to the two of them. She handed Danielle the baby. "The two of you must learn to be more careful with such precious belongings!" she admonished. She kissed Danielle's cheek. "Poor dear, you looked so shocked! I'd have thought the world had figured out the truth of your birth long ago. The king is a good husband to me— he does love me, I know. He has had his weaknesses. I didn't know your mother, and when you came into our household, she was already dead, and therefore, hard for me to hate. You grew up in my household and are like a daughter to me. Now Adrien, help your wife. Her jaw has fallen—tap it back into place, then take the babe. Don't let her drop him."

Adrien took Robin. The queen brushed his cheek and sailed on out of the room.

Danielle stared at Adrien. She was shaking, and she walked away from him. He quickly placed Robin in his cradle and followed her, placing his hands on her shoulders.

"You knew!" she charged him.

"Only since Prince Edward told me on the way across the English Channel. He does love you. He was coming to tear the

castle apart for you, whether I survived or not. Danielle!'' He
spun her around so he could see her eyes and speak directly
to her. ''Danielle, I know how hurt you are! I know how you
have fought Edward all these years, hated him for forcing you
to England, giving you to me . . . all these things. You loved
the memory of a man you thought to be your father, you were
loyal to the king you thought to be your own. Please, you
mustn't be so dismayed that Edward is your father. He is a
great king, a wise man, a brave man—and he is capable of
mercy—''

''I don't hate Edward!'' she managed to say.

''Then what is it?'' he demanded.

She started laughing, and he was worried. He held her against
himself, trying to soothe her. ''Danielle, Danielle—''

''Oh, Adrien! I'm all right, honestly, I'm all right! It's just
that . . . my mother, the wretched vow I took to be loyal to the
king! Adrien, she must have meant Edward all along. I think
she was trying to tell me when she died that I must give my
loyalty to Edward, the king, my father! Adrien, I'm just so, so
sorry! All these years, all the things I believed, the things I did
. . . the warfare I caused between us! And Edward is my *father!*
Adrien, all the plotting and planning I did for King Jean! So
much heartache between us in the past . . .''

''You have been worth it all,'' he told her softly. ''And there
are many ways to look at the picture. Edward should be content
to rule England, but lands in France have been the domain of
the English kings for centuries. And after these many years,
the royalty are so mixed with one another, it's hard to say who
had hereditary right to what!''

''You don't believe that!'' she said, smiling and shaking her
head. ''You will fight for Edward always.''

''I will fight for you always,'' he told her.

And she smiled, her eyes brilliant with tears. ''We can call
a truce now, I believe.''

''Aye, that we can. But you'll have to know, now more than
ever, I'm grateful for Aville. Grateful that the walls fell, and
grateful, with all my heart, that you exist!''

The baby began to cry, and Danielle laughed and said, ''I

can even say I'm completely grateful! Without your military mind working so diligently at Aville, Robin would not exist!"

She left him for their son, taking Robin into the bed; Adrien lay with her, the baby between them, until Robin had glutted and fallen into a deep, deep sleep. As Adrien moved him, he said, "I think it might be Plantagenet hair."

"Plantagenet eyes, I'm afraid," she apologized.

"I think there's a hint of vivid French green in them," Adrien said, carefully moving his sleeping child into the cradle.

Then he lay down again with his wife and held her in his arms, and she said, "Oh, Adrien! I still think of all the time when I did love you and wanted to be loyal and felt that I owed my fealty to King Jean. I didn't want to betray Edward, but I felt that I had to be true to my heritage. Can you imagine! When all the while . . ." she sighed softly. "I couldn't take a chance that the king's men would kill Jean."

"King Edward would never have condoned such a cold-blooded murder. Surely you know that. And your King Jean is a good man as well, noble, wise, and proud in captivity. I admire him very much."

"And still . . ." she said, turning into his arms, her beautiful eyes on his intently, "I hurt you so often in the past!"

"And I hurt you in the past. But I love you. With all my heart. It is nice, of course, to know now that you have made a vow to protect Edward the king. You should be much better behaved."

"Better behaved!"

Her eyes flashed fire and he laughed, amazed to feel himself shaking, so gratified to have her, be with her, and know that she loved him as he loved her.

"Perhaps not. You'll always fight passionately for what you believe!"

"And that is wrong?" she whispered intently.

"No, that is something I love about you. And I do love you, Danielle. I fell in love with you for so many things, not the least of which was your loyalty to what you believed in, and your honesty to me about that loyalty. The love I feel has grown out of time, out of knowing you, out of seeing all that is so right in your heart and soul.''

"Oh, Adrien! There was so much I admired and respected about you even when I was trying to hate you! I was jealous without knowing it so many times, I wanted you, but I didn't know how to have you.''

"Oh, my love. You have me for life.''

She smiled at that, and then her smile became a little wicked, surely an invitation. He lowered his head to kiss her, and when their lips touched, the fires within them flamed to life . . .

"No more talk about kings!'' he insisted. "Queens, knights, or countries!''

"The past was theirs . . .'' she began.

"And the future is ours,'' he promise.

"The king has had his pleasure—now we shall have ours.''

She nodded, and still her smile was so temptingly wicked. She wrapped her arms around him.

And the future began that night.

ROMANCE FROM JO BEVERLY

DANGEROUS JOY   (0-8217-5129-8, $5.99)

FORBIDDEN   (0-8217-4488-7, $4.99)

THE SHATTERED ROSE   (0-8217-5310-X, $5.99)

TEMPTING FORTUNE   (0-8217-4858-0, $4.99)